The Phoenix Prince

Sword/Eye, Book 2

William F. Burk

To Starlight Sara, my lovely editor.

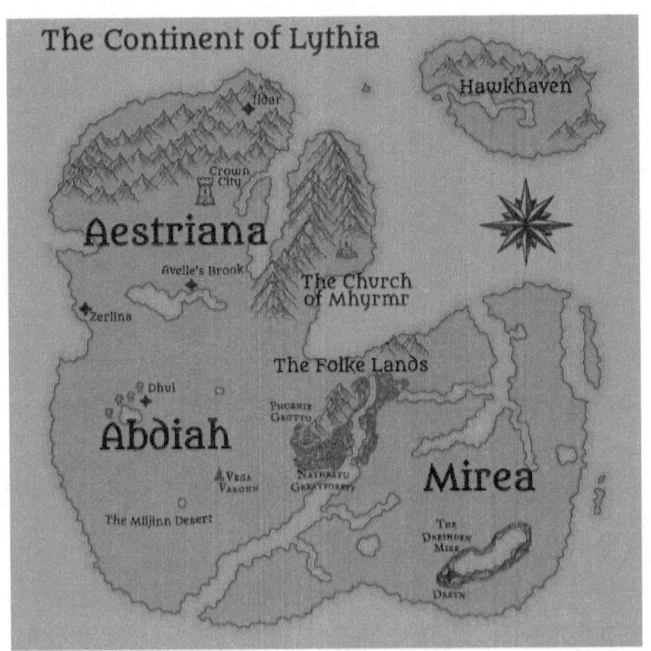

CHAPTER ONE

Under a Wistful Star

The night air was still as the frosts of winter crystallized upon the top of the mountain where the lonesome Church of Mhyrmr sat. In its gray solitude, it loomed just above thick clouds, prophets of a coming snow. The once-vibrant garden, positioned at the edge of the temple's vast courtyard, jutted out over the cliffside. Among the abounding death in the garden, only the holly bushes dared defy the cold, their blood-red berries lively underneath the defense of prickly leaves.

Zurriel stood at the edge of the garden's overhang, his crimson eyes gazing onto the clouds below. He was a monolith, his long black hair falling over his shoulder. In the moonlight, his coat of wolf fur shone like a silver beacon, reflecting onto the glass-like frost surrounding him.

He did not mind the cold, no matter its vain attempts to wrap him in its mortal coils. Try as it may (and try it did), it was all a useless endeavor. *Yes,* he thought, *useless.* For his body would not freeze. He was long past the point of that being any concern of his. He had nothing to worry about. Ever since the wretched Lunae took the Heart of Hearts from his chest—ever since he joined the ranks of the undead —he had forfeited his ability to freeze to death. *Not truly a loss,* he noted.

In all honesty, he had not even been able to *feel* the cold in one thousand years. Again, not really a loss, and he had long forgotten winter's sting. Even the warmth of the sun on summer days did nothing to comfort him. He was immune to heat as he was immune to stabbing cold.

But I don't care, he thought as he held up a finger lit with green flames. If the sun and frost were the only losses he endured in exchange for the power to carry through with his designs, then they were but trivial expenses, ones he would cast away eagerly.

For with the loss of his heart he had become an Ex Nihilo and cared not for the joys of the world.

The dark wizard summoned flames to each fingertip and waved his hand dismissively. Below him, the snow clouds obeyed and opened themselves, a curtain revealing the dark expanse of the world below. As they parted, the light of the full moon fell upon the dark visage of the continent of Lythia, exposing the vastness of its grandeur.

Zurriel dropped his hand to his side and looked out at the view. It was beautiful, and he felt an anger rise in his heart as he thought so. To the Dark One upon his perch, to think the world beautiful was futile. It was *vanity*.

"It's beautiful," he said into the air, "*too* beautiful to be so rife with wickedness."

There was silence.

"Don't you agree," he said again without turning, "Agnon?"

Suddenly, a black cloud formed within the center of the moonlit courtyard, revealing the large, taciturn Abdian.

"It is, Master," the brooding mage replied. "This world is rotten."

"Indeed it is." Zurriel smiled without turning. "Are you ready for my commands, Agnon?"

The imposing Darkling knelt to one knee and bowed his head submissively. "I will do as you wish, Master."

"The Eyes tell me of a boy," Zurriel began. "But not just any boy, no. This strange, this...curious red-eyed child walks the streets of a Beastfolk city in the northern area of the Folke Lands—in the capital city of Phoenix Grotto."

"Red-eyed?"

Zurriel turned to his servant. In the light of the full moon, Agnon could see the crimson shine of the Eyes of Lunae as Zurriel stared into him.

"I see your heart, Agnon." The Dark One smiled. "It is without fear, without contradiction; it is loyal. Tell me, Agnon, you wish to see my plans through, do you not?"

Agnon bowed his head. "I do."

"Good." Zurriel turned once more and stood upon the edge of the cliff. "We have not much time, my dear Harbinger. It shall be here before we know it."

Agnon said nothing as he stood once more.

"Go, Agnon. Bring me the third Eye; bring me the Eye of Revelation. For the time is sifting through the glass."

"It will be done, my master," Agnon said as he summoned the black cloud once more.

The wizard's minion passed through the fog again and was promptly gone. Silence returned to the dead garden. Zurriel turned his face to the night sky. Surrounding the moon, upon the highest peak in all of Lythia, he could see the stars above. The dark wizard reached out a hand as if trying to pluck one from the sky. As he reached out to touch the heavens, the moon illuminated his crimson, Aeonic Eyes.

As he reached skyward, he whispered to himself, almost melancholy, as if longing for something with great sadness.

"It is almost time...Azyla..."

The Church of Mhyrmr was long abandoned. It had been an easy transition, for no one, no matter how powerful, dared fight the raging beasts that now inhabited the church's ancient, unhallowed walls. The Ex Nihilo beasts were formidable enough just by their intimidating frames. Each creature towered over even the large Agnon, their ethereal, muscled, black skin seemed to shift into a smoky gray when touched by light; their glowing yellow eyes seemed to float in the darkness. They weren't human, and they weren't quite beast. They were something altogether...other.

It had been only a few months since the fall of Crown City, and Zurriel had promptly commanded the creatures to overtake the Inquisitors of the Church of Mhyrmr, a task he found easier than expected, but it was of no surprise to the others. These otherworldly beasts were quite enough to scare any mage, no matter their prowess.

But not all.

Larc Elliot walked the worn halls, passing these beasts with without trepidation. She knew, of course, that there was nothing to fear. Ever since she had given her allegiance to the mysterious man called Zurriel, she had sensed instantly that the beasts did not feel her an enemy.

But she did not fear them—allegiance or no. However, given that her fealty came with her release from the dungeon pits below the mountains, she felt she at least owed the mysterious old man a favor or two.

Despite this, she walked onward, her eyes unafraid, toward the harbor. Today, she knew, was a unique day—one that both filled her with hope and ambition.

Today was the day that the Archbishop returned.

She knew the truth, of course; she knew that Marven Ferrenvaal was dead. This information was privy to her, though the rest of the world was unaware. *It had to have been true,* she thought, as there was no way that that old bag would release her from prison. She knew there was no way he would become that desperate.

Five years. She clenched her fists and gritted her teeth. It had been five years since her imprisonment, imprisoned at twenty years old. *Merely a child.*

But now was different. With the old man out of the way, and a decoy coming forth, her goals were becoming closer and closer to fruition.

Soon, she thought, soon the entire church would be at her beckon.

A smile crossed her face as she pushed her long, golden hair from her stark blue eyes. Her hair had grown long during her incarceration, but now she was free.

I need a haircut.

Larc walked down the stairwell that led to the aerodock and out into the hangar. It was odd seeing the space as empty as it was, scarcely filled with Elven soldiers and guarded only by the infernal dark Ex Nihilo beasts. As each soldier nodded in respect, she saw no reason to pay them any mind. She wasn't here for them; they weren't even footnotes in the task ahead of her.

She was here for the Archbishop—but more importantly to assess his situation. She knew of the only man that could be coming to fill the position and take the place of Marven, and also be a *convincing* Marven at that. Only one man had that power, and she knew just how to play him into her clutches.

Wonderful, she thought, smiling.

She stood at the ready within the hangar that traditionally housed the airship *Orca*. Flurries blew at nice speeds, the frigid winds causing ripples in her black robes and blowing her long blonde hair frantically under its breezes. In the distance, a small speck grew closer. Larc smiled, her grin reaching her eyes.

Welcome home.

The airship *Orca* sliced through the night, slipping through the thick snowy clouds as it ascended to dock in the hangar of the temple upon the summit. Inside, the Archbishop sat in the cockpit as the Elven pilots briefed him.

"There may be a surprise once you have arrived. We have waited a few months, as you requested.

"Good," the old man replied. "We needed the time to achieve our aims. No one would believe that Eldric kidnapped old Marven unless there were some time to..." He narrowed his eyes. "'Escape' his clutches."

The Elves remained silent. They knew this was going to be a one-sided conversation. The man—the true man underneath Marven's face was...missing something...but they weren't quite sure what this something was, just that it was absent.

Outside, Larc watched as the airship docked. Patiently she stood, waiting for the impostor to make his appearance. She sighed at the thought of dealing with this wretched man once more. He was quite the headache, if she remembered correctly, and she knew that he was so old that not much would have probably changed since his release. In fact, his long imprisonment had likely made his psychological problems even more profound.

But this was a means to an end, and she told herself she must merely play the waiting game before disposing of him.

All she needed was time.

Steam billowed from the pipes of the gargantuan vessel as it landed upon the harbor. Larc swallowed once more and cleared her throat as she prepared, readying herself to hide whatever annoyances she would feel. Suddenly, the pipes beside the landing bridge whistled as they expelled hot vapors and the ramp began to slowly descend. One at a time, Elven soldiers marched down the bridge, their dress sabers held tightly in their hands. One by one, they lined the walls behind Larc, each one stopping to bow and acknowledge her as they passed.

Droning traditions, she griped in her mind. *This is so dramatic. Just come out already, you old fart.*

Six Elven officers, each dressed in their red-and-gold uniforms marched out at once, lining the ramp, three on each side. Once they had entered position, an even more decorated man stepped out, standing at the top of the ramp. Larc smiled derisively as she counted the ten medals that adorned the soldier's red coat.

"All bow!" the man commanded.

"Sir!" the other soldiers responded in unison, kneeling as one body.

Larc remained standing. "Cut the tradition, commander," she groaned. "Where is he? Valt—I mean, Archbishop Ferrenvaal."

The soldier stood startled for a moment before clearing his throat and shutting up, nodding in compliance with the Inquisitor's wishes.

"So quick to cut off the poor, poor, commander," the voice of Marven echoed into the stillness of the air. Larc rolled her eyes as the visage of the Archbishop emerged from the darkness of the large vessel.

"I have no time for foolery, Your Holiness." Larc spat. "We've some work to do."

"Oh, yes..." The old man narrowed his eyes. "How could old Marven forget such a grand purpose?"

He descended the ramp and stopped. Side-by-side, he was only inches taller than the young woman.

"Let us begin..." he said with a smile, a long bony finger placed lightly upon his chin. "We must find the boy with the Red Eye, and eliminate the goddess Lunae for good."

CHAPTER TWO

The Boy with the Red Eye

Lukas stood in a dark void. It took him a moment to register the reality of the situation, but once he became accustomed to his surroundings, he realized...

He was dreaming.

He looked around momentarily. Surely there was a reason for his being here? He didn't hear or see Lyrlark again, so certainly this wasn't the Aeon of Dream's doing. No. This...felt different.

"Hello?!" he called out into the abyss.

No answer.

"Is anyone out there?!"

Lukas listened as best he could. But nothing. Pure silence.

Am I dead, he thought as he patted his body. *I'm not a ghost. Surely I'm not dead, right?*

"Who are you?" asked the voice of a child, causing Lukas to jump.

The Heart of Hearts whipped around to see a small child staring back at him. He looked to be only eleven or twelve years of age, with pitch-black hair in a bowl cut.

"Who are you?" the kid asked once more.

"I'm Lukas!" he began. "Who are *you*?"

"I'm Alvys."

"Okay..." Lukas scratched his head. "Why are we dreaming about each other? Where are you?"

"I'm in Phoenix Grotto."

For a moment, the two merely stared at each other, the child's gaze seeming to pierce right through Lukas.

"I have to wake up now," the boy said. "But maybe we will dream again?"

Lukas watched as the child faded before him. Eventually, the evanescent child was gone, and Lukas stood alone once more.

Lukas could feel his heart race. He knew what must be done.

Alvys had a red eye.

Lukas awoke to the howls of harsh winds whistling along the mouth of the cave.

"You're awake," the voice of the Old Man said.

Lukas rubbed his eyes and blinked several times to adjust his vision to the light of the large fire in the center of their uncomfortable living space. Since his training with the elder began, the two of them had made their home inside of a dark cave carved into a cliff face. It was cold inside, and borderline inhospitable, but they made do.

In the blaze's orange glow, Lukas could see the blue-skinned Darkling. His long white hair was illuminated by the colors of the tongues of flames. The Heart of Hearts knew so little about this mysterious elder, though some things were apparent. Given his knowledge and the way he so familiarly spoke about Lucyn—and given his claim of being the smith who forged the *Sword Durandal* (one claim which Lukas surprisingly found easy to believe)—Lukas determined that this man must have truly lived one thousand years ago when these mysterious events took place.

Lukas stood and stretched his muscles, running his fingers through his shoulder-length white-blond hair. He felt better about it being long again; he liked long hair.

"I had a strange dream," he said as he approached the fire and sat upon a dead log that the Old Man had found somewhere in the snowy outskirts of the mountain forest. It had been six months since the fall of Crown City. Lukas had no idea of the status of the outside world at this point. Instead, he was here, on this icy and forlorn mountainside.

The Old Man had done as he had promised. In the past six months, Lukas had reached a mastery of his magic that he had not known before. Though his Starblood abilities remained mostly an alien mystery, he felt as comfortable with them as he thought he could be at this point.

"It is not uncommon for the dreams of a Starborn to be peculiar," the Old Man said as he stirred the small cauldron slowly. "Lucyn had many dreams such as that. It was as if the universe were speaking to him in its own...strange language. To him, and him alone."

"Lucyn..." Lukas trailed off. "The first Heart of Hearts?"

"In a sense," the Old Man said as he lifted the wooden spoon to his mouth and blew upon it. "'Heart of Hearts' is merely a title that was given to him." He took a sip of the soup and nodded. "He was in no way the first to have the Starblood. There were many Starborn before him, all of which were scions of Vespira. So, I guess, *she* is technically the first."

"Vespira?" Lukas said the name as if it were natural. "Zurriel told a strange story back in Avelle's Brook. It was a myth I'd never heard before."

"If it was the story of Vespira the Blessed One, then he told the truth."

"But I don't understand!" Lukas groaned. "Why didn't he just kill me?"

"Maybe he meant to," the elder said as he picked up a wet leaf from a small basket, tossed it in the gruel, and began to stir once more. "One cannot discern the madness that is Zurriel. Maybe he meant for you to freeze in the harsh mountains of the Folke Lands, or maybe— *just maybe*—somewhere, lost within the chasms of his lunacy, Lucyn still lives."

The old Darkling sipped from the spoon once more, his pale green eyes intent upon the food. Lukas watched silently, his mind filled with a flurry of thoughts. *Could it be*, he thought, could it be that Zurriel had indeed spared his life? *No.* Perhaps it was just as the old Abdian had said.

Perhaps it really was the power of Lucyn who had spared him.

"I dreamed about a boy." Lukas blurted out a bit louder than expected. "He was only a little kid, but his eye was red. He said he was from Phoenix Grotto."

The Old Man said nothing in reply. He picked up a small bowl, carved from a smooth rock, with his leathery blue hand and dipped it into the soup.

"Ironic," he chuckled as he handed Lukas the bowl. "It's not far from here."

"How do I get there?" Lukas began. "How do I get off of the mountain?"

"I will lead you out of the mountain," the old man said as he ladled himself a bowl. "But that is all I can do."

"That is all I need." Lukas said with a bow of his head. "I owe you so much, sir. I don't know why you've done everything you have, but I am very grateful for your training and wisdom."

The old Darkling smiled. In the orange light, his pale green eyes seemed glossy, suddenly glistening with tears. Lukas wasn't sure.

"In a sense," he began, "I'm helping a friend."

Lukas smiled. "Thank you, sir."

The Old Man remained silent for a moment.

"*Rahyu-el*," he said finally.

"I'm sorry?" Lukas cocked his head. "I don't understand?"

"Eat, boy. We have a long journey to the bottom of the mountain."

Lukas sighed at the mysterious elder's ways, but hunger seemed to win over his curiosity.

The old man looked at his young companion. Perhaps he had said too much, or perhaps the boy didn't understand. But he was content with what had been.

The old man was happy, for the first time in the span of one thousand years, he had finally told someone his name.

Upon waking, Alvys thought nothing more of the strange dream. The peculiar young man named Lukas simmered in his mind for a moment, but didn't stay long. He rose from his small bed and looked around the room. There was no light coming from the windows, and he wondered momentarily why anyone in the darkness of Phoenix Grotto even had windows. His room was lit merely by three etherlamps, each placed in a corner of the room. It was a quiet room; it was a safe room.

Safe from the streets outside.

Today, just like any other day, the streets of Phoenix Grotto were dark and brooding with the things that go bump in the night or with the ruffians and crooks who used the darkness of the labyrinthine city to hide from the bounty hunters, government officials, or anyone else that might want their heads on a spike. The better and more historic parts of the city were mainly composed of Beastfolk trying to live alongside the filth that infested the town around them. The young boy had always wondered why in Lythia the Beastfolk would decide to build a large city underneath a mountain, but since most of the folk who lived here were bears, dogs, cats, and rats, he just decided that he wouldn't question it too much. Well, it really didn't matter to him anyway. He lived his life and they lived theirs.

"You're up, kid!" a voice laughed heartily. "You'll miss dinner if you don't hurry up!"

Alvys turned to see Jalzen standing in the doorway. He was large, muscular man, with short black hair. He wore all black all the time, with several golden rings and silver chains. In the darkness, under the light of the lamps, he seemed to shimmer and twinkle because of his jewelry.

"Coming!" the young child exclaimed with a smile.

"Hurry up, kid! I'm starving," Jalzen smiled, the light of the blue lanterns glistening off of his vampiric fangs. "We're having elk tonight! And we're also having snow peas!"

"Oh!" Alvys said as he jumped from his bed excitedly. "Snow peas?!"

"Yeah! So c'mon!" He motioned with a hand, his golden rings flashing in the light.

Alvys followed his friend down the halls. *Jalzen is always in high spirits,* the boy thought. But, recently, he could tell that his friend was a bit more nervous than usual. He assumed it had something to do with the Elves. Or at least he assumed. All he knew for sure was that ever since the Elves came along, Jalzen and his friends had been grumpy. Something about being scared that they would get found. Alvys couldn't really be sure why Jalzen was so scared. Who cared if they found him? When he asked, the man simply said that he didn't want the Elves to find their *secret.* Of course, Alvys knew he was talking about the red candies that Jalzen ate with his friends, but Alvys didn't know why the Elves would care.

After all, it wasn't like he didn't have enough red candies to share. And who said that the Elves even wanted candy to begin with?

The child simply shrugged. Maybe it was just a grown-up thing. He didn't know many grown-ups who were so possessive over a bunch of candy, but, then again, he didn't know many grown-ups anyway. And who knows, for all he knew, the little red droplets were super delicious. He had asked Jalzen many times if he could try one too, but he was always met with the same answer: *these candies aren't for people like you.*

Alvys didn't know what that meant, or who "people like him" were, but no matter how disheartening it was that he couldn't taste the candies that everyone else was eating, he had let the question go. He knew more than anyone just how iron Jalzen's decisions were, so if the man said no, no meant no and that was the end of it. It was final.

"Hey kid!" the other vampires laughed as Alvys entered the room. "Glad you can join us! We got your favorite today!"

And they did. Alvys scanned room. It was cramped, that was for sure. The small den was a meeting place, large enough to hold everyone, but just not quite spaciously. He felt sorry for the people who had to eat leaning against the walls, their clothes beginning to rub off the red paint. In the middle of the room spanned a large, round table. There, among the plethora of foods, sat a pot filled to the brim with bright green snow peas.

"Well," Jalzen said, nudging the child, "grab a plate!"

Alvys smiled as he rushed to do just that. He took his plate and began to fill it with the elk and peas and everything else.

And just like that...

...the dream of Lukas was not even a memory.

The castle of Phoenix Grotto was built into the back wall of the mountain, a towering edifice. Its spires of obsidian stone were like umbral spearheads, its visage but a dark mass, its gargantuan silhouette a shadowy titan overlooking the dark city before it. Larc Elliot stood upon the balcony made of black stone under the dim lights of the blue etherlamps behind her, her vigilant blue eyes watching the city below, scanning the dim-lit maze like a hawk. Behind her, hidden in the darkened corner of the overhang, the grim figure of Agnon stood still as stone, his bulky blue features hidden by the shadow of a hooded black cloak.

"Can you feel it, wizard?" Larc began. "That strange charge in the air. I feel that something soon will take place..." She paused. "I cannot shake this strange feeling. The static in the air seems"—she casually waved her hand—"frantic."

The brooding Darkling said nothing. In the shadows, he was naught but a vague nightmare, an unintelligible mass, hardly visible to anyone not keen to seeing beyond the darkness. Still he stood, a vulture waiting patiently for its next meal.

Whatever. Larc turned her head and rolled her eyes. *Why do I get stuck with this depressing sorcerer?*

"Inquisitor Storm Slinger!" a gruff voice called out as an Elf in a gilded uniform walked through the door.

Larc turned to face the Elf, stark blue eyes meeting his.

"Your search is fruitless, commander." She tilted her head. "Why?"

"We've—"

"You're going to say 'we've been searching the city, but no sign of the Eye.'"

"We've been—" The soldier's face turned pale and his body froze. "How did you—?!"

Suddenly, a faint yellow aura surrounded the Inquisitor. The commander looked up in horror as he felt the air thinning.

"Kyrx Lygrhm!"

At the young woman's command, bright and effervescent blue lightning shot from her fingertips and webbed around the Elf like a net.

"You see, commander," she said, smiling, "electricity is a wonderful thing. It is power; it is majesty; it is the very *fuel* of life. And most of all, electricity speaks. It exists in every living thing, giving them thoughts and actions. Electricity courses through your brain, giving you thoughts, and all I have to do is listen to those sparks in your tiny little mind to hear what it has to say." Her face contorted as she bared her teeth at him. "So, I would be careful to think against me next time. Do we have an understanding?"

The gilded commander held his chest in agony as he lay upon the floor, his body convulsing from the power of the razing shocks.

"You're going to say 'yes, Inquisitor Storm Slinger.'"

"Yes, Inquisitor Storm Slinger!" he exclaimed a second later.

"Very well." She yawned as the lightning faded into small azure glows. "You have seventy-two hours to bring me that eye. I don't care who dies, but if you run out of time, the death will be *yours*.

The commander coughed and writhed on the floor as he tried to collect himself.

Larc scowled at him, then turned and waved her hands.

"Get out of my sight if you value your life."

The man crawled to his feet and rushed hastily past the large Agnon, whimpering as he held his singed clothing.

Larc turned and walked to the edge of the balcony, her icy blue eyes scanning the dark, dismal grotto below. The Elves had overtaken the city with maximum ease, so why? Why was it so hard to find a single eye?

Seventy-two hours. She smiled. *Perhaps that will kick them into full gear.*

"Agnon," she said as she turned and walked past the imposing Abdian. "They say they are superior—the Elves, that is. They boast superior sight and hearing—so why is this so hard?"

The large shadow remained still and silent, as if merely ignoring the Inquisitor's question.

"Pff," Larc scoffed as she turned and walked away from the balcony, whipping her red cloak with violent temper as she stomped past the Abdian. "Say nothing, then," she said under her breath as she pushed her now-short, golden hair behind her ear. "I don't care either way."

Pathetic, she thought, *what an utterly pathetic predicament.*

CHAPTER THREE

The Rising Fire

The forests that densely populated the surrounding areas at the mouth of the fortress capital of Phoenix Grotto were quiet. The ancient woods were large and flourishing. Giant and majestic oak trees ascended high into the sky, their mighty branches weaving above to create a blanket of emerald green foliage, home to bright birds and squirrels and venomous snakes. The dense canopy blinded the world below from the grace of the sun. As marvelous as this archaic wood was, the darkness of its forlorn terrain left it a dismal expanse, a ghastly sight to anyone who dared venture within—most of which were fools who never returned. Still, the road was braved by merchants and travelers coming through the Folke Lands to the dark markets of Phoenix Grotto.

This seemingly otherworldly forest also created an excellent cover for the denizens who knew how to pass through its forbidding lands unharmed.

Within the emerald canopies, a large red bird hopped from one branch to another, careful of the placement of his knife-like talons upon the limbs. This was much harder than flying, he admitted, but it was a small price to play to keep himself from the vigilant eyes of the Elven sentries he knew would be placed as strategically as possible. He, more than any other, knew that the now-crowned Emperor

Zilheim was no fool. He knew that damned Elven villain knew he was alive; he knew that Zilheim feared him, and if there was anyone Zilheim wanted dead more than him, it was the Elf named Lyon.

He didn't mind the sounds the branches made as he crumpled them underneath his claws. The forest was loud enough already. It was the middle of the winter in Aestriana, and the multitude of birds that inhabited that land had long since migrated to the southern warmth of the Folke Lands. The forest was so loud, so not even the acute hearing of an Elf could discern one sound from another.

It was the perfect time for him to travel stealthily to the city of Phoenix Grotto.

He was not alone, either. He traveled with the rest of his men, large brown hawk-men following close behind him. They had been together since the Heart of Hearts had released them from their prison in Ildar, about a year ago. It had taken some time; not only did the unit have to traverse deadly terrain, but the red bird leading the others had taken precautions with gaining whatever intelligence that could be offered—not much could be given other than the fact that his kingdom was under siege by the Elves and that they had claimed the capital of Phoenix Grotto, but he took what he could get.

The branches cracked underneath the claws of the multitude of birds who followed their crimson leader. They had indeed traveled far, their wings illuminated by the white gaze of the moon on seemingly endless clear nights. But now that they were only a few hours away from their destination, the red bird in front stopped, raising a wing to halt his flock.

Suddenly, the forest was silenced, as if heeding the presence of this crimson creature. Upon the ground, a small wolf stalked the brush before slowly coming to a halt at the base of the tree that housed the marvelous red hawk.

"I have word, Your Highness!" the beast barked up the tree. "But it does not involve Lyon. We still do not know where he is."

Suddenly, the brilliant red bird began to morph, steam seeping from his body as his sinews and muscles contorted to the figure of a man.

"Lyon shall wait. He is strong and does not need our worry," the bird, now a tall, muscular man with red feathers on his shoulders, said in return. "For now we must take back our homes. Tell me, Leofir, what is the current predicament of my kingdom, my Phoenix Grotto?"

"*They* are there," the wolf said. "The Elves have conquered, but they do not seem interested in governing. They prowl the streets as if searching. I have heard rumors, as well. The one who commands the thunder—she is here."

"*Storm Slinger is free once more?*" the large man said under his breath. He must admit, this information was quite worrisome. He reached to his side and gripped a dark, web-like scar upon his ribs.

"Then what guides their eyes?" he finally replied.

"They seem to be looking for something hidden within the walls."

"And the Storm Slinger, she commands their numbers?"

"I believe, Your Highness. But there is another more troubling than the thundering one."

The large man tilted his head and narrowed his fiery orange eyes. "Speak their name."

"A dark one, Your Highness. And a mighty one, at that," the wolf growled. "He is a shady wizard, far more dangerous than the Storm Slinger. We know not his name nor his purpose."

"I see." The red-feathered man scratched his fiery beard. "Go now. Prepare our way."

Without a word, the wolf nodded and shuffled back through the bushes.

"King Hallow-Talon," said one of the bird-men standing beside him on the great branch. "She is the one who gave you the scar and committed the *Atrocity*?"

"I'm afraid so..." Hallow-Talon furrowed his brow. "But I will not be so foolish again."

Another giant hawk flew to his side.

"Your Highness, I feel a storm is approaching."

"If the storm strikes," the king said as flames began to spark from his fingertips, "it shall end in fire."

Departure from the mysterious Old Man was bittersweet. Although he truly never had much time to get to know the enigmatic sage, the impact that his aid had upon the Heart of Hearts' growth was undeniable. Regardless of the fact that the Starblood still remained mostly a mystery to the young man, he felt a bit closer to the mysterious power coursing through him than he did previously.

But now he had one problem. It was simple, but not one he had honestly considered until the Old Man had long disappeared.

He had no clue where he was going.

It was a familiar feeling, and also a painful one. He was quickly reminded of the time he was lost in the maze-like city of Zerlina, and the thought of Zurriel aiding him made him grit his teeth in agony. But no one to come to his aid this time. Lukas scanned his surroundings. First of all, he was quite surprised at how drastically the biome contrasted from the frozen ranges of the mountains where he had been with the old guru. Everything at the bottom of the mountain was so green. Trees extended high into the sky, the lush blanket of their leaves blotting out the sun and illuminating the green leaves like sunlight through an umbrella; the ground was an intertwining web of roots and thick vines.

Fear had not sunk into his heart yet, though he knew he was lost. No. Instead he had simply continued walking, his mind a flurry of thoughts. How would he find this boy, even if he *did* make it to Phoenix Grotto? Say Zurriel did spare him—did the dark wizard know he was still alive? He knew that Zurriel possessed two of the three Eyes of Lunae, but what did that mean? What powers did those eyes truly bestow upon him?

Lukas shivered. The thoughts made him feel as if he were being watched.

And what of Nox? The feelings that accompanied that thought surprised him. The more he thought about her, the more he could feel a strange warmth cover his body. His heart fluttered at the thought of finding her, of embracing her.

She was alive. He knew it to be true. The Old Man was right— Lukas *knew* he was. Nox lived, and Lukas knew that she would be looking for him.

I'll find you yet, Nox, he thought as he stopped and looked at the canopies above. *Once I find this Eye, I'm coming for you next.*

Time seemed static within the ancient shroud of forest, and without sight of the sun, Lukas found himself merely guessing at what time of day it was. The birds created a mellow cacophony that descended from the canopies above down to the grassy floor. For a moment, the Starborn stopped, closed his eyes, and tuned his ears to listen to the exotic chirping. The chirping was less like a whistle (like the birds he was accustomed to) and more like a shrill laugh. Indeed, he had never heard the strange cackling and cawing noises before. He tried to imagine what these peculiar birds must look like when suddenly there was another noise among the cacophony. It seemed familiar, but Lukas couldn't truly put his finger on just what it was. Then, realization hit him like a great hammer.

They weren't bird songs. No. They were the cries of a person.

They were cries for help!

Quickly, Lukas bounded over fallen logs and sprinted in the direction of the screams. As he dashed and dodged through the ancient forest, he could feel his heart beat in his chest. What if he was too late? What if he was outnumbered? True the Starblood was powerful, but even so, he had no experience truly using it with efficiency, and if this fight involved a many opponents—

Suddenly, memories flashed through his mind of the fight with Zurriel at Crown City. He looked at his hands. They were clean, but he could still feel the warmth of Blake's blood covering them.

NO! The thought exploded through his mind, ignited by sheer rage. Numbers didn't matter in this situation. He would never let himself be helpless again! He was the Heart of Hearts! Someone needed his help, and he was going to save them. That was all he needed to know.

Finally, his sprint led him to a clearing—no—it was a road. The path pierced through the forest, its gray stones winding snake-like through the density of the woods.

Before him, two large men stood towering over a small man with dog ears, their blades drawn. Lukas stopped and crouched within the foliage, his hand gripping the *Sword Durandal* in its scabbard. It was obvious as to what had happened, the Heart of Hearts could tell by the large car that was obviously the small man's.

This was a shakedown.

"This is a toll road, see?" one of the burly men said, his blade dancing in front of the small dog-man's face.

"And it looks like you have a *lot* to pay the toll with..." the other bandit, a lanky man, said as he lowered his blade and approached the truck. "Let's see what ya got here!"

"No! Please!" the small Beastfolk exclaimed. "It's very important that I deliver these goods!"

"Somethin' valuable then!" the bandit laughed as he reached for the latch.

Suddenly, a bright flash of silver sped through the air, slicing the bandit's hand. The man dropped his blade and gripped his arm, shrieking as blood spat from the wound.

"He told you not to open the cargo," Lukas said as he sprung from the bushes. "Did you not hear him, or do you simply not care about your life?"

"Who the hell are you?!" the other ruffian said, whipping around.

"Don't worry about that," the Starborn said. "My name will be of no use to you. Now listen"—Lukas pointed—"leave now, and I won't have to hurt you, too!"

"Hurt me?! You threw your weapon over there! If anything, I'm gonna hurt *you*!"

Lukas held his hand to his side.

In a wild storm, the burly man readied his blade and rushed forward.

"I'm sick of you, guy!" the ruffian shouted.

I warned him, Lukas thought.

The man raised his blade, bringing it down with great force. Suddenly, a bright blast of white light exploded from Lukas' hand as he summoned the *Sword Durandal* to his grasp.

The sounds of scraping metal echoed throughout the forest, followed by a loud scream. Birdsong stopped, and silence filled the space.

Lukas ripped the *Sword Durandal* from the man's gut.

"Y-you!" the other bandit cried in ghastly horror. "You killed him!"

I did, he thought. *I did kill him. Why? Why don't I feel remorse? Have I really changed so much...?*

Blake's image flashed through his mind. He gritted his teeth.

After I felt your blood on my hands...

Ever since I felt this blade pierce your stomach...

Maybe that's why this man's death doesn't affect me...

*Who knows...*Lukas shook the *Sword Durandal*, slinging the blood from its slick silver blade...*the real reason...*

"You." Lukas said, his eyes mirroring the grimness of the death he just created. "Beat it."

The lanky bandit shrieked as he fell to the ground before scrambling to get up and then running off. Lukas watched the man flee down the stony road before turning to the small driver.

"Don't worry." Lukas said as he approached the round man. "I'm not here to rob you. Are you okay?"

For a moment, the man quivered, his dog-like ears folding backward as he cowered.

Lukas held out his hand.

"I'm Lukas, by the way."

"D-Darloc," the man stuttered. "I'm Darloc."

Lukas smiled.

"I'm glad I came by at the right time, Darloc."

"Yes." He nodded slightly. "Yes. I am, as well."

For a moment, neither spoke. Darloc hobbled to his feet and dusted off his blue-and-green clothes.

"What are you doing out here?" Darloc asked. "You're obviously not a bandit, so why are you prowling these forsaken woods?"

"Well, uh..." Lukas began scratching the side of his face.

"You're lost, aren't you?" the dog-man laughed. "You can admit it. It's rather common for people to lose themselves in the Nathratu Greatforest. Most just never find their way out."

"I guess it's a good thing that I met you, then," Lukas said with a laugh.

"Where were you headed, anyway?"

"Phoenix Grotto! But, I have no clue how to get there."

"Phoenix Grotto, eh?" the Beastman said as he rubbed his furry chin. "Maybe it was fate that we met, Lukas. You see"—he pointed to his car—"I'm carrying something rather special to a loyal client I have in Phoenix Grotto, and...well," he nodded, "you seem to be able to fight rather well, and I could use the protection, I guess."

"So you'll take me?" Lukas lit up.

"Of course, but I have one rule. A very...strict rule."

Lukas cocked his head. "Okay...what is this rule?"

"No questions about the cargo," he said sternly. "None."

Odd, Lukas thought. The more he spoke to Darloc, the more

22

suspicious the small, fat, Beastman became. But...he knew that this was probably going to be his only way to Phoenix Grotto.

Just grin and bear it, I guess.

"Alright, Darloc," Lukas replied. "In exchange for you taking me to Phoenix Grotto, I'll use my sword to protect your automobile."

"And..." the round man said expectantly.

"And, I won't ask any questions." Lukas held out his hand, an invitation for a handshake. "But *you* can't ask *me* any, either. No questions on how I got lost in these woods or why I'm going to Phoenix Grotto. Deal?"

Darloc smiled cheerily and slapped his hand into the embrace and shook.

"Deal! Pleasure doing business with you!"

Lukas looked at the dead body on the road.

"What do we do about him?"

"Bah!" Darloc waved his hand. "His comrade will come back for him...hopefully."

Lukas shrugged. "Hopefully, huh?"

Leofir maneuvered easily through the forest brush, his wolf form quickly slipping through areas that would halt a human's movement. And fast he had to go, for the messages of the Phoenix King were of utmost importance in the war between Elves and Beastfolk. If the Beastfolk were to be successful in driving out the Elves, then they must receive their king.

Truly, the wolf thought, *we need Lyon.*

But now was not the time for wishes. No. Now the war for Phoenix Grotto must be won with what they had and that alone. The King was alive, and with the powers of his holy flames, surely they could take back their homes.

Leofir twisted and turned through the forests until he stood at location where the walls of nature met the walls of the Grotto. He stopped. If there was one thing the Elves didn't know about, it was the underground passages beneath the city—tunnels that the beasts used rather strategically to spy and collect valuable information on their enemies.

Leofir stood for a moment as his muscles and ligaments converted back into his human form. Once fully formed, he approached the dark walls of the fortified city and felt them, searching. His hand stopped upon a single stone, which he pressed. Suddenly, several bricks within the wall began to cave inward, revealing a person-sized hole in the stone.

They have no clue, he thought as he entered. *We might just win.*

Once inside, the hole behind him slowly returned to normal, and he was in darkness. Feeling his way around, he felt the stairs upon his feet and began the climb.

But the darkness felt unusually eerie.

Why, he wondered as he felt the hair on his tail stand up on end.

In the distance, his ears detected the sound of armor clanking as someone walked toward the stairs.

We don't wear armor...

"He's down there!" A voice suddenly cried out. "The stairwell!"

Leofir jumped, feeling swelling anxiety in his chest at the clanging sound of armor. Quickly, he turned to run, but the Elves were upon him. He felt the cold metal of gauntlets dig into his skin as the soldiers dragged him to the upper floor.

"Let me go!"

"Go? Why would we do that?" the smooth voice of a woman laughed as she approached.

The wolf gasped as Elven soldiers forced him to his knees. Leofir felt the woman softly raise his chin. Sweat began to bead upon his forehead. This was bad. Very bad.

"You see, wolf," the woman said, smiling, her lips painted neatly with a turquoise lipstick. "We're about to have a nice chat."

Leofir's heart beat wildly in his chest. This was it; he was captured by the Inquisitor—

By none other than the Storm Slinger!

CHAPTER FOUR

The One From My Dreams

Darloc was a quiet man, or it might have been that he and Lukas, given that they had made a deal to preserve their confidentiality, had nothing to speak about. Being as that was, the ride was silent save for the cargo shaking in the back as the tires hit holes in the stony road. The birds cackled, but that was so common that Lukas had long become deaf to their laughter, and from time to time, Lukas could see random small, brown, furry animals (mainly squirrels and rats) hurriedly flee from the path of the vehicle as it approached them and disappear into the brush.

"So..." Lukas began, wishing to end the silence. "What's Phoenix Grotto like?"

Darloc shrugged impassively.

"It's dark." He said. "The most fortified and advanced city that you'll find in all the Folke Lands, really. Legend has it that a phoenix once lived in that cave...before it was a city, that is. The place is home of the Phoenix King"—he paused—"or at least it was. Now Elves are running the show down there, I hear."

"The Phoenix King," Lukas said under his breath. "So Hallow-Talon...?"

"I just hope we don't have any trouble at the gates."

"Why would we?" Lukas asked.

"They may not like what I'm bringin' in."

"And what exactly..." Lukas trailed of as the small man put held up a firm hand.

"No questions, remember?"

Right...right...

"Look." Darloc pointed forward.

Lukas looked ahead to see a massive wall of black stone, extending high above the forest. It was a magnificent sight. Lukas realized what the Beastman meant. This wall completely covered the mouth of the cave. Lukas' eyes widened in wonder at the sight. The idea was as exotic as it was tantalizing. To think that there was a city entirely veiled in darkness was unfathomable to Lukas.

"There it is. They call it the Ebon Shield. It's the infamous fortification of Phoenix Grotto."

"What about the sun?" Lukas asked in astonishment. "Don't they ever see the sun?"

"No." You see, before the city fell to the Elves—er—" Darloc stopped. "Before the Civil War began, really—the city was lit by phoenix flame. They say that the Aeon of War, Yeornyeim, blessed our royalty with the powers of the sun, thus creating the Phoenix Blood. But that's just an old story we tell children. If it really happened, well, who knows?"

As the automobile slowly crept toward the magnificent black wall, Lukas could see several soldiers in golden Elven armor at the gates.

"Well," the small dogman said as he pulled his humble vehicle forward. "Let's hope this goes well. I don't wanna go to prison today."

"Pris—?" Lukas started.

"You there!" the voice of an Elf called out as approached.

What is in this car, Lukas thought as he watched the well-dressed Elf come closer, two fully-armed knights trailing him. Lukas wasn't sure the Elf's exact rank, but he could tell by the Elf's extravagant dress that he was someone of high stature. He was dressed head-to-toe in red, with gold lining his coat.

"What's the cargo?" the Elf asked sternly.

"Potions, sire." The small beastly man said as he bowed.

The Elf motioned to his soldiers. "Open it up."

"No! You can't!" Darloc exclaimed with more anxiety that he seemed to have intended.

The Elf held up a hand to the other two to stop them. "Tell me," he said as he narrowed his eyes. "Why can't I?"

"B-because!" the man stuttered. "They'll ruin in the sun!"

"Now I'm suspicious, sir." The Elf motioned again. "Open it up!"

"Hey!" Lukas interjected. "You heard him! His potions will ruin in the sun!"

The Elven gatekeeper turned to Lukas.

"That is not my concern." He said as he approached the young man. "I merely need to make note of everything that comes into a city of the Almighty Mirean Empire."

"Why would you want to ruin them?" Lukas rebutted. "That's his hard work in there!"

"Open. It. Up."

"Hey!" Lukas bellowed. "Stop!"

Lukas felt his heart pulse once heavily as he channeled the Starblood. Suddenly, a wave of spiritual energy rippled through the area, causing the Elves to hold their heads.

"W-where?" the well-dressed Elf groaned. "What am I doing here?"

"You were about to let us through," Lukas said, smiling as he hopped back into the car. "You just checked everything, and said we're clear."

"Well!" the Elf snapped angrily. "Get out of my sight." He turned to the line. "Next!"

"I saw that your blade was arcane, but I've never felt magic like that, young man," the round dog-man called Darloc said. "It seems there's more mystery to you than just that sword at your side."

Lukas smiled in return. "Maybe so."

"Well, you know I have potions now, so why are *you* here?"

Lukas listened as he watched the massive wall pass over his head, revealing the brilliant city of Phoenix Grotto within. All along the streets, multicolored etherlamps decorated and illuminated the gray stones of the hidden realm.

Lukas finally answered. "I'm looking for someone. A boy named

Alvys. He has a red eye."

"Red eye, you say," Darloc sighed as he stroked his beard. "Well, young Lukas. I believe I can help you find him."

"You know where he is?!" Lukas shot up.

"I do," he replied. "But try not to be too surprised when I take you there. Things are not as they seem."

"What...do you mean?"

You'll see," Darloc chuckled. "You'll see."

Leofir awoke in pure darkness. Nothing but a void surrounded him, and he could feel he was suspended in the air. He tried to move, but found that, wherever he was, he was bound to a wall.

"Why so nervous, little doggy?" A smooth voice tittered softly from within the darkness.

"Who's there?!" he raved.

As soon as he shrieked, the light of etherlamps filled the room. At first, as he squinted his eyes, the figures in the room appeared merely as silhouettes, faceless phantoms of doom. As his eyes began to adjust, he could see a young woman clad in red robes with short blonde hair, her hair golden even in the lamplight. Leofir looked into her light blue —almost turquoise—eyes. They weren't kind; they were sharp, piercing like the thin blade of a stiletto.

"You," he said, his voice low and almost a whimper. "You're—"

"Storm Slinger, yes, yes. But you can call me Larc. What might I call you?" The young woman smiled as she looked at her long, blue fingernails.

"M-my name?" the wolf said through gasping breaths. "I'll never tell you!"

"What a shame, Leofir." Larc smirked. "And here I thought we'd be *fast* friends..."

"How did you know my name?!" the wolf cried out. He could feel his heart racing in his chest, beating against his ribcage.

"Why, you told me, remember?" she said as she approached and knelt in front of him. "You can't hide *anything* from *me*, my darling."

Leofir was silent, the sound of his breathing intensifying as the terrifying woman drew closer to him.

"Let's jump to the point, shall we? We know that you have been corresponding with insurgents somewhere in the forest; however, given that the terrain is too volatile for a search party, we have had a good bit of trouble pinpointing their location." Larc licked her finger and ran it across her lips. "That is why," she said, running her finger up the wolf's throat to his chin, craning his head back, "*you* are going to tell us where they are."

"I-insurgents?! I would never —!"

Suddenly, the wolf felt a burning sensation as his muscles vibrated and contracted, pushing against his binds.

"You're thinking that they're going to attack using the catacombs, aren't you?"

"How did you—?!"

Larc Elliot lowered her head to the wolf's ear.

"I'm just listening to those little electric signals jolting through your brain, deary." Her voice was silky and sweet. "Don't worry. You can't lie to me. It's *actually* impossible. Now tell me, *what* is Hallow-Talon planning?"

"I'll never tell you!"

Leofir screeched as another shock of electricity flared through his body, causing his muscles to convulse.

"So he's planning to take back the city? Interesting." She stood once more and ran her fingers through her short gilded hair. "I can't wait to see him again."

"How're you—!?"

"It's easy when you think your answers before I even ask a question," Larc laughed. "And where will he strike first? We already know how he's going to try to enter the Grotto, so where will he be headed?"

"I don't know!"

"Hmm..." Larc said as she narrowed her eyes for a moment, her finger rubbing her bottom lip. She huffed in frustration. "You really don't, do you? Interesting."

"I don't know! I don't know!"

"Well played, Phoenix King," She said under her breath. "But no matter. I already know enough to stop the rebellion. "Thank you, little wolf."

She sighed and motioned to a soldier as she turned toward the stairs.

"Kill him."

"*WHAT?!*" Leofir shrieked. "*NO!*"

But Larc did not hear him.

It was none of her concern.

Darloc's old automobile rustled as he drove it through the dim streets of Phoenix Grotto. The city was loud, and all the voices voices seemed to echo, probably because the city was enclosed. The streets were made of black stone, dark and inky, just like everything else in the city. Lukas kept silent, though in his mind he pondered upon the small man's cryptic words back at the gate.

Things are not as they seem? The words reverberated through his mind. *What on Lythia could that mean?*

"We're almost there," the dog-man said as he turned down a small alley, just barely big enough for his vehicle. "Mind yourself, and don't make eye contact with anyone until we're there."

"What?"

"Just do it," he insisted.

Lukas didn't complain. He averted his eyes from the streets, feeling uneasy. Where was he going? He was sure that this part of Phoenix Grotto looked rough. He readied himself for anything, his hands ready to call forth the *Sword Durandal* at the blink of an eye.

The automobile rumbled along the stone some more, then stopped.

"We're here." Darloc said. "Get out, and follow my lead."

"Darloc." A large man in a suit approached. Lukas noticed instantly how much taller this man was compared to the tiny driver. "What took so long?" The man pointed to Lukas. "Who is this?"

"W-well we got held up at the gate. Drat Elves and all. And this here is my security. He helped me get here."

"Alright," the man said, shrugging. "We'll get the potions. You go follow up with Jalzen. He's in there, and I don't think he will be happy that you're late."

"Of course. Of course." Darloc bowed and hurried toward the door.

"Hold up." The man held out his hand as Lukas tried to pass."

"I don't know you. I can't just let you into the den, ya know?"

Lukas looked up to see the man's fanged smile.

Are they...vampires? They seem so civilized. What is happening here?

"Oh! Excuse my rudeness," Darloc laughed. "I need him to come with me. He needs to give Jalzen the full report of what happened on the journey."

The vampire looked at the small Beastman, then at Lukas, then shrugged.

"Whatever," he said, calling to three more vampires, "let's get this stuff unloaded, guys!"

Lukas followed Darloc to the door.

"Okay, Lukas," the small, round Beastman said. "Just follow my lead. Trust me, it will be worth your time."

Lukas sighed, then nodded. Whatever was going to happen inside, he was positive he could handle it. *I've dealt with vampires before,* he thought, his mind reaching back to the images of Damasko in Ildar. Lukas had been a novice then. Now, however, he was confident in his abilities. Though his time with the Old Man had merely been months, the wise sage taught him much about the *Sword Durandal* and the Heart of Hearts...about the Starblood that coursed through his veins.

Lead on, he thought as he followed the small merchant. *I'm ready.*

The inside of the den was dark, scarcely lit by dim red flames. Lukas followed Darloc down a tight, red corridor until they came to an even tighter room with a large, round table.

"Darloc!" the stout vampire at the head of the table laughed as he raised his glass of what Lukas determined to be blood. "You're late, friend! What was the hold-up?"

"I apologize, Mister Jalzen!" The small merchant bowed. "I was caught up at the gates by the Elves."

"Dastards," Jalzen said as he swirled the blood in his cup.

"You'd think they wouldn't be as hard on us, especially with what they're *really* looking for." He pointed to Lukas. "Who's this guy, Darloc? You're supposed to come alone."

"He's looking for someone. He helped me through the gates, so I thought you might be able to help him out."

"What's yer name, kid?" the vampire said, burping.

Lukas looked around the table. It was odd. Instead of finding abominable things, he saw roast chickens, and pork and steaks.

They aren't eating humans?

"What's your name?" Jalzen repeated more forcefully.

"Lukas."

"Alright, Lukas." He took a sip of the blood from his wine glass. "Who're ya lookin' for?"

"I'm looking for a boy with a red eye."

Suddenly, the vampires at the table stood and unsheathed their blades.

"So you're after him, too?!"

Lukas quickly called *Durandal* to his hands.

"I don't want a fight!"

"What do you want with him?!" Jalzen burst as he pulled out a tiny red stone.

Blood Dust?!

"Stop Jalzen!" the voice of a little boy said, cutting the tension in the room.

Lukas watched in awe as a child, no more than eleven years of age, entered the room and stood by the boss vampire. *It was true*, Lukas thought. His right eye was red.

"You know this guy, Alvys?" Jalzen said as he stood. "If he's here to hurt ya, I'll send him packing!"

The young boy tilted his head. "You're Lukas, right?"

Lukas stood upright once more, sheathing the Starsword. "You're Alvys, right?"

"Yeah," the boy said, smiling, "and you are..."

The two finished in unison.

"The one from my dreams."

CHAPTER FIVE

A Ripple Heard

"You know this guy, Al?" Jalzen said as he stood.

"Yeah." Alvys said. "You're Lukas, aren't you?"

"I am," the teen replied. "And you're Alvys."

Several of the vampires stood and placed themselves at the boy's side.

"What do you want?" Jalzen's amicable voice had become rigid. "You with the Elves?"

"No!" Lukas stepped back. "I'm actually the opposite! You have to listen to me, Alvys! You are in *grave* danger! A very bad man is looking for your eye, and if he gets it, the world will be in trouble!"

"I don't buy it," the vampire scoffed. "How do I know that this isn't some trick, and you're really working for him? What exactly does this man *want* with his eye, huh?"

"Well, I...I don't know what he wants. All I know is that he wants to take it for his own. Please! You have to believe me!"

Lukas sighed. What was there to say? Could he really just come out with all of the information? Could he really just tell them everything about Zurriel and the Eyes of Lunae? What if the vampires learned of the Eye's power? Surely if they did, they wouldn't let Lukas just take Alvys away from them. If they learned of the power, even *they* might try to take the Eye themselves and hurt Alvys in the process.

Lukas stopped. *I must tread lightly.*

"And so, what? You think I'm just gonna let you take my boy like this? You may be mysterious, traveler, and you may sound sincere, but I don't believe a word you say."

"Well then," Lukas said, gritting his teeth. *This wasn't working.* Truly, there had to be another way, he was just unsure of it now. "I guess I'll take my leave."

Lukas turned to find a blade at his throat.

"Leave?!" Jalzen laughed. "And what, go tell the Elves where Al is?! I think not."

Lukas felt the cold steel of the blade placed lightly upon his throat. He looked around the room. *Too many.* There was little option here. Even if he could summon the Starblood in time, he wasn't sure he could stop the whole room without receiving grave injury. *What if they hurt Alvys?*

He was as sure as the blade at his throat that they didn't trust him, and he was just as sure that *he* didn't trust *them* in return.

Conundrum.

No. This was no real riddle. Cold metal tightened itself around his body; Lukas suddenly hit the ground with little struggle.

Yes, there was no real conundrum to be solved here. It was plain as day.

Lukas had found himself taken hostage.

Agnon sat in darkness. He was keen to the darkness; it was his kin. As far as he was concerned, he was born in it and bathed in its waters. Serenely he meditated, humming to himself in a low growl, giving himself fully to dark musings. He felt it; it was a vibration. It was a small cry from somewhere within the Grotto.

But where? That, he did not know. However, he felt, it would soon reveal itself.

He knew that the Inquisitor couldn't feel this small ripple. No. She was far too loud. Too...self-absorbed and therefore disconnected from the world around her.

Agnon had spent the entirety of his life wrapped within these vibrations—these small dents in space, and thusly he had become acute to their presence. And this was the *third* of these entities that he had felt. The first, he knew to be the Eye (though he could not ascertain where it was exactly); the second was larger. That one he could care less for; whatever it was, it was the size that disinterested him. After all, it was less his duty and more that of the arrogant Inquisitor.

It was the third ruffle in the fabric of space that piqued his interests the most. It felt different that the other presences in the area. It was louder and more vibrant; it was far more alive than anything else. He had only heard its call once before. It was loud and unmistakable; its vibration sounded like that of a choir. He had heard this same call only mere months ago in Crown City. There was no doubt in the grim sage's mind. The Heart of Hearts yet lived, and that meant one thing and one thing only...

A Starborn walked the streets of Phoenix Grotto, and he too was looking for the Eye.

Lukas sat with his head lowered. The cage was cramped, probably because it was not meant for a human. He had thought of trying to use his powers to escape, but was deterred by the chains that he now knew were probably composed of the magic-canceling Necronite ore.

"You don't want my blood, by the way," he said to the vampire meant to guard him.

"I wouldn't want it anyway," the tall man laughed. "We aren't so barbaric."

"Sure," Lukas said, rolling his eyes. "Then I suppose you're drinking tomato juice?"

"Nope. Pig blood."

Lukas paused, his eyes relaying his sheer confusion.

"You saw the dinner table." The vampire said. "Not everyone who is a vampire wanted to be that way. We never wanted to eat anyone, so we substitute human blood with the blood of animals. It tastes horrible, but it sates the blood lust. Trust me, we're vampires, but we aren't savages like the Nightshade Court. Well, at least not anymore. We detached from their ranks long ago."

"So those potions...?"

"Blood Dust made of, once again, pig blood."

Lukas froze. Memories of Ildar rushed through his mind. Damasko and his officers were so cruel and ruthless...but...but here? Here he spoke to a vampire as if the man weren't one at all.

"You aren't all that bad after all, then. Well, besides caging me and all."

"It's nothing personal, so don't take it too harshly. Jalzen just does what he can to protect the ones he loves."

Lukas couldn't help but smile.

Protect the ones he loves, huh?

For a split second, he thought of Nox. He could feel a strange warmth and pressure, as if his heart were beating outside his chest.

She was alive, but he already knew that. And, for the first time in a while, he knew he was going to see her again.

I'm sorry Nox, he thought, *but I have to save this boy first.*

"Heldor," said a small voice coming through the door. Lukas and the vampire turned their heads to see Alvys standing at the entrance to the small room. "Heldor, I wanna talk to him."

"I dunno, kid." Heldor replied. "How will Jalzen feel about —?"

"He said it's fine." The child interrupted.

"Five minutes." Heldor sighed before leaving the room.

Lukas looked at the young boy in the dim lights. It was true. His eye was just as crimson as Nox's had been.

"I don't think you're bad," the boy said flatly. "If you were so bad, why would you not be bad in my dream?"

"Alvys..."

"But Jalzen said that you were trying to trick me. Jalzen is my best friend, he's like a big brother to me, so I don't think he'd ever be wrong."

Lukas bowed his head. *How can I reach these people?*

"I have a best friend too, Alvys."

"You do?"

"Yeah, her name is Nox, and she had a red eye just like yours. But bad guys took her away and they took her eye, just like they'll take yours."

"They want to *take my eye*?!" The boy recoiled in disgust. "Why?"

"Because your eye is magical, Alvys. It belongs to a goddess, and a powerful wizard wants to take it away from you."

"That's enough!" Heldor growled as he stepped back into the room. "Alvys, you can't trust this guy. Remember that you shouldn't listen to strangers."

Alvys turned to Lukas once more. In the blue lights, Lukas could see the red eye. But there was something else there.

As Heldor led the child out of the room, Lukas could see the worry in the boy's eyes. In that moment, Lukas was sure of one thing...

He knew that the boy believed him.

Darloc drove his empty vehicle down the dismal streets of Phoenix Grotto, his mind cleared of any trouble now that that his cargo had been unloaded. Now, he knew, there would be no more complications for him. Even if he were stopped and searched, it's not as if he were carrying anything illegal. As a matter of fact, he wasn't carrying anything.

The small dog-man whistled a giddy tune as he steered his truck carefully through the darkened streets.

Nope, he thought, sighing, *nothing left to do here.* He stretched gaily. *Let's head out.*

The small dog-man drove with ease, his eyes casually glancing around. The city, which had been carved from a large cave, was vibrant. He noticed the other Beastfolk going about their day here or there. For a moment, he thought about his people.

Missing a king, he thought, frowning, *what are we to do?*

He shifted his eyes to the Elven soldiers patrolling the streets. He shivered at the sight of them. Elves were a keen race, and merely being under their gaze was enough to unnerve even the strongest of men. They were faster, more intuitive.

Before he knew it, he had reached the exit gates of the city. The giant wall at the mouth of the cavern blocked out any sunlight save for the small beams of daylight that leaked in from the gates at its base. Without fear, he lined himself up behind the other vehicles and waited his turn. Surely there would be no trouble. For even if the same guards were to check him, he had nothing for them to fine him on.

No. Nothing to worry about.

He waited patiently behind the other caravans, wondering at times what the hold-up was, but he decided that he had nothing to rush for. He didn't have another job for a few weeks, and the money that Jalzen paid him would allow him to live happily until then.

No. No rush, either.

He felt a rush of ease relax his shoulders.

As the automobile in front of him passed easily through the Elven guards, Darloc drove forward with no hesitation.

There was a pause. The guards stared at him, then whispered something to each other.

"Yeah that's him!" a voice exclaimed as it grew closer.

Darloc went pale. "W-what is the problem."

The well-dressed Elf from the gate talked momentarily with the two guards, then nodded.

Suddenly, the car hit the ground as the wheels were smashed. Several hands reached into the drivers side and ripped the small man from his seat.

"What did I do?!" Darloc shrieked. "What did I do?"

The soldiers raised the fat man to his knees. Before him stood an Elven soldier in extravagant clothing.

"I'm glad we caught you when we did," he laughed. "My name is Commander Solgus, and my men here say that you had a"—he shrugged his shoulders—"passenger...upon your entry to the city. A passenger with magic, as well." The commander's lean face became rigid. "Who was he?"

"I don't know who he was!" the round dog-man pleaded. "I picked him up on the road! Said he was looking for someone in the city! I know nothing more, I promise. Please, don't hurt me!"

Commander Solgus bent down to the terrified man's eye level. "I'm an honorable man, you see. I won't hurt you. But there's someone who would be absolutely *ecstatic* to hear your testimony. Be warned though. She's a bit more...unyielding than I am. Even if I won't hurt you, there's no promising that she will leave you unscathed."

Wh—" Darloc whimpered.

"No need to say anything." He nodded to the other soldiers. "Bring him along."

Darloc was jolted to his feet by Elven soldiers.

Nothing to worry about. Nothing at all.

But no matter how many times he whimpered those words, he

knew they were false.

CHAPTER SIX

Within the Dark Hand's Grasp

The palace was as dark and blackened as the city outside, or maybe it was just the dungeon. Darloc sat in a chair, his arms and legs bound by coarse twine. The shadows of armored men lined the damp stone walls, the light of only one etherlamp revealing their presences.

The small Beastman felt utterly forlorn and he knew that, in this room, whatever was to come to pass in the immediate future, it was not going to be bad.

Suddenly, the door opened and young woman entered the room. She was tall and lean, or so it seemed in the low light. In the dimness of the etherlight, her red robes appeared a dismal, bloody color. She ran her long blue nails through her short golden hair.

"Darloc, I assume?" she asked, her voice smooth and sweet.

"I a-am," the small man whimpered as he stared into her frigid blue eyes.

"I'm Larc Elliot," she began. "Well, you see, I'm not in this forsaken rubble because I *want* to be. No. I'm not here sight-seeing the overabundant gray and black that this filthy ruin seems to have so much of." She wiggled her fingers, scaring the prisoner with the small blue sparks that danced along her fingertips. "I'm actually here on a very, *very, special* mission. Do you know what it is, puppy?"

She lowered her head to the small dog-man's ear, her lips almost grazing his face.

"I'm looking for someone with a red eye." Her sultry whisper caused Darloc's heart to beat faster.

"A red—?"

"So it's a little boy?" She interrupted.

"How did you—?!"

"And where is this little boy?"

"He's—?"

"Nice to know." She whistled and two armed soldiers entered the room. "You've been quite a help, dear doggy, but I think we're done now."

"Can I go now? I told you what you wanted to know!"

"Can you go...? Can you go...?" She mused, rubbing her chin as she turned and walked toward the door. "No, I don't think so." She shrugged. "Lock him up."

Suddenly the soldiers drew their blades. Larc Elliot closed the door which did little to muffle the merchant's screams from within. But she didn't care; it was of no consequence. No.

She had what she wanted. She had all she needed.

The birds waited outside the walls, hidden from the enemy, concealed by the webbing of the rainforest canopy. They chirped, speaking to each other in a language that seemed to the Elves to simply be the sounds of the wildlife along the wall of Phoenix Grotto.

But this would be the wrong assumption.

"Look at them, Your Majesty." chirped one.

"They believe their heightened senses will save them," chirped another. *"Yet they cannot see us while hidden in the leaves."*

"May we claw the ones at the gate, Your Majesty? Their armor is but paper to our talons."

"No," the chirps of Hallow-Talon echoed through the forest. *"We must play their game. Let us go to the tunnels."*

The trees rustled as the birds broke through the canopy and were free in the air, carefully gliding just above the green. Hallow-Talon looked forward, toward the tall fortification that was the famed wall of the Grotto. The sheet of stone, solid black Ebon Shield, blocked the entirety of the mouth of the cave that contained his precious kingdom.

I'm coming for you, my beloved home, he thought as the birds' wings guided them to the most remote side of the mountain.

The birds landed, shifting back into their human forms as they touched the ground. With a nod from his king, one bird placed his hand upon a peculiar stone. Suddenly, the stones began to morph until a dark doorway appeared.

Once inside, the Phoenix King snapped his fingers and summoned a small flame to light the way. As if on cue, several etherlamps beamed from the top of the staircase.

"Well, well, well..." the silhouette of an Elf stood in front of the lights. "I had heard you were at large, Your Majesty, but I was naught to believe it."

Hallow-Talon raised his hand without a word, red flames exploding from his palms, climbing the staircase with a great gale of heat.

"How's that for 'at large?'"

The corridor was quiet.

"Your Majesty!" one of the birdmen cried out, pointing to the floor.

The king followed his subject's finger. At his feet, liquid flowed down the stairs. He felt his heart jump.

Water?!

"As I was saying," the man at the top of the stairs said through a cracking voice. "My name is Commander Avrik Solgus, and I—"

The commander jumped backward as another blast of crimson flames filled the corridor.

"I don't care who you are," the Phoenix King said sharply as he began ascending the stairs.

"Don't come any closer!" the Elf screeched as he hit the floor. "Soldiers! Do it!"

At his command, the soldiers suddenly tossed buckets of water down the stairwell.

"Fools!" the phoenix exclaimed as he sent another blast of flame hurdling up. The two forces collided with a resounding hiss, exploding into a giant plume of steam.

The Elves stood silent for a moment, but not for long, as the shadowy figures of hawks sped up the staircase, their talons warping the Elven armor with sickening crunching noises.

"Help!" the commander squealed. "Hel—!"

"Not so fast," the Phoenix King growled as he gripped the wiry Elf's face in his giant hands.

The decorated man began to squirm violently as red light illuminated the bird-man's hand. Within seconds, flames erupted from his hands, searing the Elf's face. The Elf's screams became muffled and then Commander Solgus fell limp.

"No, there will be no help for you today," Hallow-Talon said, turning to see the other Elves had been felled by his men. "Today is not your day," he spat. "It is *ours*."

The blood of Elven soldiers filled the tunnels underneath the city of Phoenix Grotto. Even with their renowned armor, the hawk-men made quick work of them, razor-sharp talons crushing the bones underneath their precious metal exoskeletons.

Foolish, the king thought as he passed the corpses. *So much for their self-called superiority.*

"Your Majesty," a hawk-man said as he approached his commander. "We approach the exit."

"Aye. That we do, soldier."

"What is the plan once on the surface?"

"We baptize the sinners," the king said. "We baptize them in fire. Then we reclaim the castle."

The hawk-men merely nodded, then faced forward and followed their liege to the surface.

Darkness filled the room, defied only by the amber flame of a single candle. Agnon sat, his blue face lit dimly by the light. The room was cold, but he didn't mind. He liked the cold. It reminded him of the mountains, far from the harshness of the desert sands. The more he thought about the coarse barren winds, the more he felt his ire rise. For a moment, the words of the High Priestess fluttered through his mind.

My people? The thought grated across his mind. *I have no people.*

He knew it was true. He had long absolved himself of the Abdian culture. The culture of magic-less, *powerless,* hypocrisy and death.

'You want power, don't you boy? You want to crush those who did you

wrong?'

He could see Zurriel in his mind clearly, just as it had been, all those years ago.

'I can give you power...I can give you the might to crush your enemies under your grasp,' the voice of Zurriel said in his mind.

"Agnon." Larc Elliot said as the door swung open, light spilling into the room.

"What now, woman?"

"I've found the Eye your master is so...interested in."

The large Darkling rose silently.

Larc turned sharply and moved from the doorway. "Follow me."

The two moved down the hallway without speaking. As much as the Inquisitor hated to admit it, the large wizard made her...uneasy. She was a woman of strategy and intelligence, one who valued research and information, one who reveled in preemptive and advantageous situations. But *he,* this dreary sorcerer, was different, and it unnerved her. She had tried multiple times to read his thoughts to determine his allegiances, but each proved fruitless. It was strange, and worrying to say the least. But even more so than her anxieties, her confusion proved dominant.

It was as if he were constantly thinking *nothing*.

No. That couldn't be true. Could it? The thought was ghastly, so she dismissed it. She would not show fear. She refused. Fear was weakness, and she'd dare not let herself be considered weak.

The two approached the balcony, and Larc led Agnon to the edge. Before them, the vast shadowy labyrinth of Phoenix Grotto sprawled out among the cave floor, its designs made visible by the blue and yellow etherlamps that lit the city.

"It's truly a shame," Larc said, a strange wistfulness in her voice. "To think this city is really so forlorn."

Agnon said nothing, his large, darkness-shrouded figure standing at the rail.

"There." Larc pointed to a dark area of the city. "Where the lights are darkest. That is where you will find what you seek."

Silence again.

"Who are you, wizard?" Larc said, instantly wishing she had not.

"I am the Harbinger of the Black Star," he growled, his face shrouded by his thick black cloak. "Ask me nothing more, girl." He held out a shrouded arm. *"Nuun Gravikka,"* the wizard called out.

Suddenly, the large man leaped from the balcony like a whirling wind, startling the Inquisitor with its force. Surprised, Larc Elliot looked over the rails. Below her, a dark cloud vanished.

And so the harbinger has become the hunter.

Scarce yellow lights lit the streets in spots, giving way to the darker shadows between. Given that most people avoided this area and deemed it dangerous, Agnon had no trouble appearing and disappearing as he maneuvered through the blackened alleyways. Now that he knew where to find the Eye, it wouldn't be difficult to find it among the little options presented to him along the forlorn district of the city. The area was darker than usual, with some spots being completely blackened. But it was still the same as the rest of the city for the most part. The buildings and streets were carved out of the same obsidian-colored stone, and extended tall into the air, their windows lit by vague yellow lights, indicating that they weren't vacant. He felt the presence of the Eye here, of course, but it did little to aid him in his search to ascertain it. This was his bane as far as his magic was concerned, given that no matter how close or far he got from his target, he would never be able to correctly determine his distance from it.

All he needed to do was find the Eye and retrieve it from its owner.

And the Darkling was sure he would be *quite* persuasive.

The large Abdian continued forward, concealed by the shroud of his hood, a vagrant shadow, embraced by the darkness of the dismal city. Alleyways twisted and turned, becoming thinner and thinner until he came to a small garden lit by luminous blue mushrooms. Agnon looked to the far end. Only a short distance away, two hardy men stood stalwart by a crimson door.

"You lost, partner?" one of the men asked, drawing his blade as he approached. "Because last I checked, Jalzen isn't expecting anyone today."

Agnon was silent, his pale green eyes studying the man from the safety of the shadows his hood cast over his face.

Vampire.

"You deaf, partner?"

With a wave of his hand, Agnon conjured a black cloud. The guard jolted as he felt the tip of a cold blade touch his neck threateningly.

"What the—?" he exclaimed. There, at his throat, a cloud hovered, the tip of the blade sticking out of it. He looked at his assailant. Agnon held his hand through a second cloud of his own.

"Magic!" The guard froze. "Who are you?!"

"I am looking for a red eye," the muscular wizard said in a low growl. "Is it here?"

"What—?" the guard yelped as the blade pressed harder against his throat.

"Is. The Eye. Here?"

"Inside! Inside!" he pleaded. "Just let me go!"

Agnon said nothing as he felt the dagger glide across the guard's throat, severing his head cleanly from his body. *Vampires,* Agnon thought, *be sure to sever the heads completely.*

"I thank you," the brooding wizard said as he pushed the corpse to the ground. With a wave of his hand, a black cloud formed upon the closed doorway and he entered.

The Eye was inside. He knew that much.

Alvys sat beside Jalzen, the two of them laughing at a joke one of the gang members had told. It was dinnertime as usual, and the assorted animal meats upon the table were as lavish as ever.

"That's so bad I can't believe I'm laughin' at it!" the vampire lord croaked. "What a mess that was!"

The vampires helped themselves to the plethora of foods before them, the smells of pork mixing with the baked breads and cheeses, when suddenly the smoke grew thicker and blacker.

"So here you are..." a deep voice filled the room. "O, Eye of Revelation."

Everyone rose from their seats and unsheathed their weapons, ready to fight whatever the threat may be. Gazes scanned the room. In the doorway, a giant shadowy figure formed into a man veiled by a black cloak.

"And who the hell are you?" Jalzen asked, his voice stony and gruff.

"Give me the boy."

"Listen here." Jalzen laughed with a nod to the others.

Agnon looked around. Within mere moments, he found himself surrounded by blades and knives.

"No one messes with our little bro Alvys, you got that?"

Agnon was once again silent.

"Tie him up." Jalzen spat.

"You have a choice," Agnon said, his voice grainy and cold. "If you give me the boy, I won't kill you all."

"Your lack of self-awareness is a bit stifling, brother!" Jalzen laughed. "You got blades at your neck. I don't think you should be doing any threatening here."

"That is your choice." Agnon repeated. "Be quick. I am not a patient man."

"Thick skull, huh? Too bad." Jalzen sighed. "Kill him."

At the command of their master, several blades arced, only to find themselves slicing through air.

"What!" Jalzen burst.

But it was too late. Upon the wizard's command, several black clouds formed at the necks of each assailant. With lightning-fast speed, Agnon's dagger glinted in the dim red light as he sliced through each cloud. Jalzen and Alvys watched in horror as the men they loved so dear fell to the ground, headless.

Quickly, Jalzen reached to take hold of Alvys. Just as their hands met, an arm reached out of a cloud and took hold of the boy.

What happened in mere seconds seemed like an eternity for Jalzen. Alvys' rang through Jalzen's mind as the boy was dragged into the void. *It can't be, can it? Did this really happen?*

Unfortunately, he knew it did.

Alvys had been abducted.

CHAPTER SEVEN

The Distant Thunder

Lukas could hear a muffled commotion outside the door where he was held captive. Something had happened; he knew that it meant trouble, and for some reason, he knew it meant trouble for Alvys specifically.

The air was still. Suddenly, the door swung open.

"YOU!" Jalzen's voice exploded in the room.

"Me?!" Lukas jolted, the abrupt loudness of the vampire startling him.

"*You* did this, didn't you!?"

"Did what? What happened?"

"He's gone!" the vampire erupted once more. "Alvys is gone!"

"Alvys is...?" Lukas trailed off.

"Gone." Jalzen's voice was hollow.

Jalzen...

"I know it seems dumb." The vampire said as his knees hit the ground and his posture slumped. "I know what I am. I know what I've done. I get it. I'm a *vampire*."

Lukas paused. He could see the distress upon the vampire lord's face. It was so strange. When Lukas had been a captive in Ildar, all that time ago, he saw nothing but the thirst and desire for bloodshed among Damasko and his officers. But Jalzen was different. As Lukas looked upon the vampire's weary face, was sure of that. He seemed almost...human.

"Look, man!" Jalzen fell to his feet. "I'm a vampire, I get it!" he yelled once more. "Let people think what they want about me! Let them curse my name to the other side of Empyria! Yeah, I've done some things I'm not proud of! Yeah, I've hurt people in the past! I'll even admit that I've tasted human blood before out of desperation! But Alvys? He's like a little brother to me! All of that was real! When we shared meals together, when we laughed at stupid jokes and stayed up all night telling him about our adventures...when we felt like a family...that was *real!*"

Lukas thought of Heldor's words as he watched Jalzen hit the ground repetitively, his knuckles tearing against the stone floor.

Jalzen just does what he can to protect the ones he loves. Lukas thought.

"You're right." Lukas began. "You *are* a vampire, and you've already admitted you've done terrible things."

"You..." Jalzen looked up, his reddened eyes rising to the young man in the cage.

It was unusual. Many times throughout his life Jalzen had been scorned or rejected. He *was* a vampire, after all. He was a creature of the void, doomed to never tread the path of light. But, in that moment, under the gaze of this mysterious young man, he felt different.

"But"—Lukas smiled—"you're not a bad man, Jalzen."

Maybe so, the vampire thought. Maybe this man was right—maybe, just maybe...

"Tell me," Lukas started, "this one who took Alvys, what did he look like?"

"He was tall," Jalzen said, clearing his throat, "I couldn't really see his face, but he appeared in a dark mist, then left through a black cloud."

I knew it...Agnon. That means that Zurriel knows about the Eye, Lukas thought.

"I know that man. He's my enemy." Lukas's voice was hard. "Set me free. Because if I know anything from my encounters with him, I know that he knows I'm in the city. And he won't leave with Alvys until he's killed me as well."

Lukas stared into the vampires yellow eyes. They were sheepish, like a wounded rabbit. Much different from the wolfish man who had locked him up.

"Listen to me, guy," the vampire said, his voice cracking and gurgling as he spoke. "I'll set you free! I'd give you a thousand freedoms! I'd give you money or even my very life. Just please. *Please.* Bring Alvys back!"

"Jalzen." Lukas chuckled. "You really are a great guy!"

"Whatever you say." He said, sniffling as reached for the key and turned the lock.

With a groan, Lukas crawled out of the small cage and held up his cuffs for them to be unlocked too.

"Very well," the Heart of Hearts exclaimed as he stood and stretched his worn muscles.

"You better keep your word. If you don't, or if something happens to Alvys, I'll kill you myself!"

"You don't have to worry about that, Jal." Lukas laughed. "Because I'm not going to save him."

"You—!" the vampire's ire quickly shot upward.

Lukas held out a hand to calm the angry fiend.

"WE are."

"You mean?"

"*We* are going to save him." The Starborn lowered his hands, beckoning the vampire to take them. "*Both of us!*"

Jalzen smiled as he wiped the tears from his eyes.

"What was your name again, stranger?"

Lukas smiled as Jalzen took his hand.

"Oh, me? You can call me Lukas!"

The shadow pervaded the castle, a dismal brume over the black stone. The lights from the blue etherlamps created haunting phantoms along the walls. At the end of the large hallway sat the throne room of the Phoenix King behind a gargantuan door lined with jade and obsidian.

"So this is the one that your 'master' is so obsessed with?" Larc Elliot yawned as she sprawled lazily across the throne, inspecting her blue fingernails out of boredom. "It is really *is* red after all."

Agnon said nothing.

"W-who are you people?!" Alvys cried, tears coming to his eyes.

"I suppose you'll be leaving me now, won't you, wizard?" Larc yawned, ignoring the anxious child.

"There is another." Agnon's dark voice growled.

"Oh?"

"The Starborn stalks the streets," he said, "I should not leave until I have his head as well. Such would please my master."

"And so you're going to use the boy as bait?" Larc chuckled, her eyes still upon her nails. "Devilish of you. And how do you know that this 'Starborn' is even aware that you have the Eye?"

"You are a foolish girl," Agnon spat. "If the Starborn is already in the city, then he will know that I am here. He will feel my presence as I feel his."

"'Starborn' this, 'Starborn' that." Larc laughed. "You seem a bit caught in fairy tales, wizard. But, no matter." She stretched her long legs and rose from the throne. "I have a little birdie to capture. Adieu," she said as she walked past the large Darkling.

Alvys could feel his heart ramming against his ribcage. Anxiously, he rubbed his thumbs against his sweaty palms.

"What do you want with me?" the boy cried through gasping breaths. "I wanna go home."

Agnon said nothing, not even giving the boy a look of acknowledgment. The grim mage waved his hand, summoning the dark cloud once more.

"Come, boy." He said finally as he grabbed Alvys by his pitch-black hair. "For you are now but bait for a much larger fish."

Alvys kicked and screamed as the Darkling dragged him into the abyss.

There is no hope, the boy thought, for it seemed so far away.

"*Fool's errands,*" Larc Elliot whispered under her breath as she walked down the obsidian halls. "*Fool's errands set by fools themselves.*"

Truly, she could care less about the dismal Dark One and his desires for some supposed mythical object. Aeonic Object or not, even if the Eye granted some power, she couldn't truly see why the Dark Wizard Zurriel truly wanted it. Though they shared residence at the now forbidding monument that was the Church of Mhyrmr, she had never seen him. Even when the Darkling spoke of him, it was as if he spoke of a phantom or imaginary friend. Surely if a man of such immense power acquired the Eye of Revelation, then he could perhaps rule the world.

But that was what perplexed her, for she had heard nothing of a desire to rule, no desire for political power—he had simply handed Aestriana over to the now-emperor, Zilheim, without any cause for fight or alarm. It was as if he wanted nothing to do with the world.

But that wasn't her problem. Who cared about myths and ancient relics? She held in her hands the most destructive force in the world. Larc smiled as she felt an electric charge run through her fingers. *Yes...*

She was the Storm Slinger—she was *lightning!*

When she finally made it to the balcony, she stopped and stared out into the darkness. Below her, she saw only spots of blue and yellow from the etherlamps glowing on the streets. He was out there —the Phoenix King. She knew that he was.

No reason to fret, she thought as she smiled, amusing herself. She knew why he was here. *He wants his precious cave back.*

"But you cannot have it, *bird,*" she said, laughing aloud.

"Madame Inquisitor!" a soldier said as he walked out onto the balcony and knelt. "I have news—"

"I see," she interrupted without turning to face him, snickering at the the news. "So Commander Solgus met his end in hellfire, did he?"

"Y-yes, Madame Inquisitor."

"Do you know what this means, sir knight?"

"That—"

"The Phoenix King is here, yes. And now that he walks the streets, he will come *here.*" She pursed her lips. "He wants his precious little city so, *so* badly. It's pathetic, really." Larc sighed and waved her hand dismissively. "Prepare castle defenses. It won't be long now."

"Yes, Madame Inquisitor."

Larc paid the soldier no mind as he rose and hurried out the doorway. She leaned on the railing of the large balcony, her blue eyes matching the same cold glow of the lively, dark city below.

"Foolish little redbird," Larc said, her voice smooth and sweet, "don't you know not to fly in a thunderstorm?"

"Hurry." A cloaked Hallow-talon motioned to his brown-feathered companions as he squeezed his large frame through the marketplace. In the darkness of the city, the simple brown hood of his cloak did much to conceal the Phoenix King's face and was advantageous to hide his bright red feathers. He was obvious otherwise; his crimson shoulders and hair would be instantly recognized by any Elven patrolman. This, of course, was not a confrontation he wished to have. It was not time to alert the streets.

Not yet, at least.

The busy commerce of the city was perfect. Given that most of the citizens of Phoenix Grotto were Beastfolk, it was a simple task for the king and his men to hide in plain sight.

"Your Majesty," one of the hawks approaching the king said in a hushed tone. "The streets are worse than we thought." He motioned to a building with three guards positioned at the entrance. "And I assume the castle will be even worse."

"You worry too much, Gray-wing," the king began. "Have you forgotten who you are?"

"No, Your Majesty," the hawk-man said, nodding. "But I assume you know how we will find our way to the castle? Your word is our law."

"Once again, I ask you," the Phoenix said. "Have you forgotten what you are?"

Gray-wing was silent, his yellow eyes staring into the darkness cast over Hallow-talon's face by the veil of his hood.

"You ask how we will reach our home; you ask how we will restore our dominion. I say it is easy."

The Phoenix King raised his large, leathery hand. He pointed one thick finger upward toward the ceiling of the cave.

"Gray-wing. We are birds, the freest of all mortal creation. And as birds, we shall *fly*."

CHAPTER EIGHT

A Plan and a Snare

Alvys was in darkness. He had no clue as to *where* he was, but the fear within his gut told him that, wherever it was, it was not a happy place. The air was stale and damp as he sat upon a cold floor and looked around in futility. There was nothing but darkness. The child felt his heart sink.

No windows.

No light.

No hope.

In the room, the boy could hear the sounds of someone breathing.

"Who's there?!" he asked, his voice trembling.

There was no answer. Alvys took a moment to listen, the silence tricking him. Was he alone? Was he merely hearing things?

No. Someone was in the room with him.

"Where am I?" he called out into the void once more.

"The Starborn shall come," a dark, grim voice said, resounding throughout the darkness. "And I shall extinguish his light."

"Where is Jalzen?" The boy's voice was high-pitched and shrill. "Is he okay?! Did you kill him? Where is everyone?! Are they okay?!"

"Perhaps." Agnon's voice was deep and low. "Perhaps not. That is of little importance now. You have a much greater role to play. One that involves that crimson eye."

'*Because your eye is magical Alvys.*' Lukas' words surfaced in the little boy's mind. '*It belongs to a goddess, and a powerful wizard wants to take it away from you.*'

"So you're the wizard that wants my eye?!" he yelled. "Well it's mine! It's *my* eye!"

Suddenly, the blue glow of an etherlamp lit the room. Alvys felt his heart jump to his throat. Before him stood the tall Darkling, his massive form dwarfing the small boy.

"You would dare challenge the will of my master..." Agnon's voice was rigid. "*Boy.*"

"Get away from me!" Alvys shrieked as he threw his fist at the large man's groin. In horror, the little boy watched as a black cloud appeared and swallowed his arm. Pain streaked across his face as his own fist slammed into his cheek from another cloud to his right.

"You are an abominable fool, child," the wizard said as he reached down and grabbed the boy by the throat. "And if I did not need you alive for your Aeonic Object to be extracted, I would have slaughtered you along with your friends. You may be crucial to my master's plans, but you are in no way a guest of honor. Remember that when my blade crosses your throat."

A shiver of terror streaked up the little boy's spine. His eyesight blurred as tears began to well in his eyes. He could feel the wailing deep in his throat.

What was this fear, he wondered, this frigid, ineffable fear that consumed him? Alvys began to weep, a sniveling, pitiable display of tears.

Agnon released his grip; Alvys hit the stone floor knees-first. Pain jolted through his body, sharp and cold.

"You are but bait at this point," Agnon said, and spat upon the ground. "For now, you will be the lure to catch the Starborn. But soon your usefulness *will* expire. Very soon. Remember that, *boy.*"

The dark wizard raised his hand and whispered under his breath. A dark cloud formed at his command, and he was gone.

"Jalzen..." Alvys whimpered under his breath as he held his knees in agony. "Jalzen..."

He stopped and took a deep breath as tears poured from his eyes.

"Lukas," he wailed. "Lukas, please save me!"

The market was crowded, the large town square filled with people. It was the only area of the city to be truly illuminated to a fullness which rivaled the sun. Despite the dark stones that had been used to construct the rest of the city, the streets of this vast plaza were lined with lightly colored stones that bloomed together to create the visage of a giant flower. Though it couldn't be seen because of the fullness of the area, the design of the petals was made of pink quartz woven within white marble. A stem of green jade extended from the north corner of the design and flowed like a river to the steps of the immaculate centerpiece of the square, which was the large, ebony, temple of the Aeon of War: Yeornyeim.

"So you're sure about this, Lukas?" Jalzen said as he squeezed through the crowd. "What if the guy really took Al away from the city? And even if not, how are we supposed to find Al once we get in?"

"Well," Lukas said as he halted and looked around. "I assume Alvys is being kept in the dungeon. Every castle has a dungeon, right?" the young man said with a smile that reached his eyes. "So we'll just have to find our way there!"

"And how will we do that? I don't know what's in that castle," Jalzen said, pausing to study the young Starborn. "And I'm *positive* you don't!"

"Easy!" Lukas turned and smiled with pure naivety. "We get arrested!"

The other paused, his face scrunched in thought.

"You do realize that getting arrested will put *us* in the dungeon, right?" Jalzen sighed. "It won't do us any good if we end up rotting in chains, kid."

"Don't worry, Jalzen!" Lukas said as he unbuckled the *Sword Durandal* from his side and placed it on the ground. "I have a plan. You just gotta trust me!"

"Well, it better be good—"

Suddenly, pain shot across the vampire's face as Lukas' fist crossed his cheek.

"What the hell was that for?!"

"What?" Lukas raged in return. "You just gonna go shoving

people?!"

"Shovin—?" Jalzen stopped and smiled.

Ah! You're fun, kid.

"Yeah!" the vampire yelled in return. "And I'll shove you harder next time! Keep outta people's way, you little brat!"

Lukas swung once more. Jalzen dodged and quickly replied with a fist to the Starborn's face.

"Fight! Fight!" a man called out as people began to scurry away to avoid the crossfire. "Guards! Guards!"

"You bastard!" Lukas yelled as another fist connected with Jalzen's face.

"Oi! Oi!" the voices of several Elven guards said, muffled behind their gilded metal visors.

"You want some, too!" Lukas turned to one of the soldiers, fists up.

"Yeah!" Jalzen followed his lead. "Bring it!"

Swords rang as their blades scrapped against their sheaths. Lukas and Jalzen dropped their fists as they looked at their surroundings. In the distance, people lined the walls in fear. But, what was even more evident than the fear of the citizens was that they were surrounded. The blue light of etherlamps reflected a greenish tint off the golden armor of the Elven guards who had their swords drawn.

"Come with us," one of them said, "and you'll keep your lives."

Lukas bowed his head as he raised his arms in surrender. The soldiers bound his hands and pushed him forward. Lukas was led away, followed by Jalzen.

Underneath the shadow cast upon his face, Lukas was smiling.

"You have the boy," Larc yawned as she reclined lazily upon the Phoenix Throne. "Why stay here? Isn't your master so eager to pluck his magic eye or whatever?"

The large Abdian said nothing, merely standing in the doorway. The Inquisitor looked up.

I just had to get stuck with the walking statue, didn't I? she thought as she looked at doorway to the courtroom.

She shrugged upon second thought. Actually, she determined she enjoyed the silence much more than if this mysterious magician was constantly trying to talk. At the end of the hall, the large blackened figure seemed to blend into the obsidian floor.

Truly, he was a menacing sight—a vague shadow of death that moved like a reaper to dispose of any and all he needed to. Yet one thing unnerved her.

Why can't I read his mind...?

It wasn't as if he were undead, as she could definitely detect electricity within him...but still...when she found herself trying to probe his mind, she found nothing...

As if *empty space* were all that constituted his thoughts.

But this couldn't be true. She had seen his cunning and ferocity with her own eyes. So, who was this large beast of a man...?

Or, rather, *what* was he?

She shivered and shook her head in disgust.

"It is true. My master does wish for the boy." Agnon's deep voice echoed throughout the empty space. "But the boy must wait in order to bring out..." he paused. After a moment, Larc realized she was holding her breath. "Another one. One who must die here."

Agnon whipped his black cloak as he turned and exited through the doorway.

The Storm Slinger exhaled moments after he had left.

This man, she thought, feeling her ire rise, *I'm not afraid. I can't be. I am lightning!*

But there was no denying it. Agnon made her anxious.

Agnon moved silently down the cavernous hallway, a darkened specter merging with the dim light around him. He knew that it would not be long now. The Starborn would come, just like before.

He was too virtuous, too courageous. He was too *stupid*. And the wizard knew with great certainty that he would come to rescue the boy.

Virtue. Agnon raised his hood, veiling his blue skin in shadowy black. In a way, he must admit that he found he slightly admired the boy—but it was the same admiration that a cat gives a mouse as it plays with it, the same admiration that a predator feels before it crushes its prey between its teeth.

Yes. *This,* he thought, *is my favorite type of game.* The Starborn would come, and Agnon would blot his star from the sky.

Under the cover of his cloak, Agnon smiled as she walked down the hallway.

Oh foolish boy, he whispered, *thou shalt die this day.*

CHAPTER NINE

Rescue! Rescue!

Soldiers pushed Lukas and Jalzen along, the ends of their swords poking the prisoners' backs if they slowed. Jalzen had long felt uneasy, but he couldn't decide what unnerved him more: the fact that he was being carried away into the dungeons, or how little it seemed to worry Lukas. Actually, the more he thought about it, the more asinine he decided it was that he had actually gone along with this mysterious young man's plans. He knew so little about this Lukas. He was merely a strange, alien figure who seemingly appeared out of nowhere. Had Alvys truly dreamed of him? What did that mean? The boy had never seemed to have strange dreams before. Sure, the red eye was a unique feature about the child, but Jalzen himself never thought it was in his right to judge it.

He himself was, after all, a vampire. So, he wasn't the most normal, one could say.

The corridors became darker and damper as they were led closer to the dungeon. Jalzen felt sweat begin to bead upon his brow. He was a vampire, so he knew that his imprisonment would lead to torture before death. He looked at Lukas; the young man's face showed no sense of anxiety as a small amused smirk passed across his lips. Lights became less and less frequent as the pathway extended into darkness. Polished stones abruptly became jagged bricks when the two prisoners were stopped at a stairwell.

"Jalzen." Lukas whispered. "Steel yourself."

"What—?"

"*Lucyn Rejiis!*"

Like a violent gale, white flames rode up Lukas' arms, shattering his binds like straw. Great pressure filled the space, a teeth-gritting push that caused the soldiers to fly backward, the metal of their gilded armor creating sparks as it hit the obsidian floor.

"What the hell?!" Jalzen spouted.

Without a word, the young Starborn snapped his fingers. Suddenly, a blinding light filled the hallways, its sheen glazing off of the mirror-like gloss of the dark, crystalline walls. Jalzen blinked rapidly, frantically trying to adjust his eyes to the flash.

"Lukas..." he said as his sight returned. "What are you?!"

There was no mistaking it. He knew now just how unnatural this stranger was. Lukas stood before him, bright flames breathing and whipping along his arm, which held an elegant, green-bladed longsword.

This boy, Jalzen thought, *is no ordinary boy*. No. He had heard many rumors ride upon the wind, but the wind was a fickle mistress who often whispered the lies of others.

"Oh, me?" Lukas smiled. "I'm the Heart of Hearts!"

"*You're* the—?" Jalzen began.

"Jalzen!" Lukas said, interrupting the other. "This might hurt!"

"Hurt?!"

Without a response, a bright flame spat from Lukas' fingertip. Jalzen felt a great heat as the fire caused his bindings to explode into strands of mere twine.

"Let's go, Jalzen!"

"Magic! Magic!" the soldiers screeched through their muffled visors as they sprinted down the hallway.

"No you *don't!*"

Lukas took in a breath. In a flash, the *Sword Durandal* arced, a giant blade of white light riding off of its emerald blade, spinning down the hallway.

The Elves ran, but not fast enough. Their screams were quick, then silence ensued.

Jalzen stood frozen. Lukas exhaled. The flames along his arms hissed then vanished as mysteriously as they had appeared.

"What the *hell* was that, kid?" the vampire said, starstruck.

"Oh!" Lukas laughed. "Magic! Very...special magic..." he pointed to the corpses halfway down the hall. "We're gonna need their keys!"

For a moment, Jalzen stood bewildered, unsure of what he had just seen. Sure, he knew that magic existed; sure, he knew that some people—that mainly being the Inquisitors of Mhyrmr—were conjurers of intense magical manifestations, but this was something different altogether. He understood now what the young man had meant.

A flaming buzz racked his body as the fire appeared, as if the mere presence of the flame sent an acute razing through his being—as if his heart were to be rent in two. The force of the white tongues seemed to pull him into the abyss. Never had a magic made him feel this way.

And never had he feared anyone more than he did this odd, mystical, boy.

Lukas quickly bounded down the hallway and returned with a set of shiny silver keys.

"Keys..." Jalzen nodded slowly. "Right...*right*..."

The dungeon was decrepit, depressing, and downright pitch-black.

"Great..." Jalzen whispered. "I might be a vampire, but no lamps still means no sight for me. You got a trick for this one, too, kid?"

The vampire was right. No lights lined the moist stone walls, which made the two fugitives' descent down the ebony staircase all the more treacherous. Lukas thought about summoning white flames to his fingertips to help guide the way, but soon realized that if he did so, his vampire companion might suffer and writhe in the holy flame.

No, he realized. If he were to preserve the well-being of his friend, he would have to limit the usage of the Starblood. If he did not, he might risk harming Jalzen in the same manner that he had injured the vile Damasko the Bloodletter a year prior when he and Blake traveled to Ildar. The thought of Blake made his entire body cringe. He clenched his fist.

I can still feel it...

My hands still feel the warmth...

The stains of your blood on my hands...

It was piercing sadness, a wrenching guilt, like jagged glass filling his chest.

Agnon... he thought, a cold rage icing his veins. *I'm coming for you too.*

Lukas snapped his fingers.

Of course! Epiphany struck him like a spear. *Maybe I can't see, but I can still feel!*

"I just might have a way to get us through this darkness, Jal!"

This was surely true! I just might work. The Old Man had taught him many things in the six months he had spent with him. Lukas smiled at his own cleverness. The young man took a deep breath. Slowly, his mind fell into darkness, the scattered light of his subconscious beginning to close. The world around him became acute as he felt his mind dissipate into his surroundings.

Fade away, he thought, *hear the world, unhindered.*

He exhaled.

"Well?" Jalzen said. "Can you see now?"

Lukas knew that sight was an impossibility in darkness, but he didn't need it now.

"Take my hand, Jalzen." Lukas replied. "I can hear enough to see."

Jalzen silently let the young man guide him. Wet slime made the stairway perilous. Lukas held the others' arm with caution as he maneuvered them, climbing downward. Slowly, they reached the bottom and stopped.

"So you can hear real good right now, eh?" the vampire whispered. "Then listen for Al!"

Lukas said nothing, but there was no need. They both knew what they had to do.

The hunt for Alvys was on.

In the hallway leading to the dungeon, the two Elven soldiers lay flat upon their faces; the cut from the blazing blade of light has sliced straight through their gilded plate armor. They lay there, lifeless, until one began to stir. It took him a moment to realize his luck—to realize that he was yet alive, that his mortal flame still burned. The magic that had almost extinguished his life was the strangest he had ever felt, yet, by the breath of the Aeons, he had survived its maw.

Those white flames, however, still danced in his mind. Those bright blazes struck fear into him. What were they? He had seen magic many times before, yet no magic had ever made him feel that way. The very presence of its igniting caused him ache all over. Deep within him, simply being around it, he felt as if his blood were boiling with great heat.

He turned to his companion.

He was dead, a stone-cold cadaver wrapped inside of a gilded metal sepulcher.

He must have taken the worst of the blow.

But now was not the time for mourning. No. He pushed away the sadness of losing a comrade. He had a duty, something greater than death.

He must warn the others.

There was an intrusion, and if it were not squashed quickly, the consequences would be dire. He placed his feeble hands upon the stony floor and pushed. As he rose, his tendons wiggled and muscles jerked at a concerning rate.

But this was merely an afterthought. For what was a mere amount of suffering now if it would prevent hell later? True, his hands and arms ached as he rose, but if he allowed the intruders any quarter for their machinations, he feared the one who would punish him. He feared the death he would receive.

And, most of all, he feared the wrath of the fickle Inquisitor who commanded them, the Storm Slinger.

After much struggle, the wounded soldier rose to his feet. Despite his injured arms, he determined that his legs had remained greatly intact. This made sense, of course, as the wound left by the horrific magic hit his armored backside.

He nodded, then hurried down the hall. The intruders must be eliminated, and he would not waste his time.

The gods had given him a second chance, and he was wary not to waste it.

Alvys didn't know what time it was or how long he had been within the walled, door-less, window-less room. It had been a while since the mysterious dark wizard had visited him, and it felt as if he had been in confinement for weeks.

No, he reasoned with himself, *it couldn't have been weeks.* He was hungry and thirsty, but he would have probably died already if it had been weeks. It must have been only a day. Still, he didn't know where he was, how his friends were doing, or if they were even alive.

He thought of Jalzen.

Did Jalzen die along with the others? Images slipped through the young boy's mind. He could only think of his friends with tears in his eyes.

They're gone...

All of them are gone...

What would he do now? Any other emotion evaded him as he fell to his knees and wept.

Jalzen...

Jalzen...

"JALZEN!"

He wailed. He screamed. What was the point? No one was there to hear him; no one would let him cry on their shoulder.

But he stopped and sniffled, snot running down his face, mixing with his tears.

He remembered Lukas.

LUKAS! he began to call out in his mind. *LUKAS!*

He didn't know why he felt this way, but something within him felt that peculiar young man, that strange and seemingly otherworldly Lukas would come for him.

LUKAS, he screamed internally once more.

Suddenly, he heard Lukas reply.

"Alvys?!" Lukas called out.

"*Lukas?*" the boy's reply was distant, but under his spell, Lukas could hear it.

"Where are you, Al?" Jalzen said, following his companion's lead. "Can you hear him?"

"He's in the wall!" Lukas exclaimed.

"The wall—?"

"Alvys!" Lukas repeated as he ran his hands along the cool stones.

He followed his senses to the corner and stopped.

"There's a hidden room here."

"Well?!" Jalzen said. "How do we get in?"

"There's gotta be a way! Otherwise why make a room you can't access?" Lukas said, mostly to himself. "But how...?"

"Check the stones?"

Lukas nodded, blindly running his hands along the stone wall, feeling for any sign of a crack or an out-of-line stone.

"Nothing."

"Damn!" Jalzen ignited throwing the keys in his fury. "These keys were useless, too."

There was a long silence.

"Dammit!" the vampire cried out, his fist slamming across the wall with great force.

Then, there was a mild sound—a faint click that echoed through the cavernous room. Suddenly, the sounds of bricks grinding against each other sounded from within the darkness and Alvys jumped out of the room.

"Jalzen!" Alvys exclaimed as he rushed out into the darkness, feeling around for his friend, wrapping his arms around him and squeezing as hard as he could.

"Kid!" the vampire man yelled back, grabbing the boy and lifting him off the ground. "I was so worried!"

"You came, Lukas! I knew you would!"

"Yes, Alvys! Of course I would," the young man said. His voice became more rigid. "Now let's get out of here!"

Larc Elliot and Agnon didn't talk to each other, but Larc rather enjoyed that about him. Despite how uneasy he made her feel, she respected that he was a force of little to no words. He wasn't like that fool, Valter, who constantly chattered on about his strange madnesses that never made sense. No. This dark wizard was beyond taciturn. He was brooding and grim, a specter at his master's command. He followed through with his orders to do the unthinkable, yet never seemed to show remorse, or any emotion for that matter. She had even been told that he killed the High Priestess of the White Lotus priesthood. He, an Abdian, had crushed within his hands the very throat of the woman who ruled his country. Well, who the Abdians' *thought* was their ruler. The Immaculate Ones were the *real* rulers.

Yet, still, none of Agnon's vicious actions seemed to cause him any anguish.

The more she worked with this massive sorcerer, she found herself ever more perplexed by him.

The 'Harbinger of the Black Star?' She smirked as the thought crossed her mind. *So mysterious.*

"Your Holiness!" an Elf exclaimed as he burst into the throne room and collapsed upon the ground. "Intruders!"

"As...expected." Agnon spoke up before Larc could.

"One has strange magic!" the Elf coughed as he heaved upon the floor. "White flames! They killed my companion! They—"

"Starborn..." Agnon growled as he approached the fallen soldier. "So you have taken my bait."

"I tried to stop him, but I—"

The soldier stopped as the large Abdian's boot pressed against throat.

"You *tried.*" The wizard's voice was deep. "But you did not succeed. No. It would be impossible for you to. You stood against the Starborn bloodline. You stood against a scion of Vespira. There was no hope for you against that magic."

The force of the hulking Darkling's boot left the soldier gasping for air but unable to find it. The soldier clawed at the wizard's robes as he felt his windpipe press against the back of his throat.

"And there is no hope for you here, either."

Then a popping, crunching sound, and the Elf fell limp. Larc smiled. She was right. This man was dangerous. She licked her lips.

How very, very, *ruthless, Agnon.*

"Weren't there two guards earlier?!" Jalzen said, wide-eyed.

"There were!"

Lukas, Jalzen, and Alvys looked at each other momentarily, each knowing what this meant. A guard survived. But more importantly.

The castle now knew that they were here.

"This way!" the call of an Elven soldier came from the exit, followed by the sounds of boots getting closer.

The three looked at each other, wide-eyed, then broke into a sprint, bounding down the long hallway and into the castle itself.

"You have any idea where we're gonna go?" Jalzen exclaimed from the tail end of the group.

"No clue!" Lukas replied with a smile.

And the castle interior did little to cure the confusion. Each of its hallways and stairwells seemed to be reminiscent of the last. Whatever the Elves had done to the place or how long they had occupied the fortress was unclear, but they had controlled it long enough to eradicate all decorations and royal emblems, causing each of the dark corridors to appear to be copies of the last.

Eventually, the three came to a stairwell and began to climb, each leaping over two steps at a time. They did not know if up were the right direction, yet at least up *was* a direction, and much better than the seemingly labyrinthine passages below. Eventually, they reached the top of the stairs. Before them lay a vast courtyard. Under the sapphire light of the etherlamps, the red flowers appeared a deep violet. The space seemed to extend the entirety of the rooftop of the castle. It was quieter than inside, with only the faint trickle of the fountain waterfalls extending from the center.

"Where now?!" Jalzen called out.

"Nowhere," a deep voice said from seemingly thin air.

As if an answer to a dark omen, a black mist descended upon the brightly lit garden. Lukas squinted his eyes as he peered into the brume. Barely visible, a large, blackened, spectral outline stood deep within.

"It's been a while, hasn't it?" Lukas said, pointing the *Sword Durandal* forward. "Agnon."

"I knew you would come," the Darkling said, his voice was a coarse growl. "O, foolish Child of Vespira."

"You!" Jalzen raged. "You're the one who hurt Al, you basta—"

"Jalzen," Lukas said, cutting the vampire short, "run."

"Huh?"

"Take Alvys," he repeated, his voice harder, sterner, "and run."

"But—!" Alvys cried out.

"Don't worry! He won't chase you. There's no way he'd give up this perfect opportunity to keep me from interfering in his master's plots."

The three were silent, then Jalzen took the boy by the hand and bolted.

"Don't you *dare* die, Lukas!" he called back. "If you do, I'll kick your ass!"

Lukas turned to his opponent. Just as he had remembered, the dark sorcerer stood tall and large, dwarfing him.

"So you really aren't going to chase, are you?" Lukas smiled. "You wanna kill me that badly?"

Agnon remained silent, his hand reaching to his side to pull out a long, gnarled dagger.

"I'm going to kill you here, Agnon." Lukas' voice was a low, frigid growl. "I'll never forgive you for what you did to Blake."

"Foolish Child of Vespira," the Darkling said as the last of the mist faded. "I shall blot out your starlight."

CHAPTER TEN

To Fly in a Thunderstorm

Scarlet wings sliced the air above the dreary, cavernous city of Phoenix Grotto. Hallow-Talon glided swiftly, followed by a flock of other, similarly massive birds. Following their blood-red king, they all knew that, whatever lay ahead, battle was imminent.

But they had come prepared—anything would be done to reclaim the conquered city and cast out the Elven army. Before them, the castle was lit by mere spotted beacons created by the small azure lights of etherlamp torches. Suddenly, an explosion of white light erupted from a balcony.

"Your Majesty!" one of the large hawks cried as a great wind blew past them, buffeting their wings momentarily . "What does this mean?!"

The Phoenix was silent for a moment, his eyes fixated upon the illuminated pillar before them.

Could it be, he thought, *could it truly be?*

There was no doubting it. He knew exactly what this meant.

Starborn.

"Well, my men," he called back to his flock. "It seems the stars are among us today!"

* * *

Jalzen held Alvys' arm in a death-grip as he led them through the castle at breakneck speed.

"Jalzen!" the boy cried out.

"C'mon, Al!"

"Where are we going?"

Where indeed? Jalzen had no clue. In this disorienting fortress, hallways and entrances seemed to extend forever, and the further the two progressed, the less and less familiar things became. Each hallway looked identical, with nothing to act as a visible landmark to denote any progress had been made in their escape.

Jalzen knew that the Elves had held dominion over the city for half a year now—in that time they had removed every single artifact, portrait, and flag that held any semblance of allegiance to the Phoenix King. The vampire had to admit, truly, he missed that old bird. When King Hallow-Talon was on the throne, things were definitely quieter. It was easy then, as Beastfolk couldn't contract the vampire disease, so Jalzen and his gang weren't considered a threat. At least his kind were tolerated back then.

The two rushed around a corner to reveal a massive room that held large doorway, wide open, leading to a black obsidian balcony. The cool air of the Grotto brushed their faces as they stopped at the entrance, the earthy smells of the outside leading them to the overlook.

"So it seems I've found our little mice."

The two jolted, chills of fear shaking their spines as they turned to see several Elven soldiers standing before them. A stunning young woman stood at their head, her lithe figure draped in the blood-red robes of the Inquisition.

"But all I need is the boy. I don't *have* to hurt you, vampire, and I just might let you go if you're a good sport and hand over the Eye to me."

"So Lukas was right!" Alvys blurted out. "You really *are* after my eye!"

"You see, little boy," she said. "There's someone who wants that eye and can give me what *I* want in return for it. Your eye is special, little songbird. I don't know how you came to possess it, but you hold in that little head of yours the Eye of Lunae herself!"

"That's a bunch'a nonsense!" Jalzen erupted. "Why would Al have anything to do with an Aeon?!"

Larc shrugged apathetically as a wave of blue lightning ran between her fingers, only to disappear.

"Your guess is as good as mine," she said softly. "But we don't always have to understand things in this world, do we? Some things are the way they are and some things aren't the way they aren't. Speculation is useless and annoying. In this world, the only things that matter are ambitions and the means to achieve them. Now. Give me the boy. *Last chance.*"

She shifted her stark, icy gaze to Jalzen. The vampire froze as if stopped by a frigid gale. This woman, whoever she was, was not to be trifled with.

How, he thought, *how to deal with this*? Fighting her was out of the question. He had determined that from the moment he saw the bright blue sparks run up her fingers. This woman—she clearly had magic at her command, and Jalzen knew for a fact that he wasn't too keen on finding out what kind. *But now what?*

Wait! What was he saying?! No! *I'm not afraid! I CAN'T BE!*

"No way!" the vampire said as he stood between the Inquisitor and her mark. "You think for a damn second I'm gonna let you take Al?! *Hell no!* I won't let you lay a hand on him!"

"Oh?" Larc tilted her head, her golden hair almost green in the blue lamplight. "A vampire with morals, huh? Don't pretend to have the high ground, fangfilth. You're just as much a monster as you believe me to be."

The air was cold, still, and silent for all but the ringing of blades as they were drawn from their sheaths.

"Let me ask you something, *Inquisitor*," Jalzen said into the night, his voice soft and grim. "Have you ever had a family? Not just blood relatives—no, that's not what I mean. Have you ever had people who you eat with, who you live with, who you would die for? Do you have anyone who would take the time to weep with you or laugh with you —hell, do you have anyone you'd fight the world for?"

Larc raised an eyebrow.

"What are you going on about?"

"I'm a vampire, yeah, I know." Jalzen clenched his fist. "I've done some terrible stuff. I've killed, I've pillaged, I've even tasted human blood. I've done some things I'm not proud of, that's for sure. But when I met Al, he was just an orphan on the street. Society hated him because of this eye you want so badly. Listen to me, *lady*, I dined with this boy; I laughed with this boy; I care for this boy. Yeah, I might've done bad things. But when I see Al, when I see him smile or laugh— when we all sat around to share a meal together like a family—when I saw all of the goodness within him...it made me feel like *I* could be good too! So you want Al?!" The vampire raised his fists. "I say go to hell!"

Jalzen... Alvys thought. He had no clue. He didn't know that Jalzen was a killer, a vampire; he didn't know about all of these bad things. But in that moment, Alvys felt his heart tear in two. He couldn't help but smile.

Jalzen...you really are *my family!*

"Pity," Larc sighed.

Suddenly, a flicker of blue electricity shot from her fingertip and collided with the vampire's chest, blasting him against the railing.

"JALZEN!" Alvys screeched.

The boy rushed to his friend, wrapping the vampire's large body in his small arms.

"Jalzen! Jalzen!" He bellowed as he shook Jalzen's limp body.

Emotions wrestled within the young boy, their intensities failing to register within his mind. Alvys looked deeply into his friend's lifeless eyes. Tears spilled forth involuntarily. This was his world—his life—his family.

Gone...

In mere seconds...

Don't die! You can't die!

"JALZEN!"

"Pathetic." Larc chuckled. "Your friend was an idiot, boy. After all that about family and what rubbish, too! How imbecilic!"

"*YOU SHUT UP!*"

Suddenly, bright white flames exploded from Alvys, the force of the blast knocking the Larc and the soldiers back into the hallway.

Jalzen...

Alvys felt strange. In that moment, within these odd flames, he felt his heartbeat overflow with power.

Jalzen, he called out with his mind, *Jalzen wake up.*

"Wake up, Jalzen." He couldn't tell why, but he spoke aloud.

Slowly, the other's eyes opened.

"Al?" Jalzen whimpered, his voice still weak. "You're glowing," he grunted. "What's happening?"

"Don't worry, Jalzen!" Alvys said as he stood up and faced the Inquisitor. "I won't let her hurt you!"

"Aw!" Larc jeered. "How sweet! Does the little boy want to play hero. I'll tell you something," the Inquisitor said, calling upon her Word of Heart. At the snap of her fingers, bright blue energy exploded and covered her body like a net. *"I will kill you here."* Her voice was stone. "Your newfound Starblood can't save you."

Fear struck the boy, a fear he'd never felt before. It was the sort of fear that left your body cold and destitute, the sort of blood-chilling anxiety that froze you solid in place.

This was the fear one felt when faced with certain death.

Alvys' knees buckled; his flames extinguished as he hit the smooth obsidian floor. Time seemed to slow. It felt as if he watched the sparks around the woman dance for an eternity.

"*NAY!*" A deep voice resounded from above.

Bright red flames filled the balcony, an explosion of warmth and wind. When everyone's eyes adjusted, a man stood between Alvys and the Inquisitor. The young boy eyed him. He was tall, his skin leathery and sun-kissed. Upon his shoulders, red feathers became tongues of bright red flames.

"Are you okay, young one?" The man's voice was deep and gruff.

The sight of this large, feathered man left the boy speechless. He was majestic, like an angel of burning judgment.

"Do not worry." The large bird-man said. "This battle shall be won this day."

"Oh!" Larc laughed, clapping her hands. "My little birdie has finally come out to play?"

"Silence, witch," Hallow-Talon said. "Who let you out of your cage, Storm Slinger?"

"Oh, just the new management," she said, smiling. "Seems they had a few spots available, so I took one."

"Tell me, Larc Elliot, do you remember the Night of Silent

Thunder?"

Larc smiled wryly. "Oh, you mean when I killed that whole tribe of your little birdies? How could I forget?! They made such *cute* kawking noises as they died. Why do you bring it up, Your Majesty? Tell me, are you still sour about that whole...*fiasco?*"

Flames began to spit from the large man's body. He raised his huge fist, fire seeming to move like sinews along his large muscles.

"Perish, witch!"

With a swing of his gargantuan arm, a ball of fire exploded from his fist, its blaze filling the room like an oven.

"Is that all you have?!"

She was above.

"How?!" Hallow-Talon swiped to the side just in time as a large thunderbolt hit the ground like a great arrow. Light fragmented into bright blue sparks upon impact. Both Jalzen and Alvys had to shield their eyes from the blinding light.

"You're too slow, little birdie!"

"Nay!" the king's loud voice boomed from above. Larc quickly shifted her view to the ground.

Empty.

"I know your tricks, Storm Slinger," Hallow-Talon roared from higher above her. "You read minds, but you can only do it as long as you're making eye-contact!"

Larc hastily turned in the air, but she was too late. As she righted herself, a fist of searing blaze slammed into the side of her face. There was a sudden instance of pain; Larc shrieked as the flames engulfed her right eye. The sensation of her eyeball melting under the heat caused her to rave as the Phoenix's fist held momentary contact.

"Die!" Hallow-Talon exclaimed as his punch followed through; his great strength, fast and formidable, sent the young woman speeding past the rail of the balcony and barreling toward the ground below.

They was a soft splashing sound as she hit a fountain below, then all was silent.

Alvys and Jalzen watched the luciferous blazes extinguish and become shiny ruby-red feathers. The young boy watched, overcome with awe. This bird-man was special. He was like something out of a wild fairy tale. He was powerful.

"You were very brave, boy," the king said as he landed once more, perching upon the railing of the balcony. "And your courage won you the battle today. Now tell me what you are doing here."

And Alvys did. He told the king everything—about his eye, about the man who kidnapped him, about his escape, and about Lukas.

"A young man named Lukas, you say?" Hallow-Talon said as he stroked his chin. "Tell me, did this young Lukas possess a strange silver blade?"

"Yeah, he did," Jalzen grunted as he stood. "Thing turns green when he uses his magic—not to mention his white flames. Kinda like..." the man looked at Alvys as he trailed off.

You, Al...

"He's on the roof now!" Alvys blurted out. "He was fighting a really big man!"

"Hey! What the hell!" Jalzen suddenly interrupted. Alvys, Hallow-Talon, and the other bird-men all turned to the man, who was feeling his teeth furiously.

"My fangs! My fangs are gone!"

"So you were a vampire, eh?" the king said. "One of your kind will not stay cursed so long in the light of Starblood."

Alvys stood quietly, his eyes fixed up, looking toward the top of the castle.

There was a moment of silence.

"Aye, young one," Hallow-Talon finally said, motioning his hands to his men. "Let us go, men! Let us aid the Heart of Hearts!"

"I've been meaning to give you a beating for what you did to Blake," Lukas growled as white flames rode up his arms and engulfed the emerald blade of the *Sword Durandal*. "Looks like I'm finally getting my wish."

"Foolishness, Child of Vespira." The large wizard held up a hand and a black cloud formed beside him. "You may think that you are formidable, but you are no match for me, and just as your friend did, you will not escape me." He smirked. "Perhaps I will make you scream like she did."

With a flash of silver Agnon's hand swooped through the cloud. Thinking quickly, Lukas jolted to the right as a cloud formed to his left.

So that's how he plays, Lukas thought.

"I am Agnon the All-Present," the large Darkling said as he swiped his long dagger through another cloud. "You will never escape my grasp!"

His magic is annoying, Lukas thought as he swung *Durandal,* a bright wave of light riding up its blade and sent hurdling toward the Darkling. *I don't have a way to get close!*

Unless...!

Agnon quickly summoned a dark cloud. The blast of light passed through it with ease. Lukas quickly stepped backward as the energy wave missed him and exploded into the wall of the courtyard.

His powers are simple, though...

Lukas weaved to the left as the blade of the dagger pierced through a cloud, barely swiping the chainmail under his shirt.

I wonder if...!

Lukas found his footing and reached into the cloud, taking hold of the wizard's arm and propelling himself forward.

The clouds act as portals from point A to point B...but...

With lightning fast speed, the Heart of Hearts brandished the *Sword Durandal* as he charged headfirst into the black cloud.

That should mean it can take me from point B to...

Agnon suddenly jumped backward as his opponent shot out from the cloud at his left.

"Point A!" Lukas exclaimed as he swung the *Sword Durandal* at the wizard's head.

Agnon did his best to evade, sliding upon the grass in a desperate attempt to keep his balance.

"You!" the dark mage growled as he held the side of his face.

In the etherlamps in the courtyard, Lukas smiled. He knew he'd done it, even if it were minuscule. He had landed a hit.

"How dare you!" Agnon roared as he wiped the blood from his face.

Lukas smirked. "You're not as untouchable as you think, Agnon."

"Very well." The large Darkling raised his hand. At his command, five clouds surrounded Lukas. "Let us see you escape this!"

"*NO!*" a deep voice thundered, causing the dark mage look skyward. "*LET US SEE YOU ESCAPE!*"

"You—!" Agnon said as a ball of fire collided with the ground, setting the garden ablaze.

"Hallow-Talon!" Lukas exclaimed, his face lightening.

"It has been a while, Heart of Hearts!" the giant Phoenix King smiled as he descended upon the ground.

"Foolish bird!" Agnon growled as he summoned a black cloud. "You will perish here!"

"Are you so dumb, wizard?" the king laughed as he motioned around with his hands. "There is no way you will live if you fight."

It was true, unfortunately for the dark mage. Agnon looked around the garden. Surrounding him was a wall of incinerating red fire, but even more than that, he stood surrounded by birds, sharp talons ready to cleave if he decided to do something risky.

He looked for the boy. He wasn't among them. Frustration filled the Darkling's mind. Whatever plan they had contrived, they obviously knew that he could move through space freely—but they must have also discovered that he could do only that.

They somehow knew that he couldn't use his powers to *find* his targets.

Suddenly, a dark cloud appeared behind him. The large, grim wizard said nothing as he stepped into it. Then, he was gone.

Lukas sighed, extinguishing the flames along his arms.

"Worry not, Heart of Hearts," Hallow-Talon said as he walked over and placed a hand upon the boy's shoulder. "You will have your day." He looked out off the roof at the city below. "But not all is lost. My kingdom is mine once again."

Lukas smiled. He was rather happy that the king had won his day.

"Yeah," he said, clenching his fist.

Next time, he thought, picturing the dark wizard, *and I'm coming for you, too, Zurriel.*

CHAPTER ELEVEN

Resolve

The city was speedily reclaimed. Without any leaders, the Elves were driven out with almost no effort whatsoever. The great Mirean army, even with all of its might, still feared the razor-sharp talons of the Phoenix King's men. No Elf would, even with their heightened senses, dare stand against the might of the Beastfolk without a proper commander.

So the Mirean army retreated and in a matter of days was gone.

Lukas stood before the obsidian throne as Hallow-Talon was seated upon the stone seat once more.

"I owe you for saving me, Your Highness." The Heart of Hearts said as he knelt before the throne.

"Stand, boy. I owed you, as well. If I recall, was it not you who released me from the clutches of Damasko a year ago?" The Phoenix smiled. "No. This day was merely me returning the favor."

Lukas bowed his head. "Thank you."

"Now, I must ask you," the Phoenix King said, raising a bushy red eyebrow, "where will you be headed next?"

"Mhyrmr," Lukas said. "There is a man behind all of this, a wizard named Zurriel. I'm going to find him and put him down." Lukas paused. "And about Alvys...can I ask you to keep him safe—to keep him here?"

Hallow-Talon rubbed his chin as his eyes wandered to the banners along the wall, their blood red cloth branded with the insignia of the Phoenix King.

"I only ask that because I know that this man—Zurriel—is trying to retrieve the eyes of Lunae, Aeonic Objects with terrifying powers."

"Lunae, you say? How interesting..."

"I don't know what he is planning to do with them, but I know that he has two of them—one he already had when he was the Philosopher King and one he stole from my friend Nox."

"This is much to take in, young Heart of Hearts. All of this about Aeons and legendary kings." The phoenix rubbed his temples with thick fingers. "Perhaps I was in captivity for too long—perhaps I have grown too old to this world." The king inhaled, then nodded as he let the air out. "I see. Very well, I will keep the boy here. But keep in mind that I too have ambitions. I must find the Elf named Lyon, and now that I have my city back, I must find allies to combat Emperor Zilheim."

"No!" a small voice resounded down the hallway.

"Are you crazy, kid?!" another echoed just as loudly.

Lukas turned to see Alvys and Jalzen scurrying down the hallway, Alvys first, Jalzen right behind him.

"*Lukas!*" the boy yelled as he entered the room. "Take me with you!"

"What?!" Lukas exclaimed louder than intended. "T-take you *with* me?!"

"Yeah, Al!" Jalzen said, just as loud. "Take you with him?"

"Yes! Take me with you!"

"You don't know what you're asking, Alvys!" Lukas said. "It would be much safer for you to say here."

"No!" the boy retorted. "That big man hurt my family—and...and..." Lukas watched the boy curiously as faint white flames began to dance upon his skin.

You're...

"And I wanna hurt him back!"

Starborn...

"Alvis." Lukas said, his face like stone. "Ahead there will be many dangers—there will be people who wish for nothing more than to end your life. Are you prepared to face that?"

"They hurt my family! I'll face anything!"

Lukas smiled. He approached the boy and held out his hand. "Then come along."

"I'm coming too!" Jalzen said suddenly.

"No!" Alvys snapped back. The man's face went white. "Jalzen. This is something I gotta do by myself. When that lady hurt you, it made me so mad! Stay here so that nobody can hurt you!" the boy said, smiling.

"Perhaps you could be of use to me, Jalzen," the Phoenix King said. "I need all the help I can get to restore my kingdom to its former glory. You can help with that here, while the boy goes. Neither of you know how to fight, and only the boy has magic. Calm yourself, and remember that you would just be in the way now, without your vampire strength!"

"Yeah!" Alvys exclaimed. "I don't want you to get hurt again!"

Jalzen clenched his fist, his contorted face eventually melting into a smile.

"You really are growin' up, kid." The man released his shoulders and sighed. "Just don't get hurt, and come back in one piece." He turned to Lukas. As their eyes met, it was much different from when they had first encountered each other. Eyes full of distrust and malice had now been replaced by a gaze full of trust and a bond of friendship.

"Please, Lukas. Take care of him. And remember, if anything happens to him, I'll kill you first."

Lukas returned with a smile and laugh. "You got it, Jal!"

"Mhyrmr, huh?" said someone, and a deep laugh echoed through the room as the doors opened and a round dog-man was led in. "Well I'll take you there as long as you can get me out of trouble next time!"

The three turned.

"Darloc!" Lukas exclaimed.

"In the flesh! Now, where we goin'?"

"We?"

"Yeah, how do you think you're gonna get to Mhyrmr?! There's no aerodocks in Phoenix Grotto! All you've got is my trusty auto, and since I'm not delivering any special candy anymore, I thought I'd give you a ride!"

Lukas let out a laugh. "Well, Darloc. Gotta say, I'm glad things worked out..."

The streets were jovial and bustling as a figure in a black robe maneuvered through the crowd. No one seemed to notice as the figure limped, its cloak wet and dripping, and remained unseen. It took some time, but eventually the figure made it to a dead end—but it was no dead end; she was not that stupid. She looked around to see that no one was there when she ran her hands along the cool black stones of the wall. Her hand rubbed up against a loose brick and she smiled.

Oh little birdie, you showed me some tricks...

Slowly, the floor opened to reveal a small passage—the secret route to inside the city.

Or out of it.

Her face still hurt, and her golden hair would never grow back on that side of her head. Larc Elliot ran her fingers along the burn, feeling her singed eyelid.

One eye...

Yes, little birdie...

I'll make you pay...

CHAPTER TWELVE

The Thing That Binds All Men

It was midnight by the time Agnon worked up the courage to tell his master about his failure. This, however, had been unprecedented. Ever since he was a mere child he had served Zurriel—and never once had he failed.

But this time was different, and the large wizard did not know whether to feel fear or shame. Solemnly and after much contemplation, he decided that he should face his dark master. Agnon rose from the small room he had claimed for himself within the abandoned temple at Mhyrmr and exited. Soon, he crossed the frozen gardens, his eyes scanning the courtyard, dead all but for the sanguine dots of the berries of the holly bushes. Crystalline brush crunched under his boots as he made his way to the tower where his master kept himself.

The climb was just as miserable as the trip to its first step. The dark stone of the temple was wet from the mountain snows that draped the church at its high altitude. He climbed silently until he reached the top.

"Agnon." Zurriel's voice was muffled through the door. "Come in."

Agnon entered. The room was brightly lit by great green flames— the flames Agnon feared so much—the flames of lunacy itself.

"You have failed me, Agnon. The Eyes told me the moment it was so."

Agnon said nothing. There was nothing that could be said—he had failed his master. That was all there was to it. The large Darkling merely bowed.

"You have never failed me before, Agnon. Why now?"

"I have no excuse, master. If it is enough to dispose of me, then so be it."

The other stood silently. Agnon bowed his head to avoid eye-contact. Tension filled the room like a thick mist, accompanied only by the flickering of the unholy green flames.

"Do you remember the day we met, Agnon?" Zurriel's voice was smooth, a comforting tone that ironically unnerved his servant's mind.

"I do, master."

"Hmm..." the Dark One said, rubbing his chin, thinking.

Agnon could feel the goosebumps prickling along his skin.

"Come with me, my child."

At Zurriel's command, the room began to melt and shift, the walls stretching outward until they finally disappeared.

"Look around yourself, Agnon."

Agnon lifted his head to his surroundings. The dimly lit quarters had been replaced by a bustling and sandy city somewhere in the deserts of Abdiah.

"You remember this place, do you not?" Zurriel's voice was almost reminiscent. "The city in which you were born..."

"The city of Zhyrshra..."

"Yes."

Agnon looked around as the Darklings of the city passed him by without looking his way.

"Do not worry. They cannot hear or see us." Zurriel motioned with his hand. "Now come, let us take a walk."

The large Darkling stood and began to stroll beside his master.

"All of these people walking," Zurriel said wistfully, "not one of them is innocent. Each of them hide behind the curtains of their placid facades the image of a beast. You have seen it yourself, haven't you, my dear child. You saw it clearly that day..."

Zurriel waved his hand. At his command, the world began to warp into bright colors. Agnon shielded his eyes from the shining.

"Look, Agnon. You will find this scene familiar."

And familiar it was. Agnon's skin crawled at what he saw—but his ire rose because he remembered. Before him was a small room filled with books. He noted with instant familiarity the incantation circles upon the wall.

But most importantly, he saw what lay before him.

Agnon clenched his fists; his fingernails cut into his palm. Upon the floor, two mangled, dark-blue bodies lay upon the floor. He knew he should not study them—but just as it had been the first time, this time he still couldn't look away.

"Their heads were cut open," Zurriel spoke rhetorically. "Their spines broken, arms twisted unnaturally, kneecaps cut out of their legs. This was their price—the price of defying the Aeon of the White Lotus—for defying Obsidian. But this happens all the time in Abdiah, doesn't it?" Zurriel placed a hand upon Agnon's shoulder. "Tell me, Agnon. Do you know them?"

"I..." Agnon's deep voice was a broken whimper. "I do."

"And who might they be, my child?"

Agnon pointed to the smaller mutilated body.

"Mother..."

His hand moved to the other figure, his arm shaking violently.

"Father..."

"Yes." Zurriel nodded. "Your parents." He smiled and pointed to a bookshelf in the back of the small room. "And who is over there?"

As if on cue, a small Darkling boy crawled out from hiding.

"Me..." Agnon held his head in agony. His voice shook. "It was me...they didn't find me, so I was left alive."

"Yes." Zurriel waved his hands once more. The world shifted to reveal a young Agnon wandering the streets alone. "Tell me, do you remember when we first met?"

"I do, Master."

The scene they viewed changed as a young Agnon stood before a man in a black cloak.

"I offered you power, remember? I offered you the power to extinguish your enemies. Have I done so?"

"Yes, Master," Agnon said with a shaky voice. "You have given me great power."

"Do not fear, my child. You have failed me, yes, but you are more to me than a mere pawn." Zurriel paused. The two watched as the young boy took the cloaked man's hand.

"And do you remember what I asked you all those years ago?" Zurriel finally said.

"Yes, Master." Agnon replied.

The cloaked man spoke to the child.

'What is the one thing that binds all mortal men?'

The boy paused, and Agnon replied in his stead.

"The fear of death itself."

CHAPTER THIRTEEN

The Devil's Decision

Eldric stood in a vast darkness, but he was unafraid. No. There was no reason to fear. It wasn't like the fear he had the first time, second, or even the third time. He had grown old now, and nothing about this seemed to scare him anymore.

Especially not *her*.

"Who are you?" he said as he stared at this mysterious woman. She was the same height as he was, but she was significantly younger, with a lean body and long flame-red hair draped over her ghost-white skin.

But her beauty was not important. What seemed to perplex him — what had always *haunted* him — was her eyes, solid black with white irises. In all of his lengthy life, Eldric had never met someone with the same eyes. She had the same eyes that he had.

She too, he concluded, held within her the curse of the Devil's Blood.

"Who are you?" Eldric said again, this time with slightly more force.

But she was silent. The old mage sighed. She was *always* silent. For the longest time had he dreamed this dream, and never once had this enigmatic maiden spoken to him.

No. She only stared, like a strange ephemeral phantom; she simply watched him as he spoke, trying desperately to understand what her purpose could possibly mean. Was she a harbinger of doom? A prophet of fortune? He had no clue. All he knew was her gaze.

"Father," a voice called to him. Eldric looked around. The voice was Snow's.

Eldric returned his eyes to the woman.

She was walking away.

"You were having that dream again, weren't you?" Snow's voice was soft as the old man woke. "The one about the woman?"

Eldric groaned as he raised his worn body.

"I was." He said. "I've had it all my life. Ever since I was a child."

"What does she look like?"

"She's beautiful," he said, raising a bony finger to his eyes, "and her eyes are just like mine."

"Well," the knight said, "Ayize said he needs to speak to you outside of the ship."

With his daughter's help, Eldric rose to his feet and looked around. Outside the window, the moon had set below the desert horizon, giving way to the sun, which aspired to chase away the infernal designs of the night.

As he limped down the landing ramp, he could feel the chill of the desert wind, not yet scorched by the impending sun. The old wizard looked around. A short distance from the *Prometheus* stood Ayize, arms crossed as he watched the sunlight bathe the endless sands.

"I'm going to drop you off in Dhul," the thief said as Eldric approached, not turning his eyes from the horizon. "I've kept you hidden for long enough. What you do from here is your decision, but I need you off my ship."

"Actually," Eldric began. "I have a request."

Ayize sighed. "What makes you think I'm about to take requests? *I* saved *you*, remember? If anyone owes anyone, it'd be the other way around, yeah?"

"Listen to me, lad," Eldric chuckled. "At least hear an old man out."

The thief rolled his shoulders. "You have three seconds, that's all I'm gonna hear—"

"Take me to the leader of the Black Roses," Eldric cut in, his voice sharp and hard.

"Whaaaat?" Ayize laughed in shock. "You know that if I take you to the Lioness, she'll just kill you, right? All of you! You're the Master Inquisitor; you're one of the guild's most infamous enemies, and now you wanna just walk in on us? And with your body guard and Prince Reethkilt? Certain death," he said and spat on the ground. "I didn't know you were so stupid."

"Let me give you a correction," Eldric chuckled. "I *was* the Master Inquisitor. I know two things. One, I know that, if Valter Rivyra truly escaped Avelle's Brook—which I *know* he did—he will want nothing more than to control the Church *and* the Inquisition. And two, if the Church and Inquisition knows that I survived the siege of Crown City—which I *know* they do—then they'll want nothing more than to eliminate me. As it stands I am the Church's greatest threat. You see, I'm a wanted man now—same with Snow and Prince Reethkilt." Eldric smiled. "Even if your leader wants my head, I believe that we might be able to see eye-to-eye somehow."

Ayize looked at the old man, mouth agape. *This old fool*, he thought, *even in the darkest of times, he still smiles and laughs as if he were told a funny joke. This old man*, he thought, *seems to defy the darkness.*

Ayize laughed.

"Ya know what, you old geezer? I think the Lioness might like you." His smile turned grim. "And if not, I wouldn't mind having a smoke from that pipe while we watch you hang."

CHAPTER FOURTEEN

Where Paths Diverge

The ocean winds carried their salty kisses over a vast blue expanse. Nox stood at the bow of the SS *Beartooth*, her eye observing the seas with wistful wonderment.

"The Western Sea is much more forgiving," Agmundr said with a chuckle as he approached to stand by her side. "The Northern Sea is much too cold for you Smalls."

"It's so magnificent," Nox said longingly. "It's...calming."

"There is an old legend," Agmundr began, "that Klyriai, Aeon of the Sea, loved his sister, Lunae, so much that he swore to protect those who worshiped her name. That is why we of the blood of Lyhaal do not fear the sea."

"Klyriai..." Nox trailed off.

"Perhaps that is why you survived, or perhaps it is why the sea took us to you."

Nox stopped. She had never considered it. She had never considered that perhaps there were powers at work beyond herself— powers steering her path in the course it needed to take. She turned her eyes from the sea. On the ship deck behind her, Iago stood, weaving his hands in strange motions as phantom blades danced around him.

No, she thought.

"You know, Agmundr"—she turned her eye back to the sea, smiling at its azure glints—"perhaps the Aeons willed a small part in my rescue, but I believe most of the work was done by the hearts of mortals, wouldn't you say?"

Agmundr smiled, the winds sifting through his blue hair.

"You, Iago, Caedmon, the Soothsayer," Nox said, "I think each one of you deserve just as much credit as Klyriai."

For a moment, the giant stood silent, the light of the evening sun bathing his face its glow, turning his blue beard almost purple.

"Yes," he said with a smile. "I believe you are right."

"Agmundr," Nox said after a moment. "It will be strange to part ways with you, the Soothsayer, and all of your warriors. You've done so much for me; I don't know how to thank you."

"The world is full of greetings and goodbyes, My Lady," a female voice spoke. "But, though we may part ways in the flesh, we are never far in spirit."

Both Nox and Agmundr turned to see the elegant Emalyn approaching, her long white dress almost ghostly in the way it ruffled in the wind.

"And besides," the Giant maiden said as she placed her hand delicately upon the Jarl's face, "I believe it is *we*, in fact, who owe *you*."

The young Aeon looked at the two lovers. They seemed so...inextricable. It was if they moved in unison, as if Emalyn were the moon who beckoned the tides of the Jarl's heart. Staring at them, Nox found herself thinking of Lukas. She wondered if he was even still alive. Would he have stayed at the monastery? Would she get to see him again at Zerlina? The thought of seeing him made her happy—it made her feel warm—but most of all, it made her wistful. And for the first time, she could almost say that her heart longed for him.

But, she knew he wouldn't just stay at the monastery. She knew Lukas more than anyone in the world, and if she knew him at all, she knew he would be looking for her. *What a dork*, she thought, smiling. Just as he would challenge his fate for her, she knew wholeheartedly that she would do the same for him.

Nox turned her face to the horizon. Along the lines where the night eternally chased the day, she could see the last glint of the golden sun sink below the ocean.

I'll find you yet...

Like the moon seeks the sun.

Iago stood before a giant doorway below deck and sighed. What brought him here, he wondered? He didn't have a superstitious bone in his body, so why was he standing in front of this door like a fool? Magic existed in this world to give men power. He was certain of that. But to believe that supernatural forces pushed and pulled the fates of men—to think that perhaps he had been bound to some destiny or path that he would be unable to extricate himself from? That, he felt, was foolish.

But the more he thought about it, the deeper it unnerved him. Was it foolish? Was it *truly* so imbecilic? Or was it something deeper? Did he deny it because he didn't believe it or because he didn't *want* to believe it?

Perhaps he was merely afraid it was true; the thought disturbed him. All his life, had he been running from something so inevitable—something so imminently tangible?

"Why do you stand outside my doorway, Elf?" the voice sounded as if two spoke at once. The door swung open to reveal the large figure of the Soothsayer.

"Why do you think?" Iago growled as he ground his shoes upon the planks under his feet.

"I do not know. Perhaps you should tell me?"

The Elf took in a deep breath.

"I want you to"—he sighed—"use your cards and tell me what they say."

"A reading. You want a Lunar Tarot reading?" She paused, then smiled, her giant face softening. "Come, I will help you to your seat."

The room was dark, lit eerily by azure flames that danced upon the tips of long black candles that were suspended over the table. Wafting smoke lay lightly like a morning mist within the space. Iago gagged at the intense earthy smell of the incense that filled the room.

The Giant helped him to his seat and sat across from him.

"So," Iago said, his voice unsure. "W-what happens now?"

"We ask the cards. You see, this is an ancient technique given to the Giants by the Moth Queen, Lunae. Ancient tradition speaks that Lyhaal was the first to rely upon this form of divination. According to the tale, the cards were used to guide him to the Black Moon Vigil to meet with Lunae before he challenged and defeated the Aeon of War, Yeornyeim. This Vigil is the same place that you and the little Lunae entered before the dragon attack." She placed her hands upon the deck that sat neatly before her. "We begin."

Iago stared at the black cards. *Why*, he screamed within, *why are you afraid of these cards*?! *What am I so afraid of?*

The mystic drew the first card.

"The Duality of the Friend and the Betrayer," she said as she laid it upon the table before the Elf.

Iago stared at the card. It merely held two solid colors, split in half. He raised an eyebrow. Half dark red, half dark blue, the tarot card lay upon the table, as mysterious as the Soothsayer herself.

Iago's palms began to sweat. *Why*, he thought, *why am I sitting with this woman? This is stupid! This is all so stupid!*

"The red faces you," she said, her dual voices soothing. "Tell me, little Elf, have you betrayed someone dear to you? Do you feel you have you lied or abandoned anyone?"

Abandoned? His mind began to wander.

'Iago' he heard Amalia's voice in his mind say. *'You'll protect me, right?'*

'Iago!' Another voice, a different woman's voice, entered his thoughts. *'Run Iago! Never forget—'*

He cringed and shut that memory off.

"Shall I draw the next card?"

Iago shivered, regaining focus, then nodded for the wise woman to continue.

Carefully, the Soothsayer closed her eyes and slowly drew a card from the top of the deck and placed it upon the table.

"The Gallows."

Iago shivered, cold chills coursing up his spine. In the smoky dimness of the room, he could see the image of the empty noose pointing toward him.

"The Gallows represent certainty."

"Certainty of *what*?" the Elf blurted out, but soon wished he hadn't.

"The noose is empty," she said, "which means that what will come to pass has not yet. It means that there is still hope to fulfill your purpose."

"Purpose?"

"Yes, your destiny."

Iago scoffed and laughed. "Destiny my ass! I don't believe in destiny."

"Destiny is not for all, young Elf. For most, destiny is a choice made by the person—they get to decide their purpose. They get to decide for themselves how they will live their lives." She paused. Iago looked into her eyes. They were a curious sapphire, hidden behind her long blue hair. "But that is not the case for some," she finally continued. "For some, destiny has raptured them whole. She is a dark beast who swallows even the strangest of people. For some, destiny has wrapped them in her coils and set them to do her bidding. Hear me, young Elf, for you are entwined with destiny. Do not run from your fate, for escaping its jaws with crush you surely."

Iago froze. Was this it? Was this why he hesitated at the door? He felt his blood begin to rise. Yes. He feared this all along.

These very words, he feared them.

Why?

Why?

Why?!

He loathed to hear of his purpose.

"Then there is one more card," the Soothsayer said in two simultaneous voices.

Iago held his breath as the large woman drew the card from the top of the ebony-colored deck. As she picked it from the stack, she held it to her face for a moment, her expression a twisted arrangement that showed only confusion.

"Never before have I drawn this card..." she said, her voice low and contemplative.

"That doesn't make me feel any better!" Iago exclaimed. "Just show it to me already!"

The mystic placed the black card down upon the table for Iago to see. This one wasn't as scary for some reason, yet he couldn't tell why.

The room was dim, but the candles allowed full vision of the supernatural spread. Upon the card was a gauntlet of shining black metal, embroidered in golden designs of dragons and lions. Upon the middle finger, a red ring glowed deep into the night, its sanguine light jumping from the card and pervading the darkness of the room. He stared at it for a moment, clueless, then turned his gaze to the Soothsayer for an explanation.

"The Master's Ring," she said. "Represents unity and wholeness."

The two were silent. Iago stared intently at the psychic as she looked steadily at the card. For some reason, he felt his fear melt away. It was odd to him, as he felt that his anxiety should increase with the confounding of his supernatural guide.

But it didn't, and he didn't know why.

"I see. So now I know, little Elf," the giant Soothsayer said.

"Know...what?"

"Hear my words, little one," she said. "For this is what the cards say..."

"A betrayer not of friends,
    But a betrayer of soul,
    From destiny's claws, do not defend,
    For in you the world will be made whole."

Iago felt his heart stop as sweat began to form upon his brow.

"The world...made whole?" his voice trilled. "By me?"

"As the cards have said."

"N-no! That's gotta be a mistake! I'm not the one to do something so stupid! I don't care what happens to this world! Let it burn for all I care! It's none of my business!"

"Then tell me," she said, her voice becoming eerily quiet. "Why do you have the White Bird tattooed upon your back?"

In a flash, bright rage sparked in Iago's eyes. "You shut up about that! That's none of your business!"

"Those who bear that mark, they are—"

"Your Grace!" the voice of a Giant came through the door. "We have made landing in Zerlina. The Jarl requests your presence on deck.

"I am sorry, little Elf," she said curtly as she rose. "But our time has been cut short."

Iago watched her leave the room, then followed her out the door.

The world whole, huh? Her words had stung him like whip. *What a bunch of nonsense...*

Outside, the winds carried gulls along their ways as merchants filled the docks below. Agmundr stood with Emalyn and the Soothsayer in the middle of the deck, with warriors at a knee beside them.

Nox, followed by Iago, and led by Caedmon, came to the surface and stopped.

"Young Nox," the Jarl's voice thundered over the sounds of the sea. "This appears to be where our stories diverge. I would love to accompany you upon your quest, but I am a king, so I must return to my kingdom."

Nox smiled. "It seems that is true, my Jarl. I will always remember you and the kindness you showed me and my friend."

"You think we would let you part so soon? Just like that?" Emalyn asked, nudging her husband in gut. "Stop the fluff and give her the present, why don't you?"

"I agree with Emalyn, my Jarl," the dual voices of the Soothsayer spoke as she handed him a tiny sack, which seemed even smaller held in the hand of a Giant.

"Of course! Of course!" Agmundr chuckled heartily as he took it.

"I-I don't need a present!" Nox laughed nervously. "Really!"

"No," the Jarl began as he bent down and handed the small bag to the girl. "You saved my wife *and* my kingdom. This present is but the least that I can give."

Nox opened the leather drawstrings to reveal a beautiful, sky-blue, glass eye.

"I..."

"I thought it was about time you had a matching pair!" Agmundr smiled, amused by himself. "No?"

"I love-" Nox choked. "I love it!"

"I'm going to miss you Lunae, er, Nox..." Caedmon sniffled.

"I'm going to miss my Giants!" Nox burst, joyful tears recounting the times they'd spent within her mind.

"And we will miss you as well!" the rest of the warriors cried.

Nox wiped her face and looked at the warriors before her. In their eyes, she could see tears of happy days and large feasts and tales of valor come and gone.

It was true. She would miss them *dearly*.

"The eye is not normal," the Soothsayer said among the wails and crying of the others. "It is made of Vryxn Glass, a mysterious gem, it is. It will enhance your powers."

"And," Agmundr finished, "if you ever need anything, Hawkhaven is open to you eternally, My Lady."

Nox held the eye to her chest and bowed. "Thank you once again!"

"Are we gonna give thanks all day, or are we going to *finally* walk on land?!" a sharp voice asked.

Nox looked at Iago by the ramp, looking as shrewd as ever with his arms crossed while tapping his foot. He wore an interesting wooded mask to cover his face, but Nox could tell by the grumpiness of his voice and body language that he was still good old Iago nonetheless.

She raised an eyebrow. "*We*?!"

Iago sighed, his breath silenced by the wooden mask.

"Yeah. *We*. Not like I have anywhere I can go now that I'm an *international criminal*. I might as well help you find Lukas."

"I *knew it*!" Nox exclaimed as she attempted to hug the Elf. "I knew we were friends!"

"Don't push it!" he jerked as he pushed her away. "I don't do hugs!"

"Oh! Then we need a secret handshake!"

Iago groaned. "Don't touch me."

Agmundr and other giants watched as the goddess Lunae and her unlikely friend walked down the landing ramp and off of the ship.

Ellier Vondell sat at his lavish desk in his fanciful quarters. The room was painfully white, he thought, as the lord's chambers of the castle were made of pure marble, but he liked the roominess enough to forgive the color. It had been six months since the fall of Crown City — six months since Prime Minister Eizen Zilheim became *Emperor* Eizen Zilheim. Vondell had spent fourteen years as Zilheim second-in-command, so the procurement of a favorable position was easy for him to attain.

He found Zerlina to be a town of mild winds and elegant historic sights, so when the emperor asked him where he would like to govern, the option was evident.

And thusly, he was now here in Zerlina, a consul to His Excellence.

He rose from the desk and approached the large window that overlooked the city. It was marvelous. Zerlina extended over brilliant stone roads lit by the lights within the white houses. The homes led to the dock, beyond which lay the ocean.

"It's beautiful, isn't it, Consul?" a, unevenly pitched voice spoke.

Vondell turned to see a wiry old man standing before him. This had been an easy enough transition for him, yet the only thing he truly despised about his new position was his adviser, this old man...

Cercion.

Vondell could never describe what he hated most about the curious elder. The man was thin and slinky, and his white-and-red robe had long sleeves that extended far beyond the length of his arms and almost touched the ground.

The old man pushed his stringy, floor-length black hair from his face.

"Old Cercion has news for you, good Vondell."

"Just speak."

"So courteous." Cercion smiled as he approached the empty desk and ran his sleeves upon the glass that stretched over it. "Cercion has some fun news for you"—he narrowed his eyes—"Commander."

Vondell kept his back turned. He couldn't really tell why, but something about this peculiar man...unnerved him.

"They say that a ship had docked recently, but not just any ship, *no*. This ship held Giants—*Giants!* Those are men who are not seen outside of their fortresses in Hawkhaven." Cercion snickered. "But get *this*. No Giants disembarked—no, no, no—it was a young girl and a masked man. But who, who," he tittered, "*who?!*"

"Cercion." Vondell's words were stone. "Get to the point. You better not be interrupting me at this time of night to tell me about nonsense."

"Oh, no, no, no!" The old man danced in little hops where he stood. "Old Cercion would never, *ever* think of wasting the good commander's time."

"Then why are you telling me all of these things?"

"Because they are of interest! *Interesting* interest! A mysterious girl and masked man! What could be more interesting?!"

Vondell sighed. He hated this old man. He was so furiously frustrating. "I don't find it so interesting, Cercion."

"Oh? Perhaps not you, but to the Master, it is."

The Master. Vondell shivered. He knew who this mysterious "Master" was. He cringed.

Zurriel.

"Do as you will. If this girl is so interesting to your master, then so be it. But it does not interest me."

The other pushed out his bottom lip. "Will the commander give Cercion his soldiers?"

Vondell sighed. "Whatever. Ten soldiers. That is all."

"How gracious the commander is!" the old man said joyfully, yet strangely almost in a hiss.

Vondell watched the night sky as the strange old man exited the room.

He didn't know who the old man was or from where he came. The man named Cercion seemed to almost appear one day under the direction of the dark wizard. Zurriel was trouble, he knew, and he wondered how much longer Zilheim would allow him to pull the strings before he ended him. The emperor wasn't a fan of taking orders, Vondell knew. That was why he had killed the king. So whoever this mysterious Zurriel was—this *End of the World*—his might must be great enough to earn His Highness' respect. Or, unbelievably, his fear. Whichever the case, it was the decision of Zurriel to assign the manic Cercion to his charge. Truly Vondell had no honest clue what to do with the old man. His voice was shrill; he talked too much; he was eccentric—too much for the Elven commander's tastes—and Vondell was slightly certain the fool was senile. It wasn't uncommon to hear him talking to himself or speaking in third person.

But no matter, he thought. *Perhaps this girl and masked man will keep him away for long enough to let me think.*

A masked man. He wasn't too sure if he should involve himself and frankly didn't care.

No. He didn't care.

Vondell looked out of his giant window. Outside, the rays of the full moon revealed the city as a whole, bathed in silver light.

Truly, yes. Truly all was well for him.

CHAPTER FIFTEEN

Returning Home

Nox descended the landing ramp and hopped onto the dock. The air was frigid and reeked of seaweed and salt. Nox wrapped herself in her cloak and began walking forward. The docks were rather gray in the moonbeams, almost dreary. Of course, Nox wasn't too sure what she assumed they would look like, but she had imagined that it might be more...vibrant? But that wasn't what she found here. Instead, the harbor was crowded closely with shanties of loose wood planks, constructed irresponsibly so that one could actually see the interior lights between the boards of some of the buildings. The street seemed to be all leading to the entrance of the city of Zerlina, extricated from the drab district by a mighty stone wall.

However, despite all of that, there was no stopping her sense that she was on an adventure. And, as far as Nox was concerned, that was all that mattered.

"Come, Iago! Onward!" she said gallantly as she marched forward.

Then, she stopped.

"Yup," the masked Elf said with a sneering smile. "Let me guess. You have no clue where you're going, do you?"

Nox turned, a large and stupid smile across her face. "Nope. No clue whatsoever."

Iago sighed. "How you've survived this long, I'll never know."

"Okay, smarty-pants!" the Aeon retorted. "Do *you* know where we're going?"

"Pff!" The Elf shrugged. "Why would I know? I'm an Elf! I'm not even native to this country!"

"Well you found the monastery one time, didn't you? Y'know," Nox threw her hands up in the air dramatically. "When you made the it go *boom!*"

"Well I didn't walk there or anything! That Agnon guy took me there with his weird portal stuff."

Nox pursed her lips into a sour pout. Iago disregarded his companion and continued down the dock. It didn't take long for him to notice a change in the town that even *he* could detect. This change, he didn't have to be a Zerlina native to notice. He looked at the guards at the gates and the police patrolling the city. It was obvious.

Elven soldiers.... he thought. *He's finally done it. Does that bastard Eizen finally control the whole world?*

"Nox." Iago looked over his shoulder. "Let's..."

"Ask someone!" Nox guessed.

"...be careful," Iago finished.

"Careful?" Nox asked, lowering her voice as well.

Iago pointed to the soldiers at the gate, their gilded armor silver in the moonlight.

"Those are Elven soldiers. They shouldn't be here, which means..."

"The Elves took over the city?" Nox completed the other's sentence.

"Right. And if I know Eizen well enough, he didn't just take over the city, but all of Aestriana as well." He paused. "Then what happened to King Reethkilt...?"

"Eizen?"

"Eizen Zilheim. The Prime Minister of Mirea. A bastard, that one. Arrogant and oh so high-and-mighty," Iago spat. "What a joke."

"That's no good..." Nox groaned. "So I guess we can't ask them anything, can we?"

"They're after me. I'm too suspicious. But..." Iago pointed at a large building at the end of the alley. Nox squinted her eye to read the sign in the light of the moon.

"River's End?"

"Inn and Tavern. If there's anyone worth asking, they'll be in there..."

"Tavern..." Nox said under her breath. "Okay!"

Nox had never been inside of a tavern before, but she was quick to decide that it wasn't much different from the feasting halls of Jarl Agmundr's palace in Hawkhaven.

Meat. Check.

Drink. Check.

Festivities and song. Check.

Yes, she decided that there was almost no difference save that the food didn't look as good and, well, she wasn't in a palace.

Iago nudged her to follow him to a table, and they sat. It wasn't long before the bartender came to their table, he was a short, round man with a bald head and puffy chops of black hair on his rosy cheeks.

"How old are you, girl?" he said with squinted eyes. "You don't look the age to be in a place like this." His eyes scanned her some more. "You've definitely got a sword and all, but you look awfully young."

"I'm sixteen." Nox smiled. "Why? Is that a problem?"

"Look," the masked Iago cut in. "We aren't here to eat or drink. We want to know how to get to the Zerlina Monastery."

Suddenly, the man's rosy face turned pale. "The monastery?!" he exclaimed. "Who are you? Why would you want to go there?"

"Well," Nox said, "I was raised there, I—"

"Get out!" the man growled, his cheery expression melting into a scowl. "Place is bad luck, and I'll have no one in my tavern who has touched that forbidden soil."

"But we—"

He pointed to the door. "Out!"

There was no need to argue. Both of them knew that. The two stood outside under the moonlight.

Forbidden? Nox felt her heart sink. *Unlucky?*

The feeling felt so familiar. For the first time since her adventure began, she felt the rejection she had felt as a child. Nox walked to the edge of the dock overlooking the sea. The moon above was bright and elegant, its visage crying tears of light that seemed to dance like fleeting flickers of silver upon the darkened waters. For some reason, as she stared out into the vast ocean, she could feel a tug in her heart. She sat upon the edge, removing her shoes first and dipping her feet into the pool, the icy waters flicking upon her toes.

"I had forgotten," she said as if speaking to the waves. "But that's no big deal, right? If I'm unlucky, then I'll wear it proudly. That's what I should do, right?"

"Who are you talking to?" Iago said as he approached and stood beside her. "You'll look like a lunatic if you talk to yourself like that."

"I was talking to my big brother, I think."

"Big brother?"

"Klyriai. I was talking to Klyriai."

"The Aeon?"

Nox nodded and smiled. Iago shrugged. This girl, she was so filled with life, so filled with naive hope and vulnerability...it was so easy to forget that she was a divine being—a goddess nonetheless. The Elf just assumed this was one of the rare times that this side of her came out. The two were silent, both gazing out into the dark horizon. The swishing of waves filled the salty air; the stars shone like incandescent crystals suspended within the blackened void.

"Do you think," Nox said finally, "the monastery is...?"

"Gone? Like *poof*!" a shrill voice spoke from behind the two. Nox and Iago jolted, both whipping around.

Before them, an old man in oversized robes stood, his long sleeves almost drooping onto the moist planks of the dock.

"Who the hell are you?" Iago demanded.

Nox drew the *Nightbringer* from its sheath.

"Yeah!" she said. "Who are you?"

"Me?" the old man said as he held up his sleeved fingers in surrender. "Please! Put down that *fearsome* blade! Old Cercion means you no violence."

"Well you better start telling us what you *do* mean!" Iago's voice was a rough growl.

"The monastery is gone." the old man said.

Nox lowered the black blade, her voice almost a whimper. "Ggone?"

"Yes!" the old man said, narrowing his eyes. "*Gone*! They never rebuilt it! But do not worry, little girl! No, no! There is no need to worry! The monks are just fine. They live at the abbey on the south side of town. The priests pray and work in the vineyards by day! To find your way, you must go to *Little Leaf Vineyards* today! Does that answer your question...*little Aeon?*"

Nox suddenly raised her blade once more. "How do you know that?!"

"I know what I know and I reap what I sow. Helping the Master is hard work," the old man began, walking closer and narrowing his eyes. His voice was a low hiss. "*You know?*"

Silver flashed in the moonlight. Without a thought, Nox slammed her bare foot into the old man's kneecap, the force against his withered body causing the joint to snap. The black blade was without shine as it swished through the night and slid into Cercion's chest.

"Who are you?!" her voice was hard.

"Shhh..." The old man called Cercion smiled as he held a finger to his lips. Slowly, his flesh began to bubble and quiver. Nox stepped backward as the man melted into nothingness and was gone.

Nox and Iago stood silent for a moment, the high of battle sending adrenaline through their veins. Nox looked at her Elven partner, then out at the ocean. In the distance, the horizon faded into green, prophetic of the coming dawn.

"We need to find that vineyard," Nox said with a deep breath. "If this man knew where it was, then that means that the monks are in danger."

"Do you think," Iago began, "that he might have?"

"I don't know. But I'm afraid for the worst. This man knew I was Lunae, which means he's definitely with that Zurriel guy." Nox turned her back to the sea and sheathed her blade.

"Let's go. I don't know how much time we have left."

Iago nodded. "Let's do this."

Brother Claus was in his garden as the first lights of dawn triumphed over the dark horizon. *It is a beautiful sight,* he thought, as he watched the stars give way to the azure sky. He turned to his flowers and marveled at them for a moment.

Black Moon Tulips. He didn't know why he loved them so much. Tall tulips, this particular plant grew higher than ordinary tulips and, for some reason, remained evergreen. This, however, wasn't the most peculiar thing about this seemingly alien plant. No, its most defining feature was that, during the morning time, just as the day and night collide, its ebon petals began to glow a faint silver tint. The silver, he thought, was just like the light of the moon. This, he assumed, was the reason they were given the name "Black Moon."

Black petals, that shine with the silver of the moon.

He bent down and groaned as he lifted an urn of water. Watering the plants wasn't as easy as it had been. Now, at the age of sixty, many things weren't so easy.

"Hellooo!" a piercing voice said from the entrance to the garden.

Brother Claus jumped at the high-pitched voice, dropping the urn. The cold water drenched his feet.

"Are you Brother Claus?"

The monk looked up to see a strange old man standing before him, with eight elven guards behind at his command.

"I'm not impressed..." The old man sounded disappointed as he held his long sleeves to his face. "I thought that the man that raised an Aeon would be more...*manly?*" he paused. "Is *manly* the word...yes, yes, yes...*manly!*"

"Raised an..." Chills sparked throughout the monk's body. "...Aeon?"

Brother Claus knew instantly what this meant, and he didn't doubt for a second the realization. It all made sense.

Falling from the sky...

An eye that was crimson red...

The Aeon this man was referring to...

It was Nox.

"I don't know what you're talking about," the monk said. "Now if you'll excuse me, I need to get another urn. Thanks for scaring me well enough to drop and break this one."

"You don't know? So you didn't raise the Aeon Lunae? So she has come to this town looking for a parent who isn't here?" The man cocked his head. "Do you *lie* to old Cercion?"

'*Come to this town?*' Brother Claus felt his heart leap.

"Nox is here?!" he blurted out instinctively. "She's here, in Zerlina?"

A wry smile crooked upon the old man's face. "I never mentioned such a name! But truly it is a good one! Nox, is it? So Lunae is called Nox?"

The monk felt his heart sink into his stomach.

"Take him." Cercion said with a snap of his fingers. "We will need him at the party if we wish to attract a *special* guest!"

Brother Claus fell to his knees as the soldiers in gilded armor bound his hands and dragged him away.

What have I done? he thought.

But he knew. He was the very bait to trap the daughter he loved the most.

Unfortunately, it took hours to navigate the twisted convoluted city of Zerlina, which proved a great obstacle. It was midday before Nox and Iago finally made it to the fields outside of the city and laid eyes upon the vineyards of the abbey. The vineyard, however, along with all of the vegetation that lay sprawled out along the fields outside of the town, was dead. Nox drew her cloak as a cold breeze swept past her. She was thankful for the boots and armor given to her by the Giants. They were insulated, which made sense given the harsh northern climate of Hawkhaven. But more so, she was thankful that her boots were thick enough to avoid absorbing the wetness that still lingered from the melted frosts.

It was a nice walk to the abbey, which was positioned upon a hill that, admittedly, tired both the goddess and her Elven companion. Nox couldn't tell if she was tired from not sleeping all night or from the journey to their current location.

Either way, she decided, her body was begging for rest.

There was no door at the entrance into the courtyard of the brick abbey. Nox and Iago entered and stood.

"It can't be!" a woman's voice exclaimed.

Nox couldn't mistake that voice. Ever.

"*Sister Helga!*"

And it was. The two turned to see the old nun.

I..." Her cane fell from her hands as she held her hands to her face. "I can't believe it. I was certain...I was—"

"You thought I was dead?" Nox bellowed in laughter.

Nox could see tears forming upon the old woman's eyes.

"I was. I feel so silly—so guilty now for doubting you...I just..."

The young Aeon approached the nun and cradled her hands in her own.

"Sister." Nox heard her own voice trill as she fought back tears. "I'm here now."

"And you're in armor—you have a broadsword now, and..." She paused. Sister Helga ran a weary hand past the young girl's face to reveal the glass eye.

"It was taken." Nox said, pointing out what the nun was probably thinking. "My eye, I mean. When I was taken away, a dark wizard held me in a cage in some old library. He took my eye and threw me into the ocean. I have to admit, I was really scared"—she motioned her hands toward Iago—"but my friend here saved me! He jumped into the ocean and kept me from drowning. I owe him my life, really."

The old nun eyed the masked Elf, her old eyes looking him over with a curiosity that made her look much younger.

"I thank you, mysterious Elf. I know your people have done much to oppress us, but anyone who would risk their life for Nox is welcome here anytime."

Behind the mask, Iago's face became hot.

"I will not ask you to remove your mask," Sister Helga said, "I know your reasons are your own. But may I please have your name?"

"Of course." Iago replied replied. "Lyon. My name is Lyon."

"Well, Lyon," the sister said, bowing, "you have my eternal gratitude."

"Sister Helga!" Nox finally said, looking around. "Where is Brother Claus.

The nun's face suddenly darkened, her lighthearted features melting into a grim visage. "I figured you would ask that. I mean, of course you would. He is the man who raised you. You probably came back just to see him, didn't you? Well, you see," she said, pausing, "he was taken by the Elven forces. By the consul's advisor, an old man named Cercion."

Nox and Iago looked at each other. A deathly ice filled their veins.

"But he..." Nox stopped.

"Even since the fall of our country, the Elves have been patrolling the city. They're being led by the now none other than Commander Ellier Vondell."

"Ellier..." Iago growled under his breath. "Ellier is here...?"

"Ever since then, he's been funneling the tax money to the Empire. So may orphans have come to us, so much so that we've actually run out of space..."

"And this Cercion guy?" Iago asked.

"He's the consul's adviser. We don't know much about him other than that he's old and twisted mentally, but..."

Nox balled her fist, her nails digging into her palm, knuckles whitening. "And this man—this Cercion—where did he take my father? Where did he take Brother Claus?"

"I assume the dungeon of the fortress that the Elves are using—the one in the center of the city."

Silence sat between them for a moment. Nox felt nothing but the cold winds that swooped in from atop the high brick walls of the abbey.

"Nox, you're not going to—?" the nun began.

"I am." Nox cracked her knuckles. "I'm gonna go get him. And I'm gonna thrash that Cercion for good this time."

"This time?" The nun dismissed the question. "You're being headstrong, as usual. What, do you think you're just going to barge into the enemy keep? The reason Cercion took Brother Claus is no mystery. If you've met him before, then he obviously, for some reason, wants to lure you there. And you've told me once already that your eye was taken by a wizard. He might just want to finish you off—"

"No." The Aeon's voice was firm. "I have to go. I *must*. I can't leave him there, Sister Helga. Brother Claus raised me! He's my father—I...I love him. I love him and I won't let anyone hurt the ones I love."

For some reason, Nox remembered the words of the blue-haired knight from the beginning of her journey. Back then, she didn't truly understand Snow's resolve—not like she did now. Now, she felt she understood fully. Now that she wielded the *Nightbringer*, she knew exactly how Snow felt. The *Nightbringer* rang as it was pulled from its sheath. Sister Helga marveled at it; its long, black blade seemed to show no sheen or luster—a dark abyss that spited the light of the day.

"Sister Helga," Nox said, her eyes unmovable. "I will protect the ones I love, and there is nothing that will stop me from that. Even if it means death."

The nun sighed. "I see you're as stubborn as ever, yet I commend your courage."

"Surely there must be a way into the fortress?" Iago spoke up, trying to break the tension.

The nun nodded. "There is, actually. I do not know whether it was fate that brought you here at the time of this opportunity, or perhaps if One chose to smile upon you, but there *is* another way in."

Nox lit up. "How?!"

"Rumor is that the Elves are holding a very special prisoner in the fortress. Besides Brother Claus, I mean. I don't know who it is, but this person is important enough to hold a banquet to celebrate their public execution."

"And that helps us how?" Iago sounded grumpy as always.

"The vineyard just so happens to have some choice wines and other products that Consul Vondell desires to be brought to the celebration. I guess you could say we're catering."

Nox's face lightened. "When?"

"Tomorrow evening. Tomorrow evening we will be taking the supplies by carriage. If you were to hide in a barrel—well I would assume you would be sent to the store room. I still worry, Nox." The nun sighed. "You know that if they catch you you'll be put to death, don't you?"

"I do. But don't worry, Sister Helga." Nox snapped her fingers. Suddenly, a purple flame flickered upon the tip of her thumb. "I've got some tricks of my own."

"Magic...?" the nun whispered in astonishment. "Okay, deary. I trust you."

Nox smiled, then yawned. "Sister Helga." The goddess' voice was small.

"Yes, Nox?"

"Can I...sleep here..like, now?"

The nun giggled. "Of course, dear. I'll find you each a room."

CHAPTER SIXTEEN

Klyriai

The sounds of the sea caused Nox to open her eyes. She could feel the warm waters lick her skin. The sky was empty and without stars. Above her, a bright black moon shone with an eldritch glow, but she wasn't sure how she could see it.

"I has been a while since we've spoken," a male voice distantly echoed throughout the space. Nox sat up. She had already realized that she was not going to sink into the dark waves below her, but instead she stood upon them as if they were stone.

She looked around. Nothing. Nothing but darkness and the swish of the waves below her feet.

Nox cupped her hands in front of her mouth and took a deep breath.

"*Hello?!*" she called into the darkness. "*Who are you? Where are you?*"

"I am here," the voice called again, this time closer.

Nox looked around. The voice seemed as if it were in her ear, yet no one was present. It was as if she were alone with this disembodied entity.

"Well," she said, slight frustration sparking in her voice. "Can I see you?"

"Of course."

Suddenly, the dark waves began to shift and turn violently. Nox shielded her eyes as bright light shot up from beneath the waves, illuminating the black waters a shining emerald green.

"I am glad you spoke to me earlier."

Nox turned and gasped. From the sloshing waters, a man rose from the depths. He was tall and thin, and his long hair seemed to flow like the oceans themselves, swishing this way and that that way as if twisted by an unseen wind. Nox stared into his deep blue eyes. They swirled like bright whirlpools within his head.

"Again, I say, it has been a while since you have spoken to me. One thousand years, in fact. But I am glad to see you well, sister."

"Sister...? You must be?!"

"Klyriai, yes. You seem well. It seems you have overcome the tragedies of the past. That is good."

"Tragedies?"

"You do not know? Well, I suppose it would be impossible to know anything that transpired after your death."

Nox went cold. "My...death?"

"Listen to me, little sister. You never thought it strange that you don't remember being Lunae? That you never realized your identity until that wretch Zurriel brought it to your attention?"

"Well. Yes. I thought it was odd." Nox paused. "When I retook the Sword of the Black Moon from Lyhaal, he remembered me—said that we had made a promise, even, but I don't remember him or our promise. He was so sad—it broke my heart. So you're saying that the reason I don't remember is because I..."

"Lunae," the Aeon's voice became grim. "One thousand years ago, you died."

Nox's blood ran cold.

"You were killed, more correctly. You were killed by the hand of Lucyn, the one whose Starblood heart you stole. The one you gave to *that boy*."

"That boy...?"

She remembered, sharp images cut through her mind.

"In the woods!" she exclaimed. "Lukas! I gave Lukas Lucyn's heart?!"

"Perhaps," Klyriai said, shrugging. "Perhaps not. But that is not why I came to you."

"Why, then?"

"Because you must know what truly transpired upon that day, one thousand years ago."

The glowing waters stilled.

"Lucyn struck you with the First of Three—the *Sword Durandal*—and you died. Before your death, you took his heart. But that is not all."

Nox felt her head grow fuzzy. So much information out of context caused her to feel dizzy.

"Lunae. Before you died, you gave birth to a child."

Nox's mouth gaped. "A *child*?!"

"Yes. This child walks the world right now. I do not know the gender of the child or its age or name, but it walks among us today."

"Why are you telling me this, Klyriai? What's your purpose here?"

"I have one purpose in this information. And it is that, wherever this child is, Zurriel will most definitely be after it. You must seek it out and find it before he does."

Nox paused.

"I'm sorry. I'm sorry, Klyriai, but I can't do that just yet. I may be an Aeon or have died or whatever, but right now the man who raised me and gave me everything is in dire trouble, and I have to save him."

The other Aeon smiled. "Ever the guardian, I see. Even if you don't remember who you are, you haven't changed one bit."

'*Let's protect each other,*' *Nox*. The promise she made with Lukas entered her mind. '*I'll protect you; you'll protect me.*'

Nox smiled. "To protect the ones I love. *That* is why I fight."

"I come with a warning. If you enter the fortress, you will see a man die upon the gallows. You do not know this man. Let him die, and his death will grant you an easy rescue of the monk you call your father. But, if you rescue him, you will see the truth."

"What?" Nox cocked her head. "I don't understand—!"

The Aeon of the Sea merely stared back with a grin. Suddenly, the waters darkened, and her vision faded.

"Worry not, little sister," his voice resounded. "Wherever the moon touches the seas, I shall always be with you."

***

Nox awoke less rested than when she had drifted off. The encounter with the elusive Aeon had left a strange chill over her body.

I have a...child?

The thought created odd emotions within her. She looked down at her hands. She was only sixteen. She didn't know what to think about a child. Was it a boy or a girl? If it already walked Lythia, what if it was *older* than her? Her stomach twisted. She exhaled.

I'm not ready to be a mother...

She shook her head.

Snap out of it, Nox! Think about your mission!

Brother Claus was being held captive, and she had to save him. Any ruminations about a child somewhere out there in the world weren't important now.

The words of Klyriai swam in her mind.

A man I don't know...but is dear to me...?

Genuinely, she couldn't place her finger upon who this person might be. Even throughout all of her adventures, she had only met Iago and the Giants of Hawkhaven. So, this person would be?

Who?

"The other brothers and sisters are preparing for the evening," Sister Helga said as she entered the room. "I see you didn't sleep well."

"Oh, I uh..." Nox stretched her arms high in the air. "Just strange dreams."

"I'm sure you're nervous."

The nun sat at the edge of the bed. The two sat in silence for a moment.

"You look so..." Helga paused. "Different.

Nox held her hand to her glass eye. "You mean..."

"I wasn't going to say anything. I didn't know how to, well, address it."

Nox sighed. "It's a long story."

"Well"—the nun motioned out the window to the morning light —"we have a little time."

Nox shrugged. And so she told Sister Helga everything. About her capture and her prison in the mysterious library of V'rezen Myur. She told her about the dark wizard Zurriel and how he took her eye. She smiled as she recounted her adventures with the Giants of

Hawkhaven.

But most importantly, she told her about who she was—or who everyone said she was.

"I see." The nun's voice suddenly became quiet. "So everything comes together."

"What do you mean?"

"When that man, Cercion, came looking for Brother Claus, he kept saying that he was looking for the man who 'raised an Aeon.'" She shrugged. "We had no clue what he was talking about, so we remained silent. He went to each of us, trying his best to get a confession. By the time he reached Claus, we knew. We didn't want to admit it, but we knew deep down who he was talking about."

"He meant..."

"The girl with the red eye. We knew, then. We knew that you were not human." The old nun pushed back her short, graying hair with a bony finger. "I didn't know how to bring it up, so I just thought I'd let you tell me on your own, but when you didn't...well, my curiosity got the better of me."

Nox turned her eyes to the window. Outside, two birds alighted upon the branch of a withered oak.

"I was always so disrespectful," she began. "Looking back, you were right. All he wanted was the best for me, but I always spat in his face. And now..."

A warm leathery hand embraced Nox's own. "And now you're going to save him."

"Sister?"

The nun smiled. "I believe in you, my little Nox."

The cell was dark and cold. In the distance, the sounds of dripping water was maddening, like the eternal ticking of a clock. Brother Claus sat upon the small cot that lay upon the stone floor of his cell.

How long had he been here? He did not know.

Why had they taken him? He did not know.

There were no answers; there were only an ever accumulating amount of questions.

"Nox..." he whispered into the darkness.

"You okay over there, partner?" a gruff voice called from the adjacent cell. "I hear your sniffling. I assume you're not a soldier?"

"You would assume correctly." The monk cleared his throat. "I'm a priest."

"Holy man, eh?" the voice chuckled. "Your kind don't belong here, that's for sure. Tell me, what did you do to put yourself beside me? We're in the deepest part of the dungeon. Must'a been something real bad, eh? You're in the lowest circle of hell, after all."

"I—" The monk looked down at his ankle, shackled to the wall, and sighed. "I don't know what I did. I was gardening, then that man, Cercion, bound me and brought me here..."

"Cercion..." the other spat. "I'll give you a bit of information— whether it worries you more, I don't know —but, listen." He coughed a dry cough. "There is no man named Cercion."

"What do you mean?" Brother Claus gasped. "I saw him with my own eyes! He carried me here!"

"Perhaps he did, but he really didn't. There's no real way to determine how long the *real* Cercion has been dead, but I'll tell ya, that ain't him. He's just a *face*, one of the many visages of the wizard known as *Valter Rivyra the Face Thief*."

"So what are you saying?"

"I'm saying that there's no way to know what else he has up his sleeve."

The light from the doorway pierced the darkness around the corner to the stairwell, followed by the stomping sounds of Elven soldiers descending the stairs.

"Good talk, Father," the voice said. "By the way, may I have your name?"

"My name?"

"A man should at least know the name of the last friend he ever made."

"Well, well, well..." One of the Elven soldiers smirked, his lips barely visible in the candlelight. "Oh how the mighty have fallen."

"Let me hear his name," the prisoner said.

"Cl-Claus," the monk replied.

"Good to know you, Claus."

Silence, cur!" an Elf said as the door to the cell swung open. Brother Claus' heart began to race as he heard the sounds of chains rattling and the guards giving his new friend a flogging. "Today's the day we finally rid the world of you."

In the dim light that was available, the monk watched the man be dragged from his cell. His face seemed worn and starved, his long brown beard reaching the bottom of his neck. Brother Claus shivered at the man's forlorn face. Across his face, a large scar had severed his left eye, leaving it white and without texture.

"Who are you?!" the monk wailed.

"I said *silence!*" The Elf slammed his cane against the wall, causing the monk to cower and whimper.

"Oh, I forgot," the other prisoner chuckled, slurping blood into his mouth and spitting it onto the ground.

The Elf grunted as he hit the man again.

"Havell," the man said through gritted teeth. "I'm Havell Maro."

The evening came quicker than Nox had expected it would, the golden light of the sun bathing the red bricks of the abbey in a vibrant crimson. The monks and nuns of the abbey had spent the majority of the day diligently preparing the supplies for the upcoming feast. There was electricity in the air, Nox could feel it. It was a certain pressure, a chill of fear.

Nox stood and watched them, the brown-cloaked monks and black-clad nuns working diligently, operating in pairs to heave barrels of wine and foods onto the wooden wagon.

"They don't want to do this," Iago said as he came to her side. "Can't really blame them though. They're basically celebrating the execution of one of their own—or at least that's what I picked up from this."

Nox turned to her Elven companion, his face hidden by a smooth mask of white wood, with slits cut for the eyes and two holes at the nose.

"Who do you think is being executed?"

Iago huffed. "Why do you think I would know? I've been with you all this time. I didn't even know that Eizen finally extended his slimy hands to Aestriana. But I know for a fact that, however he was able to take down this country, he probably had Zurriel's help."

Nox balled her fist. *Zurriel...*

He shrugged. "Best we can do is hope to One above that we actually don't get caught."

"Scared?" Nox smiled a clever grin, the light of the sun causing her glass eye to glisten. "You don't have to go with me, you know?"

"As if!" the Elf laughed, running his hands through his short red hair. "I'm a lot stronger now than I was. Besides, there's someone in particular at that castle," he said, his voice becoming a dreadful hiss, "someone I need to have a *long talk* with."

"It's that Vondell guy, isn't it? I heard you whisper his name the other day."

Iago opened his hand and looked down at his palm. "Yeah, me and Ellier have"—he clenched his fist—"important matters to attend to."

Nox shivered. She could feel the heat in her companion's voice. Whoever this man was, she pitied him if Iago ever found him.

The wagon was filled to the brim when Nox and Iago approached it.

"You'll be in one of the wooden barrels." Sister Helga said as she came to their side. "One of these barrels will probably be an easy fit for you, Nox." She turned to Iago. "I'm sorry Lyon, but you're going to be rather uncomfortable in yours."

Great, Iago thought.

"You're positive that you're okay with this?" Iago reiterated.

"Yes," Sister Helga said as she nodded to the bishop who stood beside her. "As dangerous as it may be, Brother Claus is innocent...and I fear what they may do to him."

"Brother Claus is a righteous man," the bishop spoke up, his bony brow raised above his old and faded yellow-brown eyes. "We would be poor servants of One if we allowed him to suffer unjustly!"

"So what's the plan?" Nox said, her sky-blue eyes wide with anticipation.

"Well, we can sneak you in with the food." Sister Helga said, pointing to the city beyond the vineyard. "If we can fit you inside of one of the barrels, you'll be put in the storage room of the palace. Then you can—"

Nox looked out at the fields, and the city just beyond. She could see the castle's spires just over the gray walls of Zerlina, the top of which were shingled with red stone.

Bloody, dangerous.

Nox nodded. She had to do this. She couldn't be afraid.

"Go it!" the Aeon exclaimed with a fire in her eyes. "Let's go!"

"Not so fast," Iago spoke up. "How will we know where we're going once we get in?"

"The dungeon is at the bottom of the fortress," Sister Helga said.

"So just keep going down..." Nox finished. "Okay! We don't have any time to lose!"

"Tell me, Captain. No. *Former* captain," Ellier smirked in amusement as he looked down at Havell, who knelt before him. "How does it feel to die as a prisoner in your own country? Oh, wait, I mean what *was* your country." The Elf chuckled as he inspected his fingernails. "My mistake."

Havell said nothing, his eyes locked onto the ground.

"Stay silent, I suppose," Ellier chuckled. "It's not as if I *want* to hear you wail or anything." The Elf walked to his desk and leaned back, sitting upon the edge. "You've lost your kingdom, your king, your home, your status, your men"—Ellier grinned—"even your prince has abandoned you."

"Shut up already, you prancing spit." Havell growled in a low tone. "You can jail me; you can chain me to the walls; you can starve me to near death and beat me; hell, you can even kill me! *But don't you dare—don't you* dare *insult Prince Reethkilt!* He would never, ever, *ever* abandon his people!"

As Ellier Vondell stared back into the former captain's eyes, he couldn't help but shiver. What was it about this man that unnerved him? How? How could this man still have such spirit after all he had endured? He didn't know where this prince was, yet still...

Yet still he would stake his life upon his lord's name.

"You're a fool, Captain." Ellier Vondell finally scoffed. "You're a fool, and today you shall die a fool's death." He nodded to the soldiers. Upon his command, they raised the prisoner and dragged him from the room. The Elf watched them leave, then exhaled deeply once the door was closed.

Good riddance.

CHAPTER SEVENTEEN

Crashing the Party

A crowd of Elven soldiers had filled the courtyard of the historic fortress. Now evening, the sun shone down upon the gallows in a golden spear of light, its setting rays dying with the condemned.

Despite the cheers and festivities of the crowd below, today was not a day of celebration. No. There were no townspeople among this group. This was a victory for the Elven soldiers alone.

For today they would rid the world of a prisoner.

As Sister Helga's wagon, filled with barrels of food and wine, approached the gates, the armored hand of an Elven guard halted her advance.

"Papers?" he said, his voice muffled behind his gilded helmet.

"Papers?" Sister Helga repeated. "I was told nothing of papers!"

"This is a private event," he said, removing his helmet to reveal his gaunt face then speaking slowly, as if she couldn't understand. "Lord Vondell only wishes for certain people to attend. No papers; no entry. That simple, hag?"

"*Hag?!*" Sister Helga gasped. "You listen here, *young man,*" she snapped. "I am carrying the first shipment of food to you lousy grunts so that you might enjoy whatever you are about to do. I don't think your Lord Vondell would be very happy with you if he found out that you denied the wine, now would he?"

"I-I-I..." The Elf cleared his throat and placed his helmet back onto his head. "C-carry on..."

"Thank you." Sister Helga smiled with an accomplished nod as she drove through the gates.

The wagon passed by the crowds to a door in the corner of the courtyard. Helga sat and watched as the Elven soldiers unload each barrel one by one as she prayed to One that their plan wouldn't be revealed. As she watched each barrel, she wondered which ones Nox and Lyon were in.

"Alright old hag!" a soldier in golden armor exclaimed as he rounded the front of the wagon. "That's the last one!"

Helga felt her heart quicken under her breath. She nodded without a word and turned the wagon around.

Nox, she thought. *Little Nox. You've grown so much. Please be careful.* She began to pray. *Oh great Starbreather, watch over this little one. Guide her and her father home.*

The wagon crossed the courtyard and left through the gate. And the nun began to pray harder.

The castle was eerily quiet. Nox sat stuffed in her barrel for what seemed like hours even though she was sure it couldn't have been that long. Cramped inside, she held the *Nightbringer* clutched to her chest. She felt her barrel being lowered to the floor with a *thud,* then the sound of footsteps walking away. A door slammed shut, then, silence.

It was time to come out.

Nox gripped the hilt of the black sword and closed her eyes. Bright flames lit the blade a deep violet as she felt her Aeonic powers rush through her veins from deep within.

"Disperse."

At her command, the barrel exploded into splinters, the tiny fragments flying against the walls.

"You think you could be any louder?" Iago said as he fixed his sleeve. "Jeez, Nox."

"Well," the Aeon pouted. "How'd *you* get out, then?"

Iago pointed to his barrel. Nox followed his finger. Before her the barrel remained intact, all but the top, which had been easily removed.

"The tops come off, Nox. The monks and nuns didn't bolt you inside."

"W-well!" Nox felt her face growing hot. "M-my way was cooler!"

Iago waved his hand in indifference.

"Sure it was." He pointed to the doorway. "We gotta go. Judging by the silence, and if I know Ellier Vondell like I think I do, then the hallways just might be empty."

Nox nodded. Silently, she followed her Elven companion as they crept to the door. The Aeon gripped the hilt of the *Nightbringer,* once again igniting its purple flames. Nox's heart beat faster as she watch Iago turned the door handle. Slowly, he pushed the door forward.

"I was right," the Elf said, smiling. "Ellier, you dumb bastard."

"You sure seem to know this Ellier guy well," Nox said.

"Yeah. He's one of the ones who put me in prison for killing the prince..." Iago balled his fist. "One of the ones who put Amalia to the sword. But today...today I'll get my hands on him..."

The hallway was long and brightly lit, with a red carpet running its length which made the directions even more disorienting.

"Which way to the dungeon?" Nox said as she scratched her head.

"How would I know?" Iago replied, walking past her.

Nox said nothing; honestly, she felt there was nothing to say. The two stealthily strode down the hallway, Nox relying on Iago's acute Elven eyes to find their way.

"There!" Iago whispered loudly. "The stairwell!"

The two nodded.

"*NOW, MY GOOD MEN OF MIREA!*" A loud voice filled the courtyard outside, resounding off of the walls, its buzz echoing into the streets outside.

Nox turned.

"Nox." Iago nudged the Aeon. "Come on. We have to go!"

"*WE BRING TO YOU TODAY A SPECIAL EVENT!*"

Nox quietly stepped to a small window and peered through.

"*Nox!*" Iago's voice echoed but was not acknowledged.

"*WITH THIS MAN'S DEATH, A GRAND VICTORY WILL BE WON FOR OUR GREAT COUNTRY, OUR NEW KING, AND OUR SUPERIOR RACE!*"

Nox peered through the tiny glass. Outside, the gilded soldiers had gathered around the gallows. Before them, upon a high balcony, a decorated man stood, announcing an event to the crowd.

FOR EMPEROR ZILHIEM! they chanted in a cult-like cadence.

"Nox!" Iago whispered more assertively, grabbing her arm. *"Ignore them. We have to go down."*

Nox stood still, her eye fixated upon the man with the noose around his neck. He looked worn and scarred, his brown hair long and unkempt—the same as his dusty beard. Suddenly, the words of Klyriai ran through her mind

'You will see a man die upon the gallows. You do not know this man. Let him die, and his death will grant you an easy rescue of the monk you call your father. But if you rescue him, you will see the truth.'

Nox paused.

I don't know this man. She knew this was true, but still, she felt a strange...*connection* to him. Who was he? Why did she feel as if they had met once before? She was certain that she had never crossed paths with this individual, yet still, she felt she had. She wasn't certain what circumstances led her to feel this way, but she could be certain of the emotions stirring within her. She could feel it—a warmth in her heart, like a faint affinity for this weathered man upon the gallows.

"Nox," Iago growled. "Don't you dare—"

The Elf barely finished his sentence as Nox jerked her arm from his grasp.

"AND NOW," the executioner announced proudly, his face shrouded all but his smile, *"TO DEATH WITH YOU, FORMER CAPTAIN—"*

Suddenly, the eastern wall exploded in violet fire, launching the red brick and grayed stones of the fortress into the air. The soldiers stopped their chanting and drew their blades, readying themselves and watching the cloud of dust for any threat they could possibly detect.

"SORRY!" The voice of a young woman roared, filling the courtyard. *"BUT THAT GUY'S NOT DYING TODAY!"*

As the dust settled to the ground, the figure of Nox came into view, the *Nightbringer* at her side. At the sight of the petite girl, thunderous laughter erupted from the soldiers.

"You're too late, girl!" the executioner chuckled derisively. "He dies now!"

The Elf turned to pull the lever. Suddenly, a bright ethereal blade shot past him, severing the rope, and dropping the prisoner to the gallows' wooden planks.

"You!" the executioner cursed.

"You really are a pain, you know that, Lunae?" Iago groaned as he walked through the hole in the wall, unmasked.

"You are—!" the decorated Elf upon the balcony exclaimed. "Iago of the Thousand Swords!"

Iago smirked as he threw his mask upon the ground.

"Good to see you again, Ellier," he called back at the commander. "Don't worry, *we* will be catching up soon enough!"

"Well," Ellier responded curtly. "I doubt that will be happening anytime soon." He waved his hand to his soldiers as he turned to enter the fortress. "Kill them."

The army of Elves simultaneously drew their blades and rushed forward.

"Damn it!" Iago spat as he summoned one hundred phantom swords into the air.

"Thanks, Iggy!" Nox smiled as she rushed in the direction of the gallows. "I'm gonna rescue this guy now!"

"And leave me with everything else?!"

"Yup!"

Iago spat on the ground. As the soldiers approached him, he pointed in their direction. At their master's command, the hundred blades shot forward, hissing as they sped to their targets. Loud wails filled the courtyard as the blades slit the throats of several soldiers.

She always leaves me with the heavy work, Iago raged as he held his hand high. "Now try *this!*"

A great gale exploded around him, pushing back the armored knights.

"Get back!" an officer exclaimed.

"It won't save you!" Iago warned.

The soldiers froze in fear. Towering above their opponent was a gargantuan phantom hammer.

"What?!" Iago smirked as the giant phantom hammer came

crashing down. "Thought I was only a one-trick pony?!"

"You really think you're a match for us, girl?" said a decorated soldier as he and his men surrounded Nox. "You've got a sword, and all five of us have armor!"

"No big!" Nox said as she rushed forward.

Reflexively, the soldiers swung their blades downward, screaming as they cut the wind.

With inhuman speed, Nox ducked and spun upon her knees, swinging the *Nightbringer* in a circular arc, spitting forth tongues of violet flame that sliced into the Elven armor easily. The soldiers screamed as their innards disintegrated in the heat of the mysterious energy. Nox passed them, leaping onto the wooden gallows.

"Hey!" she said as knelt before the forlorn prisoner. "I'm here to help you!"

"M-me?" he coughed. "Who are you?"

"Nox. I'm Nox!"

"Nox..." the man whispered, wincing. "Have I heard that name before?"

Nox could tell the man was starved and worn, his face shrunken in, revealing his scars.

"You've heard of me?"

"Yeah," he replied. "I think I have. But why would you save me? You don't even know my name."

"I don't know," Nox replied. "For some reason, I felt that you were important. But that doesn't matter right now. We have to get you out of here."

"The monk!" the prisoner exclaimed suddenly. "I heard your name from the monk!"

"Brother Claus?!" Nox exclaimed as she helped the worn man to stand. "You know where he's at?!"

The man raised his head, revealing his dulled, blind eye in the evening light. "You're lookin' for him, right? I can take you to him!"

Nox stood, the man's arm wrapped around her shoulders. She looked out into the yard that was now filled with corpses of the dead guards.

"Bout time," Iago said grumpily as he stretched his back. "Got me all worn out already."

"So you'll take me to the dungeon?" Nox asked the prisoner, ignoring the Elf's complaints.

"I will show you the way."

"Thanks Havell—" Nox stopped mid-sentence. "How did I—?"

Havell's eyes widened. "How did you know my name?"

"I don't know..." Nox said. "But I feel that...you were very important...to Lukas. I don't know how I know that...but I do."

"You..." Havell began. "You know Luke?" He smiled. "Something tells me that this little mission here is about to get real interesting..."

The doors to Ellier's office swung open as the Elven commander rushed in.

"*HE IS HERE?!*" Ellier Vondell raged as he stormed by Cercion, bumping against the old man with his shoulder as he passed. "WHY IS THAT WRETCHED BOY ALIVE?!" The Elf took in a deep breath and exhaled. "He was supposed to be *dead*. Zurriel said he drowned in the Northern Sea!"

"Old Cercion—"

"Silence!" Vondell roared as he grabbed the old man by the throat. "Enough with this foolishness! Zurriel has tricked the emperor! I'll have no more of it, and I'll start by killing *you*! I'm sick of your constant games, your freaky face, your shrill voice! I'm going to kill you and then that foolish Iago Lyon!"

Cercion gasped for air, but the Elf's grip was strong, a stern grip fueled by white hot rage. The sound of his neck cracking was a single grimacing pop before the Elven commander dropped him to the floor.

"Foolish old bastard." Vondell spat upon the old man's limp body before walking away.

"We need to go down before these halls flood with soldiers," Havell said he removed his arm from Nox's shoulder. "I can walk."

Nox stopped and gave him a questioning glance. From what she could see, he looked to be in no condition to walk. She scanned the weary-looking soldier. She could see from his sunken face that he had been fed just enough to avoid starvation. His body looked grayed and riddled with scars.

Nox raised an eyebrow. "Are you...sure?"

Havell smiled. "Please! I'm the commander of the Red Ravens. You think a little bit of torture is gonna stop me?" he held up his metal binds. "Just need to get these off...somehow."

"Here!" Nox said.

Flames rode up the blade of the *Nightbringer*, easily cutting through the chains around Havell's wrists.

"Huh?" he muttered as the binds clanked upon the ground. "Those were Necronite. What are you?"

"Oh," Nox laughed and held out her hand in invitation to shake. "I'm Lunae! The Aeon! Nice to meet you!"

Havell let out a long, drawn-out sigh as he shook her hand.

"Ya know what?" he said, as if to himself. "I'm just not gonna ask. I shouldn't have expected you to be normal."

"Alright!" Nox said in fiery exclamation. "Where to, Mr. Havell?"

"Just follow my lead! We have a little time, but not much. If I know anything, those Elves are gonna check the courtyard area for us first."

With a wave of his hand, Havell began to run down the hall.

"So lively, even after what he's been through," Iago said. "He's strong, I'll give him that much."

"I like him." Nox smiled and ran, following close behind.

Iago watched her for a moment, then began his pursuit as well.

Nox caught up just as Havell approached a corner. Suddenly, he grabbed her as she passed him, pulling her back and out of sight.

"Wha—"

Havell silenced the girl with a hand over her mouth, muffling her words. "Guards," he whispered in her ear so low he was almost silent.

He released her and motioned his thumb against the wall. Nox peered briefly around the corner. He was right. There were two Elven soldiers, their golden armor almost green in the blue etherlight. For a moment, the three of them stood in silence against the wall.

"They've moved," Havell whispered as he motioned forward. "This way."

Havell led Nox and Iago carefully through back rooms, trying his best to be as speedy as he was covert.

The Aeon and the Elf didn't speak, instead, they merely followed their guide down the halls. The corridors were brightly lit, the blue from the etherlamps casting a cerulean splash upon the white marble walls. A plush red carpet extended the length of the hallway, diverging every few feet to accommodate a doorway to other rooms.

As Nox strode down the halls, she could see paintings on the walls of important men and women—or who she assumed were important. Despite the adrenaline pumping through her, these paintings somewhat reminded her of the Jarl's home in Hawkhaven.

Abruptly, Havell stopped. Nox, in a fury to stop her pace, passed him slightly before halting. Iago merely slowed.

"We go through here. We must be hasty," the former prisoner said.

Nox nodded and followed the soldier as he descended the stairwell.

"Nox." Iago said, his voice sharp.

Nox swiftly spun around to meet his gaze. His eyes were stone, as fierce and as cold and biting as a winter wind.

"I have to leave you now," he said. "I'll catch back up when I'm done, but there's something I must do here—there's someone here I must"—he gritted his teeth—"talk to."

The two stared at each other for a moment. Nox knew that the harshness of the past was behind them. Now, she knew, they were truly friends.

Nox nodded and smiled. "I know, or at least I figured that was something that might happen. I'll see you in a bit!"

Iago watched the girl descend the stairs, then he turned away.

Ellier Vondell, he thought as he clenched his jaw. *I'm coming for you...*

CHAPTER EIGHTEEN

To See You Again

Cercion's body lay motionless for a moment, long enough for the commander to leave and move out of sight. Outside, the cadaver was stone, but it was not so inside his mind.

Cercion, the *real* Cercion, opened his mind's eye to horror. It was the same horror he had felt for thirty years—the same horror he had felt ever since that *maniac* laid hands upon him.

He could feel the nails that bound him to the cross; he could feel the agony of living one thousand lives, of dying one thousand times.

Valter, his shrill voice was but a whimper. *Why are you doing this to me, Valter? Why must you use me this way? Why will you not let me die?*

The old man tried to move, but could not. His body had long since molded to the cross that bound him in whatever dimension or reality he was trapped in now.

Is old Valter really so bad? Valter's voice said softly, almost in ironic sympathy.

The real Cercion looked up to see the old and wiry Valter Rivyra standing before him, a wild smile plastered upon his face.

I gave you life well beyond your years, Valter said, narrowing his eyes. *You would have died in your bed thirty years ago if it weren't for me. Besides, you do not like it? Do you not like being part of my* collection?

Please, Cercion cried as he writhed upon his cross, *let me die! Use me no more!*

You do not set the parameters, Cercion. Valter's voice was colder. *No. You merely must do as told. Now rise.*

The body of Cercion lay upon the floor where Vondell had left him.

Suddenly, his fingers began to slightly twitch.

The halls were painted with dark red blood; the floors were decorated with the corpses of fallen Elven soldiers. Iago, walked onward, carving a path of blood and rage. He knew where he was going; he had not been so careless as to kill without getting the information he wanted, and he retrieved it indeed.

And now he marched onward, a reaper bringing death to each and every thing that was not his mark. Only one other time did he feel this height of carnage; only one other time did he care so little about the lives of his enemies; only once long ago did he wish to slit the throat one another more than he wished to end the life of Commander Ellier Vondell.

He was a falcon on the hunt for a rat, and the treacherous rat never escapes the vengeance of the falcon's claws.

The halls were silent now, save for the grunts and groans of men taking their dying breaths as they slowly emptied their carcasses of blood. It mattered not to Iago. It was their faults, after all; it was their faults for standing in his way. But that was all over, for now he stood at a large black door—on the other side, the commander awaited him —and he would have the information Iago sought. The Elf pressed his hand upon the latch and opened it.

"So," the voice of Ellier Vondell chuckled, "Iago of the Thousand Swords! Or would you rather me call you by your true name, White Dove?"

Iago entered the room. It was just as he expected. Along the walls, a multitude of armed soldiers stood, blades brandished and ready to tear him apart. At the end of the long hall, Ellier sat upon a throne, dressed in gilded uniform.

"I suppose that it doesn't matter at this point," the commander said in a snarky tone. "There are fifty men here. Even *you* can't kill them all before they reach you."

"Ya know, Ellier," Iago said, smirking, "I never liked when people called the bird on my back 'White Dove.'" Suddenly, a heavy breeze filled the room. Soldiers turned their visors from the gale. "You see, the bird on my back is white. That part is correct."

"*Gladyus Millenio*," Iago whispered, a gray aura engulfing his body. "But the bird on my back *isn't* a dove!"

Ellier watched in terror as a gray light materialized behind his opponent, forming into the shape of a pair of large, wide wings, with bright gray phantom feathers.

"The bird on my back..." Iago's voice was heavy and grim. "Is a *phoenix!*"

"*KILL HIM!*" The words of the commander exploded across the room.

The army of armored soldiers charged forward, blades out, ready to kill.

"You poor bastards..." Iago said under his breath as he pointed a single finger forward. Suddenly, one thousand feathers shot forward from his wings, each razor sharp and slicing through the armor of the soldiers. Screams rang out, followed by gargling noises of slit throats trying to cry out. Iago did not move from his position at the door. There was no need. He had mastered this new technique with the help of the Giants, and he knew its raw, terrifying powers. He also knew the strain it put on his body, but that was secondary here.

The floor was riddled with bodies; red blood spilled from the suits of armor only to be absorbed and lost in the crimson carpet.

"Now." Iago smirked through heavy breaths as he began to walk over the armored knights and toward the commander. "Let's have a chat."

Ellier Vondell sat in horror, his body frozen, his limbs paralyzed by the carnage he had just witnessed.

"*Tell me, Ellier...*" Iago's voice was absolute, "*Where is Hallow-Talon?*"

"H-he's in Phoenix Grotto! I-I promise I'm telling the truth! Please!" he said, hyperventilating. "Let me live!"

The old fool got his city back, eh? Iago smiled. "Looks like Eizen isn't as clever as he thought he was. Losing the Grotto will cost him dearly." He turned to Ellier. "I take the information you've given me gladly, but..."

Iago turned away as several blade-like feathers surrounded the commander, dicing and mauling his body in a violent whirlwind of pain and horror.

"If you thought for a second that I'd let you live, well..." The maimed body of Ellier Vondell fell to the floor with a thud. "You're stupider than I thought."

Iago looked around at the multitude of dead bodies that surrounded him. He clenched his fist.

So much blood...

I forgot this feeling...

This truth...

He thought of Nox; he couldn't help it. Her smiling face, her innocence...

She was *good* in every way he could think of, and, he had to admit, when he was with her, when he stood in her light...perhaps, just perhaps, he thought *he* could be good too.

I'm sorry, Nox... He winced as he looked at the floors. *I'm sorry I forgot.*

Blood trickled from underneath the soldiers' armor and onto the floor, bathing the white marble surrounding the rugs in crimson red.

I forgot that, wherever I go...

I can only bring death...

It was hard to tell what the situation was outside of the dungeon. Brother Claus had nothing but the darkness and the sounds of dripping water to call his friends. It was a lonely time, and he spent most of it with Cercion's words resounding through his mind. Was Nox truly here in Zerlina? If she was, she was in danger. For a moment, he cursed himself for revealing that he had raised her. He knew Nox—he knew how rambunctious, how defiant she could be. He knew that she would come for him.

Poor Nox. That reckless child. She was in danger, and it was all his fault.

Run, Nox he thought. It was the thought that consumed his mind.

It didn't matter what happened to him. Hang him, beat him, maim him—it didn't matter. To Brother Claus, no punishment in the world was worse that someone hurting his precious Nox.

Perhaps I should pray...?

Brother Claus bowed his head.

Dear Lunae. Hear my prayer—

"It's so dark!" a familiar voice replied.

Brother Claus felt his heart rise. Could it be? His mind began to slow. "Could it *truly* be? He raised himself and peered through the bars. Before him, with his eyes adjusted to the darkness, he could determine two vague figures in the void.

"I can't see a thing!" Nox snapped her finger and a bright violet flame lit upon the end of her thumb, illuminating the room.

The monk stopped, his mouth agape. Brother Claus, his ankle chained to the wall, fell to his knees.

"Nox..." his voice broke out in a loud whimper, "is that really you?! Nox!"

"Father!" Nox exclaimed. "Father I'm going to get you out of here!"

"Nox, you're..." the monk began in a low, dazed voice, "you're covered in armor, a blade at your side—and flames coming from your thumb! Nox...what are you?"

"Well," Nox rushed her words, "it's a long story, so I'll—no—*we'll* talk when I get you out of here!"

"There's no hope!" the monk sighed. "These chains—they're solid iron, and there's no way to free them from the wall. There's no way I can get out without a key..."

"Pff!" Nox laughed, "keys are for losers!"

Nox drew the *Nightbringer* from its sheath, and with a swing of its midnight-black blade, cut through the bars of the cell and severed the chains that bound the old monk to the wall.

"T-that blade!?" he gasped. "Is it magical?"

"It is. But I'll explain later. Right now, we *need* to get out of here!"

"Nox...oh, Nox..." Brother Claus rose and swiftly embraced the girl he loved so much—the child he had found in the woods, the one who fell from the sky, the daughter who had defied him at every turn—and held her tightly.

"Nox." The monk's voice was drowned by his tears, "*I missed you so much! Oh Nox, I was so worried...I didn't know what to do! Every day, I prayed to One; I prayed to one for your survival, and now*"—he choked—"*and now you're here, in my arms.*"

"Father," Nox said softly, "of course I would survive." She smiled.

"C'mon. You didn't think I was *that* helpless, did you? You didn't think I was *that* naive?"

"No..." the monk sniffled. "Of course I didn't. Some part of me knew that, no matter what happened—no matter what happened, you would survive...I just..." he said, his voice cracking as he began to weep, "*I just thought I'd never see you again!*"

"Father," Nox said as she brought the monk to stand.

"Are we done now," Havell asked. "This place is gonna be teeming with guards soon. If we're gonna get out of here, we better do it now."

"You?" Brother Claus said. "That voice! You're Havell Maro!"

Havell cracked a smile. "Aye, you remember me, don't you?"

"You two know each other?" Nox asked.

"Let's just say we were neighboring jailbirds." Havell chuckled. "C'mon. Let's get outta here."

Havell led the party up the stairs and into the hallway.

"We can't go through the courtyard because they'd expect that. It's the only way out of the fortress. But with your fancy sword, you should be able to get us out from another area, right?" He looked at the *Nightbringer* in Nox's hand. "That thing can cut things that a normal sword can't, right?"

Nox smiled. "Good guess!"

"There's an old storage room down the hall that hasn't been used in decades. If we can make it there, then we might be able to cut our way into the sewer and escape through the waterways."

Nox and Brother Claus looked at each other, then to the captain. The three nodded, and Havell needed nothing more.

"How do you know your way around this place so well?" Brother Claus asked as the trio rushed down the hallway toward the old storage room.

"Oh, right!" Havell laughed. "I was stationed here before I became commander of the Red Ravens. I spent a good ten years here, so I know the place well."

"Wow, Havell!" Nox giggled. "You're a really cool guy! I know why Lukas liked you so much!"

"Lukas?!" the monk began.

"Here it is!" Havell stopped. "Through here—!"

"Suddenly the door opened, and hands pulled the commander and

Brother Claus through the doorway.

Nox jumped through after them to find that the large storage building was filled with soldiers—and at the middle of the room stood the old man in the ill-fitting robe.

"CERCION!" Nox roared as she pointed the *Nightbringer* toward the deranged elder.

"Hello! Hello!" he sang in return. "How are we, my dearest little goddess, Lunae?!"

Brother Claus screamed out as ropes were tied around his and Havell's hands and they were pushed to the floor.

"Let them go!" Nox exclaimed, purple flames coming to her hand.

"Oh but what fun would that be?!" the old man laughed giddily. "Say, let's play a game! A duel to the death, yes? And we'll even raise the stakes!" He clapped twice. "If you manage to kill me, your friends go free, but..."

The two soldiers put blades to their hostages' respective throats.

"If I kill you, little goddess, then they die as well."

Nox was a roaring ocean, her mind red with anger. She looked at Brother Claus, her father, the man she loved so much, the one who constantly disciplined her.

"Cercion..." The flames in her hand vanished. A great fire coursed through her veins. This was it. *I'm going to kill you!*

Suddenly, her eye of Vryxn Glass erupted with energy engulfing the glass eye with bright purple flames.

"So it really is true!" Cercion giggled as he stared at her purple glass eye. "You really *are* an Aeon! How fun!"

"Yes!" Nox smirked as she pointed her black blade forward. "Let's see just *how fun it can be!*"

Nox stood her ground, her burning eye locked onto her opponent.

Vryxn glass. She remembered what the Giant Soothsayer had told her. *So that's why you gave it to me. You knew I could do this!*

"Let our duel begin!" the acrobatic old man exclaimed as he jumped forward.

Nox readied the *Nightbringer.* Through her burning eye, she could see tiny particles floating within the man. What were they? A chill ran up her back. Never before had she seen these particles, but every instinct in her body screamed that what she was seeing—tiny orbs underneath the old man's skin—wasn't normal.

It was as if he weren't human at all. As if—

"You're a corpse!" she blurted aloud.

"Ooh!" The clown-like man jumped up and down, clapping his hands giddily. "Who is to say?" He narrowed his eyes. "*Am* I?"

"Ugh," Nox spat. "What a weirdo!"

Cercion giggled. "Come to me, little goddess. Come to old Cercion."

Nox abruptly sprang forward, her black blade alive with violet flames.

"I might not be able to read your mind, and you might not have a brain..." she roared, "so I'll just have to split your head open and find out for sure!"

The flames embracing the *Nightbringer* howled as Nox swung the blade, aiming to sever the man clean into. The limber old man called Cercion leapt into air, his body spinning at a high speed.

"Nox!" Brother Claus exclaimed as the acrobat's foot slammed into her shoulder.

"Is old Cercion too fast, young Lunae?" he cackled.

Nox stretched her shoulder and held up her hand. With a snap of her fingers, a bright violet flame engulfed her hands. "Too fast?! Let's see how jumpy you are when you lose your legs!"

"Nox..." Brother Claus said in astonishment as he watched the duel. Was this really the same girl he had raised? He saw how fluid her motions were. The swing of her sword was strong; the flames she controlled were fierce and grisly.

Nox, he thought, *I...*

"So," Havell whispered. "You ready to get out of here?"

"What—?"

Suddenly a blast of psychic energy exploded within the room.

"Hey, friend," Havell laughed as nodded to the guard, "these ropes are a bit tight. Help a guy out, eh?"

Brother Claus looked at the soldiers. He didn't know what had just taken place, but the men were looking around as if aimless.

"O-of course," one of the soldiers said as he cut Havell's binds.

"What did you—?"

Before the monk could finish, the released commander of the Red Ravens drew the Elven soldier's blade from its sheath and thrust it through his gilded armor.

"Hey!" The second soldier drew his blade as he watched his comrade writhe upon the floor, wailing in agony. In a bright flash, the captain drew the blade from the gilded corpse and, moving in speedily, thrust it through the chest-plate of the other soldier.

"What did you do?!" Brother Claus exclaimed in ghastly horror.

"Let me see your binds."

"Ooh, hoo-hoo!" Cercion giggled as he wiggled his way around Nox's blade. "So close too!"

Nox gritted her teeth and threw a bolt of purple flame at the clown. Cercion laughed hysterically as the blast exploded upon his arm.

"You got me!" he said, smiling as he dipped his hand into his melting flesh and sucked it off of his finger. "I need some friends to share this excitement with!"

Nox watched in horror as the old man bore his fingers into his skin and sprayed blood everywhere.

"Little goddess of One!" he laughed as human figures began to climb out of the blood. "*I AM LEGION, FOR I AM MANY!*"

"Legion, huh?" Havell smirked as he helped the monk to stand. "Why don't you show us your true face, Cercion," he laughed, "or should I call you by your real name? Which do you prefer, *Valter Rivyra?*"

"Clever, Commander," the old man said, his voice altered completely. "Too bad my secret will die with you."

"Valter?" Nox said through panting breaths.

"No time." Havell pointed his blade at the shape-shifter. "We have to get out of here!"

"Oh but you won't," Valter laughed as he pointed to the army before him. "No. You will die here. You, Lunae, *and* the monk."

"No!" Nox exclaimed. "I refuse to leave yet!"

"Kid, what're you—?"

"I see now." Nox began. "*Cercion*, right?" She said, her voice softening. "There's someone inside of there named Cercion?"

Valter laughed. "Oh yes! But he belongs to me. I stole his face; I stole his name!"

"That's not true, is it"—she smiled—"Cercion."

A sudden flash of discomfort crossed the man's face as his expressions began to contort.

"You're in there, aren't you?" Nox exclaimed. "You're hurting, aren't you?"

"No!" Valter's voice began to rise as if two spoke at once. "You're not—"

"—I won't," the voice of the real Cercion strained as the body fell to its knees, holding its head as two souls warred inside of it. "No—"

"I see." Nox smiled as she approached them. "So that's how it works. You don't just steal faces; you take souls."

"I won't let—you," Valter struggled.

Nox raised the *Nightbringer*. Bright violet flames exploded from along the blade.

"Cercion, I will..." She began.

Cercion shook as Valter regained control. "Die!" he exclaimed as he jolted toward Nox.

"—*set you free!*" she roared as she brought the blade down upon Cercion's body.

The blade made impact, the flames slicing through without making a cut. Cercion's body fell to the ground.

Then, silence.

"I can hear my heart," Cercion said once more, his mind returned to himself. "My old, old heart."

Nox, Brother Claus, and Havell watched as the old man became rapidly older.

"I am old now, but finally, I shall die on my own." He looked at Nox as he began to shrivel up. "What is your name, young lady?"

"Nox," she replied, her voice gentle.

"Thank you, Nox." Cercion smiled as he began to turn to dust. "You are...quite kind—"

And then he was no more.

"You know," Havell said. "You and Luke..." He shook as head. "You're both stubborn as hell."

"Nox!" Brother Claus said.

Nox jumped at his sudden sternness.

The monk nodded. "You did the right thing."

"Here they are!" the muffled voices of gilded Elven soldiers stormed the room. "In the storage facility!"

"Told'ya we should've left!" Havell groaned.

This time, the reinforcements were many.

"What now?" Brother Claus asked, his voice shrill, panicked.

Nox readied her blade. "We fight!"

"All of them?" Havell said. "We can't fight the whole fortress."

Nox inspected her enemies. Havell was right. "We'll just..."

"*Gladyus Millenio!*"

A great rush of wind swept by Nox. All around her, ethereal gray feathers swept past her as if caught in a violent storm. Screams filled the room and each and every one of her enemies was ground into dust before her.

"I can't take my eyes off you for a second, can I, Lunae?"

Nox smiled. She knew that voice. She whipped around. "IAGO!"

CHAPTER NINETEEN

Something Far Greater

Havell stood over what was the body of Cercion, now a pile of ash.

"Strange..." Havell muttered. "So he truly was someone else deep down..."

"We gotta get out of here, and quick!" Iago interrupted the commander's contemplation. "It's only a matter of time before the Elves find the corpse of Vondell, and if they do, they'll be swarming around this area with even more soldiers than we just faced."

Nox looked at the commander. "Where to?"

Havell nodded and pointed to a manhole in the corner of the room. "There."

"Right!"

"Guess the sword will come in handy for more than just stabbing things," the commander grunted as he pried the cover open with the stout, bloodied Elven blade. "Sewers are our best bet."

"Ugh," Iago gagged. "It *has* to be the sewers, doesn't it?"

"We just gotta take it, Iggy!" Nox said. "Just hold your nose or something!"

Nox turned to Brother Claus and nodded, then she followed Havell down the hole.

The sewers, of course, were dank and wet, with a ghastly putrid smell filling the corridor. Iago was last, closing the manhole behind him, plunging the party in pitch blackness. The sewers were dismally dark, and only the sound of running water could be heard.

"It's too..." Brother Claus said as Iago snapped his fingers.

"—dark?" the Elf finished the monk's sentence, a luminous gray sword materializing in the air.

The party walked on, Havell at the lead, followed by Nox, then Brother Claus, and Iago at the tail end of the line. The floor was damp, and several times Nox had to step around small puddles caused by erosions in the stony passage.

"You know where we're goin' Havell?" Iago's voice echoed down the chasm.

"No clue," the soldier replied with a laugh.

"What?" Brother Claus asked, his voice trembling. "You mean we're stuck in the sewers?"

"Maybe," the commander said, shrugging. "I really didn't think this far. I just wanted to get out of Elven grasp, so..."

"Hold up." Nox stopped walking and halted the others. "I have an idea!"

"Well, let's hear it," the commander said.

Nox closed her eyes as she extended her hand. Bright violet flames danced upon the tips of her fingers. Light filled the room as a faint breeze swept through the tunnel, causing the waters to ripple. Nox held the blazes for a moment, then inhaled sharply and the flames were gone.

A moment passed, the three men watching her looked at one another momentarily, when suddenly the flames exploded from her glass eye.

"Now," she said as she looked around. Before her, she could see her surroundings in their entirety. Above, she could see the streets of Zerlina and the people as they walked past. She searched, her vision trailing the length of the city.

"The road that leads to the abbey is this way." She pointed down a hallway and began walking.

The three men merely looked at each other in the dim light and shrugged. They couldn't understand the girl and just what she was, but being that as it may, they had merely decided that this mysterious power she had was one that they should simply trust in. Havell beckoned for the monk to follow behind. Brother Claus looked ahead. He watched Nox as she was led by whatever force what guiding her within that mysterious violet flame. He thought back to moments ago when she fought Cercion. True, he had always known she was different—falling from the sky couldn't mean she was what one would call *normal*, but for all her life, although he hadn't wanted to deny her uniqueness, he had wanted nothing more than for her to live a normal life as an average girl. He wanted a daughter, that was all. When he had come upon Nox in the woods, he knew that he was going to raise her. Perhaps he had failed in that regard. No. He looked ahead at the girl. She walked confidently, boasting dark armor and that midnight blade. The monk looked at the purple blaze in her glass eye.

Nox, he thought, *so it's true?*

The party walked silently for a long time, weaving through the tunnels, the sounds of their footsteps obscured by the noise of the water rushing by them.

"Here." Nox said as she pointed forward. Up ahead, the sewers ended as the water poured into a lake outside.

The four climbed down from the tunnel and welcomed the fresh air. One by one they emerged from the depths and out onto the coolness of the surface. They hadn't known just how long they'd been on the run, nor how long it took them to move within the dim and ghastly tunnels beneath the city of Zerlina, but it must have been quite a while, for the night was upon them. As Nox climbed out of the hole, the last of the party, she saw the gardens of the abbey bathed in moonlight. She took a deep breath and exhaled. The three men watched as the violet flame extinguished, and they stared at her glass eye.

"It's beautiful," Nox said as she looked out into the pastoral countryside outside of Zerlina.

"We need to lay low probably," Havell began.

"Not as low as you think." Iago said. "Cercion is dead, and I killed Ellier, so the Elves have a good bit to worry about before they deal with us."

"You killed Vondell?"

"Yeah. Let's just say we had a...*unique* relationship."

Havell sighed. "Nox. Iago. The more time I spend with you two, the more I feel I just need to stop asking questions."

"Then stop already." Iago yawned as he walked by. "Let's go back to the abbey."

"What about me?" Brother Claus spoke up. "Will I be okay?"

"I assume so," Havell said. "The only reason you were kidnapped was for Cercion to draw out Nox. Now that he's gone, I doubt the Elves will have much interest in an old clergyman."

Nox turned to Brother Claus and took his hand in hers.

"Let's go, Father. Let's go home."

Morning came with no interruption. The light of the sun doused the clouds in crimson as it triumphed over the horizon, beating back the infernal machinations of the night. A single ray of light peered into the window of the abbey, piercing the glass and falling directly upon Nox's blue eyes, the once-purple vryxn glass now returned to its original azure color. The girl turned in the bed, but it was too late. She was, decidedly, awake. The room was silent save the sounds birdsong. For a moment, she stared at the barren lemon tree outside of her window. She thought back to the days she had spent at the monastery and she felt a slight ache in her chest. All her life, she had dreamed of adventure outside of those ancient walls, but never did she think that one day she would miss the comfort and security of the monastery.

She thought of Lukas in that moment.

What is he doing? Is he even still alive?

She let out a long sigh. When she thought of him, it was as if she could feel him, a distant heartbeat that was almost audible.

Yes, she thought, *I know he is alive.*

Nox had long forgotten what it was like to be an innocent girl skipping along the cold stones of the cathedral. The more she had grown to understand who she was, the more she had decided upon who she would be.

"*Goddess or no goddess, Aeon or no Aeon,*" she whispered quietly. "*Lunae or no Lunae. I am Nox. Always am, always was, and always will be.*"

She smiled.

Yes. She knew it to be true.

She, was Nox.

"Nox...", low voice said, followed by slight tapping upon the door.

"Are you awake?"

Nox rose from the bed and beckoned the voice to come in. She knew who it was and what this meant.

"Nox." Brother Claus' voice was soft and wary. "I wanted to talk."

"You saw a lot of strange things yesterday, didn't you?" Nox began, bowing her head to hide herself from his gaze. "Magic and blood..." She paused. "*My* magic, too..."

Silence hung in the air. Outside, the birds had stopped and flown away as grimly gray clouds rolled in from the sea, veiling the visage of Zerlina and prophesizing dreary rains.

"Brother Claus," Nox finally spoke up. "I know I never became what you wanted me to be. I know I rebelled against you at every turn; I know I ruined hundreds of dresses and shoes, and I know that it must be hard for you to see me called 'Lunae' and to see me wield magic and swords and wear armor. I know it must be hard, so I..." She paused, her breath halted and her voice trembling, "I just want you to know that I'm sorry I never became what you wanted me to be."

Nox looked into the old monk's eyes. His face seemed so melancholy, as if it longed nostalgically for a person long passed away.

"You're right, Nox. You never became what I wanted you to be." Nox winced at his words, a sharp pain flaring in her chest. "You defied me at every turn; you were constantly causing trouble, and I may have even blamed my own irresponsibility upon that boy, Lukas. Nox"—he inhaled and exhaled, his breath quivering—"I saw many things yesterday. I didn't understand at first, but eventually it all clicked. It didn't take much contemplation. You fell from the sky, so to believe that you are some incarnation of Lunae is not difficult. But warrior or no warrior, Aeon or no Aeon, Lunae or no Lunae, you will always be my little Nox."

"Brother Claus..." Nox said softly, her heart in pain and her head bowed.

"Oh, Nox," the monk cried as he grabbed the girl and held her in a fierce embrace. "You never became what I wanted you to be," he choked, tears running from his eyes. "You never became what I wanted you to be, because you became something *far* greater!"

Those words. She had never thought in a thousand lifetimes that she would ever hear them—and now that they had been spoken, she could feel tears rush from her eyes.

"Father," she whimpered, "I love you, Father!"

The old monk held the goddess tightly. Goddess or Aeon or Lunae. She was Nox, and that was all that mattered.

"I love you too, my daughter."

The two hugged for a moment longer, then Brother Claus released her.

"Come," he said. "The others await you."

"Odd that they haven't come for us by now." Havell said as he sipped a mug of coffee. "You'd think they'd be all over this place."

"Well," Iago said with a yawn. "Most of them are dead. Give it time."

"That magic of yours, it's scary," the commander yawned in reply.

Iago shrugged. "Good. It should be."

Havell raised an eyebrow. "How does it work? I don't think I've ever seen anything like it."

"I can't give away all my secrets now, can I?" Iago said.

Havell smirked. "We're all friends here, right?"

"Alright," Iago said, taking a sip of coffee. "My Word of Heart is 'Astral Materialization.' It allows me to solidify raw magical energy in the air. I can make anything I want, really, but the larger or more complex the object, the greater the strain on my mind and body. Also, the things I make are pretty fragile. I mean, they're just condensed energy particles, so..."

Havell rubbed his freshly-shaven chin. "Interesting..."

The two turned in their chairs as the door opened and Nox entered the room.

"Mornin' early bird," Havell teased. "We almost ate your portion."

"Thanks for not." Nox said, smiling in return. "I'm very hungry."

Nox sat at the table and began to spread butter on a warm biscuit.

"Where are we headed now, little lady?" the commander asked.

Nox took a bite of her food. "Brother Claus told me that Lukas went to join the Inquisitors at Mhyrmr, but I don't know how to get there."

"Perfect!" Havell nodded. "You see, I'm looking to find out what happened to Prince Reethkilt, and one of the last people to see him was the archbishop, who happens to be at the Church of Mhyrmr currently." He took a drink from his coffee and then a bite of bacon. "I'll be coming with you from now on. You saved my life, so guess I owe ya."

Nox bowed her head. "Thank you, Havell!"

The soldier laughed. "I can't send a little girl off all on her own, now could I? If I let you go out alone and you die, I wouldn't be able to sleep at night. Besides, out aims align. The honor is mine, Nox."

"Alone?" Nox raised her brow and looked at Iago. "What do you mean?"

"I'm leaving," the Elf said with a halted voice. "I...have to...go."

Nox paused. She had known Iago for some time now. From her capture to her freedom and their adventure in Hawkhaven, she had felt that she truly came to understand him. Iago was harsh and cold and blunt most of the time, but this frigid exterior only hid the passion and fire deep within his heart. He seemed distant, but she knew that, despite how he appeared, he honestly and deeply cared for his friends. But that voice, she had never heard him speak in that tone. As if he were wrapped in thoughts he dared not entertain.

"Where are you going?" Nox said softly. "I'll go with you!"

"No. Iago's voice was stern. "I must go alone. There's someone I have to see—someone I have to face..." he said, his voice trailing off into almost a whisper. "Someone I should dare not face...I have no right to face."

Nox looked into his eyes, they seemed so hollow, so forlorn.

She nodded. "I understand. Then go, do what you must, and may our paths cross again, friend."

The Elf smiled. The expression was so alien on his face, and Nox realized she'd never seen such a genuine smile from him before. He rose from the table and put on his mask.

"You've transport for me, right?"

Sister Helga nodded to a monk, who rose and motioned for the Elf to follow.

Iago stopped at the door. "I hope our paths cross again, my friend."

Nox smiled as she watched him leave. "Yes."

146

* * *

Breakfast was finished with haste, and just before noon, Havell sat in the driver's seat of a black automobile, a black hood drawn and hiding his face.

Mhyrmr...? the thoughts floated around in his mind. He thought of the Archbishop, and when he did, he couldn't help but feel odd.

Where was Eldric?

"Ready to head out?" Brother Claus said as he trailed Nox, a large suitcase in hand. "Remember to always wear layers! And brush your teeth. And no unnecessary magic! I don't want you hurting yourself trying things that are too advanced for you."

"Father!" Nox said finally.

The monk halted. For a moment the two stared at each other. Suddenly, Nox leapt forward, embracing the monk.

"Thank you, Father. I love you."

Havell smiled as the monk began to tear up. "Oh, Nox! I love you as well!"

"C'mon!" Havell groaned. "We gotta get to Mhyrmr if we want to speak to the Archbishop."

"Be careful, Commander!" Brother Claus said as Nox opened the door and took her seat. "Word is that the previous Master of the Inquisition, Eldric of the Black Flame, is at large. The church says that he tried to take Archbishop Ferrenvaal's life at Crown City. If a traitor like that is among us, he may just try to finish the deed!"

Eldric, the commander thought, *no, that doesn't seem right.*

"I see," he said. "Thanks for the tip!"

"See ya, Brother Claus! Bye Sister Helga!" Nox called out, waving her hand outside of the window.

The clergy waved as the car drove off. Captain Maro was silent for a moment.

Marven Ferrenvaal...what are you thinking?

Valter paced the floors of the Archbishop's quarters, frantically mumbling to himself.

"The girl, the girl, the girl," he said, his voice high-pitched, perhaps even a squeal. "She knows, she knows, she knows—*yes! Yes!* She *knows!*"

The old man scurried to his desk.

"Foolish little goddess!" he said as he kicked his chair in frustration. "My secret will do you no good when you're *dead!*"

Valter laughed, and all the souls inside him wailed.

CHAPTER TWENTY

Azyla

Marko Jharres strolled through the gardens of the Palace of the Sky King, his eyes drifting from Crown City below to the Elven soldiers posted along the walls.

He smiled.

He caressed a flower with the back of his hand, plucking it and smelling its petals. How careless he was today. How lackadaisical he felt as he perused the gardens and fountains. True, he had business that *might* be important. Maybe. Sure the information might be of...special interest to the emperor. He smirked.

Emperor Zilheim, is it now? The thought amused him. *Oh the follies of mortals. Emperor, king, lord...all is naught, a foolish attempt for the temporal hands to reach the glory of Empyria.*

The idea made him snicker to himself. He had aided the emperor gain his power, true, but it didn't stop him from thinking that the Elf's lust for power was stupid. But, also, he didn't mind. The more a man sought something, the easier it was to control him. After all, everything would play out eventually, just as the wizard Zurriel had proclaimed to him.

But, he thought as he sharply turned, *that is in the future.* As of *now,* he had a message for the fool upon the throne.

The walk to the courtroom was scenic, but to Marko—one who had walked these stones for the majority of his life—the beauty had faded over time. He passed the rows and sanctuaries of icy Dawnlilies and groves of Windfish trees, the blue from their petals and leaves still illuminated even in the encroaching darkness of night. Fresh light from a young moon passed over the arbors, creating web-like shadows upon the pathway. Ahead, four Elves in gilded plate armor stood, blades always prepared.

"I've some news." Marko said as he approached. "Something that he might find..." He wiggled his fingers in the air. "Interesting."

The four guards looked at each other for a moment, wondering how Marko could have information that their scouts didn't, then nodded and stepped out of the way.

Inside, the moonlight fell upon the gray stone in pools of crystalline silver, hiding the elite Elven guards that lurked within the shadows. Marko walked down the long blue carpet that led to the throne. Ahead, he could see the Elven emperor sitting lazily upon his honored seat. As he approached, he could see the tear in reality positioned above Zilheim—the Wind Stitch. It had been silent ever since Zurriel opened it using the Antithicite. The strange zombie-like beasts called the Ex Nihilo still crawled out of it every so often. But there it hung. It was a common sight to Marko. He had lived under the roof of the House of Reethkilt since he was a child. It was no different now that he was an adult—no matter who sat upon the throne.

"Marko," Zilheim said as the other approached the throne. "Why have you come to me at this hour?"

"Vondell is dead." Marko bowed theatrically. "That's why I have come."

"Nonsense!" the emperor exploded. "You speak lies!"

"Oh, I speak no lies, Your Honor. The Winds have told me and—"

"Your sorcery means nothing to me, *human*."

Marko held up a finger and smiled. "Then perhaps you would take the word of the soldiers in Zerlina, who will arrive tomorrow before noon."

Zilheim narrowed his blue eyes.

"Or not," Marko said, shrugging. "It doesn't matter to me. After all, what do *I* know? I'm only born of Aeonic blood."

"Bah!" the Elven ruler scoffed. "Aeonic or not, remember your place, *human.*"

"Of course, of course," Marko said, bowing, the smile upon his face hidden by the shadows. "I mean no disrespect, *Your Honor.*"

Emperor Eizen Zilheim rose from his throne.

"You are dismissed, Marko. I wish not to see your face anymore, nor hear any more of your Aeonic nonsense."

Ever the fool, Zilheim, Marko thought behind his grin, *ever the fool.*

Zilheim approached the doorway and stopped. "Remember that you are here under *my* good graces. You continue to act a jester, and I'll make you into one."

Be careful, Your Honor...

"Of course, Your Grace. How could I forget my station?"

The jester might just get the last laugh...

The night was alive, the stars bright above the darkened garden. Marko walked to the balcony overlooking Crown City, the nostalgia causing his mind to ponder things he'd not considered for some time. As he looked out at the speckled lights of the city below, he thought of Clement. It had been six months since the fall of the prince's beloved home; it had been six months since Emperor Zilheim had announced to the world that both the king and the prince were dead.

But Marko knew it was a foolish proclamation, foolish words from a foolish man. The State could claim Clement's death as officially as they wished, but the Winds spoke otherwise.

Clement, Marko knew, was alive. And as long as that man drew breath, the world might have hope. The thought made Marko sick to his stomach. He knew that it would take more than what happened six months ago to kill that wretched prince.

Foolish cousin with a foolish hope. Beyond the overhang, the lights of an Elven airship glinted as it cruised above the city, the aether around its hull a beautiful blue. *You may try, cousin, but I will kill you yet. You will die, along with your stupid hope.*

"Reminiscing are we?" a voice laughed. "Caught in the tides of the past? Of lost loves and witty nihilism?"

"I was wondering when you would appear," Marko said without turning his gaze. "Zurriel."

"And here I am."

Zurriel approached and stood beside Marko.

"Tell me," Marko began. "What do the Eyes say?"

"They are waiting for their third."

"And then what?"

"I will find that which has been forgotten, something more powerful and greater than even the Aeons themselves."

"I don't understand."

Zurriel smiled a surprisingly warm smile. "Tell me, Marko, do you know anything of the ancient Morning Star Kingdom?"

Marko shrugged. "I assume you're about to tell me?"

The other laughed softly in return.

"At the dawn of the universe, Angels were created among the other races. These beings held magic greater than any mage or sorcerer who exists today. Using these godlike powers, they held dominion over the other races and enslaved them. Their empire was known as the Morning Star Kingdom."

"A fancy story, Master."

"Fancy and...a bit esoteric. What, you might ask, happened to the Kingdom? No one seems to know. And the Angels? Why are none in existence today? No one knows that answer either. But I'll tell you what happened. Long ago, there was a great war which decided the fates of the worlds."

Marko looked up at the silver stars. "Worlds...?"

"That's correct, young Marko. Lythia is but one in a sea of worlds, floating about the nothingness of Nihilo. But this was not always the way things were. No. At one point, all of the worlds were one. One world. One realm. Whatever happened during that War, it was powerful enough to sever the lands and scatter them among the stars."

"What does this have to do with anything?" Marko said, his breath a cloud as he continued gazing upward. "What are you getting at?"

"Something was lost in that war—lost with the powers of the Angels themselves. While the flesh of the Angels became the Elves, their powers were contained in one place."

Marko said nothing. The odd storyteller confused him, as he

always did.

"An artifact called the *Apotheosis*," Zurriel finished.

A silence hung between them, filled only by the humming of airships as they cruised through the air, the ethereal azure lights of their hulls a distant glow above the captured and occupied city, once a lively place that was now filled with only oppression.

Marko took in a deep breath, then watched his breath disperse into the abysmal night.

"And what do you plan to do once you find this object?" he asked.

Zurriel was silent, his crimson eyes locked onto the stars above.

"Tell me, young Marko," he finally spoke, no heat in his breath. "Have you ever heard the Legend of Azyla...?"

CHAPTER TWENTY-ONE

The Lioness

The moonlight lit the sands of the desert like reflective glass, a vast sheen of white that seemed to extend into an endless beyond. The *Prometheus* was silent as it roamed lowly, just above the sands. Eldric sat in the seat beside Ayize. Both had been sitting in silence for the majority of the cruise to the headquarters of the Black Roses, and thusly the lair of the infamous Lioness.

Eldric understood the other's caution in transporting the old man to her. He could also detect that the assassin might also feel a strange guilt for the job. The Lioness was the most wanted woman in the world—a strange, shadowy figure who cast a shadow over the most fearsome criminals of the current era. Of course, this was merely an assumption the old man was making about the assassin, but it wasn't far-fetched. Eldric had seen Ayize with his young teammate, and it was rather obvious that the ruffian was merely hiding his true self. Eldric was old, but he was not yet blind, and his eyes could easily detect that Ayize hid underneath a kind and righteous heart underneath his cold exterior.

"You seem tense," Eldric said finally.

Ayize was silent for a moment.

"I don't like the idea of carrying an old man to his death."

Eldric chuckled. "You know, young man, I stopped fearing death a long time ago. Besides, death is not certain. When you get to be my age, you will come to know that certainty is more a myth than a truth. There is nothing certain in this world other than the certainty of uncertainty. Never is never a possibility. You'd do well to remember that."

"Don't lecture me with your tongue-twisters, wizard. My head already hurts."

The cockpit was silent once more, all but the soft hum coming from the engine.

"You really have hope that she won't kill you?" Ayize said. "Or are you just so stupid that you don't fear death?"

"I've already said that we don't know for certain." Eldric bit down upon his pipe. "And you have it backward. It is the fear of death that is stupid. Those who fear death are incapable of acting when they are at risk. You cannot have courage and fear death as well. It is the suspension of that fear that in turn makes one courageous. The two are mutually exclusive."

"Bah!" Ayize scoffed. "You know, old man, I think I might actually be sad to see you hang."

Eldric smiled. "I appreciate that. Let's just hope that it won't come to that."

"Second thoughts?"

"Nay. Merely enjoying your sentiment."

Outside, the rising sun met the dark sky, creating a yellowish-green tinge upon the horizon. The airship carried onward beneath the evanescent stars.

"There." Ayize pointed forward.

Eldric followed the Darkling's finger to the silhouette of a desecrated tower in the distance. Even from a distance, Eldric could see its age. Made of sandy stone, the tower probably once stood tall and proud. *But now,* he thought, *it has become the perfect hiding place for the most dangerous of ruffians.*

"The Lioness is there, in those ruins."

"Unique building," Eldric chuckled.

"The tower was called Vega Varonn. Angelic ruins, supposedly, date all the way back to the Morning Star Kingdom."

"And you live here?"

"Wouldn't expect it, huh?"

"Never."

Ayize laughed. "Ex-actly. Not as bad on the inside as it appears, though. We've managed to do some...tidying up, I guess you could say."

"So the Lioness enjoys decorating, it sounds like?"

Ayize smiled a crooked smile. "You could say that...maybe."

The ruined tower grew taller by the second as the *Prometheus* approached it, cruising across the barren sands. The two sat silently in the cockpit once more.

"Nervous, old man?" Ayize said after a few seconds.

Eldric gave the other a wry smile as he placed his pipe into his pocket once more.

"Never."

Snow and the blinded Clement sat across from each other at a curved booth in the crowded living quarters of the *Prometheus,* saying nothing.

"You're silent, commander," Snow finally said with a smile. "You aren't nervous are you?"

"Don't give me that crooked smile, Snow," the prince laughed. "I believe you know that answer already. If I feared mere assassins, what kind of warrior might I be?"

"Likewise," she replied.

Snow looked at the prince in the light of the yellow etherlamp that hung above them. Across his eyes, the scar that Marko Jharres had left was beginning to heal, yet the prince's eyes had slowly faded to a blank white. *It's true*, she thought, *the prince is totally blind.*

"How did you know I was smiling?"

"Oh come now, Snow." The prince shrugged. "I might be blind, but do you think I don't know you well enough to tell when you're smiling?"

"You're a fool, Commander."

Clement smiled and laughed. "Perhaps I am, my friend."

"Ohhhhh!" Enlil spoke up finally, startling Clement. Snow had to admit, even she had forgotten that the assassin child sat in a chair to their left, and Snow felt her face turn red as she realized she had let the girl slip past her awareness.

"I get it!" the little girl blurted out, eyes widened. "Are you guys in love?"

Snow felt her face grow hot, thankful that the prince couldn't see her.

"I, Clement spoke up, "b-beg your pardon?"

Snow looked at the prince as his fingers began to fidget.

"W-we're..." the half-Elf knight said as she regained her composure. "Sparring partners."

"Y-yes," Clement quickly agreed. "Sparring partners."

"But Mister Prince is blind!" Enlil cocked her head. "Does that mean you'll have to find a new partner, Blue?"

"I, uh—"

"Hey!" Ayize came over the small intercom placed in the corner, "En, we're landing. Get up here!"

Snow sighed as she watched the small Darkling jump to her feet and scurry to the cockpit. She looked at Prince Reethkilt; he was smiling.

Dust exploded underneath the *Prometheus* as it landed onto the open field that served as the landing dock for the Black Roses. As the stands floated to the ground, Ayize shut off the aether gauges and stood, motioning to Eldric.

"Come on, old man. But keep in mind, you aren't going to be received as respectfully here as you would anywhere else in the world. Remember, to the world you were a hero; to us, you've always been a villain."

Eldric smiled as he struggled to stand, leaning heavily upon his cane. "Worry not. I am aware of the situation. I am old, but I am not yet senile."

Ayize said nothing.

"Home!" Enlil exclaimed as she bounced on her feet and scurried past her companion.

Eldric hobbled to meet his knight and the prince. "Come," he said, "you must guide the prince."

"I will not take my eyes off of you, father." She took hold of Clement's hand and helped him rise from his seat. "I will not take my eyes off of *either* of you."

Eldric looked at his daughter and the prince and smiled, then bowed his head and whispered his Word of Heart, low so none could hear.

"Aye," Clement said. "And I thank you, Snow."

The air outside was hot and the wind coarse. Two men, shrouded in black hoods, stood at the bottom of the ramps. As he descended, Ayize gave them a strange sign with his hands, and the two men nodded, then turned and walked away.

"Well," he called back to the old man. "They know you're here to see her now. Come on, and just hope she won't take your head upon arrival."

The outside of Vega Varonn was decrepit, ruined, and miserable, but the inside was decorated lavishly with a vast variety of swords lining the walls. Ayize led them down a hallway with a long crimson rug that ran down the entirety of the corridor.

"She's quite the fancy for swords, eh?" Eldric said, breaking the silence.

"Special ones, yes." Ayize grinned. "Each one of these swords has a 'story,' if you know what I mean."

"I don't."

"Let's just say that each of these swords helped someone 'move along.'"

Eldric's chuckling echoed down the hallway. "She's a sense of humor, too, it seems."

"You could say that. You're a strange old man, you know that?"

"Noted."

The hallway came to an end at a gargantuan double-door with two more of the hooded men on each side.

"So this is..." Eldric began.

"Yup!" Enlil sang.

"End of the line, old man. Let's just hope the Aeons like you enough to spare your dreaded life."

Eldric reached for his pipe. Ayize motioned to the two men, who nodded and pushed upon the door.

The sounds of booming revelry filled the corridor as the warm lights of a large, crowded room poured through opened door. Enlil rushed past her partner and was lost in the crowd. Eldric and Snow, who led Clement, followed Ayize down the center of the room. The inside was vast. All around, all types of ruffians from far off places reveled around the tables, feasting on various dishes. Truly, Eldric thought, this was the den of a lioness.

"Ayize!" a coarse voice exploded throughout the room. "Why the hell did you bring an Inquisitor into my hall? And why the hell did you bring the *Master* Inquisitor? Couldn'ya have brought a small fry, if you *had* to bring one?"

Suddenly, all went silent, eyes suddenly directed to Eldric. The Inquisitor looked forward. In the center of the far wall, a tall, older woman lounged upon a mat. She had a lean body, her smooth dark skin decorated by several scars that Eldric assumed were from a blade. Long raven locs fell over her shoulders like a thick mane.

Eldric didn't have to ask who this was, he just knew.

The Lioness.

"Shut it, old bag!" the Darkling said as he walked toward his leader. "You think I'd bring'ya this asshole on my own? He *wanted* to come see you."

The Lioness picked up a long pipe and huffed it. "Well, Inquisitor." She said as she blew out a thick cloud of smoke. "Ready to die?"

"I am," Eldric said as he stuffed his pipe. "How would you like to do it? Beheading? Hanging?" He lit the pipe and took in a deep breath of smoke. "Or would you rather rip me open yourself?"

A baleful stillness lingered within the silence of the room. Snow watched Eldric as she held her hand upon the hilt of *Silversong*, gripping it firmly. She felt strange in this moment. Never had she been in a situation similar to this one. Her Elven eyes quickly scanned the room.

So many...

It was impossible, even for her. There must have been five hundred outlaws filling this hall—far too many for her to stop, if they decided to strike. Even with her strength and Elven senses, the sheer number of assailants in this room was unbeatable. She turned her eyes back to Eldric. Several times had his life been in danger; several times had he faced certain peril, and several times had he prevailed. The old man still stood. Here he was, in the center of the room—a space filled with the ones who wished to kill him most. And yet, Snow couldn't believe what she saw.

Eldric was smiling.

She couldn't help but feel odd. It was that same smile she'd seen her entire life. That smile that seemed to defy the darkness of the world.

Suddenly, the Lioness burst into laughter, her deep voice resounding through the silent hall. Everyone was baffled, each person turning to their neighbor, eyebrows raised. Whispers of confusion were like soft static hanging low in the air. The Lioness clapped her hands and wiped her eyes. Eldric blew out smoke, the fumes seeping out from the corners of his grin and disappearing in the air.

"You're a fool, wizard!" she said, and took a deep breath as she wiped the tears from her eyes. "But I think I like your spirit. I haven't met many men who would suggest their preferences of death like that. I like that. I still currently want your head, but I like your attitude, old man."

"You can call me Eldric."

"I'll call you whatever I want, old man."

Eldric blew out a ring of smoke. "Very well."

"But so far, I can see you at least have some strength. I like strong men. So, tell me, old man, what is it you want?"

Eldric took another huff of his pipe, the exhaled, the plumes of smoke covering his face.

"Aid, of course."

The tall woman ran her tongue over her teeth and spat.

"Aid? Are you senile? What in all of Lythia makes you think that I would aid the Master of the Inquisitio—"

"*Former* Master of the Inquisition. I'd say that right now my bounty might even be higher than yours, eh?"

The assassin queen smiled with a wicked laugh.

"I see what's happening here. Your world has turned its back on you, so you come to me? What you really mean by 'aid' is really more like protection, isn't it? What? Scared of the gallows, are we? Well, I hate to be the bearer of bad news, but I'm not a fan of weak men."

She snapped her fingers. Suddenly, the several men seated around Eldric stood, ripping their blades from their sheaths. Snow flinched, freezing as two more men reached their swords around her and the prince and cold steel pressed lightly against their throats.

Eldric stood in the center of a wheel of death, the tips of assassins' swords held a mere fingernail's distance from his neck.

"I'm sorry, dear Lioness." The old man's voice was no longer nonchalant. The laughter of the carefree former Inquisitor had now been replaced with a frigid, eerie tone. His white eyes scanned the men surrounding him. "Tell me men. Do you fear the flames of hell?"

Bright black flames exploded from Eldric's body, throwing the room into chaos. The Lioness did not flinch. The tables and chairs flew from the ground, sending those seated flying toward the wall. Haunting wails filled the air as assassins tried to snuff out the black flames that danced upon their clothing. The Lioness smiled; her pale teeth shown fully in her crooked grin. This. *This* was what she liked.

"Lioness," Eldric said grinning once more, his teeth lit darkly by the void-like flames that surrounded his body. "Look at me. Do I look like the kind of man who would *dare* hide? The type of man who runs when the world strikes against him? Do I look like the type of man who would dare run from a world in need? Inquisitor or criminal, it does not matter. I need not protection. Nay. I need a ship and a crew. The world has been unbalanced, and there is someone I need to kill to make it right again."

The old man snapped his fingers; the assassin queen watched contemplatively as the flames began to fade. Some of the assassins who had been thrown about began to stand while others lay limp and unconscious from the impact of being slung against the tower's ancient stone.

"I see," she said, her long fingers stroking her chin. "So you want to kill someone? Such a vile way to say it, too. You've only been an outlaw for a small time and already you want carnage? I must say I'm impressed. You see, this changes things. I like strong men, Eldric. I do not waste my time with weaklings, and, as of now, I *might* be able to help you."

The tall, lean woman stood. Snow gripped *Silversong* once more as she approached. The Lioness was muscular, most her body revealed except for what was covered by a long multicolored loincloth and several tight bandages around her chest. Her exposed body was well toned from years of physical training, decorated from scars from what

Snow assumed were sparring sessions without protective measures. The knight stepped closer to the Inquisitor as the woman came closer.

"You're much taller than I expected," Eldric laughed when he realized that the woman towered over him.

"And you're not as stuck-up as I assumed you'd be." She spat upon the ground. "How about we make an agreement? A deal, if you will."

"I'm listening."

"A duel. One-on-one. Me versus you. If you win, I'll give you a ship and a crew."

Eldric raised an eyebrow. "And If I lose?"

"I execute you, right here in Vega Varonn." She held out an inviting hand. "What say you, old man?"

"Such high stakes." The other laughed. "I agree. But don't blame me if the fires are too hot."

"Very well," the Lioness said, grinning once more. "A trial by fire!"

CHAPTER TWENTY-TWO

Trial By Fire

The ruffians slowly gained their sensibilities as the Lioness called them all to a court nestled upon the northern side of the tower. Ayize walked on one side of Eldric as Enlil walked alongside him on the opposite.

"I told you that you were gonna die, old man." Ayize shook his head as if exasperated. "You don't know what you've gotten yourself into."

"Don't worry, Mister Eldric!" Enlil said giddily. "Death might not be so bad!"

Snow led Clement, who was silent, as she slowly, closely trailed Eldric, her ever-watchful eyes vigilant.

"I don't like this," she whispered to Clement. "I don't know what it is, but something here seems off."

Clement squeezed her hand firmly. "Do not worry, Snow. I don't like this situation either."

Snow looked ahead at the Lioness, who led them down the corridor of ancient, sandy stones. This woman made Snow nervous. What was this feeling? Was it fear? If it was, why? She thought back through her life as the personal knight of the Master Inquisitor. Never once had she felt this way; never once had an enemy made her feel as unnerved as this woman did.

What if he loses? The thought shot quickly through her mind. *Why? Why am I thinking that?*

But there was something more here, she could sense it. This rugged woman saw the sheer force that Eldric possessed mere seconds before asking to duel him—it seemed like a death wish...unless.

Unless she really can *win...*

The corridor ended at a worn, weathered door. The assassin queen paused as she approached, halting everyone behind her. She lightly placed her leathery hand upon the door.

"Tell me, Eldric," she said without turning. "Are you ready to lose a wager with your life at stake?"

"Nonsense," the old man laughed. "I do not plan to die here. Remember that."

The other smiled, her white teeth glistening in the faint light.

"I'll remember it gladly. And I'll shove it in your face as you head to the gallows."

The door opened to reveal a large open space. Ruined remnants of an edifice sprang up from the flat, dusty ground. It was evident that a building of some sort existed here at some point, but what remained of it were ruins lost to time—a monument of another age. All was lost and mysterious—for all but one thing that Snow couldn't look away from.

In the far center of the dusty arena, the gallows awaited like a spider upon a web.

"This is where we fight, old man."

"Spacious," Eldric chuckled as he limped forward.

"You two might want to step back." Ayize motioned with his hands. "You don't wanna get caught in this."

Snow nodded, then motioned for Clement to stop as well. She watched as Eldric limped forward, taking his place upon the battlefield.

The Lioness grinned. "Look, old man," she said. "I want to fight you, not murder you right away, so I'm going to put in to play a few rules."

Eldric shrugged. "If you wish to endanger yourself, then be my guest."

The assassin queen held up three fingers.

"First," she said, pointing to the far wall of the space. "I will begin the duel over there, far away from you. I know that your black fire works best as a ranged offense, so I will give you the advantage...well, because you're going to need it."

Eldric raised an eyebrow. "We're very confident, aren't we?"

"Not confident"—she grinned—"I'm certain." She bent a finger so that two remained. "Rule two. In order to win, you must hit me once while I must strike you three times."

"Nonsense!" Eldric exclaimed. "You shame me by giving me such an easy victory?"

"No, dearest Inquisitor." The woman smiled, the light of the desert sun glistening off of her dark brown eyes. "I'm being rather fair, honestly. I give you one strike, but you won't even dare get that far. I will get my three strikes in before you even get close to your one."

"And your third rule?"

"The simplest one. Since this is a duel, I would like for you to try to kill me. However, I won't kill you until the third strike." She ran her thumb across her neck. "It will be more satisfying that way. I'm a lioness, after all. I like to toy with my prey."

Eldric sighed. "Very well."

Snow watched the Lioness walk to the far side of the field. She had to admit that she felt bad about this situation, but now —*now* she felt even worse. This woman was so sure of herself, even when faced against the greatest mage in all of Mhyrmr. She showed no signs of fear, no signs of intimidation. Snow released her grip on Prince Reethkilt's hand and placed her hand upon her short sword, *Silversong*.

Why do I feel so tense? What is happening here?

Once far away, the assassin queen stopped.

"Enlil! We go on your signal!"

Everyone turned to the little Darkling. She held her arm skyward, hopping from one foot to another giddily. Eldric readied himself, his mind drifting to summon his Word of Heart. Snow felt her heart drop.

"GO!" the child exclaimed.

Eldric extended his arm, the void of his black aura engulfing his entire body.

"*Rex Ynfernim!*"

At the old man's command, brilliant black sparks exploded from his fingertips, spit forward and spiraling toward the woman at harrowing speeds.

Snow watched the fires erupt and turned to the Lioness.

Surely she fears the fire, right? Snow watched the assassin queen. The Lioness showed no fear; there wasn't even the slightest hint of danger within her visage. No, she was...

She was *laughing*.

The flames came closer and closer.

Snow turned to Ayize. "Why isn't she moving?"

The Darkling smiled without a regard. Snow turned her gaze back to the queen. Suddenly, her heart dropped.

She's gone!

A great wind filled the space. Eldric froze. Lightly pressed against his throat, he felt it...cold steel. Held in place, he slowly moved his gaze.

"That's number one," a voice whispered in his ear. "You're too slow, old man."

Ayize and Enlil burst into laughter.

"How?!" Snow turned to the two Darklings. "Wind magic?"

"Nah," Ayize said with a shrug. "It's called *Jumping*. Super-fast movement. One of the highest echelons of Projection magic, and also one of the most useful in battle, too. Trust me, knight, there's no way he can win this."

The Lioness lowered her gnarled dagger and began to walk back to her starting position. Eldric sighed deeply, his muscles relaxing the best they could. This was odd for him, and he felt unsure about his situation. In all of his time as the Master of the Inquisition, he had never once been daunted by an enemy as much as this woman intimidated him now. Never before had he wondered how he would reach victory—or if he *could* reach victory. Overcoming an enemy was something he'd never had to consider, rather it was something that he knew in his heart would happen. But now, faced against such an incredible speed, he knew that this fight would be different.

"Are we scared, old man?" the Lioness laughed derisively. "We can stop and hang you right now if you want."

"I never said I feared you, Lioness. No. I'm just getting warmed up."

The tall, battle-scarred woman clapped her hands as she stood again in her place.

"That's what I like to hear!" she snapped her fingers. "Enlil! Again!"

The little girl jumped as she yelled. "*Goooo!*"

In the blink of an eye, the Lioness was gone. Eldric waited for the wind to reach him.

"Now!" Eldric exclaimed as bright black flames exploded from his body.

Nothing.

"So slow!" the assassin queen cackled as she floated in the air, her blade held inches away from his skull. "That's number two. The next one you will forfeit your life."

The Lioness sheathed the mangled blade as she slowly floated down to the ground.

Snow could feel her heart begin to thud within her chest. This was it; this was all that was left...this one last chance, this one last second.

"Enlil!" the woman repeated.

The little Darkling swung her hands in the air.

"Goooo!"

"*Stop it! NO!*" Snow rushed forward with frantic speed.

"Snow —!" the old man exclaimed as the half-Elf knight came to his side. The Lioness jolted forward. Great wind exploded between them as a large plume of dirt and dust exploded into the air.

"What an idiot," Ayize said, laughing.

Dirt fell softly back onto the earth, swept along by desert breezes.

"This is...curious," the Lioness jeered and licked her teeth.

"Snow..." Eldric said as he sat upon the ground. "What did you...?"

Snow stood, the blade of *Silversong* pressed into the assassin's throat.

"If you want to kill him," Snow growled, "then you'll have to kill me first. I'm done with your stupid games, and I'm not about to watch him truly die."

"I see," the assassin queen laughed. "So the cub bears her fangs?" she pressed the gnarled dagger into Snow's waist, its blade slim enough to slither between her breastplate and her fauld. The Lioness curled her fingers around the blade of *Silversong* and tried to pull it away from her neck. "You're strong, aren't you, girl? That blue hair doesn't lie."

"And I won't move from this spot until one of us is dead." Snow's face was stone and grim. "I won't let you kill him—not while I still draw breath!"

"I see..." the Lioness said through a smile as she withdrew her slim dagger. "So this is how it is?"

Snow pointed her short sword forward as the Lioness stepped back.

"If you must fight someone, then I will take you."

"No, no, no..." the other said, twirling her finger around the long, dark locs that fell over her shoulder. "I'm not interested in hurting you, knight. What is your name?"

"Snow," she replied, curt and sharp.

"Well, Snow. It seems I have found a diamond among the pebbles. I think I might have a found a way that I could...delay the death of your precious Master Inquisitor. Only if you are open to the"—the assassin queen looked at Snow from the corner of her eyes, her glare almost cat-like in cunning and dreadfulness—"terms...?"

Snow pointed the tip of *Silversong*, using it to keep distance between them. "Trickery?"

"Dear, I have no need to trick you." She smiled, amused. "If I wanted you dead, I'd have done so already—you, your precious Inquisitor, *and* your darling prince. No, it is not my means to deceive you. All I want to do is offer a...truce of some sort—one that benefits me and allows you to, well...prolong my desire to kill the precious old man here. But, if you believe me a schemer, then I understand." The Lioness reached out and touched the tip of *Silversong* with her thumb, pressing inward until a small bead of blood seeped out, running down her scarred and leathery hand. "In that case, I'll kill you all right now." She licked her thumb and swallowed. "Believe me, knight, your blade is naught to mine, and I could kill you at any moment. *That* is no lie. So, tell me. Will you hear my proposition?"

Snow looked to Eldric, who merely returned the silent glance, then back at the Lioness.

She lowered her short sword. "Speak your words."

"I like strong men and women, Snow, and I can see that strength in you. Join the Black Roses and work for me. If you do this, I will hold your precious old man and prince captive, but I will not kill them. If you serve me as a fitful assassin, I will keep them alive. If you fail me—even slightly—I will take their heads and leave you to mourn. Do we have a deal?"

Snow clenched her fists. What was this madness? She was no assassin. The Lioness knew this, too, Snow could feel it. She stared into the other's dark eyes. There was no honor in this, but it must be done. Snow knew that this was the only way out. She looked at Eldric. There he lay, sitting upon the ground, disgraced. Ire shot through the knight's veins. How dare this woman—this gutless assassin? She was crude and menacing. How dare she dishonor the Master Inquisitor with cheap tricks? She wasn't even half the person Eldric was. Snow sighed. That was life, she knew that much. Sometimes, good doesn't always prevail—such is the way of the world.

She turned her eyes to Clement. She felt her heart sink at the thought of his death. What would she do if she lost him—her best friend, her equal? She dreaded to even think of a world where she saw him hang.

No. She had to do this. It was the only way.

The knight sheathed the glittering *Silversong* and held out her hand.

"You have a deal. Pray you don't break it."

The Lioness smiled and shook the other's hand. "Welcome to the Black Roses, Sister Snow."

CHAPTER TWENTY-THREE

Two Visits

Three days passed in strange silence. Or, well, it felt like about three days to Clement, although he couldn't truly be sure how long he had sat upon the dusty floor of his cell or how much time had truly transpired since the fight between Eldric and the Lioness. He had long decided that, whatever happened, Snow was the one who convinced the assassin queen to spare his life. As far as the fight or any further details, he wasn't too sure. After all, it wasn't as if he saw anything happen. No, he merely heard the noises of others speaking and had to guess what was happening from the clues that the sounds provided him.

He felt that three days might be a reasonable estimate, given that he could now feel a full beard had grown upon his face.

And as for knowledge of Eldric's whereabouts, he had no real answer. Several times he had called out for the old Inquisitor, but he had never received an answer. Eventually, the prince concluded that he wasn't there. Prince Reethkilt deduced that, wherever he was, he was alone. Eldric was alive, Clement was sure, but it appeared that the Lioness had perhaps placed them in separate locations. Of course, Clement didn't know exactly what that meant, save that whatever type of building the Vega Varonn was, it was large enough to have two holding areas. But, even without the presence of other prisoners, he was not without company.

The man who guarded his cell was quiet, so much so that the prince soon determined that he was probably trying to conceal his presence. But he was there. Where, exactly, was unknown. But the guard was present...somewhere. Clement stood and wandered around the cell, holding his hands in front of him to feel his surroundings. The air was cool unlike the desert outside, so it could easily be inferred that he was underground. He moved slowly, almost tripping over the waste-bin. There was no bed, so he had to sleep on the floor. He sighed. He was a prisoner, alone.

Smart, Clement thought.

What his friend Snow was should be obvious; blue hair was mythical, but everyone knew what it meant. That was the way of mythical things. The strength that came to those of blue hair was something of heroes in fairy tales told to children at young ages to fill their minds with wonder as they were whisked to sleep. And the Lioness knew that mere bars wouldn't keep Snow from rescuing them.

So you separate us. Clement smiled in spite of himself. *And if she saves one, you kill the other? That way, she can't save us both. Blackmail. Well played, assassin queen.*

They hadn't put any chains around him or clasps around his hands or feet. It was quite odd, but he couldn't help but feel like he wasn't a prisoner even despite the fact that he was sure he was in a cell. As his mind meandered in the darkness of his blind sight, his thoughts were silenced by the sound of approaching footsteps.

Suddenly, there was a clanking cacophony, as if metal were being struck against metal.

Clement sighed. "I assume you're trying to get my attention, whoever you are?"

"Seems you aren't deaf," a familiar voice spoke. Clement felt he had heard it before, but couldn't place it. "Are you used to being blind yet? C'mon, it's not *that* bad, is it?"

"Ah!" the prince said. "The assassin! Ayize, right? Is that who I am speaking with?"

"You know my name," Ayize jeered. "And here I thought the Crown Prince of Aestriana was too important to remember a mere ruffian like me. I'm touched."

"Have you come to kill me?"

There came a muffled racket that Clement could only assume to be the sounds of a key turning a lock, followed by a screeching as the unlocked door was slowly pushed open, then closed. He heard the lock turn once more.

"But you aren't Crown Prince anymore, are you? Because there is no Aestriana. Nope." There was a thud as Ayize sat down across from the prisoner. "It's all gone. Your crown, your country, your king...all of it, bye-bye."

"Why did you come to my cell, assassin?"

"And then there's Marko Jharres—your cousin, right? He's the one who took your eyes? Killed your father? What a guy!"

Clement clenched his fists.

"Why did you come to my cell, assassin?" he said, this time more gravely. "Have you come to merely mock me? If you have, then I tell you, you waste your time."

"Oh?" Ayize laughed. "Why? Is the pride of the great prince too impervious, too immovable to be shaken by the truths of his fallen status? Say, are you still a fool?"

Clement was silent for a moment, his anger dying, and unclenched his fists.

"Pride, you say? I fear you have me wronged, Ayize. There is no pride to be had with being a prince. Honor, yes, but pride? Pride is for the weak and destitute. Whether my country is flourishing or fallen, I will never leave the side of my people. If even the world were to go up in flames, I would gladly burn first if it meant saving my kingdom and everyone else. Do not misunderstand, assassin." Clement turned his face upward and smiled. He couldn't help it. He understood now. Ayize meant no harm; he was helping. "I am not a prideful man."

"So it seems." Ayize's laughter was a low cackle.

"So, tell me, assassin. Why do you test me?"

"Well, that's actually an interesting question."

Something was off. The prince couldn't really pin it down, but there was something different about the assassin now. This didn't seem like the same man who groaned and griped every time he was asked something or asked anything of. Clement was sure that that was the same one who sat before him...but this time...

This time, his voice wasn't coarse. It was wistful, as if lost in a deep nostalgia.

"I am Ayize Dya, one of the most wanted men in the world. Do you know what they call me?"

Clement paused. "The Black Lotus."

"Interesting name," the assassin laughed. "Or at least I always thought so. Do you know why they call me 'The Black Lotus?'"

"I do not."

"I'm going to help you, Prince Reethkilt. I can't promise that what I'm about to do will help you for sure—it might kill you, honestly—but I'm going to present you with the option anyway."

The prince raised an eyebrow. "Pardon?"

"Oh, shut up. You heard me, you blind bastard!"

"There's the familiar coarseness." Clement smirked. "But why would you want to help me?"

"Because. You aren't a bad man, and seeing you crawl like this is pathetic."

Clement couldn't help but laugh. "For an assassin, you've rather strange morals."

"That's because I wasn't *always* an assassin. I used to be a priest, and I'm about to help you reach Empyria."

The prince's laughter stopped abruptly. "*Empyria?*"

"You heard me. I was once a Priest of the White Lotus, so if you let me, I can take you to Empyria."

The prince said nothing, feeling breathless.

"I know the story," Ayize continued. "Marko Jharres awakened the Four Winds within himself. I mean, it makes sense and all, given that you both are of the blood of the wind serpent, the Aeon called Vhryt. But if he has the power of four winds, then that leaves zero winds for you. Don't ya hate that?"

"You...you mean?" Clement's words came out slowly.

"As a White Lotus priest, I can guide you to the gates of Empyria using a certain meditation routine. Since I'm a mortal, I can only take you to the gate, but you can enter, because..."

"I have the Blood of Vhryt..." Clement's words were a soft whisper.

"Bingo. You have Aeonic blood, so you should be able to enter Empyria without any problems. From there, why don't you go to

Vhryt and just ask them what's up?"

"Enter Empyria...you would give me this chance?"

"Well, it's more a gamble, really. Empyria isn't a...concrete place. It's a realm of abstraction and ephemeral dreams. Some metaphor, too." Ayize paused. "Anyway, if we do this, I have to warn you..."

"Warn..."

Ayize's voice became hard. "Your soul will leave your body. But what divides cannot become whole. Once body and soul have been split, you'll have three days in mortal world time to get in and get out. If you go past three days, you'll die and wander the ethereal wastes forever."

"How will I know how much time I have?"

Ayize cracked a small smile.

"You won't."

Eldric was truly at a loss for words. Never before had he experienced such a powerful opponent. Never had he even considered that someone with such speed could possibly exist. For his sixty-some years of living, he had encountered magics of all sorts and types, and never had he truly worried that he would be inadequate to stand against them. Lightning, fire, ice, water...he had seen every element manipulated by a multitude of mages; he had faced down necromancers and vampires with no worries whatsoever. But this was different.

This time, he was truly defeated, shamed, and demoralized.

The old wizard looked at his unbound hands, opened them, then closed them. He watched as small black sparks flickered between his fingertips. Never had this cursed magic of his failed him—this magic, demonic and wrathful. The devastating power of his fell bloodline, it was the blood of the Devil itself.

As he watched the ebony sparks, he thought of the woman in his dreams. That enigmatic mistress, he wondered who she was. He had dreamed of her for as long as he had been alive, her black-and-ivory eyes aglow, as if she were staring into him rather that at him. And that was all he knew of her. He didn't know her name. The only thought he had was that perhaps she was his mother.

Was that it? She was rather young, but then again, Eldric never knew his mother or father, so perhaps she had died young and it was merely her phantom appearing to him?

No. Eldric stroked his full beard. That didn't seem right. It was his mother who abandoned him at the steps of a library. It was his mother who felt shame by his existence. In that case, he deduced, it couldn't have been his mother who held the Devil's Blood.

Then his curiosity intensified. *Who could this woman be?*

This question had been with him ever since the dreams began, yet his desire to answer it had become more unbearable as he aged. Sometimes, he thought that he might die without hearing her voice or knowing her name. It saddened him, and slightly enraged him.

Why won't she speak?

"Father?"

Eldric's head snapped up as his body jolted. There, on the other side of the cell bars, stood Snow.

"Did I scare you?" Snow said with a wistful smile.

"I was just lost in thought, my dear," he said. "Nothing for you to worry about. Just the musings of an old man."

"It was unfair," Snow said, her voice cracking. "The duel, the terms. She took advantage of your clubbed foot. She knew that you can't move well. She—"

"No, Snow." Eldric sighed. "I lost. Fair and square. I cannot blame anything but my own ability. The world has rejected me all my life because of this foot. I cannot now reject myself for it, too."

Snow held the bars of the cell, her head pressed against them. Eldric could see the faint glistening of the remaining tears that wet her cheeks.

"You saved my life, Father." Snow's words were a soft whimper. "You took me in when I was hated by the world for being half-blood, when I was hated for the Giant blood within me, when this blue hair made me an outcast with no redeeming qualities to the people around me. You showed me that I was worth something and that my life mattered, and that no matter how different I looked on the outside, I still deserved to be loved."

Snow sniffled as tears began to flow. She tried to stop it; she told herself that it wouldn't happen, that she would refrain.

But she couldn't help but cry. It was all she could do. It was the only thing that justified how she felt. She knew that, in the darkness, an assassin guard watched over them, but it didn't matter at this point. No, it was too late.

Snow was weeping.

"I swore to protect you!" she wailed, the sounds of her voice ringing through the bars. "And to see you like this—it makes me think I failed you."

Suddenly, her knees gave way. Her hands slid down the bars as she fell to her knees.

"I'm sorry, Father. I'm so, so—"

She stopped as she felt the elder's hand caress her face gently

"Snow." Eldric's voice was firm. "You are placing too much upon your shoulders. My being here is not your fault; it is my own. You didn't place me in any danger or fail me in any regard."

"But I did," Snow said quietly. "I failed you."

"No. You *saved* me, Snow."

The knight raised her tear-stricken face, her deep azure eyes glossy in the dim light of the etherlamps.

"I...?"

"Yes." Eldric smiled, that smile that seemed to defy the world. "Had you not acted and locked swords with that dreadful woman, I would've been cut to pieces. But it is by your intuition, your skill, and your courage that I am alive right now."

Snow stared into the old man's wrinkled face, his expression light as his laugh-lines shown ever more apparent with his smile.

Eldric grabbed her hands through the thin spacing in the bars.

"Snow." His voice was firm and heavy. "You *have* repaid me. Time and time again, you have *always* repaid me. And hear me well..." He paused. "You owe me *nothing*."

The room was still. Snow sniffled as Eldric held her quaking hands.

"It's been three days," she said, finally beginning to calm herself. "I'm sorry I didn't come sooner. I...I was afraid that I would break down like this."

Eldric released her hands. "All is well, my dear child. I love you nonetheless."

Snow smiled. "Thank you, father."

The knight wiped her eyes and stood.

"The Lioness has called me to a mission."

"Oh?"

"I don't like it. I'm not an assassin, but"—she paused—"this mission is, well...I think she's choosing it purposefully, and I don't know why."

"I don't understand? What do you mean?"

"The mission is to go to a small town in Mirea—an Elven town named Drevn—and remove a certain troublemaker. The hit came in from the lord over the town. He said that this certain problematic character is killing people in the town, ripping them to shreds..."

"Sounds oddly like Inquisitor work..." Eldric said underneath his breath. "Are you troubled that you'll have to go into Elven territory?" he asked louder.

"Yes," Snow finally said, her hands fidgeting nervously. "I know what I should expect, I just...I don't know if I can."

"Snow," the old man said. "You're strong. You can do this."

"I'll be accompanied by Ayize and Enlil, so I guess I could say that I'll be in good company—even if Ayize is standoffish and the little girl is unpredictable. I just, I..." Snow sighed. "I can't help but feel like the Lioness is doing this on purpose, to test me or something? But I don't know why she would do that."

A silence hung between the two as Snow gripped the bars once more, her mind stirring.

"Well," Eldric said after some time. Snow couldn't help but detect a strange weightlessness in his voice. "Perhaps she's not evil."

"How can you say that, father?" Snow snapped, astonished. "She tried to kill you! She wanted to kill all of us!"

"Yes, yes, and yes," the elder man admitted, laughing. "But that doesn't make her evil, I don't think. Snow, not everyone in your opposition is evil. Some simply are wrong. Evil, no. Wrong, yes." Eldric stroked his long white beard. "When I fought her, I knew that my life was on the line. I knew that her bloodlust and resolve to end my life were both very real. But they were not evil. She played the game for the sake of her men. Imagine this: your mortal enemy walks into your den and demands your help. What do you do?"

"You help them!" Snow said firmly.

"And give up the respect of your men?" Eldric's words were firm as well. "If she had accepted my help immediately, it would have shown fickleness. If she had instantly aided me, it would have meant that she was at my command. Who wants a leader who can so easily be swayed? Yes, she is the feared and terrible Lioness of the Black Roses, but she is also a leader who must be worthy of respect and loyalty. No one wants to follow someone spineless."

"So the duel was...?"

"Merely her way of asserting her dominance."

"But that doesn't matter! She was still going to take your life!"

"That she was, but that does not make her evil. She did what she had to do. Think with me, Snow. When you fought the dark wizard, Zurriel, back in Crown City, how did his presence feel?"

Snow thought deeply, reliving her memories of the confrontation with the dreaded sorcerer within her mind.

"He felt void. Inhuman. Fighting him felt like the weight of the world sat upon my shoulders. It felt like plunging my blade into his chest would rid the world of a great evil."

"Exactly. Now, when you look at the Lioness, how do you feel?"

Snow couldn't believe what her father was saying. She thought about the assassin queen. She was coarse and unrefined and vile and vicious, but...Snow stopped. She thought of the people of the den and how they seemed to love their dismal queen; she thought about Ayize and how he complained about everything—but when he talked about his mistress, he did so with warmth. She thought about the little Darkling, Enlil...

"She loves them, doesn't she?" Snow said softly, her tears now dried. "That's why she did what she did, isn't it? She needs them to believe she's strong. But it's not selfish, like Zurriel. She doesn't want their fear; she wants their respect. And she knows that they need her to be strong, for their sakes'. They need a powerful leader because it gives them security and faith."

Eldric smiled lightly, his eyes filled with love. "You understand."

"She's not evil," Snow said.

Snow took in a deep breath.

"I will go," she began, "I have no choice but to obey, but I will also rise to this challenge. If the Lioness is indeed testing me, then I will rise to the opportunity she is offering. Not just for me, but for you, and Clement."

"You understand now." The old man nodded. "Go, child. The world is calling."

Snow returned the nod then turned to walk away.

"Thank you...father."

Eldric smiled a small smile as he watched her disappear into the darkness once more.

"Mister Assassin Guard," Eldric laughed. "I know you are watching. Do not worry. I am not going to try to escape. Wherever you linger in this room, I must say that the ingenuity of youth never ceases to amaze these old bones."

There was only silence.

Eldric thought of the woman from his dreams once more.

CHAPTER TWENTY-FOUR

Just Like Me

"And now we begin," Ayize said. "Sit upright and cross your legs. This represents the crossing of time and space."

"Aye," Prince Reethkilt said as he did as commanded.

"With your right hand, place your index finger and middle finger lightly upon your closed eye. This represents the Sight of the Eternal World."

Once more, Clement did as commanded.

"Good," Ayize said. "Lastly, place the tip of your thumb upon the center of your chest, where the heart beats. This represents the Heart of Everything, the Cosmic Tree, Yggdrasil."

The Darkling waited until the prince was in position.

"And now we begin," he said. "While I perform the meditation, you must sit still and breathe inward through your nose, wait, then out through your mouth. You must remain still and focused. If you lose your focus halfway, you'll probably die."

"Die?!" Clement gasped.

"I mean, yeah, I don't know," the Darkling snapped back. "It would be bad...probably? Don't question it! Just don't lose focus, okay."

The room fell quiet. Clement couldn't help but think just how uncomfortable this position was. But he knew that he must endure. After all, what was a tiny bit of uncomfortable sitting compared to his mission to save his country?

Ayize began to chant in a language the prince did not understand. At first he felt nothing, but soon, as he listened to the mysterious language, his breathing began to steady, the air passing through him as if it never entered him at all.

The Darkling's words slowly began to fade. Clement could feel himself begin to lift—not as if he were floating or flying, but rather as if he were simply beginning to disappear, as if pieces of him were being cast into the wind, one by one, tossed into a vast void.

"O, door to naught," Ayize said, "give us peace as we walk your gracious stairs."

Suddenly, vision ruptured within Clement's mind. He felt odd. No longer could he feel the cold of the dungeon, but instead, a fair breeze blew. But it was different than what he had felt before. The air was warm, carrying with it the sweet smells of honeysuckles and wildflowers. Chills bubbled upon the prince's skin as the air seemed to penetrate his flesh and travel through to the other side. Clement looked around. He stood in a vast grassy plain. It was empty, extending to the blue forms of mighty mountains in the distance. Light bore down from a sky of nothingness, just a white emptiness above.

"Odd, isn't it?" Ayize said.

Clement jolted when the other spoke. He stared at the Darkling for a moment, then at his own hands. Both he and Ayize seemed to be physically there, yet he couldn't shake the feeling of emptiness that filled his bones.

"This is as far as I go," the assassin said. "Best of luck to you, prince." He smirked. "Oh, and if you die, it's not my fault. I already warned you, so don't say I didn't." The Darkling closed his eyes and, in a blink, disappeared.

There was silence, dead, still, and vacant.

But there was one blatantly obvious difference in this realm for Clement. He could see. He was certain that he had indeed been whisked away to another place—one not of the flesh, for that matter—because his sight had been returned to him.

Three days to get in and get out, huh? he thought as he began to walk toward the vague and distant mountains. *Now what?*

He had no clue. Where he was going or where he was—it all meant nothing to him. Instead, he found himself hopelessly stranded in a reality so unlike his own. He wished he had asked the assassin for directions, but quickly remembered that even the mysterious Ayize was a stranger to this place.

"Hello, my man," a deep voice echoed throughout the vacuous stillness. "You look rather lost."

Clement whipped around to see a rather large, flame-haired man sitting upon a golden chariot. Clement took a moment to study his situation. This strapping man wore a full beard in the same blazing reddish hue. The horses, the prince noticed, shared the same flame-red color in their manes as the man's hair.

"You look rather foolish as you simply gawk," he said. The man's hearty laughter clapped like thunder, as if amplified by the stillness. "Tell me, do I leave you so speechless?"

"I"—Clement smiled at how foolish he must have seemed—"you merely caught me off guard."

"What is your name, young prince?"

"How did you know I was a prince?"

The large man smirked cleverly. "How can one tell that the sun rises in the day and the moon at night?"

Clement stood, befuddled.

"By sight, of course!" the man finished. "You hold yourself like one with the heart of a prince. So tell me, what is your name?"

"You are correct in your assumption," the prince said, bowing. "I am Alexander Clement zel Reethkilt, crown prince of Aestriana."

"Ah!" the other said. "You belong to *that* Aeon? Slippery serpent, it is!"

"And your name, if I might ask?"

Suddenly, the red hairs upon his head and full beard exploded into bright, red-hot flames. Clement held his hands to his eyes to block out the light.

"I am Yeornyeim, the Aeon of Flame, War, Honor, and"—he smirked—"my favorite: I am the Master of Deals, Bets, and Wagers!"

"Aeon?!"

"Yes, boy! Aeon! You heard me, didn't you?"

Clement bowed once more, holding his head down. "It is an honor,

My Lord!"

"Ah, cut it with that stuff! Other Aeons like Ymerhyl might like the worship, but I'm not a fan of it. I don't want to see that groveling stuff! Show me heart! Show me *passion*!"

Clement rose once more, regaining his posture. He stared into the Aeon's eyes. Flames seemed to dance as they swirled around his pupils, a river of molten red endlessly twisting and swishing underneath his crimson brow, their fiery tongues whipping like sunspots as they splashed outward every so often.

"Tell me, Serpentchild. What brings you here?"

Serpentchild? Clement let the thought go. Surely the Aeon could see what he was. Already, Yeornyeim had made it known that he knew the prince's connection to Vhryt.

"I want to see Vhryt."

"Brazen and bold!" the war god laughed. "I like you, Clement. You've a warrior's heart. I might just help you. After all, I think the old Wind Serpent might like to meet one of their kin. But..."

"You've doubts of my lineage?" the prince said, unsure.

"Well, let's just say that life is no fun without a little fire, eh?" the Aeon sprang up from his seat and threw his hands wide open. "What's this life without a bit of *danger?*"

"I don't understand?"

"*Passion! Drama! Volition! Heart! Courage!*" Yeornyeim laughed. "You get it, don't you prince? This world would be ruined without the salt that preserves it!"

Clement raised an eyebrow. "I don't quite understand what you are trying to say."

With a flick of his wrist, the War God summoned a wooden spear with a golden spearhead.

"I'm saying," he said as he threw the spear at the prince's feet. "That we should play a game, make a *wager*, if you will! Let's have a little duel, eh?"

Prince Reethkilt bent down and lifted the wooden spear from the soft grass, instantly noting how heavy it was.

"What are your terms, Aeon?"

The other smirked as he summoned a spear of his own.

"It's simple, prince. The first one to impale the other wins!"

Clement straightened himself and brought forth the weighty spear, pointing it directly at the tall god.

"Very well."

Snow's mind was cluttered, an unusual thing for her. Her thoughts were a storm; her palms sweaty as anxiety seemed to lay over her shoulders like a thick blanket. Never had she felt about anything the way she felt about this mission. In all of her time as the personal bodyguard to the Master of the Inquisition, she had never once been conflicted about the job she was supposed to do.

But now...now she had a bad taste in her mouth.

She had undressed, taking off her silver armor, and had sat upon her bed in her undergarments. Beside her lay clothing she had been given for the mission, yet she knew it was just another way for the Lioness to assert her dominance over the situation.

Across the room, a dusty mirror hung by a rusty nail. Snow stood and stared at her reflection. Her body was lithe and lean, patterned with healed scars from sparring matches and perilous combat situations from her past. She was twenty-nine years of age now, and she had served Eldric for twenty of those years.

Eldric, the man she saw as her father.

Eldric, the man who saved her life.

Nostalgia filled her mind as she ran her fingers along each scar of her body. Each scar was a tale; each tale was a reason she wished she could return to simpler days. In those days, she killed to protect—she killed for the sake of rightness and light.

But the Lioness was a different sort of leader. She was a mistress of darkness—one who valued the strength of her men more than their souls—one that saw the value of those under her based only upon the their respective might alone and nothing else.

Snow looked at the clothing on the bedside. It was leather armor, sleek and brown.

What was she now? Was she still a knight? Or was she simply a killer?

"Lost in thought, are we?" the Lioness laughed as she entered the room. The assassin pointed at Snow's belly, then to her own exposed abdomen, running her fingers down the scars that stripped across her sides. "We match."

"I'm not like you," Snow quickly snapped back. "My blade is honorable and just!"

"Honor? Justice?" the Lioness cackled. "Honor is for fools, my dear. It is an illusion created merely to soften the blow of reality." She sat at the foot of the bed. "Tell me, Snow, do you know *why* I recruited you? Why I allowed the Inquisitor and prince to live?"

Snow halted, her eyes staring intently as the woman scratched her head, digging her sharp nails into her thick, dark locs.

"It was because of your eyes," the tall woman continued.

"I don't understand."

"Is it really so difficult to understand? I saw everything I needed." She smiled, the light reflecting off of her teeth. "When I was about to kill your precious Eldric, you were going to kill me, weren't you?"

"I was."

"It was in your eyes. The eyes of a killer—cold, filled with rage. There was no honor in those eyes."

Snow said nothing, as she clenched her fists; her mind seemed to swirl. This cruel mistress, was she right? No. Certainly not, right? *Right?*

"We're the same, you and I," the Lioness spoke up.

"Why are you doing this to me?" Snow's voice was low as she grit her teeth.

"Doing what to you?" the assassin queen's lips curled into a wicked smile. "I have no idea as to what you might be talking about, my dear."

"This mission," Snow said, this time more forcefully. "Why are you sending me to Mirea to confront the Elves?"

"Do you have an objection? I don't understand the problem."

"You know my bloodline, don't you?!" Snow shouted, jumping to her feet.

"I don't know what you're talking about," the Lioness said with a coy smile. "But it sounds like someone has a chip on their shoulder."

Snow balled her hands into fists. She felt her body temperature rise. Rage coursed through her veins. What did this woman know? *Nothing!* She knew nothing of the anguish that a half-Elf had to experience—nothing of what *she* had to go through to just exist under the prejudices that were in play.

She thought about Eldric and the prince.

Calm yourself, Snow, she told herself. She had to play this woman's game, as much as she loathed it, for the sake of her father and Clement. *Just a little longer.*

But how much longer...?

"You know what you're doing." Snow's voice was calm yet incensed. "I don't know why you're doing it, but I know you know what you're doing."

The other was silent, her eyes carefully inspecting her long, sharpened nails. Static hung between them, a silent tension. Snow sighed as she sat upon the bed, her head falling into her hands.

"I need to get dressed," she said, her voice rigid and curt.

The Lioness remained quiet for some time.

"I'm helping you," the assassin queen finally said.

"What?"

"I'm helping you. You don't know it now, but no one ever does. We often can't see that sometimes the most fearful situations are the ones that set us free. When we can face our demons and spit at them instead of cowering—when we can see that the things that terrify us are merely holding us back, that the ghosts that haunt us are merely tricks of the light—*that* is when we find true strength. You don't know it now, but I'm doing this to help you."

"I don't understand!" Snow raged. "I'm your enemy! I'm the personal knight to the Master of the Inquisition! Why would you care to help me?!"

The Lioness smiled. It was a strange smile, one Snow hadn't seen before. As she thought about it, she realized another thing.

The Lioness' demeanor had changed. Her voice was low, wistful.

"I like strong people, Snow. And I believe that you are strong."

"And Eldric and Prince Reethkilt?" Snow shot back. "They are weak?"

"Maybe, maybe not. You see, Snow, you don't understand strength. Strength exists in all of us. It is strength of body that lets us fight, strength of mind that gives us sight, and strength of spirit that gives us victory over our enemies. The Inquisitor lost the duel, yes. But I am not done with him, the prince, *or* you, for that matter."

Snow was silent, her mind affray. The Lioness stood and walked to the door.

"Because we're the same," she said as she pulled back her hair to reveal a pointed ear. "Because we're *both* half-Elves."

Snow's head snapped up, her eyes wide as her chest leapt in shock.

"Wha—"

The door had already closed, and the Lioness was gone.

Thoughts of the event that had just happened made Snow feel dizzy. She shook her head, trying to push the surprising revelation to the back of her mind for now. The knight eyed herself in the mirror and nodded. She had work to do.

She looked at the leather armor beside her on the bed. It was obviously going to be lighter than her mail and plate armor.

Once dressed, she felt strange as she stared into the dusty mirror once more.

Who am I? Her mind was a flurry of emotions that made her stomach clench. She looked at her gloves, opened her hand, then closed it. *Father...*

"Hey! Miss Blue!" Enlil's cheery voice was muffled behind the door. "It's time'ta go! Ayize is already ready, and he gets really grumpy when he has to wait!"

"Coming!" Snow looked at her silver blades against the wall and sighed.

Snow opened the door to see the little Darkling waiting close by.

"You look weird without armor!" the child blurted out. "You're actually really skinny!"

"What does that mean—?"

Enlil beckoned the knight to follow and bolted off. "C'mon!"

Snow was right. She felt much swifter as she followed the speedy child down the halls of the Vega Varonn. The more she moved, the more she decided that she might just like the weightless feeling of the leather armor over the burden of her steel breastplate and the weight of her chainmail. Eventually, the little girl slowed and Snow followed her at a more acceptable pace. Enlil guided her follower down the twisting hallways until they came once again to the open air of the landing pad. The area was wide and dusty. Snow noted that there were several black ships, but none of them seemed even remotely like the *Prometheus*.

"This way! This way!" Enlil grabbed the knight's hand and began to pull her along.

Ayize stood at the landing deck, his arms folded as he paced back and forth with a scowl.

"Took long enough," he said, throwing his hands into the air. "Where were you?"

"Getting ready," Snow replied blankly.

The Darkling sighed and shook his head. "Well, let's get on with it. It's gonna take us about a day and a half to get there. We're going deep into Elven country, so..." he trailed off. "Well, you're a half-Elf, you get the picture."

Snow nodded.

"You don't gotta be all grumpy, *Ayize*!" Enlil shot back.

"No," Snow said, smiling a small smile. "He's right. I *am* a half-Elf." She paused, her eyes meeting his. She stared into his pale green eyes, her face hardening. "But I am ready to face whatever I might find there."

"Ha!" the Darkling's face softened. "We'll see about that."

"Just don't die, okay!" Enlil's voice was cheery as always. "Because we might not be able to bring you back, and then the old man and the prince would be sad."

Snow could feel the young girl's eyes upon her. It felt strange. If she were being completely honest, she found Enlil strange as a whole. She couldn't be older than thirteen, yet she seemed to hold no fear in her countenance. Snow thought back to when the young girl guided her and her defeated comrades out of the Palace of the Sky King. Even in the face of the horrific Ex Nihilo beasts, Enlil seemed to show no fear. It were as if the child were completely incapable of it. Here they were, going on a mission, and she was treating it as if it were a vacation of sorts.

"Are you in love with the prince guy?" Enlil asked.

"What?" Snow's voice cracked. "What do you—?"

"Hey. *Ladies*." The two looked up the ramp to see Ayize tapping his watch. "Time's ticking and that mark ain't getting any deader."

Snow gladly took the distraction.

"Yes," she said. "Let's go Enlil."

The girl smiled in return, her question lost within her spacey mind.

"Call me En! We're gonna be sisters!"

CHAPTER TWENTY-FIVE

The Prince's Gambit

"A duel, you say?" Clement held the golden-headed spear, feeling its weight in his arm.

"Second thoughts, Serpentspawn?" the large Aeon said as he stepped down from his golden chariot.

"Nay. I dare not stray from this opportunity," the prince said, striking the ground with end of the pole. "Not every day one gets to fight the god of war, eh?"

The divine raised his lance high in the air. "That's the spirit! Come at me, prince! Show me your power!"

Suddenly and with great force, Clement bolted forward, the blade of his lance shifting swiftly, unpredictable.

"The fire of your heart blazes, prince!" the Aeon said with a bellowing laugh as he pushed away the other's attack with a quick twist of his spear. "But you will have to be more creative than that if you truly wish to best me!"

"Then fare with this, Aeon!" Clement shouted as the shaft spun through his fingers and rolled around his neck. With one fast thrust, the point of the spear shot forward.

"Clever!" his opponent said as he stepped to the side.

Yeornyeim placed his hand at his side and it returned with blood from the cut upon his rib.

"I commend you, my good prince!" He exclaimed, a wide grin igniting his red hair into blazing tongues of fire. "For it has been five hundred years since a mortal made me bleed."

Clement nodded, a grin crossing his face as well. "Then I not take the compliment lightly. And I have struck you indeed!"

"Struck," the other said, holding up his hand to halt the prince, "But not impaled. You may cut me, but you are far too cautious to land a killing blow."

"Cautious?"

"Hear me, Serpentspawn. As long as you hold fear in your heart, I shall win," the god began. "It is when we discard our fears that we truly obtain powers to overcome them."

Clement took a deep breath. He thought about the Aeon's words. Perhaps he *was* afraid. But afraid of what? Was it the imposing divine being before him that frightened him so? *No*, he thought, *that couldn't be it*. What then? Was it the warning given to him by the assassin-priest, Ayize? That he had three days before his life was forfeit? He thought on it. Sure it was a daunting omen, or so he thought it *should* be. But he decided that it wasn't that he feared it.

What then?

Clement thought of his father. In his mind's eye, he relived Marko's smile as he slid his knife across the old man's neck—the old man who loved him, the old man who raised him, adopted him, fed him...

Clement clenched his fist.

Why, Marko?

Hate and love warred within the prince as he reminisced on times with his cousin—his dear brother. Then, he thought about their duel. He remembered the terrifying powers that his cousin held...

Yes, that's it...

"Have you found it, good prince?" the Aeon asked, breaking the silence.

"I have, or at least I believe I have."

"Then say it aloud!" he thundered. "Scream it into the skies! Hear, prince, as your voice fades into the distance. Our fears only hold power when inside of us, but they too, like all things, fade in the nature of the world.

"I am afraid," Clement said, his voice trembling, "that Vhryt has forsaken me."

"So your mind says," the god began. "Tell me, prince, what does your *heart* say?"

"That I will find out here. That I must win this duel."

"You have said it aloud." Yeornyeim pointed his spear at the prince. "Now face me fully, unhindered."

"Gladly!" Clement raised his spear, and with one swift motion, snapped the shaft with his strong knees.

"You desecrate your weapon? And for what?" the Aeon raised his eyebrow.

"Nay," Clement smirked. "I break this spear, and with it I break my fears!"

The Aeon bellowed a hearty laugh; his voice thundered across the field. "Then come at me! Bear your spirit!"

Without a reply, the prince shot forward, a piece of the spear in each hand. The god replied with a great thrust. As the Aeon's spear pierced the air, red flames exploded from its point. Quickly, the prince deflected the blow. The god of war reacted by raining his spear point down upon the mortal. Cracks filled the air as the two were caught in a fierce collection of volleys. With great force, Yeornyeim slammed the shaft of his lance downward.

"I have won!" Clement exclaimed as he slipped to the side and swung the bladed section of his broken spear.

"Nay!" the god replied as he deflected the blade.

"Aye!" the prince roared.

Clement dropped his bladed section, and with a great motion, threw the wooden shaft forward like a javelin, the splintered wood facing forward.

Yeornyeim grunted as the jagged wood impaled him, sinking deeply into his stomach.

"You are well mighty and fairly cunning, prince! It has been some time since I have fought a mortal such as yourself."

"Aye!" Clement laughed in return. "I can think of only one other that has given me such challenge, and to her I must return. To her I owe my life. But more importantly, I must return to my world for the sake my country and my people. I have not much time in this realm before I cannot return to my own. It is honestly a shame, for if I could fight you for eternity, I would."

"And I feel the same," the Aeon said as he pulled the wooden shaft from his belly.

"Very well. I assume that this means you will aid me?"

Clement watched as the wound in the other's abdomen shrank to nothing.

"As I have promised, young prince." He smiled. "As I have promised."

CHAPTER TWENTY-SIX

The Scarlet Secret

The storm raged over the Mirean wetlands as a little girl fled for dear life through the brumous mist of the Dreshden Mire. A mucky layer of mud and rainwater caked her legs, causing them to grow weighty as it accumulated. The Mire was dark, its forbidding expanse quiet save for the rolls of thunder and the whooshes from the heavy sheets of rain.

But she didn't care. No. Instead, she ran without thinking. She ran as hard as she could; she ran because her life depended on it. Images of her life intruded into her hysterical delirium, her breath heavy as she felt her heart pound against her ribcage.

She ran and ran, far from her life before, far from her agony, far from her torment and anguish.

What would she do now? She didn't know. Would she simply die in the Mire? She assumed she was around seven years old, but she wasn't sure. Yes, she thought. She'll die here for certain, but death was a greater paradise than the life she was escaping. Death, in her eyes, was a gift she felt she'd never receive.

She ran past a tree when abrupt lightning smote it, the force of the heavens causing the gnarled wood to explode into bright white flames.

The little girl gasped as her face sunk into a giant puddle.

Yes...

　This was it...

　　Death...

Pressure enveloped her body as she felt herself being lifted out of the puddle.

Silence.

The little girl opened her eyes to find herself held in something's grasp.

Sudden lightning illuminated the area to reveal a massive man, giant in stature. In the quick flash of light, she could see a blue skull tattooed upon his face. The two held eye contact.

Thunder raged once more, the rain mixing with the fog.

The Elven knight, Sir Vanderbilt von Rybird, strode down the reddened hallways of the Gray Fortress, the home of Count Mothrus Malroi, reigning lord of the town of Drevn. Vanderbilt had served under the count for all of his days in the knighthood, but never had he received so strange a summons. The main peculiarity of the summons was the hour in which it was received. In the dead of night he received a simple letter, slipped covertly under the door of his quarters.

It was odd, that was certain, but a summons was a summons, and it was his duty to answer the call.

The count was an...odd man. Perhaps the strangest thing (and most apparent) that Vanderbilt could say about his lord was that in the last five years, he hadn't once seen the man's face. To his knowledge, in fact, he couldn't think of a single person who had. No, none had. Once friendly and social with his men, Count Malroi had slowly become antisocial and specific. Now he hid behind an ivory mask, solid white with small slits for his eyes to peer out of. The nobleman kept his visage from even his closest officers.

The hallways of the Gray Fortress were red, lit by the peculiar sanguine etherlamps positioned among the walls. Etherlamps were usually blue or yellow, but the ones that lit this castle were a specially requested red color. It was an odd choice, the knight had to admit, but it was also out of his control, as it wasn't his castle or his place to make suggestions upon the decor. Still, the blood-red light that splashed upon the walls seemed sinister. The knight shook away the thought as he approached the count's quarters and knocked upon the heavy wooden door.

"Come in, Vanderbilt," said the count, his faint voice muffled through the wood.

The knight did as asked, closing the door behind him. The inside of the room was dark for all but a faint red glow burning above the vanity where the Count sat as he painted his fingernails a bright crimson. He was a tall Elf, thin and lanky, his skin pale as a bright moon.

"It is good to see you, Sir Vanderbilt. I hope the hour of my summons does not disturb you," the count said, his voice muffled behind the mask.

"No, My Lord," the knight said as he bowed. "Never would I dare be disturbed by your command."

"Good. You see, my dear knight"—Count Malroi glided the brush up his nails, coating them in a bloody shade—"I have an...interesting order for you to follow."

"I-interesting? Interesting how so, my lord?"

"Such a clever knight," the nobleman chuckled. "I'm glad you asked. You see, I will be having some very...*personal* guests come to see me tomorrow, and I would like for *you* to be the one to welcome them to my quarters."

"Special guests?" the knight felt a sudden shiver ride up his spine. He couldn't tell why, but something in the Count's voice was rather...grim.

"Yes," Malroi said as he held up his fingers to the light, seeming to inspect them behind the slits of his pearly mask. "They are quite special indeed. You will be good to them, won't you? Treat them nicely as I have treated you? I have treated you nicely, have I not, Sir Vanderbilt?"

The knight bowed once more. "Y-yes, my lord. You have been most gracious to me! I am forever in your debt, that I swear it."

"Good, my dear knight." He paused. "Very well. I wish for you to go south of the town, into the forest, and wait there until the morning. You will wait until a black airship appears in the sky. Three fellows will arrive with it. I want you to bring them to me."

Vanderbilt felt chills run up his arm, but he quickly pushed his confusion aside. It was not his job to be skeptical, only to do as he was told. Honestly, he found it less stressful that way.

The knight held his hand to his heart. "I shall, My Lord."

Vanderbilt nodded then promptly turned to leave.

"And, my dear knight," the count said, his face turned. "Tell no one about this. No one, you understand?"

"I won't, sir. I promise."

Count Malroi smiled behind his mask as the knight shut the door behind him. *Soon*, he thought, *very soon*. Soon he would be rid of it.

Soon, he would be rid of his scarlet secret.

Flying out of the desert upon the *Prometheus* was much easier than Snow had expected. The airship ran smoothly, and often Snow wondered how a rogue such as Ayize came upon it. Several times the idea came to her mind to ask, but each time she decided not to bother the grumpy Darkling with the questions.

And speaking of questions, the little thief, Enlil, was full of them.

"Why is your hair blue?" she asked with wide eyes. "Can I touch it?"

"I'm half-Giant," Snow responded calmly. "And no, I'd rather you not."

"Are you sure you're a Giant?" the small Darkling cocked her head. "You don't seem tall enough. I heard that the Giants are really tall!"

Snow giggled softly at the young girl's innocence. "I'm rather sure I'm a Giant. I may not be as tall as one, but I have their strength. That I know for sure."

"Is that why your sword is so heavy?"

Snow raised an eyebrow. "You touched my sword?"

"Yeah," the little Darkling said dismissively. "It was shiny. And too heavy. I tried to lift it, but I couldn't!"

Snow laughed. "You're a curious child, Enlil," she said. "But you have a good heart, and"—she turned her eyes to the door that lead to the cockpit—"I feel he is the same."

"Ayize?" Enlil suddenly smiled a big smile. "He's my big brother! Well, he's not *really* my big brother, but we're still family. He's just grumpy."

Maybe so, Snow thought. For a moment, her mind went back to her encounter with Lioness. She thought of Eldric's words. Maybe he was right. Maybe—*just maybe*—the Black Roses weren't evil after all.

"Are you in love with the prince guy?"

The blank belligerence of the question snapped Snow from her thoughts instantly.

"What?!" her voice was louder and more unguarded than she had wished.

"The prince!" Enlil said with a guileless expression. "Are you in love with him?"

W-well..." Snow shook her head to hide any embarrassment; she could feel her face growing hot. "H-he's a good friend—a...a *best* friend, maybe—and my sparring partner, that's all."

"But he's blind," the other said. "Does that mean you'll have to find a new partner."

"No," Snow began. "Not necessarily. And besides, I'd never abandon a friend."

Enlil smiled. Snow didn't like this smile, either. There was something about this mysterious little Darkling—perhaps a twinkle in her eye. The thing that made Snow most nervous was that, although the little girl's mind seemed empty most of the time, Snow knew that she hid a deep perceptiveness and cunning.

"Tell me," Snow said, quick to change the subject, "that power that you and your brother have—"

"Projection?" Enlil perked up. "It's really nifty, isn't it?" her pale green eyes became wide. "I bet you could do it too, Blue! You just gotta focus really hard and block everything else out. Ayize said that the priests told him how to do it."

Snow raised an eyebrow. "He didn't learn it from the Lioness?"

"Nope!" Enlil sang. "I learned it from her, but Ayize said that he learned it from somewhere else."

"Enlil!" Ayize called over the intercom. "Up front, now!"

"Aye, captain!" the little girl said, springing from her seat and rushing toward the doorway.

Snow debated on if she should sit and wait alone or follow the hyper child. She thought for a moment, the stood and followed.

The cockpit was a small two-seater, filled with beeping buttons and flashing lights. Snow looked out of the window. It was much different from the desert. The forests were murky and filled with a thick mist, the perfect place for any sort of evil to lurk and stalk unwary travelers.

"The Dreshden Mire," Ayize began once he noticed the knight's curiosity. "Dreadful place, really. Supposedly, an Angelic city stood here in ancient times, but for some reason, it was abandoned and left to sink into the bog. No one knows really what happened to it, but I could possibly assume that it fell with the Angels."

"I see. You know your history?"

"Maybe," he continued. "Now all that's here is this eerie mist and the dismal town we're headed to." Ayize sighed. "I just know I'm gonna hate this place."

"See!" Enlil cheered and smiled at Snow. "I told'ja! He's a really good guy, but he's just grumpy."

"Yes." Snow laughed a little at the child's innocent eyes. "I suppose you're right."

It was early dawn when Sir Vanderbilt stepped out of the town of Drevn and into the dense forests to the south. The mists of morning permeated, and dew decorated the grasses upon the forest floor, spots of crystalline water upon their leaves.

The sun was slowly rising in the distance, rising with the knot in the knight's throat. Though he couldn't really pinpoint why, he could feel his body tensing. Perhaps it was the strangeness of his lord's command. *Maybe,* he thought harder, *maybe it is the count's behavior that perturbs me.* The Count hadn't been himself for quite some time. No, the once calm and composed man had become a man of erratic thought. Perhaps it was the mask. It didn't bother him at first, but the more the knight thought about it, the more he wondered what dwelt behind its moon-white shell. The Count never left the castle; he never stepped into the midday air. The knight decided that it bothered him, but soon dismissed his concerns.

He was, after all, a knight and not a detective. He was meant to serve, not critique.

Vanderbilt wandered rather deep into the woods, making note of the small streams that flowed downstream from the cursed and forlorn Dreshden Mire to the north. He took note of the dense mossy trees, their gnarled and forbidding branches blackened and moist where moss dripped downward, almost touching the equally squishy ground. Kacklebirds, with their devilish calls, laughed in the darkness of the wood. The knight wandered for a bit more until he came to an open glade, a wide expanse, still and holy, where the sun dared peek upon the visage of the earth, and waited.

Time passed, and soon the sun rose above the horizon, a sudden vibration hummed in the air. In the distance, a black dot grew larger in the sky until an airship cruiser became visible.

So that's them, the knight thought.

"Looks like someone is here to greet us," Ayize said, his eyes taking note of the grounded Elf's gilded armor as it shone in the sunlight.

"The client-guy?" Enlil said.

"No telling." Ayize paused. "You gonna be alright, Blue?"

Snow was taken aback by the Darkling's sudden sincerity.

"Me?"

"You see anyone else with blue hair?" he growled back.

The knight nodded. "I'll be fine."

"Alright."

"But," she said, smiling, "thank you for the sentiment. It's kind of you."

"Ugh!" Ayize gagged. "Don't get all emotional. It's gross."

Outside, Sir Vanderbilt shielded his eyes from the wind as the airship *Prometheus* descended onto the ground.

Who are these people? A lump began to form in his throat as the landing ramp slowly lowered to the ground.

"I'm guessing you're the one who sent for us?" Ayize said as he walked down the ramp.

"What?!" the knight gasped as he noticed Snow.

Snow felt her heart lurch as their eyes met.

"What's the meaning of this!" Vanderbilt raged. "What shame do you bring my lord by offering the aid of a *halfling*?!"

"Spare me your god complex, Elf," Ayize spat onto the soggy ground. "I'm guessing your 'lord' is the one who we really need to talk to. Take us to him."

"Watch your tongue, Darkling!"

"Ugh!" Ayize groaned. "Look. I don't think your master would be too happy to know how inhospitable his *hound* was to his guests, ay?"

"Hound—?!" Vanderbilt's hand gripped the sword at his side.

"Watch yourself." Ayize's voice was cold and sinister. "You don't want to make an enemy of me."

The knight shot a glance at Snow before making a disgusted huffing noise and turning to lead the trio onward.

"Blasted halfling..." he said under his breath.

Snow heard him, but his words didn't hurt. How could they? She'd heard the same all of her life. All of her life she had endured this curse, so what would the rejection of some random soldier do to harm her? She looked down to see the little Enlil staring up at her with her pale green eyes.

"Don't worry, En," Snow said, surprising herself that she felt so close to this one, even after so little time. "What he says doesn't hurt me."

The little girl stared up at her for a moment more before returning the smile and walking along.

Everyone was silent then, Snow and the Darklings simply following the knight through the woods.

Finally, Ayize spoke. "What's your name, Elf?"

The man was silent.

"Vanderbilt," he said at last, gritting his teeth. "Vanderbilt von Rybird."

"Good to know."

The distant laughter of the Kacklebirds was the only sound then. Snow made note of her surroundings. Though she was born in Mirea, she had spent most of her early years (before being adopted by Eldric) scrounging the city streets to desperately to survive. For a moment, she thought about Eldric and Clement. Would the Lioness truly keep them alive? The crude woman seemed so unreadable. Snow couldn't help but feel that the Lioness wanted to help as much as she wished to hurt. The fact that Snow couldn't make herself hate the woman disturbed her.

'Because we're both half-Elf.'

The conversation haunted Snow. She couldn't shake those words; she couldn't shake the fact that, in some sick, demented way, this was the Lioness' way of setting her free.

"Here," the Elf said as they approached the stones of the town of Drevn and Vanderbilt came to a small automobile with blackened windows. "Get in."

"Quite the entrance, eh?" Ayize raised a white eyebrow.

"No one is to know you are here, whoever you are."

The Darkling sighed, then motioned for the other two to enter before he did.

Once inside, the Elven knight sat at the wheel and started the car. It was dark inside, but the shadows of the dismal town could still be seen vaguely from behind their blackened glass. Beyond the dark veil, the silhouettes of the mid-sized square buildings could be seen, but none of their details could be determined. It was dim inside the car, but it didn't bother anyone. They were assassins, and thusly, their jobs were not the most comfortable. What was a little discomfort? Nothing.

The ride seemed rather long and the silence was awkward, but eventually the seemingly endless drive came to an end.

"Get out," Sir Vanderbilt said curtly, the distaste of his lord seeking non-Elven assistance still lingering in his mouth.

"So hospitable..." Ayize sad under his breath as he stepped out of the automobile.

Before them, a regal castle stood, its imposing gray stones oddly mismatched with the ancient brown color of the rest of the town. As the automobile drove across the drawbridge, the castle became even more imposing, from its long and gnarled spires to its thick bulwarks. The structure was beautiful and powerful and chilling.

"Come quietly. Count Malroi will see you now."

The most noticeable thing about the interior of the castle were the very obvious red etherlamps. Snow felt a shiver ride up her spine as the angry knight led them down the sanguine corridors, yet she quickly decided that it would only anger him if she questioned the decorations—and, quite frankly, she didn't have the desire nor energy to argue with the Elf.

It just wasn't worth it.

"Why is everything red?" Enlil blurted out in her very spacey fashion. "It's creepy!"

"How dare you!" Vanderbilt raged as he continued leading them. "The Count has only the most beautiful of tastes when it comes to decorations. I wouldn't expect you inferiors to understand—especially you, *halfling*."

Snow rolled her eyes.

Vanderbilt, though angry, realized that he himself often questioned the oddities of his lord. But he couldn't let these *inferiors* think that. He couldn't show them weakness. No. He was greater than them. *He* was an Elf. He held in his veins the blood of a race that once held the power of the Angels. The Elves may not be Angels anymore, but they damn well had pride in the fact that they once were. It didn't even matter that no one remembered when it was or how long ago. It was what they were told, and it was the truth. And that's all there was to it!

"It's creepy," the child added blankly.

Vanderbilt merely grunted, displeased, his face rife with ire.

Snow smiled. It a weird way, seeing the little Enlil incense the knight so easily brought her an amusing joy. She had only been with the child for a few months now, but she felt that the two of them had bonded, or at least they tried to bond. Snow could see that Enlil played dumb. There was no telling how long the little girl had been an assassin, but Snow could tell that the life had probably desensitized her quite early. This trauma seemed to manifest in the girl's dumbfounded and empty-headed attitude. But Snow was a good judge. It was a farce. Beneath that absent expression, a dangerous and calculating warrior dwelt.

The reddened hallway seemed to twist erratically until they were brought to a giant, heavy wooden door.

Vanderbilt came to the door and stood to the side.

"Inside," he began, "Count Mothrus Malroi awaits your presence. I don't know who you are or why your here, but if you try anything funny, I won't hesitate to slit your throats."

Ayize looked at Enlil and rolled his eyes.

"Especially you, *halfling*," the knight hissed.

"I'll take note of that," Snow said, shaking her head in frustration, "*Captain*."

Inside, the light was dim, the room illuminated merely by a faint red glow from the etherlamp positioned upon the height of the vanity at the far end of the room.

"Tell me," said the man seated at the chair, his image upon the mirror revealing the mask drawn over his face. "Are you the ones Obsidian hath sent me?"

Ayize smiled a crooked smile. "The night answers those who howl in her midst, Count Malroi."

"Then you truly are my assassins," the count said as he turned around, the red light splashing across his pale mask.

"You need someone to disappear, I hear?" Ayize replied.

"Yes," the count said. "A vampire named Ainabel."

"A vampire?"

"Yes. She stole a very valuable treasure from me, a pendant that is dear to my family line. But be wary, for a Giant resides in the Dreshden Mire, to the north of Drevn. You will find the vampire there with him probably. I trust you can do this job." He waved his hands. "Kill her and bring me this pendant, and your payment shall be final."

"A giant, huh?" Ayize raised a pale eyebrow.

"Yes," the count said, nodding. "He seems to stick to his own space, but he has proved rather troublesome in protecting the thief Ainabel. Kill him if necessary."

Enlil looked at Snow in the low light. She could see the worry on the other's face.

"Why do you need assassins to do this?" Snow spoke up. "Why not your soldiers?"

"Tell me, halfling," the Count said calmly. "Are the Black Roses assassins?"

Snow balled her fist. "Yes."

"And assassins kill, yes?"

She could feel the anger behind her gritted teeth.

"Yes."

"Then stick to killing and stop asking questions."

She looked at Ayize, who returned an impassive expression. This wasn't new for him; she could feel it.

"Tell Vanderbilt that he is to take you to the edge of the Mire. Tell him not a word more." The Elf waved his hands. "You are dismissed."

The three turned, and, just as confidentially as they had arrived, they left the room.

Outside, Vanderbilt merely stared at them with the same implacable dissatisfaction that he had been so forthright with since their arrival.

"He says to take us to the Mire," Ayize said.

The other took up a dumbfounded expression, then motioned for the others to follow.

The Dreshden Mire was a vast expanse covering the lot of southeastern Mirea. It was not only where the nation got its name, but also a mysterious realm where a supposed Angelic kingdom once prospered before enigmatically vanishing into thin air. Now, in modern times, the soupy bog was a mere wasteland, largely uninhabitable and forbidding.

Vanderbilt von Rybird reluctantly drove the three hired assassins wordlessly through the northern part of the small town of Drevn until stopping at the end of the road, which Snow determined must be because they were entering the slums. Neither Snow nor the two Black Roses wished to speak to the Elf, and it was quite obvious that the knight didn't wish to speak himself.

Eventually, they drove as far as they could and had to park and walk the rest of the way. As they walked the muddy streets filled with gross white puddles of who-knows-what, Snow looked back at the Elven eyes that seemed so intent upon watching her. It felt so strange to Snow. These eyes felt less...jarring. They weren't full of hate, for the most part. As she walked behind the Darklings, she felt that these poorer Elves had curious eyes, like that of children.

"Alright," Sir Vanderbilt said as he came to an abrupt stop. "Here it is."

Snow looked forward. It was just as she had heard. Before her and her companions, gnarled trees twisted into the air, licked by a mist that spilled into the streets like the breath of Death himself, pluming white fingers reaching into the living world, waiting to rapture any unfortunate soul into its mortal grasp.

"So here's the famous Dreshden Mire, huh?" Ayize said. "Not as amazing as I had heard."

"Yeah, it's too misty!" Enlil pouted.

"Spooky, Snow said dryly.

The Elven knight said nothing as the three passed him and entered the mist.

Night fell upon the town of Drevn as the Black Roses journeyed into the fog of the Mire. From his quarters, Count Malroi watched the full moon break the horizon. He looked out at his humble dominion. All of the lights were out, everyone done for the day from the noble to the peasant. He reached into his desk and pulled out a small black key.

It was time to *feed*.

He had ordered his men to guard the gates—an order he had done strategically some time back, and an order that was done to protect his treasure. Carefully, he slipped down the blood-red corridors to the stairs. Shadows shifted upon the cold walls as the Elven Count made his way to the dungeon. It was cold and damp, but it had been some time since a prisoner was actually held within its hopeless chains. No. Now it had been all but abandoned, given that the common criminals were simply executed now.

The space was dark, and if it were not for his Elven eyes and the shade of his mask, he wouldn't have adjusted to the blackness as quickly.

Count Malroi walked into an old cell. Stepping over the bones of some nameless and ancient fool, he came to the far wall. It looked inconspicuous, and none would think the wiser. He smiled at his ingenuity. It was almost too easy! Gently, he ran his fingers along the brick and mortar until he felt a slight snag. He pressed inward. Dust sifted from the stones as the wall began to sink in, revealing a small, dark room. For a moment, all was silent, then he heard it: a faint wafting sound.

The sound of breathing.

"Why do you say nothing, my dear?" the Count said as he stepped into the room. "Has my hospitality meant nothing to you?"

Before him, a woman, a human, was bound to the far wall, a red pendant hanging from her neck and her body covered in tattered clothes.

"You still say nothing?"

"Where is she?" the woman finally muttered, her dry throat

cracking. "Where is Ainabel?"

"Gone," the Count said, "gone for now, but soon to be forever."

"Ainabel..." the woman mumbled as if in delirium.

"Do not worry, dear," Malroi said as he took off his mask. "Our secret is safe. When the things I have put into motion come to fruition, not a soul will remain who knows of that cursed child. No, they will all be gone..."

With what dim vision she had, the woman could see the count grow closer. Malroi smiled, revealing his vampiric fangs.

"Every single one of them..."

CHAPTER TWENTY-SEVEN

The Dreshden Mire

The fire crackled as the Giant sat in the cave, his azure eyes watching the small child directly across from him.

"Ainabel, right?" he said, his voice deep and raspy.

Ainabel looked up. In the dim light, her brown eyes could vaguely determine the large man's face. His unkempt beard was long, with greasy blue hair, indicative that he's stopped grooming a long time ago. As she looked at him, she shivered as she saw the tattoo of a skull that covered his face.

"Yeah." Her voice was slight and dainty.

"What brings you here?"

The little Elf said nothing, pushing her long blonde hair over her left ear. The Giant smiled.

"Your ear," he said, "is a human ear."

"You don't care?"

"Halfling or not," the Giant spat, "it's none of my business."

"My father cares," she began. "He said that no one should ever see me...that I'm a monster."

The Giant said nothing. Ainabel looked into the crackling fire, its orange tongues popping as it devoured the wood.

"He's not a good man," she said, bringing her knees to her chest. "I know where mother is," she said, her voice cracking. "I hear her screams."

"So you ran away?"

"I did. I chewed through the ropes and left."

"And what will you do now?"

The little girl sighed as she stood, her eyes gazing up at the Giant.

"I'm going back to get Mother. I'm going back and we'll be free."

The Giant watched the little girl wander into the mists, and, for a moment, he felt a tinge of regret in his heart.

The fog was as pervasive as it was otherworldly. The three assassins walked carefully through the muck, their eyes only perceiving the first few feet in front of them.

"This mist sucks!" Enlil blurted out, psychic energy swirling in her pale green eyes. "I can't see a thing!"

"I can, kinda," Ayize said. "It's weird. It's like this mist...isn't natural."

"You think it's magic?" Snow said. "It feels like vampire magic."

"I don't know," he replied. "I can see ahead, but my soulsight is vastly hindered. We'll just have to see what happens, I guess..."

Snow just nodded. It seemed their advantage was gone, and even with her Elven senses, she too couldn't see past the white cloud that surrounded them.

The three walked silently for a while, their leather boots trudging through the soggy sludge that was the Mire. Snow couldn't help but notice that there was no real ambiance in this place. She thought several times about how they were supposed to find their way out of the Mire, much less find and defeat a powerful vampire within it. The feeling felt oddly despairing. Even her Elven eyes couldn't see but a few paces ahead, and her two Darkling companions were greatly limited without the usage of their psychic abilities.

But, despite all of that, Snow couldn't shake the intuition that she had felt all along—ever since she had been briefed by the Lioness back at the Vega Varonn. It all seemed so strange. Why hire assassins? Surely Elven knights would be more efficient than going through the dark, secret contacts to call forth the Agents of Obsidian. And even if he *was* concerned, as he said, with using his men against a vampire *and* a Giant, there were only *three* assassins, a number quite adeptly underwhelming considering the amount of knights he had. Ten knights against a single vampire would do much more damage than three assassins wandering haphazardly through unknown territory. Even a Giant should be able to be overpowered rather easily, right? Snow knew this. She had seen several knights take down vampires in her twenty years of working as the personal shield of the Master of the Inquisition. No. There was something more here. She was sure of it.

But the Mire itself was just as peculiar. It was becoming ever increasingly quieter the farther the trio progressed into its belly. Snow had already detected the lack of sound. They had walked for what she assumed to be about twenty minutes now, and the sound of the birds had all but faded into silence. *And now,* she thought, *even the sounds of my footsteps are silenced.*

Could it be?!

"Ayize! Enlil!" she exclaimed in panic. But it was true. Even her voice had gone.

Inside the Mire, all was silent.

Or was it?! She watched Ayize and Enlil before her. Their mouths were moving. They were making gestures with their hands. Enlil laughed! They were speaking!

So only me? The sudden realization shocked her. *Only I can't be heard.*

Snow reached forward to touch Enlil's shoulder.

She could feel her breath becoming more and more halted, as if her windpipe were slowly closing.

What is happening?! Her mind raced desperately. *What...*

She could feel her mind beginning to wane.

Is...

This...

Snow felt a chill rush over her body. She could feel the wetness of the mud upon her face. Then, she felt nothing.

It wasn't long before Ayize and Enlil realized that Snow no longer followed them.

"I thought so..." Ayize muttered.

"There's magic in the Mire..." Enlil finished her partner's thought.

"Great..." the Black Lotus groaned.

"Where do you think she went? I hope she's okay..."

"Well, if she dies, I think the Lioness won't be very happy." He sighed. "I guess we gotta find her."

The two stopped and took in a deep breath. Suddenly, psychic power filled their eyes.

"See her?" Enlil frowned as she looked around.

"She's beyond my perception," Ayize began. "Wherever she is, En, she's too far for me to see."

"Same..." the little Darkling scowled, then pointed in another direction. "But there's something else out there! It's big, and I don't think it's Snow! It's bright too, really strong. You think it's..."

Ayize smirked darkly. "It's our Giant."

Enlil smiled. "Wanna go kill it?"

"I do, En. The sooner the better!"

Vanderbilt von Rybird stood and stared into the mist for a moment. He didn't really know why, but everything to do with these mysterious guests left a sour taste in his mouth and a perturbing knot in his stomach. Surely, he knew he trusted his lord; he knew that the Count had the wellbeing of the people of Drevn in mind—but, still— the Count's odd and secretive actions involving this problem unnerved him.

He was not dumb. He knew who these enigmatic visitors were. He clenched his fists.

Nothing but common assassins.

Why not just send the men into the Mire at daytime? *Well,* he thought as he stared into the brumous fumes that rose from the bog before him, *that wouldn't work.* The mists of the Mire were so thick and pervasive that he assumed even the sun couldn't pierce them.

It was the question of *what* the Count wanted that bothered him. If he had hired hitmen, then it was quite obvious that he wanted someone dead—but it seemed rather unusual for someone with access to men-at-arms to do so.

Did he want the Giant dead?

But why kill the Giant?

That was the jarring thought in his mind. It didn't make sense! They had known that a Giant was residing in the bog for about a month now, but he had never once in that time seemed to threaten or pose any danger to the town. Honestly, he seemed to not want any interaction. The town and the Giant seemed to leave each other alone, and the Giant appeared to be content with this relationship.

So why kill him?

Vanderbilt trusted his lord, that was for sure. But for some reason, he just felt...off. It was as if Count Malroi wanted to deal with this problem in secrecy, no matter how counterproductive it seemed.

But why...?

CHAPTER TWENTY-EIGHT

The Test of Strength

Night fell upon the Vega Varonn and the chill of the barren desert came with it. Eldric sat upon the cot assigned to him when the Lioness had so courteously cast him into prison. As he sat, he looked above at the small slit upon the wall that was supposed to be his window. Through the bars above, he could see the stars that glittered over the silver sands below. He couldn't help his situation from inside the cell; he knew that much was true. He was, however, thinking of a way to escape. He was trying, but his mind couldn't help but wander—he thought of one thing...

He thought of Snow, and he worried about her even though he wished he couldn't.

When she had come to him before leaving, she cried. It was the first time he had seen her cry in ages, and in that moment, he saw that little girl once more. That little girl who wandered the streets of the Elven capital city—the same little girl who, despite the hate she received, had azure eyes that still sparkled when she smiled.

Eldric smirked as his eyes became a bit watery with nostalgia.

She had become one of the most fearsome warriors in the world, but, to him—to him, she would always be that little girl...

'*Your eyes are strange,*' she'd said.

'Aye, and your hair is blue,' he had responded.

He could see her now, her face contorting as her childlike mind ruminated.

'Weird eyes! Blue hair! We're quite the pair of oddities, aren't we?! Well, Snow, I say the heck with it! Embrace your differences, child. Life is full of surprises, and if you so happen to be one of them, well...so be it!'

"Are we going to cry tonight?" a raspy voice said from the other side of the cell bars.

Eldric did not turn.

"How long have you been watching me, Lioness?"

"Not long," she said, smiling. "Long enough to watch you grovel in your memories of yore."

Eldric sat silently, his eyes directed toward the window. Outside, the stars seemed so peaceful, far away paradises, distant oases of warm light adrift in the cold black sky.

"Why did you do it?" he said finally. "Why did you spare Snow?"

The Lioness folded her arms and leaned against the dusty wall. "Whatever do you mean, old man?"

"You could have killed her. You could have killed her when she stood in your way of killing me. Why didn't you do it? Why didn't you cut straight through her and take my head? What was it? Compassion, maybe?"

"Curiosity," she said. "I spared you all because she was curious."

"I don't understand..." Eldric's voice was almost a whisper, his mind pondering her words.

"She's a guard dog whose only desire was to protect the one she called master. Nothing more, nothing less. She clings to you because you accept her, but she has yet to accept herself. She cannot live in your shadow forever, old man."

"But why? She is a knight of the Church—your enemy just as much as I am. Why show her such...special treatment?"

"*Was* a knight of the church," the Lioness corrected him. She took in a deep breath, then exhaled as she shrugged her shoulders. "It was her eyes."

"Eyes?"

"The eyes are the windows to the soul, my dear Eldric. When she stepped in, I saw her eyes. They were...ablaze with passion. Those eyes were a burning. And..." she paused. "They reminded me of my own."

"And yet you knew of her half-blooded lineage!" Eldric said in a frustrated gruff as he thought of the hardships his daughter must be having right now, as he was locked away where he could not help her.

"And now she knows of *mine*!" the assassin queen shot back.

"What?!"

"You are no longer the Master of the Inquisition, Eldric of the Black Flame. She must find who she is apart from you."

"Why?!" Eldric raged. "Why are you helping her?!"

"Because I wish to. Is my autonomy too much for your Church-minded brain to wrap around?" she stepped forward toward the doorway. "Do not worry, Eldric. If she has not learned her lessons by the time she returns, well, I'll kill you all. I don't like weak people."

And, as mysteriously as she had come, the Lioness had stepped away.

Snow, Eldric thought, *I am sorry...*

The old man turned to the window once more. Outside, the stars seemed to burn holes in the night sky.

"You're really pretty," a little girl's voice echoed in Snow's mind. *"Will you help me? You won't leave me, will you?"*

Snow awoke in pure darkness. As her perception came back to her, she realized something...

She was dreaming.

"Your hair looks like his. He's nice to me. He saved me..."

Snow turned to see a pale little girl standing in the darkness.

"Mommy is in trouble. Daddy is going to bite her again. So I ran away, but I'll be in big trouble if daddy finds me here," the girl said.

The tiny girl stood among the void, her long blonde hair almost touching her ankles. Her skin was white and luminescent in the darkness, a bright midnight moon cast upon a blotted sky.

"Are you going to leave me? I don't want to be alone. This place is cold. I'm scared."

The girl smiled smiled, but she had no fangs. Snow's eyes widened as sudden enlightenment struck her like lightning upon a lone tree.

The count! the knight thought. *he lied! Ainabel wasn't a vampire.*

"You!" Snow exclaimed as her vision began to darken.

"It's cold here..."

"You're...you're Ainabel!" Snow shouted.

She could hear the echo of her exclamation growing fainter and fainter until her vision faded, and the cold returned.

Snow felt a soft warmth against her face. She could hear now, the crackling of a fire as the wood popped under the heat.

"You're awake?" A thunderous voice growled.

Snow groaned as she opened her eyes.

"Yeah, you're awake," the voice said again.

Snow looked around. She was in a cave, that was certain. It was a tall cave, roomy. Across the firelight sat a giant man with a skull tattooed upon his face, his shaved blue hair and long beard vague in the darkness.

"A Giant?" Snow said, rubbing her eyes.

"Yes," the Giant replied.

Snow held her head. "You saved me?"

"Yeah."

"Why?"

"Why do I need a reason?" he snapped. "Would you have me take you back?"

"I would not," Snow said with a scowl. "Do you have a name?"

"Beogar. I am Beogar."

"Well," Snow said, nodding, "first of all, thank you, Beogar."

"Whatever. Keep your pleasantries."

"What happened to me?" Snow said as she stood to stretch.

"The count's magic, I guess." He shrugged his massive shoulders. "Same that happens to all of them."

"So Ainabel is that child? Where is she?"

He lifted a finger and pointed at the knight. "Your hair is blue?"

Snow could feel her muscles tense. "It is."

"Then you will fight me."

Snow stopped. "What?"

"You must show me your strength. If you are strong, we will talk more."

"And if I am not?"

"You will die here by my hand."

Alarmed, Snow's hand shot to grab her blade, only to find she did not have it.

"My blades!" She exclaimed. "Where are my blades?"

"I left them," the Giant said as he stood, his head almost reaching to top of the cave. "You will fight me without them. You hold the blue hair of Lyhaal. Do you doubt your might when you hold no weapon?"

Snow was quiet for a moment, then she nodded.

"I would never stray from a fight," she said. "I shall take your challenge, Beogar."

"Very well." A dark smile crossed the Giant's face, his yellow teeth glimmering from behind the blue ink upon his face. "The first to fall upon their back loses. But be wary little blue one, if you fall to my hand, I will kill you." Beogar dropped his knees into a fighting stance. "I will have no mercy upon the weak and unfit."

Snow readied her stance as well, only she still wondered how she would cause such a massive foe to fall backward. Never before had she faced such a towering enemy.

But she knew there was a first time for everything, and she was not too keen on losing her life here.

Silence filled the cavern as the two combatants stared each other down. Snow eyed the large man, his large body dwarfing hers.

"Now!" Beogar erupted as he raised his foot. "Show me your strength!"

Snow felt her body tense as the hammering step came down upon her. Never before had she fought so daunting of a foe—but never before had she feared a challenge.

And this would be no different!

She widened her stance, hands ready. Feeling the timing in her gut, she raised her torso on collision, catching the giant's foot and using her own force to keep it from squashing her.

The struggle was silent as the two forces repelled each other.

"So," the Giant grunted as he strained to push downward, trying his best to crush the dwarfed Snow, "it seems you do have strength."

"That I do," she replied, her voice stressed as she kept her resolve to not be crushed. "I have fought many foes over my life, and never once have I succumbed to their designs, and..." she bent her knees, the sudden shift in tension causing the Giant to jolt. "I will not fail *here*!"

217

With one great heave, Snow mustered all of her strength into her legs and pushed upward with one quick motion.

"You—?!" the Giant exclaimed as he fell backward, his booming voice echoing throughout the cave. But it was too late.

With a loud crash, the Giant Beogar fell, defeated, upon his back. Snow watched for a moment as the Giant lay there.

"It seems I win," she said.

Beogar was silent.

"It seems you are strong," he said finally. "Small, but strong. I should expect someone with the blood of Lyhaal in their veins."

"Who?"

"You are a Giant, no?"

"Half Giant," she sighed. "I'm half Elf, too."

"I don't care what you are," he said as he raised himself to a seated position. "You are strong. That is all that matters. Giant, Elf, Human, vampire...none of these things matter. No matter who you are, if you are weak you are weak; if you are strong you are strong. It is might that forges the path. I knew you were a Giant by your blue hair, but if you were weak, it wouldn't have mattered. I accept you because you are strong."

'I like strong men and women, Snow...'

The words of the Lioness came to Snow's mind. Was this the same with her? Snow recalled that there seemed to be many types of people among that assassin queen's company. She thought of Enlil and Ayize.

Was this it? she thought. *Was this the lesson I was supposed to learn...?*

"Now," Beogar said, his voice pulling her from her thoughts. "You want to know about Ainabel?"

"Yes," she said, nodding. "Yes. I do."

"She is a child who wanders the mists. She was staying with me." He stroked his full blue beard. "She was a sweet child, honestly."

"Where is she?" Snow said. "The Count said she was with you?"

"She left," Beogar said with a shrug.

"Beogar," Snow said. "The Count wants her dead, but I don't know why."

The large man prodded the fire with a small stick he could barely hold. "Look in a mirror, Snow."

"A mirror—" Snow stopped suddenly.

Beogar said nothing.

"You mean—?!"

Snow stopped and looked up at the Giant. In the faint orange glow, his long blue beard shone almost purple.

"Beogar." Snow's voice was hard and adamant. "Where is Ainabel?"

The wood on the fire popped.

"She went"—he paused—"she went home."

Snow clenched her fist. Throughout her entire life, she had lived sworn to protect those in need. That wouldn't change now.

Not this time, she thought. *I won't let you die...*

CHAPTER TWENTY-NINE

A Blood-Red Revelation

It was strange. The impoverished Elves in the slums of Drevn watched in a sort of horror as a young girl, frail and weak, with blonde hair so long it touched her ankles, stepped out of the deathly fog of the Mire. She could feel the eyes upon her, but it didn't matter. None of it mattered. All that concerned her was seeing the Count—her father...

Seeing her father, and convincing him to set Yllmaire free.

Mother. The thought raced through her mind as she walked hypnotically down the streets to the castle, her brown eyes gazing hazily forward.

Move, she thought.

Move. To save Mama. Move.

Eyes watched in strange curiosity as the child stepped onto the stone street and hobbled further toward the castle.

The citizens, staring oddly, hurried themselves out of the way as the child walked among their midst.

She could feel the numbness in her legs increasing, their sensitivity gone from the frigid waters of the Mire. Ahead, she could see two guards at the castle gate. Her vision was fading as tiny white spots began to cloud her eyesight. Ahead, a soldier took notice.

"Hey! Child!" a soldier called out as he rushed toward her. "Is everything okay?!"

Ainabel could feel her legs give way. She felt the hard kiss of the pavement, then all went black.

Soulsight defied the mist; the Darklings could see Giant in their minds' eyes. As they grew closer, they saw more clearly.

"So Blue is here after all!" Enlil smiled as they gained closer to their target.

"Looks like she couldn't find our target either," Ayize said, "and it looks like our resident Giant isn't so ferocious after all..."

As the two grew closer, the dim glow of the fire became visible, the image of Snow becoming apparent.

"Blue!" Enlil cried out as the two Darklings stepped out of the mist and into the light of the fire.

"Enlil! Ayize!" Snow exclaimed. "How did you find me?"

Enlil pointed to her pale green eyes, bright with swirling psychic energy.

"Soulsight," Ayize replied. "This mist had no chance. Now"—he pointed to Beogar—"why don't you tell us what exactly is going on."

"Well," Snow began, "apparently the one we're after, Ainabel, is a little girl."

"Little girl?!" Enlil burst out. "But who would want to kill a little girl?!"

Ayize smirked. "Someone who wants to keep a secret." He turned to the Giant. "Tell me, mister Giant, what's your name?"

"The name is Beogar." The large man shrugged and stoked the fire with the small stick.

"Okay. Tell me, Beogar, this little girl—this Ainabel—what does she look like?"

Beogar said nothing, a grim visage cast over his face in the shadows.

"I get it now," the Darkling said, smirking. "I think I know what's going on here."

The idea suddenly sparked in Snow's mind.

'Look in a mirror...'

You mean—!" she gasped.

"Ainabel is the Count's daughter?!" Enlil realized, her mouth agape.

"And there's a reason he wants her dead...but why?" the Black Lotus mused, rubbing his chin. "Why would someone want his own daughter dead?"

"I think I know why," Snow said in a low growl.

In the firelight, the Darklings stared into her azure eyes.

"Ainabel," she began, "is a half-Elf."

The girl unnerved Sir Vanderbilt. She had come from the unknown, her unkempt appearance that of a feral child or at least one who had never been properly taken care of.

But it was also more than that.

"You're sure of this?" the knight said to one of his squires as they strode down the reddened halls of the castle. "Truly sure?"

"Positive, sir," the young man said with a nod. "She only has one Elven ear."

A halfling? Sir Vanderbilt's mind raced.

"And she claims to be the daughter of Lord Malroi?" he asked.

"Aye, sir knight."

"Preposterous!" Vanderbilt spat. "There's no way that the Count would dare have a half-Elf child!"

The two continued down the corridor until they came to the infirmary. Crimson light splashed upon the light brown door, its hue staining the wood the color of dried blood.

"Wait outside," Sir Vanderbilt said to the squire with a nod. "Just in case she tries to run."

The other nodded and stood ready by the door. Sir Vanderbilt took a breath as he gripped the gilded handle of the door. Was he really ready? Was he really ready to see what awaited him beyond the door? This girl, this little *halfling*, was she really the count's? Could his very lord be harboring such a secret?

No, he said to himself. There was no way. It was absolutely unthinkable. Besides, if he truly did have a child with a non-Elf, then where was the woman? Yes. That's right! There wasn't even anyone who could be suspected as the mother. The count hadn't ever been seen with a woman, much less a *human*.

He sighed and opened the door.

Inside, the half-Elf child sat upon a wooden chair, the red light from the etherlamps illuminating her shaggy golden hair a strange orange color.

"Your name?" the knight's voice was a bit harsher than he had hoped, but he stuck to it. No one, and he meant *no one*, soils the name of his lord, be it a child or an adult.

The little girl cowered, flinching at Sir Vanderbilt's inflection.

A moment passed, and yet the child said nothing. Instead, she merely stared at the ground with empty eyes. She was a mystery, Sir Vanderbilt admitted that much. He observed her frail, starved physique. Her hair was so long that, seated in the chair, she sat on it, and it still spilled from the seat to the floor. In the red lights, it was quite obvious that there were bruises around her ankles and scratches upon the whole of her body.

The knight frowned, unable to keep his sympathy away. *What is this dismal child?*

"What is your name, child?" he said once more, this time in a calmer and more empathetic tone.

The little girl let out a breath, shaky and soft.

"Ainabel..." she said, her hands beginning to tremble. "My name is Ainabel."

"Tell me, girl," the Elf said, his words rigid with no warmth present, "why do you claim to be the count's daughter? Why do you wish to sully Lord Malroi's good name?"

Vanderbilt watched Ainabel as she sat trembling in the chair, her lips quivering as tears began to well in her eyes. He couldn't help it; he couldn't help but pity the miserable child. He could see her Elven ear on her right side, contrasted by her human ear upon her left. It incensed him. To think that this small worn girl would dare attempt to soil the name of the count pumped hot ire into his veins.

"I've already said," she said with a stutter and crack of her voice, "I'm his daughter."

"Bah!" Sir Vanderbilt huffed. "And why did you come? Do you wish for his fortune, filthy *halfling?*"

"I don't want money!" she choked. The knight watched as tears began to spill from her eyes. "I want to rescue my mommy. I have to rescue mommy before he eats her!"

"Eats her?!" a ghastly expression contorted the Elven knight's face. "What is this nonsense!" he spat. "Such made-up foolery! That's enough! I'll have your head for this—"

"Wait!" Ainabel yelled out. "I can prove it!" she sniffled. "I can take you there—I can take you to mommy!"

Sir Vanderbilt held his breath for a moment. He began to think about this choice. Should he follow this child? Was this *truly* nonsense...? It perturbed him. This child, though she spouted crazy words, seemed so...*genuine.*

Are you, he thought, *are you truly hiding something, My Lord...?*

"I suppose," the Elf began. "I suppose there is no reason for which I should deny you your offer." He extended his hand. "Come, but know this: If you are lying to me, you *will* be put to death. That is certain."

Ainabel nodded.

"Now," Vanderbilt said. "Where is this mother of yours?"

"The dungeon," Ainabel said, wiping the tears from her eyes. "We have to go to the dungeon."

Snow and the two Darklings sat around the fire, the giant Beogar sitting with him, his large body taking up most of the room.

"I mean," Ayize sighed deeply, "it's not why we're here! I don't see why we're even talking about this!"

"Ayize!" Enlil hopped up, a hand on her hip and her other holding up a scolding finger. "Remember the tenets! 'Thou shalt—'"

"'Defend the poor and defenseless.' I know, En! I get the picture." He groaned a long growl. "And here I became an assassin to *escape* the priesthood..."

"I'm not going to leave that child helpless," Snow said in a stern voice. "If you disagree with me, then feel free to not participate. Leave me, even."

"Alright, alright." Ayize stood and shook the dried mud from his leather greaves. "You two and your damn morals. We'll save her, but first we have to contend with this mist."

"There's magic in the mist!" Enlil said with a hollow smile.

"Yeah," Ayize said, turning and looking out of the cave. "I'm starting to think that our count friend didn't intend to pay us in the first place."

Snow stood. "So...the *real* reason that he didn't want to send his own men was because..."

"If one of his own men went missing, there would be questions asked, but if three unknown assassins disappeared, well, the town of Drevn would be none the wiser."

"So he intended from the beginning to kill us." Snow smirked. "What a pleasant man."

"But now..." Ayize rubbed his chin, his pale green eyes intent and focused. "How do we get out?"

"What do you mean?" Snow asked. "Can't you just use your Projection magic to see through the mist?"

"I wish it were that easy, honey," the Darkling said, laughing, "but our soulsight can only see so far and, well, we're too deep into the Mire for me or En to detect anything. The technique only sees living things, after all."

"So then how do we—"

"I will help." Beogar spoke up, his large voice bouncing off of the cavern's wet walls.

Ayize scratched his head for a moment. "C-come again?"

"I'll repeat myself only once, assassin," the Giant growled as he stood. "I will help you out of the Mire."

"Ohhh! I see!" Enlil jumped and clapped her hands together. "You can just see *over* the mist!"

Beogar smirked. "Smart one, you are." He turned to Snow. "But only because you proved your strength, Valkyrie."

"Valkyrie?"

"In my home, Hawkhaven," Beogar said, "there are legends of strong Giant women, female warriors who best even the strongest of men. They are the Valkyries, and you remind me of those tales."

"I see," Snow said with a nod. "Then I will wear the title duly."

"Now," the Giant said, stepping out of the cave, "let's get out of this mist."

Ainabel led the distressed Sir Vanderbilt cautiously down the cold red hallways of the castle, keeping herself hidden to the best of her ability. The knight knew that there was no need for her to hide. There were no knights in the hallway, and all of the servants had long been dismissed, as they were only allowed in the castle proper at certain times of the day, as per the austere and peculiar orders of Count Malroi himself.

More and more did this unnerve the knight. Never before had he considered how strange this was, but now —now with the presence of the small halfling—things began to seem more...peculiar. Why? Why would the count be so intent on being alone and unseen? But there was one thing in particular that bothered him the most.

That is that, despite his years of service, it had been so long since he had seen Count Malroi's face.

It had never bothered him before, as he simply decided that the count had his mannerisms and those subjected under him were in no place to judge their higher-ups.

But *now*...now that this little girl had appeared, well...he didn't know what he should think.

The little girl seemed to know where she was going, and eventually she and the knight came to the door that led to the dungeon.

"Do you believe me now?" little Ainabel said as she tried her best to keep her hair from her eyes.

"Perhaps a bit more," Sir Vanderbilt's voice was more hesitant than he had intended. "But no one has been locked in this dungeon for years. Why would you expect me to believe that someone has been kept alive here right under our noses?"

"Because she's got the stone. She got the stone, so she wasn't hungry anymore. I had one, too, but I lost it in the swamp."

"Stone? What stone—" He shook his head. "Listen! You're wasting my time. Just show me what you want to show me already!"

Ainabel pushed the door open and the two stepped into the deathly cold air of the dark room.

The knight reached for his belt and produced a blue etherlamp. The room lit in its cool light, shining into even the deepest corners of the abandoned cells.

"See!" he raged. "No one! Just as I thought—you're a sham!"

The child said nothing. Instead, she walked over to the far wall. Vanderbilt watched curiously as Ainabel ran her fingers down the creases in the wall. Suddenly, there was a clicking noise and the walls began to move on their own. Blue light spilled into the hidden room.

The knight retched at what he saw. There, in the new room, a human woman, despaired and beaten, stood chained to the wall.

"What?!" he gasped. "What is the meaning of this?!"

"Mother!" Ainabel rushed to the woman's side. "We have to get out of here!"

"Ainabel...who...?" the woman's voice was weak and faded. "Who is this man?"

"He's a knight!" the little girl tugged said as she at her mother's shackles. "He's gonna help us get out, right?"

"I don't..." Sir Vanderbilt mumbled, feeling a ghastly sickness fill his stomach as his head swayed in waves, "...understand..."

"It's really quite simple, Vanderbilt," a voice said from the direction of the doorway.

The knight spun around, drawing his sword from his belt. An icy chill stopped him; his heart skipped a beat in horror.

At the doorway stood Count Mothrus Malroi.

"My lord?" the sword shook in Vanderbilt's hand. "I don't understand! Why? Why would you do something so horrible?!"

"'Tis truly a tragedy, my dear Vanderbilt..." the count said as he walked slowly down the steps. "If only you had stayed the ever-faithful dog."

"Explain yourself," the knight said, his voice quivering as he spoke. "Please..."

"Well," Count Malroi said, "I suppose there's no harm in telling you since you're going to die here anyway. You see"—he pointed to the far wall—"that woman was my lover once. She was my secret from this world. I loved her. We parted some time, years ago, until she returned with that malformed *thing*..." he pointed at Ainabel as she cowered behind the knight, her shaking hands wrapped tightly around Sir Vanderbilt's arm.

"Your...daughter..." the knight's arm fell from his sword's hilt. "No...you...?"

"And well, you see, you weren't supposed to find out about this, dear knight..."

"Half-blood daughter..." Vanderbilt's hollow eyes dropped to meet Ainabel. "And she..." he looked at the woman chained against the wall.

"You were..."

"Yes," the count laughed, placing his hand upon his moon-white mask. "You see, when she returned with that child, the girl was almost seven years old. She begged me and begged me to make her my countess, but"—the count said, his voice trilling with laughter—"I had *other* uses for her. You see, my dear knight, by the time she returned to beg for my heart, I had...changed."

Slowly, he took off the mask, the vague light from the outside peering in.

He smiled a fanged smile. "I drink her blood."

The knight felt faint, the beating of his heart vague in the storm of memories that swarmed his mind. Was this his lord? Was this the man he had pledged his life to? The count was ten years Sir Vanderbilt's senior. Once, he had been a mentor, brotherly and kind. In his mind's eye, Vanderbilt could no longer remember the kind man who dined with his soldiers—the patient man who long ago trained him to use the blade...

The man before he donned the mask...

Before the man behind the mask became a monster...

"You—!"

"Ainabel!" the chained woman screeched. "Run!"

Suddenly, the child burst into a sprint, releasing the knight and bolting toward the exit.

"I wanted to stray from bothering myself with you, *thing*," the count hissed, "but I'll take your life myself this time!"

Count Malroi pointed. Suddenly, a spear of hardened blood shot from his fingers.

"Die!"

Time seemed to slow for Ainabel. In the dim light, she watched the spears shooting toward her in slow motion. In that split second, she thought of the Giant—she missed him, longing for the warmth of his fire; she longed for the safety of his cave. He was nice. He was unlike everyone else.

She closed her eyes, then she heard it...

She could hear her heart pounding. Ainabel felt no pain.

She was still alive.

Thunderous wails exploded throughout the room. Ainabel's eyes shot open, her mouth agape at what she saw.

"Sir knight!" She exclaimed.

Before her, Sir Vanderbilt writhed upon the ground where he had stood in the way, the spears sticking through his gilded armor, their dark red shafts reaching outward from his shoulder and hip.

"Run, child!" he raged as he crawled to his knees.

Ainabel could feel the tears welling in her eyes; she could feel the frigid fear rocking her legs. Her ability to stand and run was fueled by pure adrenaline and her mind's sheer desperation to survive.

"I never knew you would prove so troublesome, Vanderbilt," Count Malroi said, scowling as he watched the child scurry up the stairs and into the castle. "It seems you shall yet live, unfortunate." He smirked, the faint red light from the hallway glistening upon his fangs, coating the white teeth in light red.

Vanderbilt groaned and grunted as he tried to pull the spears from his shoulder and thigh, but to no avail.

"No matter of mine," the count said as he turned toward the steps. "You've touched my blood now. Sanguine Vampiris will take over soon. You should be thankful that I'm letting you join the ranks of the undead." He waved his hands dismissively. "And when you become a vampire soon, I'm sure that woman chained to the wall will be your first feast."

Vanderbilt could feel his ire rising within him, ire mixed with panic and raw sorrow.

Why...?

Why...?

He coughed as the tears began to flow freely from his eyes.

WHY?!

"After you've transformed, perhaps I'll let you join my new knights. My new men will now shed their Elven disguises and help me rid my city of that...abomination, and anyone who saw her."

More vampires, Vanderbilt thought despairingly, and they've been in Drevn for how long, under my nose? He was supposed to serve his lord and protect the people, and unknowingly he'd betrayed his precious town.

Malroi laughed as he ascended the stairs. Vanderbilt turned to the woman chained against the wall.

"I am sorry," he said, choking and sniffling. "But I have to get away from you! I don't want...I don't want to eat you!"

"Please..." her voice was weak and halted. "Go...save my daughter...please..."

Sir Vanderbilt stopped. That was right. His count had betrayed him—no, he decided the count that was long since dead. All that was left was a monster. The knight gripped the hilt of his sword.

"I will," he said. "I promise."

CHAPTER THIRTY

The Shield's Decision

With the aid of Beogar's height, escaping from the dreadful Dreshden Mire was much easier than getting lost within it. This, however, was to be rather expected, given that the tall Giant was able to simply stand over the mists.

"What will you do now, Beogar?" Snow asked after a long silence. "You are quite alone in your cave, are you not?"

The Giant said nothing. Snow turned to her companions, who merely responded with a shrug of indifference.

"I must be alone," Beogar finally spoke up. "I am in exile, after all."

"Exile?" Snow repeated. "Your people exiled you?"

"No." Beogar exhaled deeply, a lonely, painful sigh. "I left on my own. I don't deserve to live there," he said, gritting his teeth. "Not after what I have done."

"So you're a criminal, huh?" Ayize laughed.

Enlil lit up. "What'dya do?"

"I—" He paused. "I hurt someone. I hurt someone who loved me. And betrayed him and I wounded him deeply. I cannot face him now, so I went into exile."

Ayize shrugged. "Sounds more like running away than exile to me."

"Yeah!" Enlil added. "Sounds like you kinda chickened out, Mr. Giant."

Beogar once more remained silent; he pointed forward.

"Ahead," he said.

The others followed his finger. There, in the mist, the gnarled trees of the mouth of the Mire could be discerned, their dismal black bark visible through the sheet of white fog.

"You actually did it!" Ayize said with a chuckle. "Gotta admit, Big Guy, I was beginning to think we'd never find our way out of this stupid bog."

Suddenly, Enlil stopped, her abrupt halt causing Ayize to stamp his feet to keep from knocking her over.

"Damn, En!" he cursed. "Don't stop so quick when I'm trailing you like that, I'll knock you over —"

"Something is strange," she said, cutting him off.

"Yeah," Snow added. "It's too quiet here."

"Ya know..." Ayize rubbed his blue chin. "You might be onto something. I don't see any people out either..."

"Hail! Hail!" a frantic voice burst from the silence. The three assassins' heads turned quickly to the voice.

Before them, a soldier, his armor torn and his mail shredded, was bumbling to them.

"By Obsidian's grace, guy!" Ayize exclaimed as the man tripped and fell into his arms. "What in all of Lythia is going on?!"

"Th-the count!" the soldier began, his eyes wide with fear. "He's gone mad! We tried to stop him!" the man began to choke as tears welled in his eyes. "He was...he was too strong! He killed so many guards! It was —!"

"What?!" Ayize shook his head. "Spit it out, man!"

"Vam..." the man said, his voice beginning to fail, "...pire..."

"Vampire?!" Snow's eyes opened wide. "The count?!"

"Well, well..." Ayize said as he softly placed the dead man's body upon the ground.

"I bet he was hiding his fangs behind that mask!" Enlil said, frowning. "No fun! He just lied to everyone!"

"And, it also means..."

"Ainabel's in big, *big* trouble!" Enlil finished his sentence.

"And Vanderbilt!" Snow's words left her mouth before she realized what she said. "He's in danger, too!"

"The Elf you were telling me about?" Beogar said as he too stepped out of the mist. "The same one who spat on you and gave you nothing but hatred?"

Snow's heart stopped. Beogar was right. That knight, from the moment he had laid eyes upon her, had been nothing short of unpleasant...

Yet...

"Beogar," Snow said, her azure eyes meeting his. "I know that he hates me; I know that, if given the chance, he would do nothing short of ostracize or even end me. But still...deep down...some sick, *sick* part of me..."

Snow smiled. As the Giant stared into her fiery eyes, he saw it. In those eyes, even for a split second, he saw his brother, Jarl Agmundr.

"Beogar, Ayize, Enlil," Snow said, clenching her fists, "*I want to save him.*"

The air around them was stale and silent. Suddenly, the Giant let out a thunderous, booming laugh.

"You fools and your stupid moralities."

"You can say that again!" Ayize smirked. "Snow, you're a terrible, *terrible* assassin, you know that, right?"

"Yeah, Blue," Enlil said, smiling. "I don't understand you sometimes."

Snow nodded and held out her hand. "I know it. So, what do you say? Shall we save them?"

"Ugh!" Ayize gagged.

"Hmm..." Enlil held her finger to her chin. "I mean, that guy did try'ta kill us..."

"Yeah..." Ayize sighed. "Alright, Blue," he said finally. "But you owe me, and I don't forget my debts."

"Aye," Snow agreed, turning to Beogar. "What say you, Beogar? Will you help?"

Beogar stood still, his eyes upon Snow. This woman. He never thought he'd meet someone like her outside of Hawkhaven. *Perhaps*, his mind drifted, *perhaps this is my chance to change.*

"The bastard count tried to kill me, as well," he said with a smile, his teeth pale against the blue skull tattoo that covered his face. "Let's give him a visit, shall we?"

Ainabel sprinted down the cold halls of sanguine light, her floor-length blonde hair trailing behind her. She didn't care where she was running, as long as she escaped her father, that was all that was important. All around her the corpses of soldiers littered the halls, such a plethora of cadavers that she found herself swerving and jumping to avoid falling. Her vision blurred; she couldn't help it.

No matter how hard she tried, she just couldn't stop the tears from falling from her eyes. Streams of crystalline sorrow were warm and salty on her tongue; despair filled her heart.

Why, father? she thought, her sorrow melding into anger. *Why did you do this?! Why?*

Am I really so horrible?!

Is my existence really such a bad thing?!

Bumbling down the hallway, she felt her heart slamming against the walls of her ribcage. In that moment, she thought of the Giant.

In that moment, oh, how she wished he were here.

Snow, accompanied by Ayize and Enlil and followed closely by Beogar, rushed down the ghostly streets of Drevn, her eyes set upon the castle ahead.

"Alright!" Ayize said. "Been a while since we've fought one of those fangfilths, hasn't it, En?"

"Yeah!" her tone was almost elated.

"You remember the rules?"

"Yup!" she laughed. "Don't let 'em hit ya! And Projection magic works great!"

"We have to find Ainabel and Vanderbilt, too," Snow added.

"Right, right..." Ayize groaned.

Enlil frowned. "But how are we gonna get *inside* the castle?!"

"Leave that to me," Beogar said. "That measly drawbridge is nothing compared to the strength of a Giant."

Snow nodded. "Very well."

By night the town was deathly quiet. The squares once filled with commerce were now desolate and reminiscent of the despair happening around them. Despite the silence, Snow kept her Elven eyes ever astute, her vigilance enhanced by both her Elven blood and the psychic scouting abilities of her two Darkling companions.

"Dead quiet..." Ayize said in an almost breathy whisper.

"There's no one here..." Enlil added. "My soulsight isn't detecting anyone. It's like no one is here—"

"Or no one *alive* is here," Ayize added.

"You think?" Snow said as a chill rode up her spine.

"Not ruling it out, that's all."

This wasn't the work of one vampire. Snow suddenly realized they were walking into a bigger fight.

The four rushed down the streets for a short time. The town was a rustic kaleidoscope of architectural styles, a hodgepodge where the fashions of histories collided together. It was obvious that the city had been around for quite some time. Tall buildings of white marble ascended into the sky—signs of the competence of ages long passed. Snow couldn't help but notice the out-of-place feel the newer buildings held, their rough, dirt-orange bricks coarse and unsightly.

"Hey, Blue." Ayize pointed his finger forward. Snow turned her gaze ahead. Before them, several soldiers stood at the drawbridge, blades drawn.

"They're vampires," Enlil said, her blank eyes filled with swirling green energy.

"Easy enough," Beogar said, stepping forward. "Watch."

The Giant took the lead, walking speedily toward the vampires. Ahead, the vampiric soldiers brandished their blades, yelling curses in a desperate attempt to stop the Giant's charge.

But it was to no avail. As Beogar began to pick up speed, the vampires rushed forward as well, their blades high in the air. The two parties met. Swords rained down as the giant Beogar lowered his fist in one giant sweep. It was over in a matter of seconds. Beogar, his large fist swooping with immense speed, ignored the sharpness of the blades. Collecting the limp bodies of all the small soldiers all at once, he slammed against the stone walls of the buildings. Snow scowled at the crunching sound of the bodies as their bones broke. The corpses fell, and blood began to flow.

"That's...good and all," Ayize yawned as he and the others caught up to the Giant. "But those cuts on your hand are riddled with vampire blood. And we don't have any way of healing you once you become one of them."

"Heh," Beogar huffed. "Fret over your own self, assassin. I am a Giant, one of the blessed blood of Lyhaal. Vampires mean nothing to me. I am immune to their curse."

Immune, huh? The thought hung in the back of Snow's mind.

"That's cool Mr. Big Guy!" Enlil giggled. "You really showed them though!" she threw up her hands. "*CRUNCH! SPLAT!*"

"Alright, Beogar." Ayize pointed to the drawbridge. "Do your thing."

Beogar smiled darkly. "With pleasure."

The Giant approached the moat and stepped into it without caution. The cold waters sank to his waist. Deliberately, Beogar curled his fingers around the sides of the wooden bridge.

"Watch carefully," he chuckled.

The Giant began to heave the bridge upward, his muscles flexing as he gripped the wooden bridge. For a moment, nothing happened, then, suddenly, the wood began to crack and pop under the pressure. With one massive pull, the Giant bent backward, and the large wooden bridge popped ripped of the hinges.

He had done it; Beogar had removed the drawbridge, and the doors to the castle were now open.

CHAPTER THIRTY-ONE

Nothing Like You

The dark courtyard was surprisingly and eerily empty.

"It's as if all life has left this place entirely..." Ayize said as he scratched the side of his face.

"It's like a graveyard..." Enlil's voice was as soft as a breath.

"Just less resistance for us, really —" Ayize started.

"Look!" Snow shot forward, interrupting the Black Lotus.

The two Darklings and Beogar looked forward. Ahead, the silhouette of a child was sprinting toward them through the blackness.

"Hey!" Snow said as the child, a little girl, ran into her arms. "Are you alright?"

The girl said nothing, her body quivering, chest heaving in and out as she desperately tried to catch her breath.

"Don't worry, dear," Snow began, when suddenly she stopped.

As the child looked up at her, Snow could see her mismatched ears, one human, one pointed, Elven.

Snow exhaled in relief. "Ainabel!"

The girl looked up with flooded eyes. "You?"

"Yes. You remember me?" Snow stroked her hair in an attempt to calm her. "Beogar told me all about you. Don't worry, child. You're safe."

"B-Beogar?" she sniffled. "He's here?"

Ainabel wiped her eyes and smiled when she saw that the Giant was indeed among them.

"So this is the kid?" Ayize said as he caught up to Snow. "Poor thing."

"Don't worry, Annie!" Enlil bent down beside her and smiled. "We're gonna help big time!"

As Beogar approached, the small girl broke from the others and sprinted toward him.

"Tell me, kid," the Giant said as he bent down. "What happened here?"

"Daddy," she choked. "Killed everyone. Everyone except mommy and that nice knight! That knight saved me!"

Snow bent down beside her. "Tell me, Ainabel, what was the nice knight's name?"

The little girl scratched her head with trembling fingers. "Daddy called him Vanderbort...bild...I can't really remember..."

"Vanderbilt!" Snow stood immediately and turned to Ayize and Enlil. "He's alive. I knew it!"

"Alright," Ayize groaned and pointed a stern finger at her. "I'm in, but remember. You. Owe. Me."

Snow smiled and nodded. "Gladly."

Vanderbilt could feel his body growing colder as he ran down the halls of the castle. He knew what was happening.

He would be a vampire before long now.

But that was not important. Right now, the only thing running through his mind was one loud, indomitable thought: he had to kill him. He had to find and kill Count Mothrus Malroi.

Finding him wouldn't be hard. He knew that the vampiric count would have probably gone to ballroom. He didn't know why he thought this, but the idea seemed plausible. Every hall in the castle eventually lead to that room, so it would be a safe assumption that the lord would guess Ainabel got lost and wound up there.

Vanderbilt knew he didn't have much time. He pushed past his wounds, limping down the halls as fast as he could, his blade hungry for vengeance.

This time he wouldn't be made the fool.

This time he would soak his blade in the blood of his lord.

Beogar, at the urging of Ainabel, stayed behind with her, but it was not like he could have entered the castle doors anyhow.

Snow, trailing behind the two Darklings, rushed down the hallway.

"I see something ahead," Ayize said. "It's alive, so I'm guessing it's our Count Malroi."

"There's two," Enlil added. "One isn't very strong."

"Vanderbilt," Snow said.

"His light is fading," Enlil continued. "He's hurt."

Snow nodded. "We must hurry."

Sir Vanderbilt entered the ballroom, his blade drawn. The pain from where he removed the blood spears had long since stopped; his body had become cold.

The room was vast and well-windowed; the night sky behind the glass bathed it in black void. It was just as the knight had expected. Just as he had anticipated, there, at the far end of the courtroom, stood Mothrus Malroi.

"So you yet live, dear Vanderbilt?" the count said.

"Silence, fangfilth!" Vanderbilt shot back. "Your time is at its end!"

"Foolish knight." The count's voice was low and soft, almost like a caress. "You were the one I wished I would not have to kill, yet behold where we stand—*with blades at each other's throats...*"

"Just tell me...why?" Vanderbilt's sword began to lower. Never in his life had he ever thought that he would have to point his blade at the man he respected most.

No. *Once* a man...

Now, Count Mothrus Malroi was a monster.

"Why not?" the count smiled. "Do you not understand the context of the world, sir knight?" he held out his red-painted fingernails and began to inspect them. "We are the Elves, scions of the most powerful race to ever exist—scions of the Angels of the ancient Morning Star Kingdom. Once, our people ruled the world with an iron fist! We prospered because we were strong! We lived with the greatest advancements known to man! We were like *gods*!"

The count held up his hands.

"And it is our time once again! Emperor Zilheim will lead us to a new future! A *second* Morning Star Kingdom! Tell me, Sir Vanderbilt, do you not have pride in your lineage? Do you not have joy in the future your people are creating?"

Sir Vanderbilt could feel his heart begin to race, fluttering against his ribs. His body felt cold and dead; the knight fell to his knees.

"My Lord..." he began, his armor clanked as it fell to the stone floor. "...I...I don't know..."

The count's face darkened, his pale eyes growing wintry and hard.

"Then," he said, holding up a finger, "perish with your weak uncertainties!"

Sanguine spears of hardened blood shot from the count's fingers, speeding rapidly toward the fallen knight.

So, Vanderbilt thought, his mind a whirl, *so, this is it? This is where I die?*

The knight closed his eyes and accepted death—

Suddenly, a great wind passed him, followed by the sounds of footsteps. Vanderbilt waited for a moment, awaiting the sting of the spears and the embrace of death.

But it did not come. The knight opened his eyes.

"*Halfling*?!" he exclaimed in ghastly surprise. "What are *you* doing here?!"

Before him, between Vanderbilt and the maniacal count, stood Snow, holding the spears of blood in her hands.

"You're asking me?" Ayize said as he rushed to her side.

"Blue wanted to save you, that's why!" Enlil gave the knight a scowl.

"You..." He turned to Snow, who was facing forward. "You wanted to...save me?"

Snow said nothing, her stark azure eyes set forward, locked onto the count. She knew that this man—*this monster*—had gone too far. She thought of Ainabel, small and frail, beaten and broken. She thought of Ainabel's story of her mother and how the count held them as slaves.

This man. Snow's mind was set. *This man must be stopped, right here.*

Right now.

"But *why*?!" Vanderbilt suddenly erupted.

"Why what?!" Ayize shot back in an annoyed tone.

"Why, halfling?!" the knight raged. He couldn't help it, but tears began to well in his eyes. "I spat on you! I cursed your name and your lineage! I gave you *nothing* but hate! So why? Why save me? Why fight for my sake? Why would you shed blood for the very man who ridiculed and rejected you?!"

The room was silent.

"It's easy, *Elf*," Snow finally said, her voice strong and hard. "You did hate me. You did curse me. You did spit at me. But I still fight for you..." She thought of Eldric and smiled.

You're right, Father. Her heart was happy. *I don't owe you anything anymore. I'm my own woman now, but that won't stop me...*

"I fight for you despite it all..."

...from living how you taught me to live!

"I shed blood for you even in your hatred, Vanderbilt, because *I'm nothing like you!*"

"H-halfling..." the Elf's word was a single breath of surprise, a sigh of relief.

"My name," she said, "is *Snow*."

The knight felt a strange feeling. Deep in his cold chest, he could feel a small warmth. It made sense, and didn't, at the same time. For the first time in his life, he felt far from his station. It was if, for the first time, he felt truly weak—and in his true weakness, this woman—the one he hated most—had been the very one to save him.

It made sense now. He was wrong. He was *very* wrong.

"Enlil," Ayize said, "take the knight out of here."

"Wait—" Sir Vanderbilt began when suddenly a piece of thick cloth gagged him.

"No biting, Mr. Meanie!" Enlil smiled as she held up a reprimanding finger. "Now follow me!"

"Mmmph—"

"I said c'mon!" Enlil yelled once more, hoisting the Elf to his feet.

As the knight followed the small Darkling out of the room, Snow reached down and picked up the sword that Vanderbilt had left behind.

"Troublesome." The count's voice echoed throughout the large ballroom. "To think that the assassins I hired would have honor and morals," he hissed. "Despicable."

"She's the one with the morals," Ayize said, grinning darkly. "I'm just here to kick your ass for leading me to die in that stupid Mire."

The count chuckled. "So you figured it out, did you? Yes. You were meant to die in the misty wastes of the Dreshden Mire once you found and eliminated the Giant and Ainabel." He sighed, his head cocking slightly to the left, a devilish grin crescent upon his lips. "But it seems that is not the case."

"Ainabel," Snow began. "She's your daughter?"

"Yes. A worthless child-thing of a daughter."

"I think I understand now," Snow added. "Ainabel is a half-Elf, so if you were to accept her as your own, you'd lose reputation points and likely loyalty—and money too."

"Ah," the count said, smiling. "So you pieced it together?"

"You're a sick freak," Ayize growled.

"And we know your secret now," Snow said as she smiled, pointing the blade forward. "There's nowhere left to run."

The room was still, the tension of the two parties static and heated. Suddenly, the count burst into laughter.

"Run?!" he wiped a tear from his eye with a long red fingernail. "I wouldn't *dare*!"

Suddenly, spears of hardened blood shot from his body, spiraling toward Ayize and Snow.

"Blue!" the Darkling yelled.

"Right!" Snow said as she sliced through the spears with her Giant strength.

Speedily, the two broke forward, sprinting and weaving as more spears of blackened blood shot forth.

"Ayize!" she exclaimed as she watched a spear of blood shooting directly for her Darkling companion.

Suddenly, psychic energy filled his eyes. With trained speed, his hands came up to his chest. Snow watched as a multicolored aura of energy engulfed his hand. The spike of blood came fast, but not fast enough. As the spear was about to pierce his heard, he pushed his hands closed. There was a great cracking noise as the magnetic push of the two poles of his hands collided, disintegrating the hardened blood into sheer atoms.

"Go!" he yelled back.

Snow shot forward, slamming Sir Vanderbilt's sword against the spikes with incredible strength. The spikes came out like overgrown vines, twisting and shooting forward as the nervous Count Malroi cowered behind them.

"Now, Ayize!" she yelled out. "Black Lotus time!"

"Don't tell me what to do!" the other griped. Ayize spread his arms out wide as he moved forward.

"*Third Commandment*," he exclaimed. "*Lotus Genesis!*"

At his command, a blast of psychic energy exploded from his body, tearing through the thorns of darkened blood, eviscerating them down to a molecular level.

Count Malroi shielded his eyes as a phantasmagoria of light filled the room.

"Now!" the Darkling called into the air.

Suddenly, the silhouette of Snow erupted from the glow. For a moment, time seemed to slow as her fierce azure eyes meet the count's fearful gaze.

She thought of Eldric. In her mind, she could see him walking away. It was if she could hear his voice.

'*Snow*,' she remembered him saying, '*you owe me* nothing!'

"Ayize!" she roared as she leaped through the air, long disbanded from the knight's broken blade. No. This time, she was above her opponent, fist reared back. "I'll try it *your way!*"

"What—?" the Darkling shot back.

Count Malroi froze as their eyes met. Snow inhaled sharply, recalling Enlil's words, psychic blue swirling in her eyes.

Focus, Snow thought, *block it all out!*

Like a great war-hammer, blue energy exploded from her fist as it collided with the count's face. Immense force ruptured from the blast, blue light rending the ground beneath them, the tile and foundation of the entire ballroom collapsing into the dungeon below.

Dust filled the air as Ayize fell to the bottom along with the others.

"Did you...?" He said as the veil finally settled. "Was that—?"

"Projection?" Snow finished his sentence. "Yes."

"You!" the voice of a woman called out from the darkness. "You—Malroi—he..."

"Wow, Blue..." Ayize said in a mix of shock and a chuckle of amusement. "You killed him."

He looked down at the count. The once vampiric lord now lay upon the ground, his face vaporized and his skull crushed inward.

"Yep," Ayize said casually. "He's one-hundred-percent dead." He turned to see Snow breathing heavily. "Good job, Valkyrie. But, you use power like that again and, well, you'll melt your brain."

"Really?" Snow said, a ghastly expression washing over her face.

"I dunno," Ayize said, snickering and shrugging. "Maybe."

"Wh-who are you people?" the woman called out again.

Snow and Ayize turned to see the faint vision of a woman chained to the wall.

"We should be asking you the same thing," Ayize said. "Who are *you*?"

"Ainabel!" the woman cried out. "Where is she? Is she okay?"

"I see," Snow said as she stepped over stone and rubble to approach the woman in chains. "You must be her mother."

"Yes," the woman said, nodding frantically. "Is she okay?"

"She is." Snow turned to Ayize and nodded her head in the woman's direction.

"I know, I know..." he groaned.

"Who are you?!" the other woman said, this time louder.

"Don't yell," Ayize said, scowling. "You wanna get outta here or what?"

The woman cowered as the Black Lotus held his hands to the chains, first to one shackle holding her to the wall, then the next. Each time, psychic energy appeared in a rainbow of colors between his hands, and, each time, the chains disintegrated under the pressure.

"Alright," Ayize said, letting out a deep breath as the woman fell into Snow's arms.

"That technique," Snow began. "It tires you out, doesn't it?"

"Yeah," he said. "All Projection magic has a price. Soulsight is low risk, but the higher echelons command greater risk to my mental state. Don't wanna melt my brain or anything."

"Where is Ainabel?" the woman said, Snow helping her to stand.

"First is first." Ayize held up his hand. "What's your name?"

"Ayize," Snow warned. "She's a bit traumatized. Can't you be a bit softer?"

"I don't care. What's your name?" he pointed to the bite marks on her neck. "You've definitely been fed upon, but you're not one of those fangfilth. How?"

"My name is Yllmaire..." the woman's voice was dry and hoarse as she fell to her knees. "And I don't know." She held up the red stone around her neck. "He gave me this—said that it would keep me..." she said, beginning grow short of breath, "fresh."

"Well," Ayize muttered to himself, looking at the smooth crimson stone. "Sounds a lot like the one Enlil saw in Ildar..."

"What?"

"Here," Snow said as she scooped the woman up to carry her in her arms. She was unsurprisingly light to the half-Elf knight, but between the starvation and the strength given to Snow by the blood of Lyhaal, that was to be expected.

"You're very strong for an Elf," Yllmaire commented.

Snow smiled. "I'm only half Elf, actually." She turned to Ayize. "Let us go to Ainabel and the others."

CHAPTER THIRTY-TWO

The Half-Blood Key

Ainabel sprang up and ran to her mother as soon as Snow and Ayize emerged from the castle doors. Snow had carried Yllmaire for a while, but eventually the woman decided that she wanted to try to walk some herself. After a moment, she finally had the strength to take her first steps, though she still needed to stabilize herself by holding Snow's arm. Snow and Ayize slowed their walking to her pace.

"Mother!" Ainabel cried, tears beginning to flow from her eyes. "You're safe!"

"*We're* safe," Yllmaire began to weep as she fell to her knees to embrace her darling daughter.

"What happened to father? Is he still going to hurt us?"

"No, child. I don't believe that he'll ever hurt anyone again."

"What happened?"

Yllmaire turned to Snow. "Our friends...got rid of him."

Fear left the little girl's eyes. For once in her life, she felt the air of freedom. Ainabel ran to Snow and embraced her waist.

"I knew you would do it! Your hair is blue, just like nice Mr. Beogar! I knew you were just like him! I just knew it!"

A small, soft smile covered Snow's face. "Ainabel," she said as she stroked the young girl's hair. "Where is Sir Vanderbilt?"

"He's over here!" Enlil called out, pointing downward to the knight who lay still upon the ground.

Snow smiled at the child once more, patted her on the head, then walked over to the knight.

Ayize raised an eyebrow. "Is he dead?"

"Nah," Enlil said, scratching her head. "He was trying to be all bitey and stuff, so I knocked him out."

"Jeez, En..."

"So, he's a vampire now?" Snow sighed as her eyes filled with sorrow.

"He doesn't have to be," Beogar spoke. The Giant had crawled out of the moat and now sat in the clearing of the courtyard.

Snow's head snapped up. "What do you mean?"

"We of the blood of Lyhaal are blessed by the Aeon Lunae, and as such are immune to the dreadful vampire disease. There are ancient legends that our bloods were once sought as panaceas for the illness. True or not, though, I do not know."

"Well"—Ayize threw his hands up—"let's use your blood. We didn't save this bastard for nothing, did we?"

Beogar shook his head slowly. "My blood is pure. His body would reject it and he may die."

Silence fell upon the others. In the distance, a faint sliver of the encroaching dawn was turning the horizon green as the golden day met the bruise-blue night.

Beogar looked at Snow. He watched her as she stared intently at the fallen knight, then he smiled and laughed softly to himself.

Maybe, he thought, *just maybe I was wrong, my dear brother. Maybe you were right. Maybe honor is worth something after all...*

"I'll use *my* blood," Snow said suddenly, her eyes rising to meet Beogar's. "I have Elven blood as well, so his body won't reject it. My blood will heal him!"

Snow bent down on her knees, her eyes fixed on the unconscious Elven knight before her. She inhaled and exhaled deeply.

"Here we go," she said.

Suddenly, Snow bit down upon her thumb, her teeth bearing down with as much force as her nerves would allow until, finally, she pierced the skin. She held out her hand. Her Giant strength had allowed a deep cut, which now bled freely.

Enlil contorted her face. "That's gross."

"Now," Snow said. Slowly, she put her bleeding thumb into the knight's half-open mouth and held it there. His body was cold as the night air, and she could feel that his breath was beginning to falter. With her other hand, she closed his jaw and his lips automatically closed as well.

In the distance, the rising sun was beginning to break the horizon, its aurous eye opening to peer upon all of Lythia.

"The sun!" Enlil held her hand to her mouth in a mixture of anxiety and awe.

Snow could feel her thumb throbbing, the blood flowing from it and into the knight's mouth.

Come on. Her mind was a flurry of feelings; her heartbeat quickened. *Please. Please wake up, sir knight.*

Then, she felt it: warmth. Her mind spiked. Warmth was returning to his body. Sir Vanderbilt opened his eyes slowly, and Snow removed her thumb from his mouth.

"You..." he said in a hoarse voice, their eyes meeting.

In the distance, the sun had now shown its face. The pristine light of the sun had triumphed the night, splashing everything in gold.

"I'm not..." the knight gasped as he felt the warm morning rays upon his face, "I'm not turning to dust?"

"Because you aren't a vampire anymore," Ayize said, eyes wide. "Snow's blood saved you...she actually did it. She cured your vampirism..."

Sir Vanderbilt looked at Snow once more.

"You...saved me?"

"That is what it appears to be, sir knight," she said with a smile. "Good thing I'm a halfling, no?"

The Elf said nothing. Instead, he merely looked at Snow in silence, though it was obvious that he was trying with his entire might to hold back tears.

"Thank you," he said finally, "Snow."

A day passed. With the help of the now Count Vanderbilt von Rybird at the helm, the town of Drevn was beginning to rebuild. He had denied the title ferociously, insisting the woman kept captive by his lord deserved the castle, but at the urging of the Lady Yllmaire, he had accepted the seat. The townspeople were not harmed; their absence the night before was facilitated by the surviving knights who were able to escape the massacre caused by Mothrus Malroi. These few heroes who risked their lives to warn the citizens of Drevn all unanimously bowed to Count Vanderbilt once they heard of his bravery and valor in his confrontation with the vampiric Malroi. Vanderbilt, now the standing lord, swore lifelong asylum to Ainabel and Yllmaire, swearing to treat them as royalty until Ainabel came of age and could become countess, if she wished.

No one knew about Snow or the other Black Roses. And it was nightfall when the trio stealthily left the castle and ventured back toward the *Prometheus*. The forest south of the town was as dense as they had remembered, lit in spotted areas by the ivory light of a full moon. They were silent as they moved. The forest was still as well, with only the sounds of the soggy floor present in the lonesome wood.

The *Prometheus* wasn't far away, and Ayize had no problem leading them in the correct direction (when asked how he knew where it was, he merely shrugged). The three pushed through the brush and into the clearing, when suddenly they stopped in their tracks.

Ahead of them in the clearing, between them and their escape, stood a solitary shadow—the silhouette of a man, lit merely by the silver light of the moon.

"Halt!" the shadow said as it threw its hands up in surrender. "I mean you no harm!"

"That voice?" Snow said. "Sir Vanderbilt?!"

As she approached, he became more visible in the midnight light. It was him; indeed did Sir Vanderbilt, newly a count, stand before them.

"What brings you this far out?" Snow asked.

"Well," he started. The Elf's voice was different. It wasn't coarse or vile like it was when they first met him. It was small and soft, contemplative even. "I wanted to return here—I hoped I would catch you."

"I don't understand?" Snow's tone met his softness.

Count Vanderbilt looked upward, the moonbeams reflecting white upon his light eyes.

"When we first met," he began, "I wanted nothing more than misfortune for you. I derided you; I spat on you; I gave you nothing but hate—hate that had sat within me my entire life. But you saved my life—you saved me. Even after I rejected you, you still put your life upon the line for me."

In the moonlight, Snow could see the knight's eyes began to glisten with tears. His voice began to crack.

"I thought about your words to me. You made me look inward, and when I did, I did not see the pride of Angels. I saw a *coward*, and I hated myself for it. You were right, Snow. You are nothing like me. Were I in your position a day ago, I would not have put my life upon the line for you." He took a deep breath. "But never again. I see now. We are many people, from all walks of life—from all shapes, sizes, genders, races—but we are just that: First and foremost, *we are people*. We are beings with dreams and aspirations, we all seek love and we all hold value. We are people, and we should be treated as such. *You* taught me that last night; *your* actions have shown me the truth."

"Sir Vanderbilt..." Snow whispered, wide-eyed.

Suddenly, the count fell to one knee, kneeling before Snow.

"Lady Snow," he said, his voice shaky and filled with purpose. *"Thank you!"*

Snow smiled, crouching to his level.

"Sir knight." She placed a comforting hand upon his shoulder. "You are too hard on yourself. You saved Ainabel, correct?"

"I—"

"You were misguided," she said. "You were ignorant and belligerent, and, yes, you were hateful, and your words were vile, even. But you risked vampirism to save a half-blood child. You may have been a man filled with terrible things, but when it came down to the courage to save a child, you cared naught what she was. You are no coward, my friend."

Count Vanderbilt relaxed his shoulders as he let out a deep breath. A small smile formed upon his lips as tears began to flow freely down his cheeks.

"Lady Snow," he began, "I do not know where you came from or where you are headed. I do not know your life or your past." The count stood and brushed off his pants at the knee he had knelt on. "But should a day come that you need anything whatsoever, you are always welcome in my court. You, and your friends, are always welcome in the town of Drevn."

Snow smiled and nodded. "I will remember, my friend."

The other nodded.

"Are we done with all the emotional..." Ayize made a sour face. "Mush?"

Snow smiled at the discomfort of her companion, then shared a final nod with Sir Vanderbilt before turning away. The count watched in silence as the three boarded the airship. Thoughts swam in his mind as the ship rose, and, before he knew it, it was gone. As quickly as they had come, they had left.

The night was silent then, and Count Vanderbilt stargazed for a while before returning to the town.

CHAPTER THIRTY-THREE

The Devil-Eyed Lady

The red-haired woman stood before Eldric in his dreams, saying nothing. *Of course she said nothing,* he thought. *She's never said anything, so why would this time be any different?*

Eldric looked into her demonic eyes.

"Why are you here?" he asked.

No response. She just merely smiled at him and drew herself closer.

"Who are you?" Eldric snapped. "Why are you in my dreams?! Are you my mother? My grandmother?! Who are you?!"

The woman said nothing. Instead, she came close to the old man, taking his hand in hers. Her pale skin was soft and warm. Slowly, she raised his hand. Eldric watched intently as she took the tip of her index finger and placed it lightly upon his.

"I don't understand?" Eldric's voice was noticeably irritated. "What are you trying to say?"

The woman released the old man's hands and stepped away.

Eldric watched questioningly as she raised her index finger, pointing it forcefully forward. For a split second, small sparks rode up and down her finger; tiny whiskers of black lightning seemed to surround her fingertip.

"Are you...?" Eldric began.

But he never finished his sentence before he woke.

Eldric awoke on the ground of his cell. He knew he wasn't alone. He knew that somewhere in the room, an assassin waited, concealed by the shadows that seemed so common in the worn interior of the Lioness' tower. But, for all purposes, he simply acted as if he were alone in the room.

Alone in the room, maybe, but not alone in his thoughts.

No. As the old man tried to get comfortable upon the coarse burlap sack that was meant to be his bed, his mind began to whirl, set aflame anew. He couldn't take his mind off of the dream.

Could it be?

Eldric was in his sixties by now, and all his life, his devilish black flames had been the strongest force he had ever conjured. Those flames were cursed and wrathful, and many a foe had found themselves undone by the power of their unholy brilliance.

But, all this time, was he not truly at his potential? He held up a worn, bony, leathery finger. His body's aging was accelerated by the Devil's Blood within him. Could it be? Could the mysterious red-haired maiden in his dreams be telling him something more—showing him something he had never seen before, something he'd never dare to imagine?

"*I see...*" he said in a low whisper. "*So that is how it is?*"

CHAPTER THIRTY-FOUR

The Bird and the Snake

The room was lit silver, the full moon bringing with it the cold that was so usual for a night in northern Aestriana. No wind howled or stirred, and this deeply concerned Marko Jharres.

It was unusual. The wind spoke to him every night, whispering in his ears the secrets of the world and ancient wisdoms. But most importantly, the wind told him of Clement. It told him that his cousin had survived, but Marko could have ascertained this without the esoteric magic of the Four Winds. He knew quite explicitly about Clement's resilience and perseverance. It almost sickened him. Of all of the hardships in the world, it was quite often the most difficult to snuff the heart-fire of the honorable.

A wry smirk curved his lips.

No. That's not right. There is one thing that is harder than that...

It is hardest to silence the stupid.

Of course, the fallen prince no longer had the might of his Red Ravens and he was now a blind man. He was no longer a lion, but a lamb awaiting slaughter.

Yet, Marko still worried.

What to do...? What to do...?

He didn't know why, yet he knew that as long as his cousin lived, there was hope for the future.

And Marko *hated* that hope.

I know what I shall do, he thought with clever amusement.

"I believe," the trickster said to himself, "I believe I will go to Empyria and pay the kings a visit."

Time meant nothing here, but Clement knew that his very life was on a mortal clock, its hands ticking ever closer to his doom. The burning chariot barreled over the blurry fields of ethereal grassland below, burning its path through the sky. Clement took in his surroundings. The realm of Empyria was such an alien world compared to that of his own. It was as if everything seemed like oil paint upon a canvas that had not yet dried. The grasslands below seemed to sway even though there was no wind blowing. He looked upward. The clouds were a wild phantasmagoria of blues and yellows and oranges and purples, all seeming to shift around like droplets of ink splashed into a glass of water. Above these cloud-like formations, the sky was a blank white, a bleached veil lit above by a single black star, distant and forever unobtainable.

"You fight well, young prince!" the large Aeon of War bellowed with a deep and hearty laugh. "I haven't met anyone of Vhryt's blood to be as much of a warrior as yourself. Usually they are more...bookish types."

"I don't mind books," the prince replied with a chuckle. "As heir to the throne, I am not without my classical education; however"—he looked at the jolly Yeornyeim and smiled—"I understand swords more than I do books."

The other erupted into joyous laughter. "I like you, Serpentspawn!"

"Tell me, Great Aeon," Clement began, "where can I find Vhryt?"

"You seek them?"

"Yes. There are things I must know, things I must ask them."

Yeornyeim was quiet for a moment, then sighed.

"Listen to me, young prince," he said. "I will fulfill my promise to take you to them, but"—the Aeon paused, a sudden tension formed cast over his face—"do not be surprised by what you will find there. Sometimes, things are as they seem, but most of the time they are not.

You would be best to go without expectation, especially where Vhryt is concerned, for they are a fickle sort. Wise, yes, but more so mercurial."

"I don't understand?"

"Soon you will," the Aeon said, the red flames of his beard flickering as he rubbed his chin. "Your Aeon is as unpredictable as the wind. I do not know what will happen to you once you step off of my chariot, but I can be certain it will be uncertain."

In the distance, Clement could see a white spire, its strong ashen form unlike the rest of this peculiar realm. The longer Clement stared at it, the more he could be certain that, unlike the sky and earth around him, this structure did not have the ephemeral appearance everything else did.

"You see it?" the god of war asked, pointing at the encroaching monolith. "The Spire of the Sky Snake. *That* is where you will meet the one you seek: *there* is where you will meet Vhryt."

A silence hung between them. The chariot rode through the air briskly, the chilly Empyrian air whipping Clement's short brown hair about his face. As he watched the spire approach, he bowed his head.

"Prayers will do you no good here, prince," Yeornyeim laughed. "No. In this land...well, you only have *yourself*."

Marko had no problem navigating the ethereal world of Empyria. As the wielder of the Four Winds, he simply rode upon a gale and entered the Spire with no fear of denial.

Inside, the Spire was just as white as its exterior. Marko stood at the door to the throne room. He was not afraid of what he would find beyond the door, though the wind told him that he would not find Vhryt within. No, Vhryt had long forsaken their kingdom. A mercurial god, bound to the inconsistencies of passion, scattering dust wherever their heart takes them.

So what will I find beyond?

The massive stone door loomed as Marko approached, opening almost as if it knew he was arriving.

Of course it does. Marko smiled. He *held the Four Winds; he was the master here.*

The door opened to reveal an empty room, vast and open. He

stepped inside. Before him, five thrones were upon the far wall; specters sat in four, but the middle seat was empty.

"Why have you come?" said the specters in unison. "Why have you come to our throne room?"

Marko stood in the middle of the room, his eyes studying the ghosts before him. He recognized only one.

"You all wear crowns," he said with a conniving smile. "So you four must be the kings of Aestriana? All of you are of the Serpentblood."

The four kings stood, drawing blades from their sides.

"And you are the traitorous trickster!" they all spoke in unison.

"No, I am the Kingsnake," Marko chuckled. Suddenly, a great gale swooshed about the room, whipping his long hair upward. "And I am here to devour you all!"

The flames of Yeornyeim's chariot became smaller as the Aeon descended to the stone floor. Once it landed, Clement stepped down onto the pure white marble and looked at the Spire before him. It was a marvelous edifice, a pale spear shooting into the heavens above, eternal and stalwart.

"So I will find Vhryt here?" the prince said without turning.

"I do not know what you will find here—or *who* you will find here," the Aeon said impassively.

"I see," Clement said softly, his voice almost a whisper.

The Aeon did not reply.

"I don't know why," Clement spoke up, "but I feel like I don't belong here."

"Maybe you don't," Yeornyeim said. "No one said you have to belong. That is merely an illusion you have created for yourself. It doesn't matter your lineage, or your birthright. Just because it is something that *has* been done thousands of times in the past doesn't mean it *must* be done in the present." The Aeon laughed. "You are a strong warrior, prince, and I can feel that your heart is true. Maybe you were not made for this type of magic, and there is nothing wrong with that."

Clement looked at the entrance to the Spire and sighed.

"I guess I will find out soon," he said as he stepped forward.

Yeornyeim watched the prince as he walked away, his form disappearing as he entered the spire.

"Good luck, young prince."

The Aeon turned to his horses when he heard it.

Tap-tap, came the noise, *tap-tap, tap-tap...*

The Aeon turned toward the sound of the tapping.

"It has been quite some time," he said, laughing. "I should have expected to see you here, I guess."

Before him stood a small and wiry old woman with a cane, her eyes shut tight under her stringy hair, pulling a small wagon with an urn in it.

"Who are you, again?" she said, her voice tremulous and sickly. "I forget."

"My name is not important," Yeornyeim laughed. "Tell me, what brings you here, old woman?"

"Here..." she held a long bony finger to her dry lips. "There...well, I don't know where places are. I am blind, you know. Well, I'm blind just as long as I don't want to see. Seeing gets tiresome these days."

"You're as odd as ever," the god of war said, smiling. "Tell me, old woman, do you remember your name on this day?"

"My name...my name..." she muttered, tapping her nose, "the wind has forgotten it, I believe...yes, that's right..." she coughed and waved her hands dismissively. "I don't have time for your questions, Mr. Whoever-You-Are. I must get this water to the shrine!"

Yeornyeim looked at the large urn in her wagon. It was empty.

Wait a minute, he thought, chills rushing up his spine. *If you are here, then... no...*

"Would you like to help me carry it?" the old woman said. "It is quite heavy and my bones are quite old."

"I cannot help you," the Aeon said, his eyes drifting to the Spire, "but I think there is someone who will. And I don't think he knows it yet, either..."

CHAPTER THIRTY-FIVE

The Feast of the Kingsnake

"Kingsnake," the ghosts of the four kings said in unison. "Usurper of the birthright!"

"I see you don't like it that your powers are mine as well?" Marko said, smirking. "But the Four Winds have chosen *me*, not him."

Suddenly, light flashed from the thrones and the four apparitions were gone.

"Usurper of the Wind!" one raged as he appeared in front of Marko.

"Vile defiler of the blood!" cried another as he appeared behind.

"Sick reveler of wickedness!" said the third as he was summoned to the right.

"You who have betrayed my trust!" called the fourth as he materialized to the left.

"You who soil the name of Vhryt!" the four proclaimed in unanimously, drawing their blades. "You shall relinquish that which you hold most precious!"

A sardonic chuckle escaped Marko's mouth.

"No," he said. "It is you, Your Highnesses, who shall die this day." Suddenly, a slight gale filled the room, softly brisking Marko's cloak. "I have come to take the rest of what I have stolen!"

"Vile serpent!" the kings exploded, their voice a great rumble that seemed to shake the entire Spire itself. "You will perish!"

Marko calmly raised his hand palm-up. A small whirlwind sat in the middle of his hand.

"Hear me, Kings of the Winds"—a hungry grin crossed his face —"and know that you shall fall this day!"

Clement walked up the blindingly bright staircase that was the main hallway of the Spire. There were no windows, no etherlamps to light the ascent, yet somehow the seemingly infinite climb was illuminated.

And lit so brilliantly that Clement was forced to squint his eyes at times.

After a while, Clement began to feel as if the stairs *weren't* going anywhere. He looked around; this entire Spire was...disorienting, to say the least. It seemed as if he had been climbing for hours, yet he simultaneously felt as if he had made no progress. He looked behind him. Cold fear filled his veins. There—*right there*—was the doorway to the exit.

I haven't, his mind screamed, *I haven't made any progress at all!*

But why? His mind raced, remembering the Darkling's words before they performed the ritual.

Three days until I'm stuck here...

But how long had he been here? Time seemed so trivial in this odd, incorporeal realm. Had it been a day? An hour? Four hours? He had no way of knowing.

All he knew was that, however much time he had left, he didn't have enough.

"Drat!" he exclaimed, slamming his fist into the wall as frustration filled his mind.

"*Poor Clement,*" a familiar voice laughed in his mind. "*So righteous and good. Have you become so jaded, hm? Are you now so quick to anger?*"

Clement had no problem deciphering the voice.

"Marko?!" he exclaimed. "So *you* did this?! You cursed these stairs?"

"*Of course, dear cousin.*" Marko's voice inside Clement's mind was smooth and low. "*I wouldn't want you to interfere as I killed the Kings of the Four Winds, now would I? No. That wouldn't work. No,*" he said, laughing, *"enjoy your endless trek!"*

"Damn you, Marko!" the prince raged.

The voice faded in his mind, and he stopped.

What to do now? He ruminated for a moment before deciding. He couldn't shake the deep ire filling his veins with heat as he grit his teeth. Above was the man that killed his father, sold his kingdom, and took from Clement his very sight.

Above...

Clement clenched his fists as pain ravaged his heart.

Above was the man he truly loved as a brother.

Clement turned to the entrance and froze. A grim and visceral chill ran up his spine. He rubbed his eyes.

Was he dreaming? Was he mistaken?

No. It was true.

Behind him, the door to the exit...was gone.

Marko stood in the center of the throne room, surrounded on all four directions by the Kings of the Four Winds, each one of them armed with an exquisite sword and intricately decorated shield.

"So," Marko laughed, a crooked grin accentuating his laugh lines underneath his dull blue eyes, "which one of you dies first?"

The phantoms did not flinch. Marko scanned the room. He was surrounded, but the apparitions of the kings did not scare him. No, perhaps in the past, their burning blue eyes might have intimidated him, but now...well...

"Well, then," he said, a sharpness forming in his voice.

Marko extended his arm toward the ghost on the right, his finger pointing directly at the specter. A thin spear of pressurized air needled from his fingertip, shooting forward, piercing right through the ornate shield and impaling the King through the chest.

"I'll make the first move," Marko said, laughing. "Too bad. This could have been a bit more interesting, I guess."

Marko snapped his fingers. Suddenly, magic-infused air exploded from within the King's ghost, evaporating the phantom into faint ethereal strands of light and dust.

"You see," Marko said, returning his hand to his side, "*I* have the power here. *I* control the wind. And once I eliminate the remaining three of you, it will be completely within my control."

"Usurper!" the ghosts of the kings roared, their combined voices rocking the foundation of the Spire. "Now you shall die!"

As their voices became greater, they began to grow in size, the three kings rising into the ceiling as they raised their blades high in the air.

"Perish!" they raged in unison, swinging their blades downward, the swords' lengths scraping against the ceiling and causing rubble to fall to the floor below.

Marko merely smiled. "Fools."

As the blades struck downward, rushing toward the Kingsnake's head, their destructive rage wanting nothing more than to snuff out his flame, they stopped.

"What?!" the voices of the kings said together as they pushed and pushed downward to no avail.

"What is it?" Marko laughed, his hand held above his head. "Can't go any further down? Can't hit me? C'mon, try a little harder. I'm sure if you push down a bit more, you'll be able to cut me down."

The massive spectral Kings pushed and pushed, but the blades did not budge.

The Kingsnake shrugged. "Hm. So sad. Too bad I have to kill you all now. This could have been a lot more fun, to be honest. Gotta say I'm disappointed."

A great gust wind exploded from the usurper's hand, invisible blades of air spiraling upward in a cyclone, sharper than a thousand razors. Shrieks erupted from the kings as their insubstantial forms were rent to shreds in mere seconds.

The wind ceased, and there was silence. Marko stood in the center of the court as sparkling and otherworldly dust fell from the sky like snow. He could feel it now, the rush of power entering his body. No longer would the winds deny him. No, he was in full control.

Marko smiled. Then, he laughed.

CHAPTER THIRTY-SIX

Old Crow/Final Song

It was an instant shift when Clement realized Marko's spell on the stairs—whatever he did to make them infinite and unclimbable—had lifted. It was easily noticeable, though the prince himself wasn't sure how he knew. It was just a feeling, a certain sensation of weightlessness that was present in the air that made him think things had...changed.

Clement looked up the stairwell, the vast spiral stairs that corkscrewed and wound along the interior walls of the wide, cylindrical tower.

He knew what this meant...

It meant that, above, Marko was waiting.

"Why, Marko?" Clement said under his breath as he rounded up the spiral steps.

But that was it. Clement didn't know why. Sure, he was the prince, but Marko had never seemed jealous—or even interested—in the royal throne. Even six months ago, when they fought in the Palace of the Sky King, Marko didn't seem to have any goals of claiming the throne.

It seemed so unnerving, like it was all a game that the two of them were playing. Clement felt as if an icy pick was piercing his heart, a cold pain of stilling regret.

What went wrong, Marko? Where did we fail you? Where did I fail you...?

Climbing the stairs was a long trek, especially given the height and breadth of the spire. As he ascended, Clement couldn't help but lose himself in the stressful rumination that lay before him. And he knew that before him was no trial. It was a battle of wills.

Lost in thought, he suddenly realized that the stairs had stopped and that he now stood at the top.

Before him was a door, and beyond that door was the pain of the past and the grimness of the present.

Clement sighed.

Marko...

The door was heavy. Clement's large muscles flexed as he pushed it open to reveal the spacious white throne room and stepped forward. The room was so starkly blank that the disembodied light within was a blinding sheen. Clement squinted and blinked rapidly in order to adjust his eyes to the change in brightness.

Suddenly, the sound of someone clapping echoed throughout the hollow room.

"Just on time," Marko's disembodied voice said, chuckling. "Oh, how punctual you are, *cousin*. Welcome to the Kingsnake's court."

Clement's eyes adjusted. There, at the far end of the room, Marko sat upon the middle throne, his legs crossed laxly as he rested the side of his head upon his fist.

"What?" the self-styled Kingsnake laughed. "Did you expect anything less, cousin?"

"Marko..." Clement said, his eyes scanning the four empty thrones. "What have you done...?"

"They were weak, cousin," he replied. "Caught in their rapture of glory and honor, blinded by their chivalry. Just like you. Just like your fool of a father." Marko's face contorted with disgust. "And just like my devil of a father."

"Your father was a good man!" Clement shot back. "He was honorable. He was—"

"Shut your damn mouth, Clement!" Marko seethed, his face twisting with rage. "You know nothing of my father!"

"Cousin! Your father cared for you and your mother dearly! He was a good man—"

"He was a monster!" Marko stood, ripping his shirt from his body to reveal the deep scars upon his back. "You know nothing of my pain! Nothing of my struggle!"

Clement froze, his blood curdling in horror.

"Marko..." His voice was a breathy whisper.

"Look, Clement!" Marko raged. "Look what demons your *wretched* chivalry hides!"

Clement could believe what he was seeing. There, upon his cousin's flesh, the scars of vicious lashings covered his back, leaving nothing but the remnant memories of what could only be abuse.

Then, it all clicked in Clement's mind. The reason Marko was so secretive, the reason he never showed his back when they swam as boys at the lake, the reason he hid himself away...

Marko, was hurting.

The Kingsnake turned to face a stunned Clement. Suddenly, a light breeze filled the room, blowing Marko's shirt. Marko extended his arms as the shirt floated back onto his body.

"Honor is a false god, Clement," he said, his voice low and grisly. "It is a thin gild covering a broken idol."

"Marko," Clement said as he felt involuntary tears begin to spill from his eyes. "I had no idea! I—"

"Silence!" Marko fumed. "You know *nothing*!"

The breeze exploded into a great gust, howling and whipping off of the white stone walls of the throne room.

"I hate you, Clement!" Marko said as magical blades of pressurized air began to form behind him. "*You* and your honor! *You* and your righteousness! You're false, just like *him*!"

"Marko!" Clement yelled above the wind. "Marko I didn't know! Had I known, I would have—"

"Would have what?! *Saved me*?! You bastard! You always have to be a hero, don't you?! And for what? Your own wretched *pride*?" Marko laughed a strange laugh, a mixture of sarcasm and derision. As Clement stared into his cousin's eyes, he could see a wild insanity within them. "You say it's your duty as a prince, but we both know that's the *only reason you do it*!"

"The only reason...?" Clement felt as if his heart stopped.

My duty, the prince thought, *I...*

"Die, Clement! Die your *honorable* death!"

Marko pointed forward and the blades heeded his command. At the snap of his fingers, the winds shot toward the prince at harrowing speeds.

Clement felt as if his legs were made of stone. He closed his eyes.

Marko...I...

I didn't know...

Had I only known...

Tears ran freely down the prince's face as memories filled his mind. In that split second, he could see cousin's smiling face as a boy. How Clement longed for those days now...how he longed to end the pain he was so blind to...

Then, there was a loud crash.

"*WHAT?!*" Marko shrieked.

Clement opened his eyes. There, before him, the apparition of his father stood between the two men.

"Clement," the ghost of King Reethkilt's voice echoed. "You must run, my boy!"

The prince's mind raced. "But father, what about—"

"RUN!" the phantom's voice was louder, more violent.

"There is no escape!" Marko shouted. "You can't run—"

"You have no power here, Kingsnake!" the king cut him off. King Reethkilt turned to Clement. "Your time is almost done here. You must return to the living world. If you die here, Aestriana will truly be lost!"

"I won't leave Marko! I'll—"

But he never finished that sentence. The king snapped his fingers.

Clement blinked. He looked at the world around him. He now stood outside, facing away from the entrance to the Spire behind him.

"You damned old man!" Marko raged. "I've killed you twice already! Is a third time the charm?"

"Be my life or soul," King Ahmaal zel Reethkilt said, air-blades of his own surrounding him. "I will not allow your madness to harm my heir! Do you understand, *usurper?*"

"Oh, Uncle." Marko's lips curved into an unnerving smile. "You only care about your heir, your status! I always knew you were so vain." He pointed forward. "Thanks for proving my *point*!"

Suddenly, three blades of air shot forth from Marko's side of the room, speeding forward and directly toward the king.

"Silence, child!" the king raged, pointing forward.

At the commands of their masters, the pressurized slices of air collided into a great explosion, the shock forming cracks in the floor of the throne room.

"You..." King Reethkilt grunted as he fell to one knee, holding his shoulder. He looked at the wound. It was more than that. His entire right arm was missing. "How did you overpower me in such a way?"

"You're a fool, Uncle," Marko said, grinning as he towered over the kneeling king. "And now you will die for good!"

"Kill me if you desire, Marko," King Reethkilt gasped as his body slowly began to fade, starting at the wound on his shoulder. "But even if I fade into nonexistence, the power of the Wind will never truly be yours. The power waits for a righteous soul, not a"—he coughed —"savage like yourself!"

A stricken scowl cracked the laugh lines on Marko's face, a look of sheer rage filling his grayish blue eyes.

"Savage, eh?" he asked, his voice as soft as snow, calm and frigid. "I'll show you how *savage* I can truly be!"

Marko extended his arm upward, and the winds reacted. Pressurized air began to wrap itself around the fallen king, lifting him high into the air.

"Truly sorrowful, *Your Highness*," the Kingsnake said with a bitter derision in his voice. "How I could almost thank you, but..."

King Reethkilt grunted as the winds wrapped tighter around his body.

"We're beyond that now"—Marko closed his fist—"aren't we?"

The winds constricted, crushing the phantom of the king, who exploded into bright ethereal dust.

Sparkling aether fell onto the ground like silvery rain around Marko.

He smirked. "Yes...we are *quite* beyond that..."

CHAPTER THIRTY-SEVEN

Wind Talk

Clement stood, speechless, gazing up at the Spire that now rejected him. He sighed. Only the kings had resided in the tower; the Aeon was nowhere to be seen. *Perhaps it is true,* he thought.

Perhaps Vhryt had forsaken him.

But his mind was on other things now. The prince stared up at the sky. Above was white and clear, with only a bright black star hanging suspended among it.

Marko, he thought, *my duty, I...*

It was odd. Never before had he thought twice about his honor or his morals or his duty to his people. But now...

But now...

Was Marko right? Were all of the things that he thought were his best qualities just an illusion? Did he *really* embody the virtues he held so highly? Or was it all a sham? Did he truly feel the way he did, or was he simply raised—*brainwashed*—to feel that way?

Clement's mind was a raging wildfire, the blazes of which razing everything he held dear.

Who am I? He felt his heart sink. *Who am I really?*

The world was silent then, its peace drowned out by the loud flurry of emotions trapped within the prince.

Tap-tap.

There was a noise, but Clement did not hear.

Tap-tap.

It came closer, but the prince did not turn.

Suddenly, Clement felt a force bump into him. Quickly he turned to see an old woman as she tripped over him.

"Madam!" He exclaimed as his arms swiftly wrapped around her to keep her weary body from hitting the stone ground.

"I didn't see you there," she said, her voice soft and small.

Clement guided the woman to her feet once more and dusted her shoulders with caring hands. She was much smaller than he; her long wiry white hair was thinning and ran like yarn over her white, filmy eyes.

She's blind. The thought was quick in his mind.

"Worry not, madame," the prince smiled. "I know the feeling quite well. I'm blind in the mortal world, actually."

The old woman looked blankly forward, her expression empty and vacant.

"I am sorry, child," she said impassively, then turned around. "Now where did I put my wagon?"

"Wagon?" Clement's gaze passed her to see a simple wagon, holding only a large a stone urn.

"Yes," she said, "I am off to the shrine to offer the water, but I can't seem to keep track of my wagon."

Clement walked past the elder and picked up the handle.

"Please," he said, "allow me to carry you and your wagon to this shrine."

"No," the old woman said without hesitation. "It is my duty, not yours."

Clement paused. *Duty, huh...?*

"Nay." He said. "I will not aid you out of duty. I will aid you because it is what I desire to do and nothing more or nothing less. Please. I insist."

The old woman's face scrunched in dissatisfaction, then she sighed. "If you insist, young man, then I cannot stop you. Those with good hearts are too tiring to argue with, and my bones are very old."

The prince smiled. "Aye. Then why don't you ride on the wagon as well and rest those tired bones?"

The old woman was silent.

"You are a kind stranger," she finally said. "Tell me, what is your name?"

"You may call me Clement," the prince said as he helped her to her seat.

The old woman smiled. "Very well," she said. "I thank you for this, Prince Reethkilt. I know you do not have much time yet to live. You should listen to your heart and not doubt yourself as much."

"How did you know—?"

"—that you are a prince? It doesn't matter. Now, carry on."

"The mountain in the distance?" Clement said as he carried the urn and old woman through the grassy meadow. "It does appear far away. You were going to try to find it all on your own—blind?"

"I was." The elder's voice was blank. She pushed her wispy hair from her dulled eyes. "It takes me about a century each time, but I always end up finding it."

"That's quite some time," Clement laughed amicably. "By the way, madame, I never got your name."

The old woman turned her head and gazed at the meadow, odd, because she was definitely blind.

"I don't know it, either," she said with a shrug.

Clement gasped. "Pardon? You...don't know...your name?"

"Forgot it is probably a better term. My name was older than the wind, and after so long your brain isn't as sharp." She smiled, revealing yellow teeth. "You win some and you lose some, I guess."

Clement chuckled at the old woman's simplicity.

"You don't have much time," she said after a moment. "Two and a half days have passed in your world."

Two and a half, Clement thought. *That much time has passed*?!

It felt as if he had only been in this realm for about a day...

He sighed, collecting himself. "Then I'd best hurry, eh?"

"The mountain is forward, is it not?" she asked.

"Directly so."

"Very well."

The old woman took a deep breath and then exhaled. Suddenly, a great cyclone began to form around them.

"Shall we go faster?" she said.

"But I thought you needed help getting there?" Clement gasped as the wind lifted him from the ground.

"Well, I need help knowing the general direction," she said, waving her hands, slightly agitated. "Don't ask so many questions, young prince!"

Before Clement could speak again, the winds were beneath his feet, lifting him, the woman, and the wagon into the illusory sky. The prince looked at the ground far below him now, the strange grasslands of Empyria swirling like fresh paint guided by a thick brush. He closed his eyes as the air whipped about his short brown hair, howling as if speaking a language long lost. The winds grew louder and louder until, finally, there was dead silence.

Clement held his eyes closed a moment longer. The air was still, and only the soft chirp of some distant birds singing filled the void.

Suddenly, he felt the ground beneath his feet once more.

"You can open your eyes, child," the old woman said.

Clement opened his eyes. They had definitely traveled far in short time—that was certain. Around him was a thick forest of large trees with translucent blue leaves. He had no idea of where he was exactly, only that he was now standing on the edge of a mountain. Clement turned to look beyond the cliff. In the distance, the stark white marble of the Spire could be determined as a mere vague line ascending into the sky.

"We are here, I think," the old woman said. "Is there a statue here?"

Clement turned around. Before him was a small statue, a tiny idol in the shape of a winged serpent.

"This statue," he began, "it's..."

"...Vhryt," the old woman finished the sentence for him.

Clement smiled. "I see now...your urn, it is an offering to Vhryt?"

"More of a personal gift, really," the blind woman said, shrugging. "But whatever. It is all the same."

"The urn, then," Clement said as he lifted it from the wagon, "allow me to offer it in your place."

The old woman smiled. "What a devout young prince."

The urn was lighter than he expected given its large size; this, however, the prince determined was because it was *empty*.

"Madame," he said, one eyebrow raised. "I believe that you have forgotten the water."

The old woman held a long weary finger to her chin.

"Then offer the air. Trust me, I don't mind, either way."

Clement decided that there was no argument to be had. Instead, he approached the small shrine. It was meager, composed of a crude stone, the carving rough and jagged, doing no justice to the smoothness of a real snake. *It's odd*, Clement thought.

But, once again, there was no use arguing.

The prince lowered the empty urn to the basin at the foot of the small shrine, pouring into it. Of course, nothing came out of the urn, but he knew that was to be expected.

But then, as if adhering to the wind within, a green light glowed faintly in the eyes of the snake carving. Clement looked into the idol's emerald eyes for a long moment, hypnotized as if charmed by a cobra. The color soon faded, leaving the prince kneeling as if nothing had ever happened.

"Come here, young prince." The old woman's voice was suddenly cold and hard.

Something was different now. He couldn't tell exactly, but Clement could detect an odd static in the air.

"Madame?" he said slowly as he approached.

Something was definitely different. The woman seemed more...alive. Her long wispy hair and worn features seemed to be changed into...something else.

He stood before her for a moment, when, suddenly, the woman leaped forward from her seat on the wagon. Clement yelled as the ancient woman's fingers dug deeply into his ears, her thumbs pressing forcefully against his eyes—so forcefully he felt as if she were going to push them back into his head.

"Listen to me, Alexander Clement zel Reethkilt!" she shouted. The old woman's small and shaky voice was now replaced by a loud, booming thunder. Clement gasped as a great wind began to swirl around him, taking the air from his lungs. "And hear my voice!"

"You—" Clement couldn't hear his own voice. "You're—"

Then there was silence, and all went black. The prince could feel himself breathing once again. He could feel the cold ground of his cell once more.

Could it be...

And it was.

Clement had returned to mortal world. But something felt different. He could feel the air. It felt as if he could feel a distant breeze or a vibration all around him, as if a voiceless presence were whispering into his mind, saying nothing, but at once also, all it needed to.

He gasped. Clement could feel the room from where he sat; he could sense the placement of the cell bars; he could feel the presence of the assassin guard hidden in the shadows.

"You're in the left corner," Clement said loudly. "You're seated in the ceiling above the left corner, aren't you, assassin?"

"How?" the guard gasped. "How did you know that?"

Clement smiled. He knew now what this meant.

"I know," the prince began, "because the *wind told me.*"

Marko had long since returned to the mortal world after his attempt to kill Clement had failed. The stones of the Palace of the Sky King were dull compared to the shining marble of the Spire in the afterlife.

But he was distant now. Something bothered him—a sudden shift in the winds. The Four Winds were still fully his, but...he couldn't shake it.

Clement was out there. He now knew that much for sure.

Clement lived, and that alone was cause to worry.

CHAPTER THIRTY-EIGHT

The Final Duel

Eldric managed to raise himself to a standing position by pushing upward upon his sturdy cedar cane.

"Guard," he said into the air.

There was no reply; silence filled the dungeon.

"You're hiding in the shadows to the left," the old man said, this time grimmer in tone. "You'd do best to speak when your elders ask of you."

A man garbed in black stepped out of the shadows. He was tall and bulky, only his eyes visible through his black garments.

"Release me," Eldric stated once more. "I have a bone to pick with your mistress."

The assassin laughed in disbelief.

"You think it's that easy?" he said, his mask moving as he talked.

"Well," Eldric said, smirking. "Let me put it this way..."

Suddenly the air became thin as a black aura enveloped the old man.

"I still have some tricks up my sleeve," he said, "and surely your mistress would rather take my head in battle, no?"

The guard took a deep breath in, trying his best not to faint from loss of air.

"Then come," he said with a gulp. "We'll see how that goes."

The *Prometheus* returned to the Vega Varonn without any trouble. As Snow stepped down the landing ramp and onto the warm sands, her nerves flared and her stomach twisted. She knew what it was that she had to do, and she didn't like it one bit.

She had to defeat the Lioness.

Ayize and Enlil passed her as the three of them approached the entrance to the ruins. The hallway was busy with assassins and ruffians, just as it had been and probably always was. She followed the two Darklings down the hallway and into the main den and stopped.

There, on the throne at the opposite wall, sat the tall and vicious assassin queen.

"Ayize, Enlil," she said, her smile clever and charming, "you've returned with good news, I assume?"

Ayize scowled. "What do *you* think, you old crone? I'm here, ain't I?"

"Good," the Lioness said.

"We killed the count!" Enlil said, her voice cheery. "He was a nasty vampire!"

The Lioness crossed her battle-scarred legs and folded her arms.

"How quaint," she said, pointing forward. "And what of *you*, girl?"

The room fell silent. All eyes turned to Snow. Snow looked around the room, glancing over the ruffians, thugs, and assassins. She turned her eyes to the Lioness, trying her best to intimidate and pierce the assassin queen's composure.

"I want my father and the prince released," she said, her voice hard and absolute.

The room fell deathly silent, suffocating, everyone's eyes gravitating to the Lioness upon her throne.

"Big words from someone who lost her precious swords," the assassin queen said, sneering. "How do you plan to fight me?"

Snow extended her arm and took a deep breath. As she opened her eyes, blue psychic energy began to swirl around her fingertips.

The Lioness' eyes widened. "Ah! So you have *other* ways of fighting? And you believe that with this new inkling of strength you can save your friends?"

Suddenly, there was a loud bang from the entrance hall.

"Hey! Y-you! St-stop!" a voice cried out.

"You—" another shrieked, "how did you get out if you can't see?!"

"Lioness!" Clement roared as he opened the doorway, dragging two men along as they tried to restrain him.

"Clement?" Snow gasped, her eyes widening as she watched the prince move confidently. He had moved so uncertainly since he had been blinded "how are you?"

"Ah!" the Lioness smirked an amused smile. "So the prince *can* see after all? But how, I wonder?"

Clement shook the men off of his ankles.

"Nay," he said, smiling, "I see not, but the Wind shall guide me."

The Lioness laughed, pushing her long raven locs from her shoulder.

"So," she said, "what now, girl? Will you still fight me for the release of your father? Or will you both try to fight me and die trying?"

"Neither, actually," a voice said as Eldric's chuckle echoed down the hall.

Everyone in the room was breathless as the old Inquisitor limped into the den.

"You will fight *me*," he said, "and me alone."

"You have already lost, old man," the Lioness said, her faded brown eyes narrowing in annoyance. "I have no more desire to fight a weak man."

"Or perhaps you are afraid?" the old man said, cracking a clever smile. "Afraid that you might lose your life this time?"

The Lioness bared her teeth.

"It will not be my life that will end, old man." She sneered. "But I'll take your challenge simply so I *can* end you!"

Eldric pointed forward with a long bony finger. "Here are my terms, Assassin Queen!" he held up one finger. "If I lose, my life is forfeit"—he turned to Snow —"with no intervening this time."

The Lioness rubbed her chin with scarred fingers, carefully taking into account her sharpened fingernails as not to cut herself.

"And If I win," the Inquisitor continued, "you will give me an airship to go where I please and you will let us leave here in peace."

The eyes of the room gravitated expectantly to the Lioness upon her throne. Snow looked at the matriarch's face. The Lioness gripped her chair angrily with one hand; her other hand balled into a fist as she grit her teeth.

Suddenly, she smiled—a gut-wrenching, derisive smile, filled with devious intent.

"I like strong men, Eldric," she said through her teeth. "Perhaps I had you pinned as a slimy old cleric who had no backbone whatsoever, but"—she stood, her strong and scarred body standing tall, immovable, and graceful—"perhaps you have some guts after all."

Eldric smiled as if unaware of any danger.

"Then you will fight me?" he said.

The Lioness smiled, almost sweetly. "Fight you? I'm going to *kill* you!"

As Snow watched her father walk toward the exit, her eyes gravitated to Clement, who stood by the door.

"Snow!" he said in an exhale of relief, as if he could feel her eyes upon him.

"Clement," she exclaimed as she rushed to him and took his hand in hers. "I'm so glad you're safe! I was," she started, "I was so afraid for you!"

The prince smiled a small, almost bashful smile.

"And I, you," he replied as he took her hand as well. "But all is well now, and it is because of your strength." He nodded. "I owe you, I do. Truly."

"No, you don't," Snow said, her voice softening as a smile relaxed upon her lips. "I care about you, my friend. You owe me nothing."

The prince smiled, his blank eyes almost tender. Snow felt warm as she looked at him, then she turned her eyes to Eldric.

"What is he thinking?" Clement whispered as if detecting her gaze.

"I don't know..." she said, "but we must follow..."

The two of them stood for a moment, collecting their nerves, then began to follow Eldric to the battleground.

And what indeed? Snow wished she knew; she wished that it were her fighting the vicious woman in his place—she knew at least *she* would have a chance! Eldric was physically disabled; he was too slow to fight against her supersonic movement, against her "jumping" technique.

My father, Snow thought as she felt her heart rise to her throat, *what are you thinking?*

The area was just as large and empty as Eldric remembered it. The unforgiving winds of the Miljinn Desert blew coarse kisses across his face.

"Remember that you did this to yourself," the Lioness began as she stepped ahead of the crowd and took her place on the dueling grounds. "You die today, Eldric of the Black Flame."

"I beg to differ," Eldric said, smirking as he limped to his place. "I've never entertained thoughts of suicide."

The battlegrounds were silent all but the low rush of the desert winds that blew between the two contestants. Snow, looking onward, could feel her heart pounding in her chest.

What is he doing? Her thoughts raced. *What are you thinking you, old fool?!*

Her mind was a swirl of emotions as she tried desperately to understand any reasoning behind her father's decision to fight. He lost last time; what would be different now? Why didn't he let her fight for him? Why—?

Snow felt a hand firmly take hers. She turned her head to see Clement beside her.

"Fear not," he said as he squeezed her hand reassuringly. "Something is different. I don't know what, but he's more confident now."

The prince released her hand, and, for some reason, she felt slightly lighter.

"Alright, Eldric!" the Lioness laughed as she dropped into her fighting stance. "Now you die!"

Eldric said nothing. Instead, he closed his eyes and extended his hand skyward.

Snow narrowed her eyes. She had never seen this before. She

looked at his hand. His fingers were not pointing as they always were for his attack. No, his first two fingers were extended in a "V" shape. She watched as she had a million times as a devilish black aura engulfed him.

"Fool!" the Lioness shrieked as she jolted forward at an inhuman speed.

Time seemed to slow, at least for Eldric. That split second was vast as memories of the crimson woman from his dreams filled his mind. He could see her, her strange eyes watching him, and in that moment, he remembered what she had showed him.

I must say, he thought, *O Crimson Lady...*

"*Rex Ynfernim!*" he called into the air.

"Too slow!" the Lioness roared. Her gnarled dagger came down, imbued with all of the malice in the assassin queen's soul.

I will, Eldric thought, *take your lighting!*

"*...Ymperio!*" Eldric added to his incantation.

Suddenly, great webs of black lightning exploded from the old man's body. The Lioness roared as she was thrown back against the ground, raging as she held her arm, engulfed a cloud of smoke.

The desert winds carried the smell of burnt flesh to everyone surrounding.

"Your Word of Heart?!" the Lioness shrieked. "Has *three* words?!"

Eldric stood firm, black lightning jumping and dancing along his skin.

"You proposed a problem for me," he began as he lifted off of the ground and levitated just above the sands. "It was honestly foolish, but I had never considered that such ultrasonic movement was possible. Given my condition, you were the natural antithesis to my ability. That said, I needed something...*faster.*" Eldric lowered himself to the ground once more. "*Rex Ynfernim Ymperio* is what I like to think as my 'awakened' Word of Heart. Or, in other words"—he smiled a devilish grin—"even you can't outrun *black lightning.*"

The Lioness looked the old man over her, then burst into laughter.

"You old bastard!" she said as she stood, standing as if the burn on her arm were nothing at all. "It appears we are even."

"Yes," Eldric chuckled, "and it appears *you* owe me a ship."

CHAPTER THIRTY-NINE

Setting Course

Eldric stood before the Lioness' throne, both Clement and Snow at his sides, all the eyes of the ruffian audience upon them.

"The scar is bigger than I assumed. Honestly, I didn't expect it to physically burn its target," Eldric said, chuckling as he puffed his ivory pipe. "But you're lucky that it didn't eat your soul."

The Lioness smiled an almost uncomfortably warm and kind smile.

"You're the first to leave a scar on my body in many years. You should feel special, Eldric," she said sweetly as she held up her injured arm. The scar was unnatural-looking, void-black streaks arcing down her forearm. "I will wear it as a sign of friendship. I like strong people, Eldric."

Eldric blew out a ring of smoke and waved his hand through it.

"And about our deal?"

"Ha!" the Lioness scoffed. "Not as straight-laced as you seem, are you?" she waved her arm dismissively. "Fine. I entrust Ayize and Enlil to your command. As of now, the *Prometheus* is your personal vessel."

"*WHAT?!*" Ayize erupted. "Who do you think you are, you old hag? That's *my* ship! *My* ship, *my* rules!"

"Is there an issue, Black Lotus?"

"I—"

"Is there," the Lioness asked again, this time harder, "an issue?"

"You don't scare me, old woman!" the Darkling raged, his fingers upon the daggers at his side.

"Well, captain," Eldric spoke up, "your services are gladly received."

"Ayize!" Enlil said, grabbing his hand, "Mister Eldric is *helping* us! Remember the fifth tenet! Friends help friends!"

"They're not my friends, Enlil!"

"But they're *mine*!" the little Darkling said, pouting. "And I'm *your* friend, so help *me*!"

Ayize let out a long-exasperated groan.

"You have fifteen minutes until I blast outta here."

Enlil turned to Eldric as they watched Ayize storm out.

The little girl smiled. "He likes you," she said.

"Didn't seem like it," Clement laughed.

"Now," the Lioness said, "before I dismiss you from my court, I'll give you a hint, a friendly gesture, if you will."

Eldric raised an eyebrow. "And that is?"

"It happened about a month ago, but the rumor is that the Phoenix King has regained his throne from Elven control in the fortress city of Phoenix Grotto. If you wish to do...whatever nonsense you wish to do, I would at least give him a visit, no?"

Eldric puffed his pipe once more.

"And lastly, Eldric." The Lioness grinned a devilish grin. "If I ever see your face again, I will kill you."

The Master Inquisitor laughed.

"Likewise."

"Clement," Snow said as she walked beside him, both of them following Eldric, who was following Enlil down the worn halls of the Vega Varonn.

"I know what you're going to ask, friend," the prince said, smiling, "but go ahead."

Snow smirked. "Aren't you"—she pointed to her eyes—"blind?"

"It's a long story," he began, "but the Winds guide me now. It's like...I can feel vibrations in the air. It's...odd, but," he trailed off, smiling, "I have Ayize to thank for leading me to Empyria."

"Empyria?" Snow asked, smiling in disbelief.

He grinned in return. "Aye, I had some help from Ayize. For an assassin, he's rather kind." He paused, an amused grin upon his face. "And at least now you won't have to find a new sparring partner."

Ayize was angry, and it was obvious to Eldric why. He was a free spirit, that much the old Inquisitor could discern. But he was still agreeing to help, and as far as Eldric was concerned, that was enough.

"Where to?" the Darkling said as Eldric took a seat in the cockpit.

"Phoenix Grotto," Eldric replied. "If the Phoenix King has indeed reclaimed his seat, then he will be our greatest ally."

"The Folke Lands, huh?" Ayize mumbled as he flipped switches and prepared for takeoff. "Well, at least this will be interesting."

CHAPTER FORTY

You Cannot Run...

The ocean shifted, crashing against the rocks below. Iago stood high above the waves, peering downward into the dark greenish-black waters of the Western Sea.

He had long since decided that he wouldn't go home.

How could he? After everything that had happened? After all the loss he had caused? After Amalia died...

Amalia...

The name was bitter in his mind. His body shook with anger at her fate.

Zilheim...

The man who had caused him all of this trouble, all of this heartache. The man who chased him now and had been chasing him for as long as he lived across all of Lythia.

Iago sighed. He couldn't help his feelings. He knew this would happen; he knew he would want to die.

He thought of Nox for a moment and smiled. When he was with her, he felt lighter, as if he had an annoying little sister constantly barking in his ear. For the time he was with her, she almost—*almost*—made him believe he was what she said he was; she almost made him believe he was *good*.

But he knew better. He looked at his fists. There was too much blood on his hands. His existence had warranted the deaths of so many. He cringed. The world would be better without him. And now, as he stood on the precipice of the cliff above the Western Sea, he knew that he would not—could not—return home.

He knew the waters would be cold, even in the west. The bottom of the cliff looked rocky, and he hoped that he could jump just right to where he wouldn't feel as much pain.

Suddenly, the words of Ellier Vondell ran through his mind. He thought of Hallow-Talon.

I'm sorry...

He could feel pressure behind his eyes as he stepped to the edge of the cliff.

I'm sorry I mucked this up so badly. I wish I could face you—oh Aeons, I wish I could. But I'm a coward...

Tears began to roll from his eyes. He promised himself he wouldn't be dramatic, but...here he was, moments from his death, and dramatics were all he had left. The guilt...

It was all he ever had...

...just tears, regret, and the hatred he felt for himself.

Iago closed his eyes and stepped forward. The air was cool as he fell. For a moment, his fear gave way to freedom.

The water was cold.

And the world was black.

Hallow-Talon stood alone on the balcony of his palace, his fiery eyes peering down at his domain, the city of Phoenix Grotto. The dark, subterranean city was lit only by the blue and yellow etherlights glowing along the streets.

He peered down, but did not see. He had not paid much attention to anything really—not with his mind whirling like it was.

He's out there...

The thought pervaded with anxiety. He knew that, somewhere in the largeness of Lythia, the hope of the world—the key to peace and salvation—was out there. *He* was out there.

Hallow-Talon took a deep breath.

Lyon...

* * *

"You're an idiot," Iago heard a voice say. "I don't know what my sister saw in you. Perhaps her current incarnation is a more credulous than the previous ones. One thousand years ago, she would have cast you out to dry, I swear."

Iago opened his eyes to a sudden realization: he was underwater, the ocean cold, black and salty, and he needed air badly.

"Take a breath already!" the voice groaned. "You mortals and your air, I wonder what the Starbreather was thinking when he made the lot of you!"

Iago paused reluctantly, then opened his mouth to exhale. It was true.

He could breathe.

"Now," the voice said, "what were you hoping to accomplish with that little stunt?"

"I—" Iago stopped himself. "Wait, who are you?"

Suddenly, the waters around him began to rage; bubbles swirled in front of him in a violent cyclone. The swirling stopped, and a man was present. Well, he *looked* like a man; his tall, chiseled body was definitely that of a man. But his from his long blue hair that seemed to fall like a waterfall from his head to his swirling, oceanic, eyes, Iago was certain that he was definitely *not* a mortal.

"I am Klyriai," the Aeon said, "Aeon of beauty and guardian of the oceans." He paused. "I am also the older brother of Lunae, Aeon of Wisdom and the Black Moon."

"Aeon?!" Iago blurted out, sounding a little naiver than he intended.

"Yes, yes, don't be so surprised," Klyriai said, waving his hand dismissively. "I saved you once in the Northern Sea when I brought the Giants to you. I saved you then because you saved my sister..."

Iago balled his fists and grit his teeth.

"And..." the Elf began, "you saved me this time because...?"

He wished he had never asked. He closed his eyes. Iago knew the answer, or at least he thought he did.

"You know this answer," the Aeon spoke, "don't you, Iago Lyon?"

Iago was silent. He knew. He had *always* known.

"Do more have to die?" Iago finally said with a twinge of pain in his voice. "Do more have to die to make sure that I live?"

The Aeon said nothing.

Iago's mind raged. He could see it; he could hear it all.

'*Run, Iago,*' a voice returned to him in bitter memory. '*They cannot catch you! They mustn't!*'

"Lady Malorya is dead, Iago. She died protecting you when you were a child," Klyriai said, his voice hard. "There is no escape from death for your kind."

"She died for nothing," Iago spat back.

"She died for *you.*"

Iago was silent.

"And the man who raised you is waiting to see you again."

Iago shook his head as if trying to deny everything as hard as he could.

"I can't, you stupid Aeon! You're just like Lunae—acting like you know anything about me, like you understand at all! Hundreds have died to keep me alive—how is that fair?! Lady Malorya, Hallow-Talon, Amalia, everyone...they all suffered so that I could survive! Why?! Why must I be cursed to live?" Iago's voice cracked as tears of anger began to well in his eyes. "Why can't I just die already and save everyone the trouble?"

The Aeon's eyes were cold. Iago suddenly felt a chill down his spine, as if he had said something he shouldn't.

"You mortals and your stupid, mercurial emotions," the Aeon said, waving his hand. "Very well. Perish in the cold black sea!"

"I—" But Iago did not finish.

Instead, he felt the cold.

CHAPTER FORTY-ONE

The One Who Watches the Sea

'*Run, Iago!*'

In his mind, Iago wasn't sure he was dead or not. He felt cold, but no pain.

'*Never let them catch you!*' The voice resounded through his mind, and he knew he recognized it.

It was the voice of the knight who protected him as a child; it was Lady Malorya's voice.

He felt as if he could see her just as she was on that day, when she rushed him to her horse. He felt the gallop of the steed jostle his body...

...or was that the motion of the waves?

'*Halt!*' He could hear the sounds of horsemen behind them, their harsh commands causing his heart to thump in his throat.

Did we get away that night? The thought seemed to float with him, sloshing with the waves.

No...

*I did, but her...*she.

'*Run, Lyon!*' He could hear the faintness in her voice as if she were there before him. He could hear her cough and gurgle on her blood.

He ran. He ran as fast as he could. As far as he could. As far away from that evil man and his horrible regime.

He remembered falling...and then what...?

The birds...hawk-men...

Did they come to my rescue...?

Iago felt the cold fill his veins as he sank beneath the sea. This was it. *This* was his darkest moment, wasn't it?

He was dying, and all he had were the words of Lady Malorya in his mind, clear and painfully bitter.

'*Lyon, never forget...*

'*Always remember...*

'*...who you are!*'

Light filled Iago's eyes when all of the water left his lungs as he vomited salty water.

"Ah!" a deep voice laughed, "so you yet live!"

The young man opened his eyes and rose as fast as he could, holding his throat as he coughed and retched the remaining water from his chest.

He looked around. The air was warm and briny, which made sense, because he was by the sea...

...on the beach?

Yes. He was.

Then that means...

Yes, Iago was alive!

"You're a lucky one, little Elf!" the thunderous voice said again in a jovial chuckle. "But it's good that I was here. Perhaps it was fate!"

Iago turned his eyes from the ocean to see a large old man, a Giant, standing behind him.

"You saved me...?" the Elf's words were hoarse from the coughing.

The Giant smiled, the wrinkles in his cheeks reaching his eyes. "That I did."

Iago looked at the ocean once again. *Did Klyriai do this*? Was he giving him another chance? No, for some reason, that felt wrong. This felt like...something else.

This was something higher than gods or fate. *This* was sheer chance.

"Who are you?" Iago finally asked.

"Me?" the Giant said. "Why, I am the One Who Watches The Sea."

"I meant your name..."

"I already told you; I am the One Who Watches The Sea."

Iago sighed at the fact that this man was just as puzzling as the Aeon, if not more.

"Why do you watch the sea?"

The Giant grinned a wide, proud smile filled with all the purpose and optimism in the world.

"I watch for people like you."

Iago raised an eyebrow. "People like me?"

The man pointed to down the length of the beach. Iago followed his finger. There, at the end of the sands, was the cliff he had bounded off of.

"I watch for those who have forsaken themselves. I watch for those who wish to run. I watch because there is always a new soul who wishes to leave, and I must give them a reason to stay. *That* is why I saved you."

"I don't want to stay," Iago retorted, his voice beginning to shake. "I want to run away!"

The Giant was quiet for a moment, his smile melting away.

"There are many things in this life, Elf. You can run from all of them—almost all of them—but the one you cannot extricate yourself from, the one that will pervade after your flame is snuffed out, well...you cannot run from who you are."

Iago fidgeted. He could feel his mind burning.

"There's somewhere I have to go," he said finally, his voice becoming halted and tremulous. "There's someone waiting for me, and I've run from him my entire life. I've scorned and abandoned him when all he ever gave me was fatherly love. I just..." Iago looked up at the Giant. He could feel the tears begin to flow from his eyes once more. "I don't know how to face him!"

"You face him with an open heart," the Giant said, a softness and wisdom in his voice. "You face him the same way you just faced me."

It was odd. Iago couldn't tell why, but he felt as if, for the first time, his path was clear.

"I need to go then, don't I?"

"Yes you do," the Giant said.

"How will I get there?"

The Giant pointed to a large wagon led by giant horses.

"Elf," he said, "perhaps, all this time, it is because of *you* that I have watched the sea..."

CHAPTER FORTY-TWO

...From Who You Are

Iago wasn't too sure how, but the strange old Giant's cart arrived at the encompassing wall of Phoenix Grotto in only a day's time. When he thought about it, between his distracted mind and the giant horses' bounding pace, it might have possibly made sense. Though it definitely was odd, and Iago considered that magic might be at play, the Elf was too distracted by what lay ahead and merely accepted it as it was.

Right now, as he stared up at the obsidian wall, his heart rose to his throat.

How can I face him...?

The thought was loud in his mind. He took a deep breath, then turned around to thank the Giant for the ride, but...

As mysteriously as he had appeared, the Giant was gone.

"Papers!" a hawk-man guard demanded as Iago stepped closer to the wall.

"My name is Lyon," Iago replied with a tinge of frustration in his voice.

The hawk-man narrowed his eyes.

Iago sighed. "Look."

The Elf removed the cloak around his neck and lifted the back of his shirt to reveal the burned and mutilated tattoo of the White Phoenix.

"By the Aeons!" the guard gasped. "It's you!"

Iago lowered his shirt and cloaked himself once more.

"You're home," the guard said with a gasp, "Lyon..."

Eldric's group stood at the gates of the Palace of the Phoenix King. It was imposing. A dark shadow looming over a darkened city, the edifice stood as a guardian from the umbral streets just below.

"We've traveled almost all of Lythia, my girl," Eldric mentioned to Snow as they approached the door. "And never have I seen something so majestic."

"I agree, father."

"We've never stolen from this place," Enlil sang as she skipped just ahead of them.

"Might want to keep that a bit quiet, En," Ayize said with a sigh.

"This place is vast," Clement began. "The Winds show me its magnificence."

"This wind thing is quite..." Snow began, "odd."

"Aye it is," the prince said, smiling, "but it sure beats not knowing where I am."

Ahead, two hawk-men stood guard, their yellow eyes following the old Inquisitor as he approached.

"The name is Eldric," he said. "Eldric of the Black Flame."

He held up his hand. The guards were silent, their eyes trained intently upon him. Suddenly, a single black flame engulfed his fingers.

"And I would like to speak to the Phoenix King."

The two hawk-men looked at him, then nodded.

"Come with us," one said. "His Majesty has been awaiting you."

Eldric smiled. "Has he now...?"

The court of the Phoenix King was magnificent, or at least it was to Eldric and his companions. Before them, on the far wall, the throne sat, the Phoenix King upon it.

Eldric hobbled down the red carpet until he came to the steps and bowed, motioning with his hands to the others to do the same.

"Eldric of the Black Flame," Hallow-Talon's voice boomed. "What brings you here to my throne?"

"Your Majesty," Eldric began, "We have lost Aestriana, Mhyrmr, and the Heart of Hearts. I have come to you in desperation; I have come to seek aid against the dark forces of the world."

The Phoenix's eyes beheld the ones before him.

"You," he said finally, "you are Reethkilt's boy, aren't you? Clement, was it?"

"Aye," Clement said, nodding his bowed head.

"Then what they say of Aestriana is true? That Zilheim truly has it in his clutches?"

The room was silent.

"Nay," the Phoenix King finally said. "The Heart of Hearts still lives. He visited me himself. If all else, we know he is well, but..." he paused. "There is only one *true* hope for peace in this world of political unrest, and it is not the Heart of Hearts. Unfortunately, this hope, I do not know where *he* is."

Eldric raised an eyebrow. "'He?'"

"Only the—"

Suddenly, the doors swung open and a soldier rushed in.

"Your Majesty!" the hawk-man wheezed.

The Phoenix King jumped to his feet in ire.

"How dare you?!" he raged. "What have you to interrupt my court?"

"But, sire," he coughed, "he's here..."

The king's eyes widened. "He's..."

The soldier nodded. "Lyon."

Iago entered reluctantly, his head bowed in shame.

"Lyon..." Hallow-Talon said as he slowly walked down the steps.

Eldric narrowed his eyes in curiosity as he watched the Elf enter.

"Iago of the Thousand Swords...?"

"Nay, Inquisitor," Hallow-Talon said, his words hard as he stopped in front of the Elf. "He is Iago Lyon, and *he* alone can save this world from chaos."

"Why do you say that?" Iago's voice was bitter and rigid. "After all I've done, after everyone who has died because of me—after your daughter's death, Amalia." He sighed, his head still down. "How can you even look at me after my mere existence has taken all you had?"

Suddenly, Iago felt himself choke as the king embraced him.

"I have lost much," Hallow-Talon said, his voice strong, "but I still have *you*!"

Iago felt his heart shatter. His tears were unavoidable, flowing like rivers down his cheeks.

"Why?" the Elf cried. "Why don't you hate me? Why don't you just make it easy?"

"Because," the Phoenix King said as he squeezed. Iago could feel the warmth of the other's tears. "I could never hate the one I call my son."

"I don't understand," Eldric finally said, in awe of what was before him.

The two embracing broke apart. Snow looked at the weeping Elf with quizzical eyes. What had happened here? Iago of the Thousand Swords stood before her, yet he did not seem vicious.

No, this was not the same young man she fought back in Zerlina long ago.

"There is one thing that needs to happen in order for Lythia to be at peace," Hallow-Talon said with a smile as he returned to his throne. "We must put the Prince of Mirea on the Elven throne."

"Well, that would be impossible," Eldric said, chuckling as he bit down on his pipe. "There is no prince of Mirea thanks to Iago here, who murdered him in cold blood."

The king smiled a devilish smile. The smile gave way to a chuckle, then an outright laugh.

"You were never a good liar, Lyon," he said. "But Zilheim is clever."

"I'm lost," Eldric said, his voice slow and filled with hesitation.

"Well, Inquisitor," Hallow-Talon began. "Iago did not kill the prince of Mirea. He would not have survived such an encounter. You see, Iago did not kill the prince of Mirea, because Iago *is* the prince of Mirea!"

"*What?!*" Eldric laughed.

The room turned to Lyon. To Iago. No.

The room turned to the Prince of Mirea.

"You see," Hallow-Talon began. "Lyon was born in secrecy, as the king of the Elves was privy to Zilheim's lust for control. He was given to a knight, a certain Lady Malorya, to bring to the king's ally—me. It was here that he was to marry the Phoenix princess, my daughter, Amalia. This political bond would strengthen ties between Mirea and the Folke Lands. But there was one problem. Zilheim has long been operating a slave trade—giving my people to the vampires of the Nightshade Court in exchange for large sums of money. So, in short, Lyon's existence, and the political bond he represents, is the one thing that has the power to undo the evils brought upon by the current Elven regime."

"I see..." Eldric mused, rubbing his chin. "So *that* is why I'd never heard of him when we received the bounty, because it was..."

"A forgery..." Clement said.

The room fell silent. Iago froze as he felt all eyes upon him.

Eldric smiled.

Iago jumped as he felt the old man's leathery hand clamp down firmly upon his shoulder.

"Then, as former Master of the Inquisition," he said, "I stand by the prince of Mirea"—Eldric smiled—"for a better future."

"Y-you..." Iago began. "Master Inquisitor..."

"Aye!" Clement said as he stepped to the prince's side. "And I as well. As heir to the throne of Aestriana, I stand by you, Prince of Mirea."

Iago stood silent. Why? Why did they accept him so easily? Why was the path so clear to them when it was so muddled to him?

Iago took in a tremulous breath.

"And I as well," Snow said, gripping his other shoulder with a bit more force. "I have to pay him back for the wounds he gave me back in Zerlina."

Iago went white. For a moment, he remembered their fight back in Zerlina. They were now allies, and the Elven prince was certain that Snow was not someone he'd like to face in battle again.

"W-wounds?" Iago gulped. "R-right..."

"I wanna help!" Enlil hopped to join the group.

"Ugh," Ayize groaned.

"Very well," hallow-Talon laughed. "It seems we have some friends, Lyon. It seems we have a *Phoenix Union*."

Iago was silent. He turned to the Inquisitor.

"You would really accept me?" he asked. His voice shook; his whole body shook. "After all I've done?"

Eldric smirked that dark-defying smirk.

"Of course we accept you," he said, "young prince."

Iago's smile was a weak one. As he looked into the old man's devilish eyes, something about them brought him...peace.

The Elf wiped his eyes and nodded. "What do we do now?"

Eldric beamed, his eyes filled with cleverness.

"I'm glad you asked..."

CHAPTER FORTY-THREE

Little Red Bird, Sing Thy Name

Lukas and Alvys were talking in the back of the car when suddenly Darloc screeched and the caravan came to a stark halt, the suddenness of it throwing the two of them against the wall.

"Hey, what's up, Dar?" Lukas groaned, rubbing the new knot on his head.

"Soldiers!" the round dog-man said, pointing forward.

Lukas looked ahead, his eyes scanning the road in front of him. Darloc was right; there were two, three, no, five soldiers. His eyes gravitated to the outlier. Running from the gilded soldiers, a young woman in red was coming toward them.

"Darloc!" Lukas said as he barreled out the door. "Stay put!"

"What?!" the man raged. "Are you crazy! There's *five* of them!"

"Don't worry!" Lukas smiled back. "It'll be alright."

"Get back here, woman!" an Elven soldier shouted as the woman ran toward Lukas.

"A little help, please?" She said as Lukas rushed past her.

"Gotcha!" He said, summoning the *Sword Durandal* to his hand.

The soldiers stopped their chase, each drawing their blades and surrounding Lukas.

"Listen boy," one said, his voice muffled behind his sallet, "you're interfering with imperial business, get lost—"

Suddenly, Lukas raised his blade in the air.

"*Lucyn Rejiis!*" He called out.

"White flames!" A soldier exclaimed. "You're—?!"

But it was too late. In a quick arc, spiritual energy exploded from the blade, slicing into the soldiers in a great flash of dust and light.

"Well, damn..." Darloc said with a shrug.

"Woah!" Alvys gasped.

As the dust cleared, the soldiers lay dead upon the ground.

"You took down *all* of them?" the young woman said as she approached her savior. "What kind of magic is that? I've never heard of white flames before."

"Oh, that," Lukas said, laughing as he scratched his head. "It's nothing."

"Ah," she said, straightening her posture. "Why, thank you."

Now that he had a moment, Lukas could see what was so strange about her. She was definitely a Beastfolk, red feathers that ran down her shoulders. He looked at her fiery orange eyes and blazing red hair.

"Are you...?" he began.

"Oh!" she exclaimed, holding her head high and straightening her shoulders austerely. "How rude of me. You save my life and I don't even offer you my name." She extended her hand to shake. "Please, call me *Amalia*."

Lukas smiled as he shook her hand.

"Name's Lukas! Pleasure to meet you!"

Follow Me on Socials!

Facebook: www.facebook.com/BurkWillWrites

Twitter: www.twitter.com/BurkWill

Instagram: www.instagram.com/williamf.burk4

My Website: www.williamfburk.com

Also!

Cover Artist's Twitter: @YasuStudio

* * *

About the Author

William F. Burk is an award-winning author of novels, poetry, and flash fiction. Inspired early on by stories such as *One Piece*, *His Dark Materials*, and *The Shannara Chronicles*, his one goal is to write stories that people will enjoy.

www.ingramcontent.com/pod-product-compliance
Lightning Source LLC
Chambersburg PA
CBHW030803210726
48290CB00002B/403